PERILS OF LEADERSHIP

BY

S. J. RITCHEY

www.bookstandpublishing.com

Published by
Bookstand Publishing
Morgan Hill, CA 95037
3095_3

This is a work of fiction. Names, places, and institutions are the product of the
author's imagination. Any connection to an actual person or place is unintentional.

ISBN 978-1-58909-700-1

Printed in the United States of America

PERILS OF LEADERSHIP

ACKNOWLEDGEMENTS

Sincere gratitude to members of Blue River Writers—Judy Beale, Carter Elliott, Amy Kander, Paul Poff, and Margot Wadley for their helpful critiques and unwavering support. A special thanks to Dr. Herman Doswold for his review of the manuscript.

CHAPTER 1

The searing pain caused him to gasp and clutch at his midsection. Beads of sweat on his brow, Henry Rogers, the department head of Biology, pulled the yellow pad from the middle drawer of the desk and scanned the list of things to be done. Crossing off one he'd accomplished, he added two others. Trying to focus on the paper, but unable to concentrate, he pulled a pill from his jacket pocket and swallowed it. He was taking too many of these opiates, but he couldn't tolerate the throbbing across his abdomen without some relief. He rubbed his shirt sleeve across his head to erase some of the moisture.

Taking on another of the tasks on the list would be too much today. They'd have to wait until he returned from the clinic in three or four days. The remaining problems were tricky, maybe impossible to solve without getting nasty with people. This stuff with Harris would have to stop. Too many times he'd let his appetite for women exceed acceptable limits. Boseman, a surly little bastard, presented a challenge—should have kicked him out of here three years ago. And this thing with King, almost unbelievable he'd manufacture data, but who knows what faculty will do when the pressures get to them.

Pain shot across his gut. His forehead became wet and clammy. He clamored to his feet and shoved the pad back into the desk drawer. Everything would have to wait until this thing inside him was under control. And goodness knows how long that will require. He hadn't believed his doctor when he told him the issue was digestive upset in nature. It was something more drastic.

As Henry wobbled into the hall, Jason Spradlin, a young professor in the department, came along the corridor on his way out at the end of the day. Jason saw Henry drop his keys and almost topple over when he reached down for them. Henry leaned against the wall as Jason retrieved the brass ring with a half-dozen keys of different sizes and shapes.

Handing the keys to Henry, Jason asked, "You okay?"

"I'm hurting like hell." Henry shook his head as though shaking off a temporary condition, moving with shuffling steps as though concerned about his balance, a hand on the wall.

Jason watched him take four or five steps, then said, "I read your memo about having tests, but maybe you shouldn't wait. Go straight to the emergency clinic. I'll drive you."

Shaking his head, Henry said, "It'll be okay when these damn pain killers take affect. Just help me to my car."

Outside in the warm air of an early September afternoon. Henry grasped onto Jason's shoulder as they walked slowly to Henry's Chrysler sedan in the front row of the large faculty-staff parking lot. Each step seemed to be a struggle for Henry, but he was no longer clutching at his midsection.

At the car, Jason said, "I'll follow to make sure you get home."

Henry nodded as he settled behind the steering wheel, then he looked at Jason, saying, "If this thing in my gut is what I think it is,

I'm going to ask you to help with the administrative stuff for a few weeks."

Sitting up straighter as the pain abated further, he continued, "There are a couple of difficult issues that may take more energy than I can give and stay on top of the routine things."

Looking into the sweat streaked face of Henry, Jason said, "I'll help if I can." He couldn't refuse Henry who'd done so many things for him over the years he'd been at State University, although he had no interest in the problems of a department head.

Pulling the seat belt across his chest, Henry nodded, "I'll talk to you in a couple of days." He slammed the door and started the engine.

Jason watched Henry pull out of the lot, then jogged to his own car. He caught up with Henry when he stopped at the four-way stop sign a block from campus. Although Henry weaved across the mid-line at intervals, he maintained control. Jason kept pace until his boss pulled into the drive of his home. Jason pulled in behind him, waited until Henry had disappeared through the front door, backed out and headed for home.

Jason muttered to himself as the telephone drilled into his concentration on the second morning after his interactions with Henry. He glanced at his watch and reached for the instrument—eight-fifteen—too early for a crisis in the research lab on the next floor. Might be a problem at the clinic where his research group was running a study with four children with Wilson's disease, a genetic disorder involving copper metabolism.

An unfamiliar voice said, "Dr. Spradlin, this is Bridget Dawson in Dean Hawthorne's office. He would like to see you and would appreciate your coming to his office."

"Immediately?" Jason wondered what the problem could be to cause the Dean to summon him so abruptly. He wasn't aware of any student complaint or an error in his research accounts. In his eight years at State University he'd never been summoned on such short notice and never by the Dean. It had to be some disaster.

"If you will, please."

Jason tugged on his brown sports coat, raked a hand through his unruly brown hair, checked his tie in the glass pane of the office door, and walked through his research laboratory out the back door of Quincy Hall. The Dean's office was in Ragsdale Hall across the quadrangle of the huge campus of State University, the land-grant school in the state, twenty-five thousand students and six thousand faculty and staff spread in nearly a hundred buildings. Shading from the large oaks brought temporary relief from the sun, already bright in a hazy September sky and promising to bake the community with stifling heat yet another day. The grass had turned brown and the usually bright marigolds had faded as though weary of fighting the heat and drought. A few students, dressed in shorts and ill-fitting tee shirts and late for their early class, hurried along the sidewalks and cut across the lawn to save steps.

The comprehensive university of the state had been founded as Stanley College in 1830 by the Methodist church for the purpose of giving a classic education to young men who would become ministers, physicians, lawyers, educators and other professionals.

After the passage of the Morrill Act in 1862 creating the land-grant schools, the trustees of the financially strapped institution approached the state of Missouri for that designation and agreed to relinquish all rights to the property. The agricultural interests of the state immediately became strong proponents of the idea because it would give them a college they could readily identify with and potentially shape to meet the needs of their children for a practical education. The Grange and other farm related organizations lobbied the legislature for the small college and for the purchase of two thousand acres of adjacent farm land to be used for research and demonstration of improved production practices. The institution was renamed Missouri A. & M. College.

As the population grew and the demands for higher education escalated, the state appropriated funding for new buildings and additional instructors. A medical school was established and by the early twentieth century, schools of engineering and agriculture, coupled with the core of arts and sciences, provided a solid nucleus for the institution's emergence as a place of excellence.

In 1934 the school was renamed the State University of Missouri and became known by most alumni, students, faculty, and government officials simply as State University. The full title appeared only on official documents and was used only by those not knowledgeable about the history and traditions of the school. Newcomers were easily identified if they used the full name.

The burgeoning school soon dominated the small town of Spencerville. At one point university officials, citing precedents of College Station, Texas and University Park, Pennsylvania raised the issue of changing the name of the town to University City. However, the mayor and town council, refused to go along with a name change.

Bridget nodded and smiled at Jason as he entered the spacious suite of the Dean of Arts and Sciences. "Go right in. He's waiting."

David Hawthorne glanced up from a paper on his desk when Jason knocked lightly on the door frame. "Thanks for coming on such short notice." He pointed to a dark gray upholstered chair, one of five in a three-quarters circle around a glass coffee table. Jason hadn't been in this place in four years. Nothing new caught his eye, but he remained impressed with the walnut desk, matching credenza, and leather chair.

Bridget placed a ceramic coffee pot and assorted containers of sugar and whiteners on the table, closing the door softly as she departed.

"Help yourself, " Hawthorne said, as he poured two mugs of the dark brew, the aroma inviting, and pointed to the sugar and cream. His broad face and brown eyes exuded confidence, as he smiled at Jason. Jason relaxed a bit and reached for the mug.

Hawthorne continued, "Jason, we have a major problem in the Biology Department and I want your help." Now frowning, he added, "Henry Rogers called me late yesterday afternoon from the Medical School hospital. The pathologists have confirmed pancreatic cancer and insist he begin treatment immediately. It's clear he won't be back

6

in the office for some time." The look of concern in Hawthorne's eyes suggested a more dire outlook.

Jason muttered, "Oh geez. I saw him after work two days ago." He placed the mug on the table and rubbed his face. "I thought he was battling his ulcer again. Nobody suspected this." Four days earlier a brief memo from Henry had revealed he was having a battery of exams and he'd be away from the office for several days, but there'd been no hint of a life-threatening problem. It was common knowledge that Henry had endured a long running malady of intestinal problems he referred to as his signal to slow his pace.

"Somehow, I believe Henry knew it would be bad news before the diagnosis. He didn't seem upset when he called around four." Hawthorne shifted his feet and moved a stack of papers on the table.

"He seldom does, no matter what." Henry had been Jason's department head for eight years. Rarely during that period had Jason seen Henry truly agitated. One of those times involved the illegal antics of Jefferson Bell, a senior faculty member who had been sentenced to a long prison term for activities designed to sabotage the gene therapy research of Jason and his colleagues. Images of Henry telling Jason of his support throughout the crisis flooded his memory as he watched the Dean.

Hawthorne said, "The bottom line is I need help. Henry wants out of the department head position now, rather than waiting until a replacement has been identified through the search process, and I've agreed with him. Fighting this disease will consume all his energy. Then he plans to retire and not attempt to return to work." At the beginning of the fall term, only ten days ago, Henry had informed the faculty he would reach age sixty-five in three months and planned to retire at the end of the academic year. A memo from Hawthorne yesterday had requested nominations for the screening committee, the first step in the search process for a new department leader. But there had been no hint of other problems—just normal retirement plans.

"I'd like to appoint you as the interim head."

Jason stared at Hawthorne, forgetting momentarily the plight of Henry, his friend and leader. Looking directly at Jason as though to hold his complete attention, Hawthorne explained, "After Henry called, I came to the office last evening and reviewed the personnel files of the professors in Biology. Based on Henry's comments about you over the years I've been here and your record, I called four senior faculty in the department to get their opinion. Without exception, they recommended you for the position."

Jason knew his face revealed his dismay. "Dean Hawthorne, all this is too fast, about Henry for one thing. Now this department head position—I don't know."

He paused, looking into the Dean's eyes. "I'm not sure I want to tackle those kind of responsibilities at this point in my career." He didn't want to admit openly to a long time administrator like Hawthorne that he'd always vowed to shy away from administrative roles, remembering the hours Henry Rogers worked and the problems he confronted on a daily basis. Plus, he didn't even know about many of the things Henry dealt with routinely. Jason worked diligently to stay clear of departmental politics, spending his time and energy on his

8

research and teaching responsibilities. The head's job might be worse than he'd imagined.

"Both Henry and your colleagues think you have the right temperament, and express confidence you'd always place the interests of the department above your own."

Hawthorne paused to sip coffee. "And your record supports their opinion." Hawthorne's broad face, alert brown eyes, and erect position exuded the confidence of someone who usually got what he wanted. His blocky build, two hundred pounds on a five-eleven frame suggested a determined force, much as a mother bear blocking a trail in defense of her offspring. Jason wasn't sure he could turn him down.

Jason grinned. "And none of them want the headaches involved."

Hawthorne smiled in return, but ignored the aside. "Jason, I realize this comes as a surprise, but think about my question for a few hours, and let me know by the end of the day, tomorrow morning at the latest. I need to move forward with this decision. I don't want to leave the leadership of the department in limbo any longer than necessary."

Jason scrambled to find some plausible protest. "Dr. Hawthorne, you know I'm loaded with teaching and research projects."

Hawthorne nodded his head. "We could relieve you of some teaching responsibilities this semester, and not schedule any for the spring term."

His essential message delivered, Hawthorne stood, looking down at Jason. "I'll give you whatever support and assistance you need. The year will go quickly, and as far as I know, there are no pressing problems in the department."

Jason stood, realizing he and the Dean were the same height, but Jason's one hundred and seventy-five pounds was substantially less than Hawthorne. "I'll think about it and let you know something by five today."

He passed Bridget's desk in a daze. The whole conversation had gone too quickly, his mind overwhelmed with the ideas of taking on the administrative duties with all the hassles he knew would come, in spite of Hawthorne's analysis.

From his office, he called Lucy, his wife of seven years and an Associate Professor in English. "I need your advice. Can we meet for lunch?"

"That's unusual," she said, "for you to admit such a dilemma." He heard her gentle laugh, and could picture her dark blue eyes lighting at her rejoinder.

Jason blurted, "Henry has cancer and has asked to be relieved. The Dean wants me to serve as interim head. And he wants my answer by five today."

"That is a dilemma." Her tone more serious, she said, "See you in the lobby at twelve." Both worked in Quincy Hall, one of the older academic buildings on the campus, but they seldom commuted to the building together, trying to juggle schedules around work and two pre-school age children.

At a corner booth in Mortimer's, a restaurant two blocks from campus, they shoved aside the critical question until they'd placed orders. Then Lucy asked, "So what do you want to do?"

Jason fingered the ice tea glass, wiping moisture around in a pattern. "Tell him to find someone else."

"Who else is there?"

"George Stuart, Joyce Krause, Ben Rankin—any of them could do it. They're all established and respected." He mumbled, "Too bad Fred Adams left. He would have been great at it." Adams had been Jason's mentor and confidant from the very start in the department, but he'd left two years ago to become a department head at Penn State.

Lucy reached across the corner of the table to take his hand. "But, could any of them do it as well as you?"

"Sure, they all could, probably better."

"But Hawthorne doesn't think so, or he would have hit on one of them, since they're all older than you." Lucy argued, her voice sincere and calm, her fingers pressing his.

"You know, Lucy," Jason rebutted, "I've always vowed I would avoid administration. It looks like boring drudgery, not to mention major conflicts at times."

"Well, Hawthorne has offered a good opportunity to prove it to yourself. It's only for a few months, and it'd give you a chance to know absolutely you'd never do it on a long term basis. Now, you have no experience on which to base your decision, only rumors and hearsay."

"You're supposed to help me find a way to turn him down." Jason grinned, watching her eyes as she smiled back.

"I know, but I think you should try it. You're always moaning and muttering about the lack of common sense and short-sighted vision of department chairs and deans. Now's your opportunity to do something about it." Jason watched her face, deep blue eyes piercing into the depths of his soul and knowing his thoughts before he revealed a single clue. In his view, she was beautiful—slightly oval face, small nose upturned slightly, crisp jaw and chin lines, creamy skin requiring little make-up. During the first month of their marriage he'd discovered she kept her thick black hair long enough to cover most of her ears she thought protruded excessively in spite of his opposing opinion. As he looked at her, he recounted his fortune in finding and marrying her, and his continuing inability to predict her reactions.

But he trusted her judgment as she smiled, revealing perfect teeth and said, "Try it. You don't have to commit long term."

At four forty-five, Jason called and asked for Hawthorne. Bridget responded, "He's in a meeting now, but he wanted me to take your message."

Jason hesitated, still thinking about jumping into the unknown, "Let him know I'll probably take on the interim head job, but I'd like to talk to him about several things before I commit myself."

"He thought you would. Come at eight tomorrow morning."

Jason replaced the receiver. Staring into the research lab, he saw four graduate students at their benches, and a post-doctoral fellow at a computer, analyzing data from a completed experiment. Jason wondered if this challenging, but exciting phase in his professional life was about to end.

It was too soon. He had turned thirty-five four months ago, made full professor last spring, had a solid footing with granting agencies, found a good consulting arrangement with a pharmaceutical company, and had his choice of bright graduate students seeking his guidance. He had carved out his niche and settled in for a long and productive academic career, enjoying his work, sustained by the continuous excitement of discovery and interactions with students and colleagues, and comfortable with his position at a fine university.

But the conversation with Lucy over lunch had caused him to think more about the issue of an administrative role. He had some responsibility to the department, a place where he'd been supported and nurtured as he started his academic career. Maybe he could pay back some of the debt by serving for the few months until a permanent replacement for Henry could be found. It couldn't be too bad for a short time, he reassured himself, when you could see the end.

CHAPTER 2

David Hawthorne, now in his ninth year as Dean of the College of Arts and Sciences, was at his desk when Jason knocked at ten before eight. "I apologize for being early," Jason said, taking one of the chairs, "but I teach a class at nine." He dropped his worn cowhide briefcase on the plush gray carpet.

"It's fine." Hawthorne sat across from Jason and crossed his legs, revealing spotless black oxfords and dark socks that matched his navy suit. "I'm always in the office early. I'm able to get a lot done before the others arrive." He returned a pen to his shirt pocket.

Jason said, "I wanted to ask about several things before I commit to this interim appointment." He and Lucy had made a list of issues after dinner the evening before, and they'd wondered how flexible Hawthorne might be. They had debated on the proper manner in which to retreat if certain conditions weren't met without alienating the Dean, someone he'd have to work with for years.

"Okay, but first let me say a few things that may resolve some of your questions."

Jason nodded and waited, while Hawthorne stood and moved to close the door into the outer office. Sitting across from Jason again, he said, "First, I'm pleased you've agreed to do this. It'll be a big help to both Biology and to me."

"Second, while your appointment will be interim until a new head is on board, there's nothing to keep you from becoming an active candidate for the position on a permanent basis." Jason had told Lucy the evening before that there was zero chance of him doing such an irrational thing. "The search committee will be appointed by the end of next week and they will request nominations and applications nationally, including current members of the department. Based on comments from some of your colleagues in the department I'm sure you'll be nominated."

Jason ignored the implied question, waited until Hawthorne continued, "Also, your responsibilities and actions should be conducted as though you're the permanent head. Don't be reluctant to change things if you believe they're needed. The department shouldn't be in a dormant state for a year while the search goes on. You'll have certain decisions which must be made and tasks which need your attention for the long-term well-being of the department. So I encourage you in that vein, knowing you'll use good judgment about what needs to be done in the near term, and what can be set aside until the new head is on board.

"For example, tenure and promotion recommendations must be submitted. Budget issues must be attended to. Salary raises for faculty must be evaluated at the department level. Put in motion necessary actions to fill any vacancies of either faculty or staff." Jason mentally erased those items from his list.

"Dr. Hawthorne, as of today, I have no idea of who is coming up for tenure this year."

16

The Dean smiled. "Neither do I, but your office will have the records, and Henry notified the individuals last spring that their credentials must be submitted by November first."

The Dean went on. "Most things, such as the hundreds of details related to operating expenditures, salary savings, leaves, purchasing,..." he shrugged, suggesting a lengthy list, "are typically handled by staff with your endorsement and approval. From what I've observed, they're competent people and will support you without question. So depend on them, and use their experiences to guide any changes you think appropriate.

"As for the teaching, I know you have a large section of General Biology and a graduate course in genetics. I'll allocate money to support a graduate student or a post-doc to teach the beginning course during this year." Jason tried not to show his surprise the Dean had bothered to find out his teaching duties or that he was running through these issues without benefit of notes. But he'd confirmed his earlier opinion about Hawthorne—organized, prepared, keen mind focused on the issue at hand.

Hawthorne added, "Just tell me within the next couple of days how much money we're talking about."

Jason made a note in his mind, before asking, "Any major problems I should worry about?"

"None that I know about," he smiled, "but likely there are some." He shifted in the chair, glanced at his watch. "Call Henry in a few days after things have settled down for him. He'll tell you, although he didn't confide in me very often. He took care of issues in Biology."

"What about using Henry's office?"

"Henry said he'd get his wife to remove his personal things by the weekend. I'm sure the department secretary, Audrey, can assist. But yes, you should move to that office to be near the departmental core functions. It'll be very inefficient, if not impossible, to work out of your lab office. Use your judgment about that space until the head's job is filled. "

Running down his mental list, Jason said, "I have several commitments to participate in conferences associated with my research projects. I assume I can keep those." Some of the usual meetings could be skipped if necessary, but he didn't want to lose out on his increasing number of contacts.

"Certainly," Hawthorne said, "there's no reason not to. There may be times when the department should be represented at a meeting, but if you're scheduled away, someone from the department could substitute for you." He paused, then added, "But sometimes it's essential the head be present. You'll figure out those times, but if you have doubts, give me a call."

Jason thought about the possibility of major conflicts, but said, "I'm sure I'll have other concerns once I get started, but none hit me now." He realized he had committed to the position. He could envision Lucy smiling at his self revelation.

"To be certain everyone in the department is up to speed, I'll send out an announcement of your appointment today. You may start functioning and signing official papers." He glanced at his watch. "So you have time to get to your class."

As Jason stood and picked up the briefcase, Hawthorne added, "By the way, there's a ten percent salary increment for administrative appointments. I'll get the paper work done to start yours immediately." An item not on Jason's list of concerns, but a bit of extra income would be nice.

The memo from the Dean was distributed at two in the afternoon. Jason, buried in his office, trying to complete a manuscript, became aware of the release when George Stuart, one of the senior professors in the department, stuck his head in to congratulate him. Several others followed, a few of whom Jason suspected of insincerity, making sure they got on the right side of the new guy who might influence their work loads and salaries.

Amidst the parade, the lead secretary for the department, Audrey Ennis, knocked. "Dr. Spradlin, I brought a master key for you. I thought you might want to get in the office tonight or early tomorrow morning." Her eyes were sad and her hands were trembling as she gave him the key. "I'll miss Dr. Rogers after twelve years of working closely with him."

"We'll all miss him, but he'll be okay." Jason wondered if she understood the severity of the disease facing Henry, and thus would understand his promise had little substance.

After five, when all the staff had left for the day, Jason used the master key and entered the office of the man who'd hired him and had guided him through the early stages of his academic career. He experienced both guilt, sadness, and to his dismay, a measure of excitement, as he surveyed the square shaped room, the large desk and credenza in one corner, the single straight chair next to the desk. Four brown upholstered chairs arranged around a square conference table dominated the other side. Several abstract paintings added color and texture to otherwise drab beige walls. Jason opened the middle desk drawer from which he'd seen Henry pull a pad with notes and reminders.

Jason removed the small yellow tablet. Among the dozen items Henry had listed as things to be done, the top four jumped out at Jason.

* Call Ingraham re pathology tests.

* Talk with King re possible unethical publication.

* Review credentials of Boseman for tenure.

* Check about Harris' rumored harassment of female graduate student.

* Assemble stuff for budget submission

Jason stared at the list for several seconds. Conscious of a rising dampness across his forehead, he plopped into the chair, staring out the window, seeing nothing. A sense of foreboding overwhelmed him briefly as he thought about problems he didn't want to tackle and his lack of experience in confronting faculty colleagues, some older and more seasoned than he.

Acknowledging his promise to the Dean and his new responsibility after five minutes of battling his frustration of having agreed to this job, he scanned the list again and returned it to the desk. Then he scribbled a note to Audrey requesting that she set up appointments with King, Bosesman and Harris as soon as possible.

Leaving the office Jason took a chance he could drop in on Henry at the hospital. At six he entered the immense structure, a six-story main building with four wings obviously added as demands intensified and funds became available. Any coherence to the architecture had disappeared much like those temporary units at elementary schools scattered around like toys in a playroom.

After two wrong turns in the maze, he retraced his steps to the main building and asked directions from a young woman dressed in a white lab coat with a stethoscope dangling around her neck. At the nurses station, he identified himself and said he needed to ask Henry Rogers a couple of quick questions.

The buxom gray-haired nurse eyed him suspiciously, asking, "Is this important or are you just some acquaintance dropping by?" She punctuated her skepticism by whamming a stapler fixing together a set of records.

Thinking she must wreck a lot of equipment, he said, "It's important. I'm taking over his job at the University for a while and I need to clarify an issue with him."

She banged the stapler again, causing paper clips to bounce on the desk. "Okay—five minutes. Then I'll see you out. Room two-twelve, to your left, half-way down." She jabbed a large finger in the direction.

Jason eased open the door to find Henry stretched on his back, two catheters in his left arm leading to electronic monitors blinking his vital signs.

Henry turned his head slightly, saying, "Jason, thanks for your help the other day."

Jason wanted to just sit for a while with his friend and tell him by his presence he cared, but the martinet at the nurses station would be after him. He said, "You may know, but Dean Hawthorne has asked me to fill in until a permanent head is selected."

Henry nodded. "I suggested he consider you."

Rushing ahead, Jason said, "I saw the list of problems on your reminder pad. What can you tell me?"

Henry twisted a bit, his face contorted for a brief moment. He said, "Potentially the worst is this business with King. I'm surprised, but after thirty-five years in this game, I shouldn't be."

"You think he actually published based on trumped-up data?"

"Stranger things have happened when a faculty member is under pressure." The tubes in his arm were extended to their limit as Henry twisted and turned. His frown deepened as he added, "Audrey will find the correspondence. I didn't get to talk with King, but I don't like it. Those things give a department a reputation that takes years to overcome."

Jason asked, "Boseman?"

The burly nurse walked in, pointing to her watch. "Time's up."

Henry said, "No hurry about Bosemen. I'll be out of here in a few days, then I'll talk to you about him, but review his file. The Harris

22

thing—scare the hell out of him by threatening to send any complaint to the University Ethics committee."

Jason moved toward the door, the nurse eyeing every step.

CHAPTER 3

The following day turned into a blur. As soon as Jason arrived at his office next to the lab, Audrey called. "Dr. Spradlin, would you mind signing some papers this morning?" Jason had noticed the stack on the corner of the desk the previous evening, but he'd paid little attention to them. Henry's reminders crowded his thinking—so much for a problem free time. He should have known better than to get suckered into this position. But he'd have to tough it out for a few months. Backing out was no longer an option.

Settling at the desk in the department head's office, Jason was aware of Audrey moving about, removing several bric-a-brac, paintings from the walls, while he signed a stack of forms. He attempted to scan each one before signing, but admitted to himself, he didn't know in some cases to what he was committing department resources, or giving approval for some action normally beyond acceptable boundaries.

Audrey stopped her activity, closing the lid of a box. "Dr. Rogers always called the signings mindless work." She smiled, "He was usually in a good mood, even when there were major problems."

Jason recalled Henry telling him how valuable Audrey had become to him personally and to the department. She seemed pleasant always, smiling, blue eyes lighting easily regardless of the pressure; neatly dressed, usually in a dress or skirt and blouse, medium heels; not pretty, but neat; short stature, sturdy frame; blond-brown hair, cut short. She'd started work in the office after high school and Jason thought she must be in her early forties. Everybody in the department respected her professionalism, loyalty and good sense.

Jason sighed, fixing his signature to the last form in the stack, "How much should I worry about these things?"

"If you have questions, I can explain, or Miriam can tell you about the purchase orders and things involving personnel and accounting."

"Can you tell me," Jason asked, pulling the reminder pad from the desk, "about these items on Dr. Rogers' list?"

Audrey came to stand next to his chair. After a moment, she said, "There's correspondence about the ethics thing. I'll find the letter for you. And I know he had Dr. Boseman's file out a couple of days ago. I'll get that for you."

She stepped back, the faint aroma of her perfume dissipating from Jason's senses. "I don't know about the harassment question."

Jason glanced at his watch. "I have a meeting with a research group at nine for a couple of hours, then I'll be back." He rolled the leather chair away from the desk and picked up a folder.

"Mrs. Rogers is coming by at eleven," Audrey said, "to get Dr. Rogers' personal things, if you'd like to see her."

"Tell her I'll call her, and I plan to go by as soon as he's back home." He'd learned Henry was scheduled to have chemotherapy treatments as an outpatient after he was released from the hospital. As he turned away he decided the list could wait until he'd talked to Henry again, hopefully out of sight of the Amazon nurse holding the stop watch..

Jason rushed into the research lab to be met by the comfortable smells of organic solvents, the warmth of a flask in a heating blanket and the dripping sound of condensate at the end of the apparatus. Glancing at the familiar equipment caused a momentary nostalgia, although he knew he would return at the end of the year in purgatory.

Five doctoral students, a lab specialist, and a post-doc were waiting around the table in the lab. Jason said, "Sorry I'm late." He looked at the group. "Okay, who wants to report first?"

The weekly meeting usually consisted of two reports about current research work followed by a discussion period and ending with plans for next stages. Jason liked these conferences as students learned from the interactions and often added important ideas to improve the next experiment or another possible interpretation of data. He used these sessions to judge how the students were progressing toward independence, a point in their education when they no longer relied on him.

Ann, a stocky woman in her mid-twenties and in the second year of the doctoral program, volunteered. "I'm in the last phase of an experiment to test the impact of non-nutrients in the food supply on the gene which causes juvenile diabetes." She reminded the group of the experimental approach, getting up from the chair to show an overhead transparency against the white wall. "This specific test is examining the possible effect of a mixture of carbohydrate-like compounds on the gene and the subsequent release or production of insulin."

Jason struggled to focus on the update, as his mind wandered to the list on Henry's desk. What was Henry's concern about Boseman? Jason had regarded the young faculty as a bright, productive member of the department. He'd liked his occasional comment during faculty meetings, but perhaps there was something he didn't know about, some quirk in Boseman's record not obvious to faculty colleagues. Jason remembered that Henry jumped to conclusions quickly, but then he examined the situation carefully and sometimes changed his thinking.

Ann concluded her presentation, switching off the projector. "Any questions or suggestions." Jason jerked back to the immediate scene.

Steve, a first year student, asked, "How will you know about the production of insulin?"

"I intend to measure blood insulin in another two weeks, after the compounds have accumulated in the system to the point the pancreas may have been affected." She smiled at the group. "As a reminder, the mice will have been on the experiment eight weeks at that time."

"So you believe the compounds prevent the flow of insulin to the target cells?"

"No, we think the production of the hormone is lessened in the organ because the genetic capacity to produce insulin has been impaired." Jason enjoyed the exchange.

Steve persisted, "What if the effect is not on the production, but on the release mechanism or on the uptake by target tissues?"

Ann frowned and glanced at Jason, who waited for her response. He rarely rescued a student from a difficult query. Finally, she said, "I'll have to think about a different measurement to show that."

Jason was pleased when Ann jotted a note, he assumed a reminder to check further the possible mechanism. They moved on to the next student who would discuss an experiment on the cystic fibrosis project, a long-standing research line in the lab.

Jason listened carefully for several minutes, then his mind drifted to the lecture he'd prepared for his graduate class scheduled at two this afternoon.

The electronic device announcing the four o'clock class change buzzed throughout the academic buildings on campus as Jason strode into the main office. Lecture notes for the graduate class were still in his hand.

As he passed Audrey's desk, he said, "Sorry I didn't get back sooner, but it's been one thing after another since I left this morning." He started to explain further, but stopped when he saw her face—ashen, tears in her eyes and seeping down her cheeks. She pushed herself upright, touched his arm and led him into the inner office.

"What's happened?" He'd never seen her distraught before and didn't now if small things triggered this reaction..

Audrey choked. "Dr. Rogers died." She tried to wipe away the tears by rubbing her hand across her face.

Jason felt the blood drain from his face. His mind rushed through the consequences and reasons, trying to cope with his own shock and watching Audrey struggling to maintain her composure. He muttered, "When?"

"The hospital called here," she struggled to talk, her voice a whisper, wiping her eyes, "at three-thirty. He had a massive stroke just after noon today and never recovered consciousness. They were trying to find Mrs. Rogers and thought she might be here."

Jason sagged into one of the familiar chairs around the conference table and Audrey sat next to him. They looked at each other.

Finally, Jason muttered, "What next?" He rubbed his head.

"I haven't told anyone else yet." Audrey stared at him through glazed eyes. "I was too upset to talk. I just sat at my desk and . . . ." Her voice drained away as though the sound volume had been lowered.

Jason forced himself to focus on the immediate issue. "It's difficult to accept and deal with at the moment, but we should let everybody in the department know as soon as possible." Jason continued, trying to think what Henry would do under similar circumstances. "Maybe I should write a short note, and get the secretaries to put copies in offices of everyone who's here, then in the mail slots of the rest. Or better, you can E-mail it to everyone. That would be more efficient."

With something concrete to accomplish, Audrey stood, grasping the corner of the table until she could control her emotions. "I'll get it out before five today."

30

She took three steps and turned back, saying, "I've scheduled appointments with Dr. Boseman and Dr. Harris for tomorrow. The times on your desk calendar."

Jason scribbled the terse announcement about Henry's death, then leaned back in the chair. Staring into space, he recalled his desire to discuss those notes with Henry. Feeling empty and deserted, he reached for the telephone to call Lucy then he'd call Dean Hawthorne in case he hadn't heard about Rogers.

Following a custom they'd enjoyed for several years, Greg Harris, Peter Townsend, and Hugh Riley met each week after normal work hours to share a beer and rehash events going on in Biology and the University. During the last two years, Terry Boseman had joined them. They'd received the E-mail about Henry late this afternoon and now sat around a table in Randolph's, a bar and grill near campus that catered to students and those faculty willing to tolerate the noise and chaos of undergraduates talking loudly and yelling across the room to friends.

Riley, the acknowledged leader of the group, said as they each took first sips and leaned back, "Too bad about Rogers. Most people I've talked to were shocked at the suddenness of it."

Townsend, his ever-present pipe emitting fumes, shook his head. "Yeah, Henry will be missed. He'd been around a long time."

Riley, who's primary goal in life seemed to be that of criticizing people, particularly those whom he regarded as having authority over him, said, "Now we have to deal with Spradlin for a few months."

Harris twisted his beer mug. "That may not be bad. Henry could be a bastard and Jason is still finding his way in the administrative world."

Boseman, usually quiet until asked a question or ranting about some deal he considered an injustice to him personally, said, "I have an appointment with Spradlin tomorrow. I'd guess it's about tenure but the secretary didn't know or wouldn't tell."

Townsend puffed, exhaled a stream of smoke. "You should be okay with a bunch of publications and a couple of grants. He just wants to confer as a matter of course. Henry always did that."

Harris spoke up. "I'm to see Spradlin tomorrow also. I have no idea about what."

"This will be the first test for Spradlin," Riley injected. "I'd bet he'll be tougher than you guys think."

Always enjoying an opportunity to needle Riley, Townsend grinned. "You can't hold Spradlin responsible for reassigning your old lab to him. Henry did that."

"Sure, but I've had other encounters with Spradlin. He can be a tough character."

CHAPTER 4

Greg Harris rapped lightly on the door of the department head's office, now occupied by his younger colleague considered the fair-haired hotshot by Henry Rogers and others. Harris had been at State for twenty years and now in his fifties had an established research program with several graduate students and two technicians. His hair, turning gray at the fringes, had been combed to conceal balding spots. Heavy eyebrows, a mix of gray and brown, shaded his eyes.

"Jason, Audrey asked me to see you." Harris took a chair at the conference table before Jason could move from the desk. Obviously, he'd been in the office numerous times and assumed Jason would follow Henry's routine.

As he pulled one of the chairs away from the table, Jason said, "Greg, a note on Henry's to-do list indicated a conflict between a female graduate student and you. What's the problem?"

Harris felt the blood drain from his face and moisture popped out on his hands and underarms. He shifted in the chair. "There's no problem I'm aware of."

When he looked at Jason, he was confronted by a steady stare, confounding his notion he could bluff his way with the younger man.

Jason asked, "Has a student complained that your attention to her borders on harassment? Any talk around your lab about relationships exceeding the accepted boundaries?"

Harris blurted, "No." His eyes couldn't maintain contact. He wiped his hands on his pants below the table.

Jason noticed the motion and understood he'd hit on the key issue. "You realize if this is true and the student files a suit, you could be in big trouble."

Mustering his resolve, Harris glared at Jason as though challenging him to raise the question at all. He said, "Trust me. There's no problem."

Jason said, "I'll take your word that this is strictly rumor and there's no substance to it. I hope I'm correct. But be careful. You don't want to be confronted by a hearing before the university ethics committee to defend your actions."

Harris stood, muttering, "That's the right thing to do."

When Jason stood, he walked out, but thinking Riley and Townsend might be right. Jason Spradlin might be more of a bastard than Henry Rogers. If Spradlin stood for the permanent appointment they'd have to marshal their forces in opposition. He decided to bring it up at their next session.

But some student must have complained to Rogers. Henry hadn't gone around the halls looking for problems. And Spradlin hadn't pressed for details, raised his voice or accused him outright of trying to hit on women under his supervision.

Jason turned to the stack of papers, but his thoughts remained on Harris' reactions to the rumor, wanting to believe him but not at all comfortable with the obvious defensiveness of an older colleague much like a young boy caught in some misdemeanor..

An hour later, Terry Boseman arrived for his appointment. In his sixth year at State, Boseman confronted the mandatory tenure review, the most critical hurdle in the life of a young faculty member. Jason watched the walrus-shaped Boseman rake a chubby hand through his thick brown hair as he approached.

Boseman appeared wary, ready to argue, as he shook Jason's hand and perched on the edge of the chair next to the desk, as though he might run for the door. He brushed a hand across his face.

Jason said, "Terry, I asked you to come by to discuss the tenure situation with you. As you know, your credentials are be submitted soon and I wanted to meet with you about those. I know you may be concerned about the sudden change in department administrators at this time, but I'll do my best for you and the department. I need to know how you see the situation. Any worries, hints of things needing improvement from Henry's past discussions with you?"

Boseman shifted on the chair, obviously still not comfortable. "I think I'm in good shape. Eight publications in solid journals. Last year I received a grant from NIH. I've completed three M. S. students and have a doctoral candidate in the pipeline."

"Teaching evaluations okay?"

Boseman stared at the floor. "My scores from students haven't been the best, but it's okay."

Trying to make Boseman comfortable, Jason smiled. "It sounds like you're on solid grounds, but Henry had a reminder on his list to check your dossier. You have any idea why?"

A puzzled frown on his face, Boseman shook his head. "No. I believe my record is good enough."

Jason said, "I admit I don't know at the moment why he was concerned and maybe it's not important. Perhaps he only wanted to confirm you understood the process. Let's see how the department review committee recommends, unless you have questions."

Boseman scrambled to his feet, saying, "Thanks. I think I'll be okay."

Jason watched him disappear through the door, then made a note to review Boseman's file before the department tenure and promotion committee met. Henry didn't raise questions without a reason and he wished he'd had a chance to talk with Henry more about Boseman..

The First Methodist church filled early for Henry Rogers' funeral service at eleven on Saturday morning. An overflow crowd reflected his thirty-five years at State University and his interactions with hundreds of people within the institution and throughout the city.

Jason took Lucy's hand as they waited in the middle of the large sanctuary for the service to begin. She squeezed his fingers, and whispered, "It'll be okay." She understood his deepening concern that he was following a legend, thus bound to fail or perhaps be resented if he succeeded. Plus, both she and Jason were going to miss deeply the steady experienced presence of Rogers.

Jason retained little of the hour long testimonial to Rogers, his mind occupied with his personal memories of Henry. He remembered his many talks with Henry when the department head had given him advice or prodded him to take on greater challenges. These memories and the solemn faces of department faculty, university administrators, graduate students, and staff would be his recollection of the event. Jason left the church, holding Lucy's hand, speaking quietly with several acquaintances from the university who knew of his interim appointment through the university newspaper's blurb on Friday. But thoughts of Henry wouldn't go away. He wanted to disappear into a private place and cry.

Jason entered the quiet department office on Sunday afternoon. For the first time he noticed the faint aroma of Henry's pipe, likely captured by the fibers of the carpet. He placed personal items, an electronic calculator, a desk set given to him by Lucy, a handful of pencils held by a rubber band, a couple of rulers, and a pocket calendar taken from the lab office on the table, turned on the lights, and then focused on rearranging the desk so he knew where things were. He turned the pages of the desk calendar. He moved the telephone to a different location. He adjusted the chair to accommodate his longer legs. He shifted the conference table and the four chairs to make it easier for users to get into the seat next to the wall. Marks on the walls advised him to look for pictures to brighten up the place or at least cover the faded areas. He walked to the window facing one of the major quadrangles of the campus and realized he could look down on pedestrians using the sidewalks. Quincy had been constructed so the basement floor was approximately one-half above ground thus giving those on the main floor a better perspective. From his lab office without a window, he'd never given attention to the difference.

The stack of files and papers on the corner of the desk reminded him of Audrey's promise to respond to his questions raised by Henry's last notes. He picked up the manila folder on the top.

In it was a single page letter addressed to Henry. He read, "It appears very likely that the authors of the paper, *"Calcium Dependency of Viral Induced Reactions in Epithelial Cells"* have made a serious miscalculation of the data on which the manuscript is based. Two investigators working in the same area have recommended the paper, published in the June issue, be withdrawn since it conflicts with evidence from two independent laboratories attempting to replicate the same set of experiments. Based on those opinions, I arbitrarily selected two different reviewers, both active in the field, to give their independent assessments. They agree with those who raised the concern. Thus, I have concluded the paper is flawed, although two reviewers of the manuscript prior to acceptance for publication did not flag the problem.

"I am corresponding with you as the responsible administrator, since letters, E-mail notes, and faxes to the senior author, Preston A. King, have been ignored. Frankly, his failure to respond has become a worry. I'm concerned because two of the laboratories have stated in strong language the data were manufactured, and those who critiqued the paper for me concur with the possibility, but admit some quirk in

38

the methodology could have resulted in the reported outcome. Thus, four different investigators have testified independently the data in King's paper could not have been generated using the techniques described in the methods section of the article. Although I'm reluctant to make such a charge, the unanimous agreement from other researchers and reviewers, and the lack of acknowledgment by the senior author tends to support suspicion. By the way, none of the reviewers were given the name or affiliation of the authors, but they could well know first hand about the paper. I am certain they all read this journal.

"I am requesting that you discuss the matter with the author, and give me the benefit of your wisdom in dealing with the issue. As you know, it could be nothing more than an error in calculation, a mistake in the analyses, or even some slightly different approach in the protocol, but because others have persisted, I feel it necessary to try to settle the question. In my judgment, failure to clarify the issue will jeopardize the integrity of this journal."

Signed by Arthur J. Brumfield, Editor, Journal of Cell Biology. Copies to Luther E. Fowler, Vice President for Research, State University; and to Nancy Thompson, Project Manager, National Institutes of Health.

The letter was dated September second, and stamped received by Biology on September seventh, the day before Henry left for the hospital. He hadn't had time to evaluate the situation, or see King about the problem.

Jason flipped the desk calendar back to the seventh. Three hours spent in a department head's meeting with the Dean. No appointment was listed for King, but Jason knew Henry often went to a faculty's office or lab to discuss some issue without setting up a meeting. But, if he had seen King, the reminder would have been crossed off the memo pad or another one added about the matter. Too, Henry would have told him at their last meeting about King's reactions.

He paced across the office, a exercise he couldn't have done in his other office, and stopped to stare out the window. He knew King pretty well, and couldn't believe he'd be involved in outright falsification of data. King had come to State a year before Jason, established a solid reputation for work in viral replication in mammalian cells, and now had several graduate students and a couple of post-docs in an active research lab. There would be no reason to cut corners, thus the problem must be an error. But why hadn't King responded to the editor?

Jason watched a couple strolling near the building, holding hands, stopping to kiss, laughing at each other. Where did a department head start to get at the bottom of this mess? He couldn't talk to other faculty and risk the news being leaked, unless he had absolute trust in the person's ability to keep rumors to himself. Maybe George Stuart could be a sounding board. Maybe the thing to do was lay the problem in King's lap, but avoid outright accusations. He couldn't tell Lucy for fear she'd be placed in a vulnerable position when the problem became public knowledge. She wouldn't be embarrassed and have to hedge the truth, if she could say forthrightly that Jason never tells me those things. Maybe he'd ask her advice on what she would rather know in these situations.

Jason turned away from the window and glanced at his watch. Time to go. He'd promised a trip to the park with Lucy and the two kids. Maybe he'd have an inspiration overnight about how to deal with this problem. As he closed the door, he remembered he'd not looked at the rest of the folders in the stack and thought he'd have to learn how to deal with issues more quickly.

Jason and Lucy watched their two children fly down the long metal slide and scramble to get back in line for the next turn. Jennifer, age five, a smaller version of her mother, and Tony, age three, had changed their parents' lives. The once quiet house, purchased as soon as both obtained tenure, had became overnight it seemed, a bustle of uncontrolled activity, at times bordering on bedlam.

Running to get in line, Tony fell but bounced up immediately to keep up with his sister, looked at his parents, sitting on the wooden bench a few yards away. He grinned and waved.

"Did we ever," Lucy smiled, touching Jason's hand, "have such energy?"

"Can't remember, but I expect so," Jason responded. "They really like this equipment, don't they?"

As Jennifer waited at the top of the slide, Lucy said, "It's too bad I can't bring them here every day."

Jason looked at her somber features, knowing she was thinking about the dual roles of mother and professional. "It would get boring for them."

"I suppose, but I know that's your way of making me feel okay about them."

"I'm not that devious," Jason grinned at her, "but regardless, they're doing well. Happy, bright kids without a worry in the world."

"We're not objective judges of their brightness, but what parent is."

Jason put his arm around her shoulder. "Of course we are. How can they not be with your genes?"

Lucy chuckled. "I know where this might lead to later." She continued to watch the group of children, then said, "We're lucky they're not afflicted with some disease, like those Donald kids you dealt with."

The Donald's had been born with Wilson's disease, a genetic defect that impaired copper metabolism and usually resulted in an early death. They had been the subjects in Jason's research to remedy the problem. Interventions by Jason and John Hadley, a senior faculty member in the Medical School, had prolonged their lives and improved their condition. The problem had not been solved yet but recent breakthroughs using stem cell replacement of defective genes promised permanent relief. The research investigation continued with other children and two young adults under an NIH grant.

"I haven't seen the Donald's in a year now. I heard through Hadley they're doing okay."

Lucy glanced at her watch. "Let's get them to the swings. I don't want to have a major ruckus when they've missed something." She stood, trying to gain Jennifer's attention.

Jason gathered their things, wondering why the kids had brought a toy gun and the set of dolls, but his mind turned back to the issue with King and his intent to pose the question with Lucy about her learning of problems in the department. He picked up the green ribbon Jennifer had dropped in her rushing from the slide.

On Monday morning Jason used thirty minutes to review notes for the nine o'clock lecture, reminding himself he should locate a substitute within the next couple of days. When he returned at ten-fifteen, he asked Audrey to come in. She took the chair next to the desk, straightened her skirt, a notepad and pencil in her hand, waiting for him.

He pulled the King letter from the desk, reminding her of its content. "Do you know if Henry talked to Dr. King about this?"

"I don't think so. Dr. King was out of town on the seventh and Dr. Rogers asked me to set up a time to see him." She looked at the floor. "But it was too late."

"Had there been any other discussion or correspondence about this problem?"

Shaking her head, she said, "Not to my knowledge." So Henry hadn't been copied on the earlier letters to King. Audrey opened, scanned and sorted the head's mail into stacks ranging from important to junk. She seemed to remember everything.

"Okay," Jason said, "please set up a time for King to come in as soon as possible. And see if Dr. Stuart is available. I want to ask him about a substitute for the General Biology section. I'll go to his office if he's free."

George Stuart was regarded as the most knowledgeable and least political member of the Biology faculty, the individual who would give advice when asked, but seldom questioned decisions or policies. A small man in his fifties, gray-hair thinning across the top, pale blue-gray eyes set in a round face, Stuart looked up from his computer station when Jason knocked. "How're you doing?" He pointed to a side chair, as Jason closed the office door.

"I've been better. Right now, I need your help in finding someone to take over the General Biology section I have."

George pushed his chair back, looking at Jason. "There's a person in the community we've used at times to fill in—Dorothy McGinnis. She's worked on a doctoral degree with Krause, but dropped out because of young children. I could call her, if you'd like."

Jason stood. "That'd be helpful, George. We can pay her the equivalent of an assistantship or maybe a little more."

"I'll let you know by the end of the day."

Jason headed for his research lab, thinking there should be more faculty like Stuart.

An hour later, Audrey called. "Dr. King is coming in at two-thirty this afternoon."

44

Scanning a set of data collected by a graduate student, Jason's mind kept thinking about how he should approach King. He didn't look forward to the encounter.

CHAPTER 5

Preston King, a tall, gangly man in his mid-thirties, black hair, gray-blue eyes, glanced at Jason when he entered the office, then looked away as Audrey closed the door behind him. Jason shook King's hand, noted the clammy touch, and pointed to a chair by the conference table. The aroma of some solvent from King's clothing reminded Jason of his research lab.

"Things going okay with your work?" Jason asked, watching King's reactions.

King nodded, crossed a long leg over the other, pulled at his khaki pants. "Yes, everything is going well. Too bad about Henry. He was a good man."

"We were all shocked by the suddenness of his passing. Especially me."

King glanced around the room as though noting changes in the arrangement, avoiding Jason's eyes, clasping his hands together across a knee. He pulled at a thread on his brown sock.

His hope King would broach the critical issue reaching a stalemate, Jason took the lead. Leaning forward, elbows resting on the table, Jason said, "Preston, we have a problem. I learned about the challenge of your paper yesterday when I was going through Henry's work file." He handed King a copy of the letter from the journal editor.

Two minutes passed while King read the letter, twisted the paper around in his hand before returning it to Jason. "I just haven't gotten around to responding," King said, his eyes fixed on the floor. He pulled a ball point pen from the pocket of his plaid sport shirt and rolled it between his fingers.

"I assume there's a logical explanation." Jason smiled, hoping King would open up and talk about the situation.

"Of course." King barely nodded.

"You should reply to the journal and give them your interpretation of the differences between your paper and other published reports. You know the longer you delay, the more suspicious the episode becomes. You can tell from Brumfield's letter, he thinks you've been dishonest because you've ignored him."

King looked directly at Jason for the first time since entering the office. "I'll E-mail a response to him in the next couple of days." He returned the pen to his shirt pocket.

"That'd be wise, even if you know there's an error in the work. Just admit it and move forward." Jason understood that acknowledging an error had been published would be embarrassing, but it would be worse if King refused to clarify his data.

When King stood, Jason added, "Send me a copy of your response. I'll be called by the Vice-President, since he received a copy of this letter from Brumfield." He watched King stride out, closing the door softly. He hoped King's communication would terminate the conflict, but he didn't like King's reluctance to discuss the situation. Something was wrong, more than a routine disagreement about a publication. And

48

the fact that the original reviewers, selected from a pool of investigators working in the area of King's research, hadn't picked up on the problem, posed another puzzle.

Jason signed five purchase orders and scanned the stacks of mail. Nothing urgent, mostly informational memos from several university administrative offices. He stuck them in his briefcase for tonight's reading. He tossed the pile of advertisements into the waste basket.

He pulled the next folder from Audrey's stack related to Henry's list, opened the file on Terry Boseman and scanned the credentials submitted for the last annual review, his fifth year in the department. State University followed the guidelines of the American Association of University Professors that included a six year probationary period. Institutions were forced to make decisions about permanent appointments by the end of the sixth year or the faculty member received automatic tenure. State deviated slightly from the guide in that they sometimes granted tenure or terminated an appointment at the end of a three-year probationary period. Passage of this critical hurdle served as a guarantee of a life-long contract except in those cases of criminal behavior or continuous failure to meet minimum job expectations. Removal of a tenured faculty for poor performance was so torturous and time consuming most administrators wouldn't bother. By the time sufficient documentation to prove incompetence had been assembled, either the faculty or the administrator had retired. This was Boseman's critical year to clear the hurdle.

Jason flipped pages of the dossier. Eight papers dealing with the physiology of the thyroid and the mechanisms involved in the secretion of thyroxin, all published in reputable journals. Jason had heard of them all, and published in two of them himself. All of the work had been supported by NIH grants. Boseman had completed three Master's students, and now had a doctoral candidate, plus three other master's level people progressing toward degrees.

Toward the end of the dossier a summary of Boseman's teaching scores and peer reviews caused Jason to lay aside the folder and stare into space. Evaluation scores were terrible, usually an average score of less than two on a five point scale, with one being poor and five representing excellent. Regardless of the course or the size of the class, Boseman's evaluations from students were the worst Jason had ever seen. But student scores were always suspect, even discounted sometimes because of the growing inclination of students to reward teachers who gave high grades and punish those who were more demanding.

However, the faculty peer review letters were equally discouraging. Four letters from other faculty, who'd been assigned by Henry to review Boseman's teaching techniques and materials used in classes, offered no expectation of improvement. Every letter described a disorganized instructor who rambled through lectures and responded ineffectively to questions from students. Explanations of basic theories were characterized as weak and confusing. Now Jason understood Henry's note—this was a problem.

Boseman represented the classic case of a solid researcher and a lousy instructor. Jason knew the department tenure and promotion committee would have difficulty with Boseman and no doubt

50

represented the basis for Henry's reminder to be alert on a crucial decision for the department, as well as for Boseman. Jason knew the department head also made a recommendation regarding tenure separate from the committee. Both opinions were forwarded to a college level panel and in theory were weighted equally.

As he laid aside the file on Boseman, Audrey buzzed the telephone to say Dr. Stuart was waiting to see him.

George plopped into the side chair. "I caught up with Dorothy McGinnis and she'd like to teach the section. The stipend is okay."

"When can she start?"

"Next Monday. She needs to locate a day care for her daughter, or arrange for a sitter a couple of hours each morning."

"That's great, George. Thanks for taking care of that."

"Would it help if I did the lectures tomorrow and Friday?"

Jason said, "No, I'll take care of those. The truth is I could probably keep up with the class once I figure out what this job entails."

George grinned and rubbed a hand along the knee of his gray slacks. "Don't try it. I remember Henry wanted to teach the course, but discovered he couldn't after a couple of weeks. Too many conflicts." He leaned forward, starting to rise.

Jason said, "While you're here, would you be willing to talk about Terry Boseman and his teaching problems? I'm asking because Henry had left a note in his file, and I see he's received dreadful marks from both students and reviewers."

George leaned back in the chair, crossed his ankles. "I was on the department personnel committee when Terry came up for the three-year review. We had a long debate on whether to recommend termination then, but we finally agreed to continue him because he's been a productive researcher—publications, grant money, all the right things. We believed his teaching would improve if sufficiently warned."

"I'm sure the files will have letters about the recommendation," Jason asked, "but do you recall if he really was warned about the teaching issue and unless improvements were evident, he could be turned down at the sixth year?"

Nodding his head, George said, "The letter the committee wrote recommended he get help and fast, to improve his communications and organizational approach to courses." He leaned an elbow on the desk. "I critiqued a couple of classes during his fourth or fifth year at Henry's request. Jason, he's the absolute worst teacher I've seen in all my years around this place. It would be impossible for the kids to learn anything they didn't dig out of the textbook. No doubt the good ones do, but the run-of-the mill student won't be able to learn that way."

"So what's the problem? George, has he tried to improve?"

He shrugged and shook his head. "I honestly don't know, but it's hard to believe he couldn't do better. He's a bright guy and his grad students like him," George smiled, "except in a formal course. I suspect the bottom line is he just doesn't give a damn and thinks research is all he must do."

"I haven't reviewed the tenure materials from the three year evaluation or his personnel file," Jason said, "so maybe there are clues in those."

52

George stood. "It'll be a tricky case for the department committee." He smiled. "I'm glad I'm not on this year." He picked up the glass paper weight on the corners of Jason's desk and then put it back in place, saying, "Maybe the more recent reviews suggest he's improved."

Jason shook his head. "Afraid not. And it's going to be tricky for me too. An interim head will be suspect regardless."

George said, "Do what's best for Biology."

Hugh Riley, a long-time Associate Professor in the department, wandered into King's research lab on the third floor of Quincy. Three students huddled near a microscope, but didn't look up as Riley passed behind them noting the intense odor of formalin.

From a desk in the corner of the lab, a young woman spoke, "May I help you?" She came toward him.

Riley's pulse skipped a beat. She had to be one of the most alluring women he'd ever seen. Five-five, slender with definite female curves, tanned skin, dark eyes, black hair cut short, dressed in a blue dress and heels, she personified Riley's perception of sexiness. He wanted to touch her and stuck out his hand, saying, "I'm Hugh Riley, a faculty member in the department."

She took his hand. "I'm Kathryn Helweg, a post-doc with Dr. King." She pulled her hand away when Riley continued to hold it.

"I'm looking for King. Is he around?" He continued to stare at her face, mesmerized like a moth around a flame.

"He's in his office.   Just knock." She turned away and Riley watched her lithe figure until she was almost to her desk. She didn't have a wedding ring, but there must a bunch of guys hot after her.

King offered Riley a chair, saying, "What's up?" He shoved aside a lab notebook, dropping a stubby pencil into the fold, and clicked the mouse so the computer went to the screen saver.

Still thinking about Kathryn, Riley said, "I just met your post-doc. She brightens up the scene."

"She's very bright and professional."

Riley wanted to find out if Kathryn had a serious relationship, but didn't know how King would react to his prying. He focused on his original agenda for coming and said, "I've heard you're having conflicts with Spradlin."

King shook his head, "We've had a discussion about an issue, but I wouldn't characterize it as a conflict." He knew Riley's major goal in the department was to stir up problems and challenge administrators, always searching for a slip-up he could use to embarrass those in leadership positions. King tried to avoid him as much as possible without an overt turn-off.

Riley looked around the office, shelves overflowing with books and pamphlet holders. A photo of King's wife, whom he'd met at a department function, and a two boys rested on the corner of the desk. He said, "Rumors are Spradlin is not interested in the permanent headship and several of us are pleased. They wouldn't want to work with him in that role."

King reopened his notebook, hoping Riley would get the hint. He said, "He might not be bad." He'd been relieved he hadn't been confronted by Henry Rogers about the Brumfield letter. Jason hadn't yelled at him and seemed genuinely interested in getting to the bottom of the puzzle, although he'd insisted King do something quickly.

Riley leaned forward as though to confide important information. "I know personally he can be a bastard, so if he becomes a candidate, I'll oppose him as vigorously as possible. And so will others."

King stood. "Let's wait a while. He's likely not interested." He'd heard about Jason threatening Riley once when Riley had lambasted one of Jason's graduate students over a conflict between the two faculty members. And that Riley wanted to blame Spradlin for Rogers reassigning a lab space which Riley hadn't used in years.

Riley nodded. "He'll apply, so we have to be ready." He walked out, detouring to pass close to Kathryn's desk and was disappointed she wasn't there. He determined to find out more. For all he knew, King was banging her. He'd been too closed mouthed when he'd brought up her name.

Riley had been disappointed in King's reaction. He had expected King to complain about Spradlin and be ready to join any group against Spradlin. But if he's playing around with a post-doc and others know, he could be persuaded.

Five minutes after Riley left the lab, Kathryn entered King's office, sat in the chair and asked, "Who is this Riley? I felt very uncomfortable around him."

"He's the department busy-body. Always trying to stir up a controversy. Today he was eager to enlist my support against our interim department head should he become a candidate for the permanent post."

"Is he a womanizer? He was staring at me at every opportunity."

"I don't know about that, but if he gives you a problem, let me know." King knew several males around campus had tried to hit on Helweg without success. When they'd failed, they started the rumor she must be lesbian.

Jason retrieved Henry's pad and made a note to look at all the files regarding Boseman. Jason wondered why the case should be such an issue. If the performances were reversed and Boseman was an outstanding teacher, but without a research record, there'd be no doubt. He'd fail without any debate in the committee.

His thoughts were interrupted by the telephone. Audrey announced, "It's Nancy Thompson from NIH."

"Nancy, how are you?" Jason said, as he nestled the instrument against his face. During the last seven years, he'd developed a comfortable working relationship with Thompson, who'd been the agency representative responsible for most of his NIH projects.

"Doing well, but I'm distressed over the news about Henry Rogers. We heard today. And the secretary confirmed you'd been appointed as interim. You'll do it well."

"It's devastating in many regards," Jason said. "We were adjusting to his announced plans to retire, but then . . . he was gone." He waited for the issue with King to be next.

"He'll be missed in the profession," she said, a slight pause, "but the reason I called was to encourage your department to submit an application for our Center of Excellence grants. The announcements are going out later this week and we're calling those departments we'd like to become involved."

She continued, "We think Biology at State would fare well if you focused your proposal on the genetic therapy work going on there."

Jason asked, "Tell me the intent of the Center?"

Thompson said, "Our idea is to support teaching-research centers at places where physicians and others could be exposed to the cutting-edge techniques. We would hope physicians from medical centers around the country would study at the Centers for three to six months to learn those skills necessary to treat major diseases. We've thought of such things as updating on research testing that could be applied to their practices, review of basic information, and giving them exposure to the more recent publications. We've realized in the past couple of years that we support all this sophisticated research, but the utilization in the larger medical community lags too far behind. We want these grants to change that and give us other ideas about enhancing the continuing education of the typical physician."

"The concept sounds interesting," Jason replied, "but we're in such transition now, I don't know what the department would want to do. I'll need some time to explore the interests of faculty."

Thompson hesitated, then said, "I hope you'll be interested. But I called to alert you to the announcement so you don't miss it when it comes in. After you've looked at the package, call me if you have questions. I'll be glad to work with you."

"I'll let you know what we might do." He scribbled a note on a pad and drew squares around it while they talked.

Jason waited, then asked, "Have you received a letter from Arthur Brumfield about Preston King?"

"Yes, but I didn't know if in all the confusion of Henry's death and the transition, you knew about it." She paused then added, "It's disturbing, but I don't know what to make of it. King has done excellent work on viral replication in understanding basic cell processes."

"It was on the top of Henry's to-do list, so I learned about it immediately. King has promised to respond to Brumfield soon. I hope that will solve the thing."

"Let's hope so." She sighed. "Jason, the climate around NIH with all these Congressional committees looking over our shoulder, is scary and nasty. I'm afraid if Brumfield or other researchers make a big issue of this thing, we'll be brought up before the Oversight Sub-Committee or the full Science and Technology Committee of the House because we supported the research. We'd be forced to involve King in the review."

"Let's hope it doesn't reach that point." Jason said, but he didn't want to reveal the depth of his concern, based on King's defensive attitude and unwillingness to explain immediately the problem. The

58

demeanor contrasted sharply with King's usual candor and eager openness.

"Whatever happens, it's good experience for a new department head." She laughed. "Let me know about the Center application."

"I will, and thanks for calling."

Jason added an item to Henry's list on the pad. To discuss the potential grant application with key faculty. The agency alert was a signal the department's proposal would receive serious consideration. The department shouldn't pass up such an opportunity, but it would mean a lot of extra work by several faculty. Being in a favored position didn't eliminate the demand for a creative and plausible proposal, a task that would require numerous hours of writing even after the essential ideas had been formulated and sifted. While the agency might favor a particular group because of some unique expertise, study committees composed of outsiders may have quite different ideas.

Perhaps he could provide enough stimulus to formulate the basic concepts around which a group of faculty could work out the details, then pull the pieces together into a coherent proposal. Then, if successful, there'd be the challenge of getting the work accomplished. There might be sufficient resources to bring on short-term people to handle some of the effort.

He'd begun to understand why department heads never had time to give attention to research or proposals such as this Center idea. They exhausted themselves with issues like the King controversy and

Boseman's apparent refusal to spend sufficient time preparing lecture that made sense to undergraduates.

After the department seminar, Greg Harris followed Pete Townsend to his office. The square space epitomized disorganization, books and papers stacked randomly in every possible place—on top of file cabinets, on the window sill, and on much of the floor. A small figurine perched on top of the stack in the window caught his eye.

Townsend lighted his pipe, puffing away to get it going, adding to the heavy odor of tobacco already pervading the office.

Harris said, "What do you think about Spradlin? Seems awful young to become department head."

Taking another puff on the curved pipe, Townsend nodded, saying, "He's told George Stuart he won't be a candidate. Just fill in until a permanent appointment is made."

Glancing at the chaos around him, Harris shook his head. "He'll want the job after he's been at it a while."

"That worry you?"

"He could be hard to deal with."

"He's stayed out of department politics pretty much. Sticks to his lab. Big research program with scads of money coming in. But you're right. He can be tough minded."

Harris nodded, saying, "I know he confronted Riley once. Threatened to punch Riley if he ever took advantage of his graduate students again."

60

Townsend bumped the pipe on an ash tray, pieces of ash flying around, then said, "I remember, and he didn't back down when Jefferson Bell challenged his research on gene therapy."

"But Bell went too far. Doing all those things to destroy Spradlin's research."

"Henry Rogers liked Spradlin. Remember the big argument about Jason's promotion. We all thought he was too young to be a full professor, but Henry took a strong stand for him." Without pausing, Townsend asked, "You had a run-in already with Spradlin?"

Harris shifted in the chair, and said, "He called me in about some rumor in my research group. Nothing to it, but I don't think he believed me."

Townsend knew about the rumors of Harris' philandering as he made it his business to learn about all the department gossip. But he said, "If you want to organize against Spradlin, talk to Riley."

Harris stood, saying, "I'll think about it when the time comes. I'd prefer someone with more experience for the leader's job."

Townsend smiled. "Let's see how the next three months go. Spradlin has a big problem with this King issue. That could do him in if it blows up as I suspect it might."

CHAPTER 6

Preston King's face and carriage suggested frustration and aggravation as Jason watched him slump into a chair at the conference table in the head's office, now becoming familiar territory to Jason.

Jason confronted the situation. "Preston, I read your E-mail to Brumfield and I'm disappointed. You didn't tell him anything new." Jason struggled to hold back his own irritation, but knew his tone revealed his feelings. When he'd first read King's response, his impulse had been to yell at his colleague as soon as he walked through the door, but he restrained himself. King's terse note saying they had not found errors, but were continuing to check the data had not been sufficient explanation in Jason's mind.

Looking at the floor, King said, "We're still rechecking our data, so I can't be more specific at this time."

"I don't want to make a huge issue of this," Jason continued, "but Brumfield was anticipating more. Either an explanation of why your work doesn't agree with the other labs, or an admission of an error. Just to say you're still checking won't satisfy him. At least, I'd be surprised if it will."

King's face contorted into a scowl. "You don't know that."

"You're correct, I don't. But from the tone of his letter, he's convinced you've made a significant error or worse."

"Meaning?" For the first time King's voice challenged Jason. He straightened up, squared his shoulders, and glared at Jason.

"Preston, he believes you've manufactured data, or somehow manipulated the experimental methods beyond the usual limits to reach your conclusions."

"Do you believe I've cheated?" His tone carried defiance. His face darkened.

"Frankly, Preston," Jason said softly, but returning the stare. "I don't know what to think. I've known you for several years and I can't imagine you cutting corners at all. You've got to admit you've not been forthcoming with Brumfield. Ignoring him was the worst thing to do. Now this E-mail," he picked up the copy, "only adds to his suspicion. You've got to give a better explanation."

"He's trying to make my lab look bad." King shifted in the chair, and leaned his elbows onto the table, his eyes glued to the surface. "Probably those other bastards got to him."

Jason knew from his own experience that the competition between laboratories striving to make cutting-edge breakthroughs and achieve notoriety and fame was increasing, slowly but surely eroding the tradition of open sharing between investigators. The continuing decline of research dollars had exacerbated the situation, but as yet he'd not heard of anyone setting out to sabotage another researcher. Jason said, "That doesn't seem likely. Brumfield has no reason to favor one place or any group of investigators over another." He waited, then added, "But from his letter, he's being pressured to obtain some retraction or explanation from you." He paused, looking at the top of King's head, hair in disarray. "And you owe him that much."

When King continued to bow his head over the table, Jason asked quietly, "Preston, what's going on with this paper? I've interacted with you on numerous occasions and you're reacting differently than I've ever seen. You've always been straight forward, but now you're stone-walling any question about this piece of work." Jason felt as though he was addressing his five-year-old daughter.

King stood, and turned toward the door. "I'll send Brumfield something by the end of the week to satisfy him . . . and you." He pulled the door open, retreating through the clerical office, his head down and shoulders slumped.

Jason watched until the outer door closed, then he walked to Audrey's desk and motioned for her to come in.

"Would you get me a list of everybody working with Dr. King, including post-docs, graduate students, technicians, whoever? And I don't want him to know."

Audrey hesitated. "It might be hard without asking him directly."

Jason thought about the situation, then said, "Then get Miriam to make a list all the appointments for King's post-docs and graduate assistants."

"You're worried about that letter?"

"You're right, and he isn't being very helpful in solving the issue, so I have to find out what's happened some way." He paused, glancing at her face. "I don't like to go behind his back, but there seems to be no other choice."

Audrey sat in the side chair. "Dr. Rogers was upset when the letter came. He almost yelled at me to get King in here."

"If you know a better approach, tell me. You've seen a lot of strange things during your time in this office."

She shook her head. "I don't know how else to find out what's going on if you want to talk to people in his lab, other than confront him directly."

Jason considered her advice, thinking Henry would have gone directly to King and demanded a roster, but Jason remained uncomfortable with that approach. Maybe interim heads were more cautious, more insecure, although the Dean had told him to act as though he was in a permanent role. But he didn't think such advice applied in all situations. He didn't want King to become even more defensive at the prospect of Jason talking with students in the lab, nor having King jump down their throats when he learned Jason had questioned them. Given Preston King's apparent state of mind, Jason could envision him threatening students to the point they'd be afraid to open up. But perhaps that had already happened.

Jason suggested, "I could let it ride and hope it'll disappear."

Audrey smiled. "Dr. Spradlin, things never just go away on their own."

"Do one other thing. Set up an appointment with Dr. Fowler, the Vice-President for Research. Tell him it's about this letter."

Luther Fowler greeted Jason with his usual grin and bright outlook.. "I'm glad you came by. I'd planned to call you, but thought I'd give you a few days to settle in." His ruddy face changed to a frown. "Sorry about Henry. I always respected him—direct, never cut corners." He laughed. "Maybe too direct at times." They were silent for a moment, both recalling confrontations with Henry.

Jason said, "You always knew where he stood on things."

Fowler grinned. "I see we're getting ready to screw up another good researcher by making him a department head."

Jason said, "I plan to get out as soon as possible."

"Be careful, it's addictive, this administrative stuff." Fowler had been the head of electrical engineering before taking on the central administrative role four years ago. Jason had dealt with him on rare occasions about grant management issues, and knew he was well liked and regarded as a competent administrator across the university.

Fowler continued, "But department heads are key people to improving the place. You'll do well."

Jason ignored the opportunity to discuss his potential candidacy for the job, but said, "I came to talk about the letter to Preston King from Arthur Brumfield, the editor of *The Journal of Cell Biology*."

Fowler pulled the letter from beneath a bronze paper weight on the top of his desk. "It reads like he thinks King has cheated."

"I've encouraged King," Jason explained, "to inform Brumfield what's happened, but he's very defensive about the entire matter. His E-mail sent two days ago didn't help. He avoided Brumfield's concerns."

He continued to look at Fowler. "I need advice on what I should do. Obviously, if Brumfield's allegation becomes public, the department and the university will be damaged."

"Have you done anything yet?"

"Other than talking with King, I'm getting a list of people in his research group. I'm thinking about talking with people associated with the paper to try to discover what they think went wrong."

Fowler shoved the letter into a drawer, leaving the desk top clear. "Jason, there's not an established procedure for these things. I'm uncomfortable with too much stirring of the pot until we know what's likely to bubble up." Jason realized Fowler was searching for logical steps to approach a potentially career-damaging situation for King.

Jason said, "Suppose I call Brumfield. Attempt to find out what he plans to do. He could be key to this deal, unless some other investigator goes public based on their suspicions. I've had nightmares about letters to editors, revelations to the media, complaints to granting agencies, and others that are completely off the wall."

"But you think that's unlikely unless Brumfield approves."

Jason shrugged and frowned. "From the little I know, two different labs have approached Brumfield essentially demanding a retraction from King or at least an explanation. So, yes, I think he could trigger something, but that would be unusual for a journal editor. But who can predict. He doesn't want the journal to get the reputation of publishing papers which have been questioned, but he can't control those researchers who might do something on their own."

Fowler twisted in his chair, and said, "Okay, call him. Tell him we'll do an in-house investigation. See if he's willing to hold back until we can find out what's wrong."

"Should I talk to the people around King?"

"It might be useful, but you won't know until you do it." Fowler asked, "Has King ever been accused of such actions before?"

"Never to my knowledge," Jason said. "He's regarded in the department as a productive, dependable investigator and solid faculty member. He gets grants consistently and to my knowledge his work hasn't been challenged." Jason recognized that Henry might have known about such problems, but he wouldn't have shared them with anyone else on the faculty. But he hadn't hinted at past problems in that last conversation in the hospital. Jason wondered if the pain and medication had been to much for him to recall any incidents, but it seemed unlikely. Henry had been surprised, perhaps even mystified, by the accusation against King.

"Any chance King's correct and the others would like to know more about his approach or techniques?"

Jason shook his head slowly. "Maybe. I've considered the possibility, but why demand withdrawal of the paper. And you'd think they would contact King directly if they wanted details of his methodology." Most investigators were willing to respond to questions to assist those working in the same area. Sometimes a brief conversation saved hours of trial and error attempting to make a procedure work.

"Have you seen the letters sent to Brumfield by those challenging King's work?"

Shaking his head, Jason said, "No, although I assume King got copies."

"It might be worth looking at those. Maybe King missed something and became so irate he can't think straight about his response."

Jason didn't think that likely, but nodded. "I'll ask him for a copy."

Jason knew the history of science was filled with tales of other researchers, now famous, who'd been out in front of the crowd with a new theory and had undergone close scrutiny, mingled with disbelief and skepticism, even ridicule, for several years. Maybe King was one of those and didn't want to reveal too much until he could be certain of his finding. Or, he was so unsure of his findings, he didn't want to reveal his ideas even to close colleagues yet.

Fowler stood. "After you've talked with some of the lab people, let me know and we'll move forward from there."

When Jason reached the door, Fowler added, "And think seriously about the department head slot. You could do it well." He was grinning when Jason glanced back at him.

Two days after Harris talked to him, Townsend followed Riley from the department mail room, a small space in the administrative suite with four by six inch slots for each faculty member. Packages were piled on a table to be picked up in response to notes from the secretary who sorted the mail dropped twice daily by the campus mail service.

70

In the hall, Townsend asked, "You have a minute?"

As students continued to move about, headed for a classroom or on their way out of the building, he touched Riley's shoulder, saying, "Come by my office."

As Townsend closed the door, Riley asked, "What's up?"

Moving books from the single side chair not completely inundated, Townsend motioned for Riley to have a seat, then said, "Harris is worried Spradlin will become the next head. I don't know if he talked to you about it."

"I heard Spradlin called him in. Harris was trying to get this grad student into the sack and she wouldn't go along, then complained to Spradlin."

Townsend grinned. "I think she complained to Rogers actually. Anyway Harris says it's not true—only rumors. But you know Harris. He thinks Spradlin didn't buy his story and is concerned Spradlin could be a real bastard if he becomes head. On the other hand, George Stuart tells me Spradlin isn't interested."

Fingering his tie clip, Riley nodded. "I know George likes Spradlin. He may be encouraging Spradlin to apply."

Townsend nodded and waited.

"Anybody who hasn't had a conflict with Spradlin sees this hard working guy who brings in money and publishes a lot. But if he disagrees with you . . . ." Riley shrugged and frowned, remembering his fear Spradlin was going to hit him over some argument. He added, "If he had any power, he could be tough."

Townsend twirled his rack of pipes, eight arrayed on a circular stand, all shaped different, all smelly. He selected a short stem one off the rack, saying, "Well, I wanted you to know where Harris stands."

Riley smirked. "And if he lives up to his reputation, he'll keep pressing this woman until she goes along or complains again."

Riley paused, watching Townsend struggle with a lighter, puffing at the pipe, then he added, "Then Spradlin is going to jump his ass and there'll be hell to pay."

Smoke billowing around his face, Townsend said, "Spradlin is a good looking guy. Didn't he have something going with a student once."

"Yeah, when he first came to the department he had an affair with Elizabeth Abbot. Couldn't blame him, she was some sexy broad. But since he married, I haven't heard anything."

"His wife is a real looker herself."

Riley coughed as the smoke filled his nostrils. He stood, saying, "I'll talk to Harris and I'm surprised he hasn't tried to hit on that post-doc in King's lab. She's the sexiest woman in the building."

"I think he has and came away feeling he'd been slammed across the head. According to Greg, she's a cold one. Wouldn't even talk to him when he invited her for a drink after work. Just told him to get lost."

On the way out, Riley reached for a Kleenex, wondering how long it would be before Townsend came down with lung cancer.

CHAPTER 7

Jason's hopes that Brumfield wouldn't call before he'd had time to investigate the matter further by talking to King's lab personnel were dashed when the telephone rang at eight-fifteen the following morning. As Arthur Brumfield introduced himself, Jason admonished himself for not telling Audrey to stall any calls from Brumfield. Then Jason thought quickly about the issues involved with King as Brumfield spoke.

"I was trying to reach Henry Rogers, but the secretary told me you've replaced him and the circumstances. I'm sorry to hear about Henry." With only a brief pause, he continued, his voice taking on a coarser, almost belligerent, tone, "but I want to talk about Preston King and this paper that's causing such a ruckus."

"I read your letter to Dr. Rogers," Jason responded softly, "and I've encouraged King to give you enough information to clear the air." He added, as Brumfield attempted to interrupt, "He's promised to do that within a few days."

"Hell fire, Spradlin, he told me that two months ago. He ignored my requests for a clarification, then sends me this damn E-mail which says nothing. Another stall."

Jason ignored the outburst, but said, "We're planning an internal review of the situation. In fact, certain steps have been put in place already. We're unclear about what actions you intend to take, but we'd appreciate your waiting until we've done our work."

"I'm not sure I can hold back some of these guys. They're mad as hell and threatening to go public with their concerns. They've as much as charged King with outright fraud in the paper." Even on the telephone, Jason could detect the underlying frustration of Brumfield, a person caught in the middle of a controversy and not liking it.

Something in the conversation and thinking about the challenges struck Jason as out of line with the typical give and take of scientific advances. Jason asked, "So what's so urgent? If King's paper is wrong, subsequent work will demonstrate that."

A slight pause, then Brumfield said, "The others think King's paper is so far off the mark it's likely to lead the field astray for several years. From what I can figure out, they've all been trying to demonstrate the mechanisms by which viruses influence the replication of cells, but the King report goes so far as to suggest viral impact is negative under the conditions previously reported or unless certain factors are present. Nobody believes his data. At least two other reputable labs say they've tried to replicate his methodology without success. To be candid, Dr. Spradlin, had King responded in good faith, this thing would have disappeared."

Brumfield paused, then continued, "I've been sitting on two letters to the editor, both of which castigate King personally and accuse his lab of sloppy work, including hints of outright dishonesty. I can't hold back much longer."

"Were copies of those letters sent to King?"

"Yes, when I first asked for a rebuttal."

"Have those other investigators contacted King about details of the methods he used? Maybe they've missed something in trying to replicate his work."

"I don't know about that since there'd be no reason to involve this office."

"What about the initial reviews," Jason asked. "Didn't questions get raised at that point?"

Brumfield growled, "I can't understand why not, unless the paper got assigned to people who were on the fringe of the field and they didn't catch the problem, or they did a lousy job and failed to raise a flag." He added, "Sometimes we don't know the reviewers very well and their expertise may not be the best fit for the manuscript we've sent them. Things are changing so fast people are out of date before they know it."

"Have you considered the possibility these two objectors have somehow not understood what King published or it throws a monkey wrench in their pet theory and they can't tolerate that."

Brumfield was silent, either considering the implications of Jason's question or thinking he'd been bamboozled by those two labs ranting against King's work. When he didn't respond, Jason said, "Give us ten days to attempt to find a resolution or an explanation."

After a clear pause, Brumfield muttered, "Okay, but that'll be the limit."

"We appreciate your cooperation. I'll get back to you within the time frame." Jason leaned back in his chair, wondering if he'd committed to a deadline he couldn't meet, but feeling relieved Brumfield hadn't told him to forget any further delays. And the notion that the entire episode seemed completely out of character for scientists seeking the correct mechanism to a biological event continued to ramble through his thoughts.

Jason called Fowler to let him know of the need to move the timetable faster than they'd agreed to earlier, but Fowler was out of town.

Audrey stuck her head in the door. "Dr. Spradlin, you're scheduled for a department head's meeting with Dean Hawthorne in ten minutes."

As he grabbed a folder, Jason said, "Audrey, would you ask Dr. King for copies of the letters sent to him by Brumfield. He'll know which ones."

Jason recognized several faces as he found a chair around the large walnut table in the Dean's conference room. He nodded to them, while three late comers found seats.

Hawthorne started on time. "First thing, I'd like to introduce Jason Spradlin, who is serving as the interim head of Biology. Since this is his first meeting with this group, let's take time to go around the table and introduce yourselves by name and department."

Most of the names were a blur to Jason, but he placed faces with three or four names of men he'd heard about within the university. Two women were conspicuous, heads of English whom he'd met through Lucy, and Math, whom he'd read about recently for having won a national award. He made a note to look in the university directory and learn the names of these new colleagues.

"I'm sure you'll know Jason better," Hawthorne continued, as the introductions ended, "as the year progresses. And, I know each of you will make yourself available to orient him to policies and procedures of the college."

As everyone waited, Hawthorne said, "Now to the agenda I sent out." Jason found the one page list of discussion items that Audrey had put in the folder he'd picked up on the way out the door.

"First item," Hawthorne continued, "is budget submissions for the next annual cycle. Those are due in my office by October thirty-first, an appropriate date for the mystery of the process" Jason made a note to talk with Audrey and the accountant about budgets.

Someone asked, "Any specific guidelines this year?"

"I've been told by the Provost to think about stable budgets overall, although there will be some shifting of resources across college and department lines. Thus, I'd like you to prepare three versions—a stable one, another showing a five to seven percent increase, and a third representing a five to seven percent decrease. In your justifications or explanations, show what the impact would be if you received a decrease, and how you propose to utilize an increase. New uses of technology, new curricula initiatives, innovative program components might get my attention, but remember, I'll have to defend the changes to the Provost and Vice-Presidents group." Faces of department heads turned grim, all thinking about the work involved and the potential for loss of resources. Jason recognized he would be competing with other departments to keep Biology's share of resources.

Ninety minutes later, Jason walked out, his pad filled with notes and reminders about fifteen different items. He thought about the budget thing, remembering he'd read in the newspaper that the institution had received a twelve percent increase in its overall budget for the two year cycle. He wondered what games were being played in central administration and where the money was destined. Too, in this critical year, he had no experience with budget games, sighing with relief he'd have to do this only one time, but he didn't want his department damaged by losing resources. He didn't like the feeling of pressure and responsibility for all his colleagues and support staff.

Audrey was pulling the outer door closed when Jason approached the office at five-fifteen. She waited, holding open the door, then walked back in with him.

"Miriam brought the list of people from Dr. King's lab in. It's in the middle drawer of the desk, along with copies of those letters to Dr. King you asked for."

She added, "And Ann, one of your graduate students, wants to talk to you. She's on your calendar for seven forty-five in the morning."

Jason scanned the list of people in King's group, recognizing no one. Then he scanned the letters. The message from Brumfield was straight-forward, telling King other investigators had raised questions about his paper and requesting a response. He wanted to publish the set of letters together as soon as possible. Brumfield's short note contained no threat, and Jason recognized it as the typical approach by an editor when disagreements about papers were brought to his attention.

The letters from two investigators, names and affiliations blacked out, were similar and direct. Both began by making strong assertions about the validity of King's data and suggested his experiment must have been terribly flawed, but no specific details were included about the basis of the charge. In a following paragraph, both bluntly stated that King must have manufactured the data since no other such information was in the literature and recommended, almost demanded, that King retract the publication. Both closed by saying the journal should publish a retraction even if King disagreed.

Jason read the letters twice. Two things jumped out. First, he tried without success to discover the actual basis of the demand. Usually the scientist suggesting problems would focus on some aspect of the paper in question—the experimental design, some specific methodology, or even a suspected quirk in the thinking of the authors. But there was nothing like that in these letters.

Second, the letters were almost mirror images of each other. A few phrases were different, but in his thinking, there'd been collusion. It seemed one had drafted the letter. The second had copied it with a few changes in wording, but not in focus.

He placed the correspondence in the drawer. Maybe talking with King's people would reveal the real issue. But deep inside, he understood why King had not responded. And why had Brumfield blocked out the names of those accusing King of wrong-doing?

CHAPTER 8

Jason looked up from the neatly handwritten list Miriam had left under the glass paperweight the previous afternoon when Ann rapped lightly on the door, promptly at seven forty-five. The outer office remained in darkness.

"Come in," Jason beckoned, pointing to the chair next to the desk. "How's your project coming?"

"Okay. The animal phase will end next week, then I'll have a lot of lab work to do." Dressed in her usual slacks and tee shirt, she appeared not completely awake yet. She remained near the door and seemed reluctant to venture farther, unlike her usual direct manner.

"Did you check out the questions Steve asked in the update last week?"

Nodding her head and taking a step inside, she said, "I did, and I think I'm on the right track."

"You want me to look at the background papers you examined?"

"If you like, but I believe I'm okay. I checked with Angela who agrees with me."

"Make certain. He raised a good question." Remembering how easily colleagues working side by side every day could support another's idea, he said, "Tell you what. Bring me those papers for my own satisfaction." He smiled and added, "I might learn something new."

Ann took another step toward the desk. "I'll bring them by in a few minutes, but the reason I wanted to see you is about a friend of mine. She thinks there's something strange going on in Dr. King's lab. Dr. King seems upset all the time and is making all of his people repeat experiments they completed months ago."

She smiled sheepishly, looking at Jason for his reaction, "And, while we were talking about the situation, my friend said there were big rumors that Dr. King and a post-doc in his lab are having an affair. I didn't know whether to tell you or not, then I thought maybe that's the reason for all the fuss." Ann took steps toward the door as though to escape after telling a forbidden tale

"Does your friend know this? Who is he or she?" Jason's voice elevated a notch, almost demanding a response.

Ann hesitated, looking away as though she shouldn't reveal her source, then looked back at Jason and said, "Another graduate student."

"Does he or she work in King's lab?"

Shaking her head, Ann said, "She's a teaching assistant assigned to Dr. Riley for General Biology. She believed the story because Dr. Riley told the group at the beginning of their weekly meeting about attendance and grading of quizzes. And she's talked to another student who works with King."

At the mention of Riley's name, Jason assessment of the situation changed. He thought for a moment about an appropriate response to a younger professional, one still learning the about the undercurrents that pervaded any academic unit. He stood and walked closer to Ann, saying, "You should understand certain people feel the need to pass along gossip and rumors without having any facts. In this instance, the information may have some validity, but it may be strictly rumor based on someone's supposition." He stopped short of telling her anything coming from Riley should be questioned for credibility.

When Ann's face revealed her confusion, Jason said, "Thanks for telling me, but let's keep it to ourselves. In fact, that's good advice in almost all of these circumstances."

Ann persisted, "I guess she believed it because Dr. King and this associate seem to be together a lot and she's really sexy looking, so my guess is it's true."

"But you can't be sure?"

Ann nodded. "That's right, but I'd bet on it under the circumstances."

Jason said, "Let's see how things turn out." He watched Ann disappear through the door as lights blinked on in the main part of the suite.

He scanned the list again—seven graduate students, a technician, and two post-docs, all supported by grant money. He shoved it back in the drawer, still thinking about the gossip from Ann, wondering if it was significantly related to the larger problem or if it was another of Riley's ploys to embarrass King. The discussion of the possible affair by Riley was reason to dismiss it. But if this post-doc had made a serious error and was involved with King, he could be shielding her through his reluctant responses about the problem.

He called Fowler's office to learn he'd be back tomorrow.

In the morning mail a memo from the search committee requested nominations for the department head position. Attached was an announcement being sent to several journals and newsletters soliciting nominations and applications from interested and qualified individuals. Jason noted a November fifteenth deadline for applicants.

Jason went to his lab office and in the membership roster of the Experimental Biology societies he found the listing for Fred Adams at Penn State. He dialed the number.

After a secretary answered and Jason waited for the call to be put through, Fred responded, "Jason, how are you? I was devastated when I heard about Henry. He was a good person and we'll all miss him."

"You probably know I'm the interim head."

"Yeah, I learned through someone I saw at a meeting in Washington last week. That's good, you'll do it well."

Ignoring Fred's comment, Jason said, "I called to ask if you'd consider applying for the head's position here. If you are, I'd like to nominate you." He rushed on, trying to convince his friend. "I know you've been at Penn State only two years, but you liked State a lot. And we're going to become better in the next few years."

Fred laughed, not a good sign. "You're kind to think about me and I enjoyed my time there, but this is a fine university and things are going well. I'm not interested in moving, but I hope State attracts a good person. Henry will be a hard act to follow."

Jason thought Fred had closed the door on applying, but he pushed. "I'd appreciate your thinking about it. You'll see the announcement in a few days, so there's plenty of time."

After a brief pause, Fred replied, "I'll think about it, but I doubt I could be persuaded to submit my name." His voice taking on the tone of an advisor giving guidance to a junior colleague, he added, "You should do it yourself. You've got the right mind set and have enough experience as a faculty. Your reputation in the field is solid and getting better all the time."

"I'm reasonably certain I'll not become a candidate. I can see the opportunities, but the time demands can be overwhelming and I'm not ready to give up my research work."

"You could keep some projects going. A lot of heads do." Fred continued, "And how are Lucy and the kids?"

"All are well. Lucy's working hard, teaching a full load, writing another book. Kids are growing like weeds and have more energy than we can cope with."

Through the receiver Jason heard another voice in the background, then Fred said, "Jason, I've an important visitor, so I need to cut this off, but think about applying. If you wish, use me as a reference. Or call again and let's talk more about your taking it on."

Jason glanced at the position announcement again, then shoved it into his work file. Fred's encouragement was unexpected and in some uncomfortable way, posed a challenge. It seemed everybody he talked to recommended he apply for the position he vowed not to be interested in for the long term.

Audrey buzzed the intercom. "Dr. Spradlin, a call from Brenda Fallon at Redlake Industries." The image of Brenda, the Vice-President for Development at the small pharmeuctical company in Chicago, flooded into his mind, pushing aside thoughts of the application process.

"Hi, Brenda," Jason said into the phone, as he heard Audrey cut away the extension. "How are things with you and Redlake?"

"Wonderful. The bovine growth hormone cleared Food and Drug yesterday. All indications are the market will be great." Jason thought about the lengthy process of getting the approval for any additive to animal products destined for human consumption. Redlake had invested six years into the research, field testing, and review of their formulation which promised to increase the percentage of muscle tissue in beef cattle, making for more efficient weight gains and potentially lower costs to the consumer. It also could mean huge profits for the company, and since Jason had led the research effort under a contractual agreement, some money for State University and for him personally.

"That's good news, but I assume you wish to discuss our contract." The present agreement terminated at the end of the year and they'd talked some about next steps, all dependent upon the outcome of the FDA decision on the hormone. The urgency had crossed Jason's mind several times in the past few days, but other things seemed to require his immediate attention and the need to act.

Brenda said, "We've discussed some possibilities, but we'd like to meet with you in the next few days and see if there's some common interest in another collaborative project."

"I'd like to, but it would help if you could come here." He explained about the interim head job and the time constraints imposed by the administrative issues.

Brenda hesitated and Jason realized she was considering Jason's increased responsibility and how that might impact his relationship with Redlake. "I'll work it out so we can visit next week."

Jason responded, "That'll help, but are you free to tell me what you're thinking?"

Again, some hesitation on the line before she said, "You know this is confidential, but we've been tossing around the idea of establishing a production unit to clone a domestic animal for possible sale to the public."

"You mean a mass replication approach?" Excitement of the potential conflicting with the unpredictable hazards flashed through his thinking.

"Right. We could be the first to do this on a large scale and it could put Redlake in the forefront."

"Brenda, being first, especially in this kind of endeavor, is risky, even treacherous. I can envision all the ethical issues, not to mention the scientific ones, that must be overcome."

She didn't retreat or become defensive. "We know, but think about it. I'll let your office know our travel plans."

Jason replaced the phone and walked to the window to stare across the campus. Students meandered across the quadrangle. Two mocking birds fluttered in one of the oaks, beginning to drop some of its leaves. But none of those visible actions captured Jason's attention enough to draw his thoughts away from Brenda's idea. This cloning business might be too fraught with unknowns and political traps to warrant the risk, both for Redlake and for him. The science itself would present enough problems. He needed guidance from someone, but he didn't know where to turn for such help. To his knowledge nobody had previously tried to produce meat yielding animals through cloning, but he could envision resistance throughout society. He remembered the outcry with the artificial tomato. Cloning of animals could make genetic intervention in plants seem like child's play. The right wing would go berserk, screaming about changing the biological process the Almighty had created

But, someone would do it and soon. Maybe Redlake was on to something. He had to admit they had courage.

CHAPTER 9

Preston King edged into the Biology conference room as if trying to remain unseen, scowled at Jason and Fowler, and dropped heavily into a chair across from Fowler. His blue plaid sport shirt seemed more wrinkled than usual. His hair, usually neatly combed, hadn't been touched recently.

From the end of the table, Jason glanced at Fowler, and said, "Preston, you know what this is about. Arthur Brumfield is threatening to release letters complaining about your paper. I talked with him two days ago and he promised to hold off until we can discuss the situation with you and attempt to find a resolution." At this point he didn't want to threaten King further with an internal investigation.

Jason looked directly into King's eyes, belligerent and challenging as he stared back. "Dr. Fowler and I hope to avoid this allegation getting into the media and making it difficult on everybody, most of all on you and your co-investigators."

Fowler added, "Preston, let's do everything possible to prevent this becoming public. When that happens, nobody wins. So let's start by you telling us what the problem is with the experiments reported in that paper." Fowler's voice sounded like a grandfather gently encouraging a youngster to tell the truth.

King remained silent, staring at the table top, for several seconds, then he looked at them and said, "The truth is I don't know what's wrong, or if anything is."

Jason remembered the letters and his thinking that something didn't quite add up but, he asked, "What does that mean? You know other investigators are challenging your methodology and can't understand how you obtained the results you reported."

"I know," King croaked, "but the post-doc and graduate students have assured me the data are correct. I've checked every step in the process and cannot find an error. The methods are appropriate. We've used the same approach numerous times with no problems."

"Have you tried to do the experiment yourself? Fowler leaned forward on the table, his brow furrowed, trying to comprehend, trying to help King explain the difficulty.

King shrugged. "No, but I trust my people."

Jason realized King may not be able to do the experiments alone. Most senior investigators found themselves so removed from the routine work in the lab they became out of date quickly. You had to depend on others. He asked, "Have you asked the team to repeat the experiments, not just check the calculations, but start from scratch?"

King nodded. "They did, with the same outcome." A hint of a smile crept across his face "And they're all pissed because of the extra work."

"Maybe you should have a different group run the experiments," Jason said, then added, "Maybe the original team consistently makes the same error." He knew from experience how easy it was to get so accustomed to doing an analysis, you ignored all directions and continued to do it the same way, repeating any errors you'd made previously.

King said, "Others in the lab are doing different techniques and would have to learn these procedures. That could take a month and would likely be a waste of time and resources. I don't have enough slack in my grants to do that."

Fowler asked, "Would it be useful if I gave you enough money from the Research Office to have a second team duplicate the work?"

King thought for a moment. "It'd solve the funding issue, but I suspect the results wouldn't be different. And it wouldn't speed up the process or avoid the loss of time."

Jason said, "But you'd have confirmation within your own group. It seems to me that would go a long way in proving your results to outsiders."

"It's worth a try," King conceded, "but I hate to do it. My other work will be set back."

Jason said softly, feeling a breakthrough "Preston, you have to make the effort. You can't have a possible charge of fraud hanging over your head. You'd be blacklisted for the rest of your career."

"Okay, I'm willing to try it." King agreed, throwing up a hand in surrender and staring at them for a moment, then he looked at Jason. "Would you call Brumfield and tell him what we're doing? Repeating the work will take longer than the ten days he promised you."

"Can you estimate time you'll need?" Jason asked.

"A month to six weeks. The new team will need to be brought up to speed and do some trial runs before I'd be comfortable. I don't want a set of data that only confuses the issue further."

Jason stood, picking up papers from the table. "I'll call Brumfield today. I think he'll go along. Now he's caught in the middle and just wants to find a solution." The others followed him toward the door.

Near the door, Fowler added, "Give me an estimate of costs in the next day or so and I'll transfer funds to one of your accounts."

As King left, his long legs striding quickly as though escaping tormentors, Jason closed the door and said, "He really doesn't want to do this, but it's probably the right step."

Fowler nodded, his face frowning, "Let's hope it doesn't add another unknown."

Brumfield wasn't enthused when Jason called him. "I don't know if these guys will hold off."

"If their goal is to discover the truth about the experiments, then I can't see what they have to gain by making a public issue of the disagreement. King is willing to try in good faith to prove the data are either correct or not."

Brumfield growled, "And if they refuse?"

"Then I'd question their motives and so should you. Are they after the facts or are they trying to discredit Preston King?" He added, "I've examined those letters and frankly, neither has given a solid basis for their demand. Nothing but generalities and charges of cheating. I'd expected more concrete questions about the paper."

"Are you suggesting these other investigators are out to do King in?"

Jason thought about his next statement for a moment, then trying to project calmness in his tone, said, "Time is not so critical they can't give King six weeks to redo the experiments. How will they look if they go public with their differences, then discover King is right? And knowing King, I'd bet he is."

"I'll talk to them this afternoon." Brumfield's voice suggested he didn't relish the coming conversations with King's detractors.

Attempting to mask his curiosity about the letters, Jason asked, "I'm also surprised the names were blocked out on those letters to King. That seems unusual and counter to usual communications between scientists who are all seeking the truth."

Brumfield's voice became authoritative as explaining a simple theory to a novice, saying, "Sometimes questioners request anonymity, trying to avoid personal conflicts, so this journal instituted a policy to respond to that desire when requested."

Jason accepted the explanation, still believing it unusual, then said, "While I have you, would you tell me how the second set of reviewers were selected, the ones you said were independent, but agreed with the investigators doubting King's paper?"

Brumfield hesitated, apparently considering carefully his response, before saying, "When I received the letters, I called the two people who'd challenged King's paper. They recommended a couple of possibilities and I used those suggestions. I prefer not to reveal their names."

"I understand, but I'm surprised. I would have guessed you would not have asked for recommendations, especially from the dissenters, but would have chosen reviewers by some other method. I understand editors select reviewers because of their expertise in a given area, but wouldn't solicit advice from someone with a disagreement."

"I had no reason to think there was collusion. In fact, I resent your implications."

"I didn't intend to suggest the episode was planned, but I would have preferred reviewers who were absolutely anonymous and not aware of the challenge, like a third reviewer when the first two disagree."

Brumfield persisted, "I'm comfortable they were objective."

Suspecting Brumfield was somehow protecting the initial accusers, Jason pushed his growing skepticism about the validity of the charges against King. "You know, Dr. Brumfield, the more I learn about this, the more I'm convinced those two people have an agenda different than a simple disagreement about a paper. And I suspect if they can't be satisfied with King's repetition of his experiments, this whole thing is going to come apart. If they've charged King with cheating with no more proof than they've presented thus far, I can visualize this going to court."

"Are you threatening this journal?"

"I'm not threatening anyone yet, but you must admit both those two accusers and you have acted in strange manners."

The phone went dead as Brumfield refused to continue the debate, solidifying Jason's concern there was more involved than other investigators challenging King's paper. Maybe the other researchers had decided on a theory and King's work had demonstrated they were wrong. But that didn't seem likely as Jason had never heard of collaborative efforts intended to shut out other opinions. And, why had King been so defensive about the paper, ignoring Brumfield's request for an explanation? Was it the first time King had been challenged and he didn't know how to respond or was something else at play? If he didn't understand the basis for the questions, he could have asked for clarification or more specifics. Or had King become so irritated at the charge, he'd ignored the whole thing, hoping it would wither and die.

On top of the stack of mail was the packet from Nancy Thompson about the Center of Excellence grants. He scanned the cover letter and the instructions. Responding with a solid proposal would be time consuming and would mean several Biology faculty plus related disciplines, including the Medical School, would need to coalesce around a central theme with all the details of their specific involvements spelled out in a coherent presentation. He dropped the packet into his briefcase for further perusal this evening.

As the bell buzzed at three Audrey came in and sat in the chair next to the desk. "Dr. Spradlin, a reporter from the Associated Press just called Dr. King. I thought you'd like to know." Her face carried a deep frown, suggesting her experience with reporters meant problems.

Jason responded quickly. "I hope this doesn't mean what I think it might."

"The reporter wouldn't say what the call was about, but I knew you've been meeting with Dr. King about that paper and those letter." She stood and eased toward the door.

Thirty minutes later, King walked into Jason's office. His face was pale as he collapsed into the chair. He mumbled, "The AP called, wanting to know about my purported cheating." He shook his head. His hands were trembling.

"Did he accuse you of cheating," Jason asked, "or did he begin asking about the conflict with other's work?"

King sat up straighter and clasped his hands together. "He started by saying two other investigators had called the bureau office and said they'd confirmed without any doubt that I had deliberately published false data and wrong conclusions. Then he started asking questions, all of which seemed slanted to prove his sources right."

"Do you know who these "others" are?" Did the reporter tell you who had called?"

King shook his head. "No, he didn't and when I asked, he refused to tell me. And no, I don't know who my accusers are. Brumfield wouldn't tell me, kept saying it'd become clear when the next issue of the journal appeared. I assumed he meant their letters would be published."

Jason thought again about his earlier idea of a conspiracy to discredit King's work. "Preston, have you been at differences with other groups in this work?"

96

When King looked confused, Jason asked, "That is, have you been publishing results suggesting a mainline theory might be wrong, or have your data disagreed with researchers who are pushing some pet theory?" After a slight pause, he added, "You know some of these guys have big egos, plus big money might be at stake."

King looked blank, shook his head. "Well, I've published a couple of papers that disagree with certain things that have been accepted as the final explanation. If this last paper is correct and I think it is, the current thinking of several others would be altered substantially."

He stared at Jason as the implications of the question hit him. "Jason, what are you suggesting? These guys are out to get me?"

Jason walked to the window, watching the crowd of students rushing through the afternoon cool to four o'clock classes or leaving the campus for the day. "I don't know, but several things have bothered me about this challenge from the outset and the more I hear, the more I'm convinced there's a hidden purpose. Why is there such a ruckus and such a push to make you cave in to their demands? Science doesn't usually work that way, so what's the agenda."

He turned back to look at King, still slumped in the chair. "Preston, come clean with me about why you delayed in responding to Brumfield."

King stood and stepped toward Jason, a hand rubbing his face. "Jason, when Brumfield first wrote, we set out to repeat the analyses and I told him by phone we'd stand by our paper until we could prove otherwise. We believed we were right because we'd checked everything. Nevertheless we set out to check those tests again."

He leaned against the window sill, staring across the quadrangle. "Then, when he persisted, I began to doubt my own people, thinking one of them had manipulated the data. The post-doc was flabbergasted and mad as hell I'd accuse her of such actions and threatened to resign. I decided to ignore Brumfield and keep working. I guess that was a mistake but he seemed unwilling to accept any thing but an admission of error."

"Preston, this is a strange episode," Jason said, placing his hand on King's shoulder, "but if you're convinced your research is correct, let's work through it. Having another team replicate the experiment may prove valuable. But remind me of the potential implications of this work. Could it lead to a commercial product?"

"It might be the basis for the formulation of a medication to combat viral infections, but I think we're a long way from that."

"But if money is the goal, many people use every ploy to establish their authority to create a useful product or medication."

King ignored the implications. "What do we do about this reporter?"

Jason shook his head, "I don't know at the moment. Let's hope he was probing to get your reaction and won't publish anything without some official statement from the university."

Jason watched King shuffle out of the office. He hoped King hadn't come across with the AP guy in a defensive, irritated fashion, suggesting he was covering his tracks. He wondered how he would have handled the situation if he had been accused of cheating,

98

acknowledging it would be almost impossible not to sound frustrated and belligerent under such circumstances.

CHAPTER 10

The most prominent headline of morning edition of the *Chronicle*, **State Professor Accused of Fraud,** confirmed Jason's worst fears and reminded him of his inexperience and naiveté about the news media.

Jason scanned the text, a recitation of the story revealed by Brumfield and quoting two other investigators as having irrefutable evidence of King's paper being based on manufactured or rigged data. Neither their names nor affiliations were revealed. Derek Vick, the name on the by-line, wrote he'd encountered a defensive and obstinate King whose attitude suggested his guilt. The remainder of the two-column article focused on the increasing number of questionable practices by scientists and the decline of public trust in researchers out to make names for themselves and gain monetary rewards.

"So, you were right," Lucy said, as she scanned the article, "about Preston coming across as guilty."

Jason sipped black coffee from a mug, "But, in his defense, who wouldn't under the circumstances?" He reached to wipe strawberry jam from the side of Tony's face, the three-year old squirming to avoid his father's attempt to keep his shirt clean, at least until he'd arrived at nursery school. "The reporter is searching for an angle to make his story attractive to readers. And I was wrong about their getting an official statement from the university before publishing."

Lucy, smiling at the struggle, asked, "What are you going to do?"

Jason shrugged. "I don't know yet. Maybe start by calling Fowler or Brumfield." He shoved his plate and utensils into the dishwasher, then pulled Tony from the seat. "Let's get going, young man. Don't want to be late for nursery school." He looked at Lucy. "This is the kind of thing I wouldn't have to deal with as a faculty member."

She grinned, ignoring his complaint. "You'll figure out the right thing." She watched as Jason and Tony disappeared through the garage door, then turned her attention to Jennifer and another day at kindergarten.

At eight-fifteen, Jason telephoned Brumfield, who responded in a hoarse, sleepy voice, although his time zone was an hour ahead.

"You promised to hold these guys off," Jason barked, "until we completed a repeat of King's experiment."

Seemingly taken aback by the gruff tone, Brumfield muttered, "I'm sorry I couldn't convince them to delay. I'm looking at the morning paper now."

Jason said, "I'm reasonably well convinced now there's a different agenda than disagreement with King's paper. I want to know the names of his detractors."

Brumfield hesitated, then said, "I don't think I should tell you. When I called yesterday, both withdrew their letters from the journal. For all practical purposes, I'm now out of the loop."

Jason's voice hardened more. "If this thing progresses as I suspect it will, you'll be called to testify in either a court proceeding or before some ethics committee." He added, "I'll make sure of it, because I

102

believe you fostered the efforts of King's accusers." Jason knew he was pushing too hard, but he wanted those names. Knowing who they were might be key to the puzzle, if in fact, King hadn't cut corners.

Brumfield mumbled, uncomfortable with doing anything, "I'll have my assistant send the names and their letters to you. Then, I don't want to be involved further."

Before Jason could reply, he heard the phone bang down. He grinned, pleased he'd put Brumfield on the defensive, then thinking he'd been too forceful. Brumfield could have published the letters without contacting King at all, then let him send a rebuttal to the journal. But, on the flip side, Brumfield had thus far shielded the antagonists and had bought into their suggestions for the second set of reviewers.

When Jason responded to the ringing phone, hardly back in its cradle, Audrey said, "It's Dean Hawthorne. He wants to see you and Dr. King." Jason's his pulse quickened, knowing Hawthorne was getting heat about the news article.

As they returned from the Dean's office, moving quickly to keep pace with the crowd of students headed for classes, Preston said, "Well, he took it better than I thought he might."

"He's upset about the negative publicity," Jason said, "but he knows we're trying to solve the problem. That's about all he could ask at the moment." As they entered the front door of Quincy Hall, Jason continued, "I expect by the time we got there, he'd had calls from the President and the local press."

"So everybody gets involved when suspicions are cast."

"Preston, if this thing goes badly, you'll be damaged, but so will the university and the department. It's a big public relations concern."

They stopped walking at the foot of the stairs leading to floors above the entry level. "Should I do anything?"

Jason didn't respond immediately, looking at King and thinking if he'd been more forthright with Brumfield, this issue probably could have been contained, but he said, "Follow Hawthorne's advice. Do your work. Refuse to talk to the press, but refer them to the Public Relations office. And warn people in your lab to do the same. We can't afford someone making an embarrassing comment because they were pushed by an aggressive reporter."

Remembering Ann's bit of gossip about King's affair, Jason asked, "Has Riley been around your lab recently?"

King looked startled. "He came by a few days ago."

Jason said, "As best you can , keep him from knowing about this problem. I won't say more, but Riley has the urge and the capacity to blow things out of perspective."

Wanting to tell Jason something about Riley's visit, but not about his vendetta against Jason's potential candidacy for the head's position, King said, "He was interested in one of my post-docs, Kathryn Helweg. She's a good looking woman, but Riley seemed carried away. I know she refuses to talk to him."

Jason nodded. "Knowing Riley, he was scratching around for some tid-bit he can stretch into something to embarrass people. This may sound petty, but warn your people to avoid Riley's inquiries."

King muttered, "I will and if he keeps prying, I'll throw his ass out." He started up the stairs.

Jason called Fowler, who as soon as he came on the line, said, ""So Brumfield couldn't contain it."

"No, they refused to wait. Both called the AP. Now we have a major problem." Jason told him about the meeting with the Dean and their decision to plow ahead in obtaining confirmation of King's data.

"I'll support doing that, but you know we'll be bombarded by the media. I've had three calls already this morning, but I've taken the position we're looking into the matter and can't comment yet."

Jason muttered, "That's the position all of us should take until King knows the outcome of his repeated experiment. If I know the media, they'll lose interest in a couple of days."

"Unless his accusers keep the story hot."

"Then, I'd be more convinced they have an agenda intended to discredit King rather than find the facts. Frankly, the more I learn about this deal, the more I'm convinced there's a different agenda."

"You sound like you've become convinced King is innocent of any wrong doing."

Jason considered for a moment. "Maybe I'm stretching a bit, trying to find a way out for him, and us, but I'm irritated by the actions of those guys questioning his work. There's no reason not to be patient a few weeks and see if King can replicate his own experiment." He didn't elaborate on the letters which had triggered his misgivings about their motive.

He continued, "If he can't, then we should push him to retract the paper or publish a corrected version."

Fowler growled, "But you have to admit King acted strangely—just like you'd think a cheater would."

"I know," Jason muttered, "and that's why we've got to keep our wits about us—don't take a firm position until we see the outcome of the repeated work."

Fowler said, "While I have you, I received a letter from the president of Redlake Industries yesterday, telling me the FDA had approved the growth hormone you were involved with. He included an estimate of sales for the next three years."

"I know. They called me about a possible follow-up project."

"If this guy knows what he's talking about, the proceeds for our share could come to as much as a hundred grand annually."

Jason almost dropped the phone. The contractual arrangement with Redlake was such that State University and Jason would split the amount allocated to the university. He shoved aside his thought about the potential windfall and said, "Redlake has been thinking about trying to clone a domestic animal for meat production, but I'm concerned about the problems we'd have with that. I suspect they don't understand the societal implications, not to mention the difficulty of the science itself. I wondered if you have ideas, reservations, outright objections, if State became involved."

Fowler didn't respond immediately, obviously thinking about the ramifications. "Jason, this is out of my element You know there'll be major problems of marketing, ethics, maybe objections from the

106

President and the Board of Regents if it becomes a political problem. And that seems likely given the conservative bent of our society."

"I know, but think about it, maybe talk to the President to get his potential reaction. Redlake is scheduling a meeting soon to come and discuss the initiative and if the university administration is firmly opposed, I'll back out."

"The real problem, Jason, is nobody knows how the public will react. If there's a huge outcry, then we'll be dealing with state government and all the politicians." Fowler continued, "And none of us want to open the door to those guys and all their posturing."

"I understand," Jason said, "plus I'm not so sure it can be done economically yet. Remember those people who cloned the sheep in England went through a couple hundred trials before it worked. Seemed like playing the lottery."

Fowler laughed, "I know, but the technology is improving and industries will try it because it offers such monetary rewards, if they can succeed."

Jason laughed. "I had the same thought while talking to Redlake. Let's touch all the right bases before we jump into this venture."

The Friday after-work sessions organized by Riley continued on schedule as Harris, Townsend and Boseman assembled at Randolph's for beer and conversation. The weather had turned cold overnight as fall season progressed toward winter with a heavy frost overnight. They draped their heavy coats on the backs of the chairs, not trusting the security of the coat racks near the entrance of the establishment.

The atmosphere of the bar filled with warm bodies emitting vapor took on a steam bath aura. Then Townsend added to the smog by lighting his pipe and blowing smoke into the immediate area.

Townsend, goading Harris about his focus on women, said, "Greg, I hear that post-doc in King's lab gave you the cold shoulder." He puffed at his pipe, his eyes on Harris through the cloud.

Riley jumped in before Harris could respond. "She's something, isn't she. I go by just to look at her."

"The cold shoulder is too tame a description of her reaction," Harris smirked. "I introduced myself in the hall one day when we were walking in the same direction and asked if she'd like to have a drink after work hours. She essentially told me to get lost and that she'd heard about my womanizing. She threatened to call security if I came around again. But you're right, she is one of the most beautiful and sexiest women I've ever seen."

Boseman piped up, "King is in big trouble. I assume you guys saw the newspaper article about his cheating."

"I've seen him with Spradlin a few times in the last week, no doubt plotting a way out for King," Riley commented. "Maybe the problem will sink Spradlin and take him out of the head's consideration. You know central administration is all over them about these charges."

"So, Riley, are you going to make a serious play for this Helweg gal?" Townsend banged his briar on the table leg, spreading ashes across the floor.

Riley watched a group passing the table. "I'm content to just observe, but if the opportunity came along, who knows."

His encounter with Helweg still an irritation, Harris said, "Forget it Riley. I suspect she's lesbian and out of bounds."

CHAPTER 11

At ten-thirty, Jason turned off his computer, feeling good about the draft of the budget proposal he'd completed. After aborted attempts to focus on the task during normal office hours, he'd returned to the office for three nights now, pressing to formulate the budget package requested by the Dean. It had taken him a couple of hours to understand the process and to sort through the numbers Miriam had summarized for him, although she'd oriented him to the base data and the jargon during an afternoon session. He'd review the document once again tomorrow morning and then print it. He rubbed the weariness from his eyes with the back of his hand and secured his notes under the empty coffee mug given to him by a former graduate student..

The budget process had been interesting and revealing. Several faculty had responded to his request for suggestions about new initiatives and additional resources. Sorting through those ideas had been an eye opener, revealing two or three who advanced novel ideas about the future of the department contrasted to the majority who were self-centered and plugging for their own pet agendas. Several had not bothered to respond. Thinking about the potential NIH proposal, Jason attempted to frame the university budget in support of a focused effort for the department, mesh the two as much as possible, and still meet the needs of the unit. He felt comfortable, even excited, the case statement would grab the imagination of administrators. He leaned back in the chair, acknowledging for the first time he'd done something creative and potentially important for the department. He hoped the Dean and Vice-Presidents would agree and support his proposal on behalf of the unit.

Leaving the office, Jason turned instinctively toward the door leading to the parking lot, the halls quiet and almost eerie with no one scurrying about, then he decided to walk through the department to see who was working and if things were secure. Passing his own lab, he saw three graduate students bent over their desks, no doubt studying for quizzes or reading assignments. He climbed stairs to the third floor. Lights blazed from King's lab area, but at first glance, Jason could see no activity. Through the maze of lab benches and equipment, he could make out two figures huddled around a desk in one corner of the large lab. Altering his position a couple of steps for a better view, Jason realized he was staring at Preston King and a woman he didn't know. They were talking quietly, heads close together and leaning over papers on the desk, but Jason couldn't see their faces or hear the conversation. He moved on, his curiosity whetted, remembering the gossip Ann had passed to him. As he retreated down the stairs, he was chagrined about his eavesdropping. But he reminded himself to talk with some of King's people and not delay until the lab experiments were completed. He wanted to be prepared for all possible outcomes.

Outside the building the early fall humidity had yielded to drier and cooler air. Jason breathed deeply, slight odors of drying leaves

112

mingled with exhaust fumes as he found his Honda Accord near the front of the asphalt parking lot, now empty except for a half-dozen cars scattered randomly in the large space.

Jason's premonition about the media and King proved correct. Within two days, the papers no longer carried articles about the charge against King or the evils of scientists generally. But, he wasn't prepared for the call from the President's office asking that he and Dean Hawthorne come for a meeting.

In the plush reception area of the President's suite, gray upholstered chairs surrounded a coffee table covered with magazines related to higher education and the university. On two corner tables, pink and white daffodils provided color to the conservative aura of the space. After five minutes, the receptionist, a pleasant, middle-age woman in a dark suit, ushered them into the inner office of Roger Snyder, now in his twelfth year as President of State University. Jason hadn't been here since his second year at State when his research project in the university vivarium was besieged by a religious sect, several faculty were demanding he remove his work from university facilities, and the Secretary of Education was pressuring the university to stop the research. The President had rejected the demands and supported Jason after Henry Rogers had threatened to resign if the administration caved in to the pressures.

Snyder looked up from papers on the desk, then moved from the desk to the conference area, several soft chairs and a sofa arranged in a circle. He smiled at the two of them and said, "Dr. Spradlin, I see you've moved up. Congratulations." Snyder's dark hair had turned to more a salt and pepper appearance since Jason had last seen him.

"I'm not so sure it's a change I like," Jason said, shaking the President's hand. As he glanced at Snyder's expensive suit and matching silk tie, he was glad Lucy had insisted he wear better clothes rather than his usual khakis and sports jacket. At her gentle insistence, he'd purchased new suits and matching ties.

"The Attorney General has inquired about the charge against Dr. King." Snyder began. "Although I'm not certain of his agenda, he's threatening an investigation."

Hawthorne nodded, chopped the air with his beefy hand, and said, "He's playing politics with any issue that keeps his name in the papers. He's already running for the Governor's job."

"Maybe," Snyder grinned, "but nevertheless, he's demanding an explanation of the news articles about King's paper." He turned toward Jason. "Tell me about the problem."

Jason outlined the controversy between King and other investigators, yet unknown from other institutions, the discussions with King and Luther Fowler and their pressure on King to confirm the work. He concluded, "We're waiting for the outcome of the experiments to know if King's first report was correct or to discover any discrepancies. Then King will either let the editor know through a letter to the editor type communiqué or retract his first paper and submit an amended version."

Snyder asked, "Do either of you believe there's fraud involved? Has King really cheated and published a fraudulent article?" His eyes shifted from Jason to Hawthorne.

Jason looked at Hawthorne, then said, "To be completely honest, I don't know. But we thought King deserved the benefit of the doubt and an opportunity to clear the air before we investigate further. In his favor is a lengthy faculty tenure of solid research, good teaching, and service to the department. There's no reason for him to cut corners."

Hawthorne added, "I've agreed. It's a sensible way to approach the issue."

Snyder continued to look at Jason. "From your tone, I take it you have some doubts about the validity of the charge against King." His face was a blank, his eyes quizzical.

"At first, I thought he or someone in his group had manufactured data because of his behavior by not responding to the editor's letters, closed to any discussion about what happened, things you'd typically characterize as defensive or evasive. But now I'm not so sure." He didn't want to reveal his suspicion that King's accusers were pushing their own interests at the expense of King's reputation. He continued to tell himself the idea was unlikely, especially when more than one lab was involved.

But when Snyder continued to look at him, Jason said, "I know this seems absurd, but I have a faint suspicion there's something more at play. I've considered the possibility King's accusers have a different motive."

Snyder said, "That's hard to believe. What would be the point?"

"I know it's a long reach. But why are they insisting on an immediate retraction of the paper?"

Snyder said, "How long before we know the outcome of the effort to substantiate the findings?" Snyder glanced at the grandfather clock inscribed with the university seal near the door, his thinking apparently drifting to his next appointment.

"He's promised six weeks or maybe less." Fowler and Jason had urged King to move quickly, but Jason knew training a second team could be unpredictable, and he'd rather have King take more time and have confidence in the outcome. King was right that a sloppy job would serve only to raise more questions and confuse the issue even further.

"I'll call the Attorney General today. Tell him what we're doing and try to convince him to hold still." Then he stood. "I'll let you know his response."

At the door, Snyder shook Jason's hand. "I know you're in an interim role under lousy circumstances, but I hope you'll stand for the headship permanently. The university needs bright young people coming through leadership positions."

"I'm thinking about it," Jason smiled, looking at Hawthorne. He had scanned the job announcement again yesterday as he flipped through the work file, but returned it without doing anything. In addition, the search committee had sent a note telling him he'd been nominated by colleagues in the department. He knew he'd have to get off the fence soon.

116

Snyder said, "We've not interacted much, but I've heard good things about your research work. Give the headship serious consideration."

"Thanks, Dr. Snyder. I will."

"And solve this problem before we're all bowing and scraping to state officials." The President's voice carried a commanding tone. His features were stern, no evidence of the smile that had been present throughout the meeting.

Jason experienced a mixture of emotions as he left the administration building and walked toward Quincy. He didn't know if Snyder was pressuring him, encouraging him, or just being pleasant and supportive. But there had been no reason for the President to inquire about his intentions if he weren't interested. Jason realized the comments by the President, coupled with Hawthorne's encouragement and Fred Adams urging had increased the internal pressure to submit his application. But he missed his lab and the constant interactions with graduate students and the aura of the research experience. He'd worked hard to build a solid research program and wanted to maintain it. Maybe Fred's idea of hanging on to a reduced research presence had merit.

But the President's last remark left no doubt he wanted this issue with King cleared and soon. And he expected Jason to get the job done.

Jennifer and Tony finally fell asleep as Jason read a Dr. Suess story for the umteenth time. After he put the book away, Jason settled next to Lucy on the black leather couch in the den, the comfortable space where they spent free time. From the television in one corner, the laughter and antics from one of the early evening sitcoms cut through the quiet.

He told her about Snyder's comments, then said, "I felt some pressure there, but I don't know how he intended to come across. Maybe he was just passing the time of day."

"From what I've heard about him," Lucy smiled, "he doesn't go out of his way to do things like that or make small talk. If I were you, I'd take it as an endorsement. At the least, some encouragement to submit your application. If he thought you couldn't do the job, he would not have said anything."

Jason took her hand. "I'm not ready to give up research projects and cut back on teaching. Those are the reason I struggled to finish a doctorate, not to shuffle papers and worry about problems like tenure, budgets, and this debacle with King."

"Then," Lucy said, "you have to be happy with whoever takes the job, even if you disagree with the way that person leads the department."

"I can do that. We're bound to get some good applicants."

"You never know. Some won't apply because they think it'll be too hard to follow Henry." She squeezed his hand. "And others won't because they think you have the inside track as the interim, so why waste their time with the application process. And some will be afraid to have their egos damaged when they aren't successful."

"How do you know all of that stuff?" Jason looked into her eyes, watching the gleam and wondering what she was leading to.

118

"I've observed faculty in English who became candidates and lost out. They never got over being turned down and have become bitter and unproductive."

"That won't happen to me."

"Probably not," she said, twisting around to rest her head and shoulder against his chest, "but it could, if some bozo comes in and wrecks the department."

He caressed her back, thinking about the conversation. "So you want me to do this?"

"I think you'd like to—deep down."

"It'll mean more time at the office, away from the kids and you."

She shifted her position so she could see his face directly. "Jason, you can't possibly spend any more time at work.. There aren't any more hours in the day. It's what you've done as long as I've known you. And you'll always be that way. Your job is much like total immersion."

"I'll keep thinking about it."

He didn't want to prolong the discussion about his work habits, an issue about which they'd had the only major disagreements during their marriage. He ran his fingers across her neck, feeling her warmth.

He leaned to kiss her. "You interested in early bed tonight?"

"I might be," Lucy said, her eyes bright, "if I interpret your intentions correctly." Her arm tightened around his neck and her lips found his.

CHAPTER 12

Jason handed the disk with the budget information to Audrey. "I'd like you to check this for errors and make sure the format is correct. And have Miriam check the numbers before we print it." She switched on her computer and moved a stack of papers to a corner of her desk.

"I'll do it this morning, then give it to her. And remember those people from Redlake are coming this afternoon."

"I'm ready for them." Scheduling the meeting with Brenda Fallon and her colleagues had proved difficult, but after she had shuffled her schedule twice, things were arranged for the planning session.

Remembering his observation from two evenings ago, Jason said, "And, I'd like you to set up thirty minute individual meetings with Kathryn Helweg and James Ho from Dr. King's lab." After scanning the list of King's assistants again early this morning, he'd decided to start with those who were co-authors of the disputed paper. They might be more defensive but should know the details of the procedures better than colleagues who'd not been directly involved with the analyses.

"And if they ask about the reason?"

"Tell them, but ask them to keep it confidential." Jason knew keeping the talk about King's problem from spreading was impossible as the environment of an academic institution seemed to foster rumors and speculation. Although most of the employees seemed to honor requests to suppress talking about problems, a few seemed to thrive on spreading news, often embellished and altered to become more exciting than it really merited. And every department had someone like Riley who worked at the task of discovering and spreading rumors.

Jason had just dropped used coffee containers left by another group into the waste basket when Brenda Fallon, the Vice-President for Research and Development for Redlake Industries, and two colleagues appeared at the Biology conference room at one-thirty. She smiled, shaking Jason's hand. "Good to see you. It's been a while." As usual, she had on a dark business suit, gray blouse. Shoulder length black hair framed her round face.

Without waiting for his reply, she turned to the others. "Dr. Jason Spradlin, meet Cynthia Pease and Eric Thomas. They're both on our research and development staff, but you've never met them." Cynthia, short, brown-blond hair, blue eyes, oval face, dressed in a dark blue suit and white blouse, reached to shake Jason's hand, a bright smile revealing perfect teeth. Eric, five-nine, dark features, black hair combed back from a prominent forehead, almost black eyes, waited for Cynthia to shift position, and grasped Jason's hand. Both looked too young to be in this business.

Jason pointed to chairs. "Please, make yourselves comfortable. Anyone like coffee or soft drinks?"

Brenda spoke for the group. "We've just come from lunch, but thanks." She pulled folders from a bulging briefcase.

122

She handed Jason two files. "These are the credentials of Cynthia and Eric for your information."

Jason laid the thin folders aside and said, "It's good news about the growth hormone. I assume sales are going okay?"

Brenda's face lighted. "Off to a great start. Everybody's really pleased and optimistic we'll be ahead of the competition for at least three years." She paused, her face becoming serious. "And we have you to thank for the breakthrough. It'll make Redlake a major player in the production agriculture world."

Jason responded, "Thanks, but several others contributed a lot to the process and the final product."

"I know, but you got us started with the idea and did the initial research. Without that, we would have floundered for a long time." She didn't add, but both she and Jason knew, that without the new product, Redlake was in jeopardy of folding. The company had been limping along for several years, never able to find a profitable niche in a rapidly changing market. Redlake, through Brenda, had approached Jason five years ago with a proposal to work through a contract mechanism to develop one or two new products. Development had moved quickly, but clearing all the regulatory agencies had been slow and tedious. Having jumped the hurdles with a revolutionary product to increase the percentage of muscle in food animals, the outlook now loomed brighter for Redlake.

Brenda moved to the reason for their visit. "As I told you on the phone, we're looking for the next big development at Redlake and wanted to bounce some ideas off you." She nodded to her associates.

"I've asked Cynthia to take the lead, but Eric and I may add our comments at times. Of course, you react at any time. We want to brainstorm, not convince you, and we certainly don't have firm ideas at this time."

Cynthia shifted in the chair to lean forward on the table. Looking at Jason, she said, "We've considered several possibilities during the last few months and have come to a tentative conclusion that the most likely next big advance in food protein production will come through cloning of domestic animals. Actually the news from Scotland about cloning started our thinking. Now, we're speculating that most of the big food industries will move fast to capture the potential. Redlake should be able to compete because of our past work with similar laboratory techniques."

More comfortable now, Cynthia leaned away from the table, shifted in the chair. "We think the market for us is to take one of the swine breeds which has a high percentage of muscle mass but is low in fat and establish a reliable mechanism for cloning the animal. In short, mass produce an animal product attractive to consumers concerned about health and longevity. We think it's possible to produce meat less expensive than present approaches primarily because we could bypass the unknowns associated with the breeding phase. We could market a consistent product. The consumer would always know what they're buying just as they do when they purchase a box of cereal."

Jason interrupted to ask. "Is Redlake planning to get into the actual feeding of animals?"

124

"We've talked about it," Brenda responded, " but decided we'd fare better by contracting with growers to take the baby pigs and grow them to market size. Otherwise, we'd have to purchase farms and build facilities which would be expensive. Plus, we don't really have people versed in the management and feeding of animals."

Cynthia added, "We'd insist on a specific regimen for feeding the animals. Otherwise, we could lose the advantage of the body composition we've sought. We don't want some grower changing the ration to make the pigs grow faster and add a lot of fat."

Jason looked at the three. "No doubt you've considered the scientific risks involved. Remember, the biologists in Scotland, and more recently, investigators in this country have reported on the problems."

Cynthia said, "We've talked with one of the Scottish researchers by phone and Eric and I are scheduled to visit them next week. In fact, we leave Chicago on Sunday night."

Brenda said, "We'll know more after their visit, but we wanted your opinion before going. And I know also you're concerned about the ethical problems."

Jason leaned forward, dropping his ball-point on the pad of paper on which he'd made notes. "You know the obstacles as well as I. A lot of our society get bent out of shape over any new revelation that supplants the natural processes they're accustomed to. They're eager to accept new gimmicks from an engineering feat or find excitement in the exploration of space, but come close to changing the traditional way food is produced generates resistance from a lot of different groups in the country."

"So," Brenda asked, "how do we hedge our position, so to speak? Is it possible to get some reading from the regulatory agencies before we invest heavily into this? Or should we hold off until we can demonstrate the potential?"

Jason shrugged. "You're out of my realm with that question. You know the agencies better than I after your experience with getting approval for the hormone, but, I suspect it wouldn't hurt to talk with the Commissioner of Food and Drug or some deputy close to him."

He paused, thinking about where the opposition would come from. "You know the politicians will get involved and pressure the agencies to take a position they personally favor or more likely, support the position of some lobby group they're beholden to represent."

Not knowing how Cynthia nor Eric viewed the world, Jason didn't want to suggest the conservative religions would more likely be in opposition and could view the change as interfering with God's plan for reproduction. If they raised the question, several prominent politicians would support their position, not wanting to alienate the growing number of conservative voters nor their organizations who gave significant sums of money to favored candidates.

Eric said softly, "And there may be opposition from the traditional agricultural community. They might view it as another attack on the small farm and rural life."

Jason nodded in agreement. "You're correct, but if you involved growers you might alleviate some of that opposition."

Brenda glanced at her watch, always mindful of schedules and deadlines. "Assuming we are not squashed by a representative of FDA and if Cynthia and Eric return from Scotland with a favorable impression, will you be in a position to assist with the science phase? If we can't find the right species, it might mean starting at another point and genetically altering animals to establish a base." Jason understood she meant genetic manipulation via laboratory techniques rather than the traditional approach of breeding to obtain the desired progeny.

"As I told you when you called, I'm serving as department head now and my time is limited by those responsibilities and my on-going research projects . . . ."

"Are you going to become the permanent head?" Brenda was smiling as she asked.

"I've not even submitted my application yet," Jason said, "and the process is unpredictable even if I do, so I can't answer your question."

Having known Brenda for several years and having developed an easy working relationship with her, he wasn't surprised when she said, "I can't imagine the department passing you by if you're interested, so let me phrase the question this way. When you become head in a few months, would you like to be involved with us and what kind of arrangement might work best for you?"

Joining the soft laughter around the table, Jason said, "If that happens, then the best I could do would be as a consultant to you and maybe find a couple of post-docs to work directly on the project.

There wouldn't be time for me to become actively involved with the research itself but I could be an overseer of the basic experimentation."

"Good enough." Brenda said, standing and shoving files into her briefcase. "We have to catch a plane in forty-five minutes."

In the hall, she continued, "We'll get back to you after Scotland."

Jason closed the door and watched the Redlake trio hurry away, considering the potential of their idea and a possible personal role. Brenda's statement about when he became department head seemed another endorsement. Walking toward the office, Jason acknowledged his desire to be closely involved with the Redlake venture, one that could revolutionize food production. Somehow he could make this dual role work out. If the problem arose.

Shortly after four and his brain still churning with ideas about the Redlake project, the President called. "Dr. Spradlin, I wanted you to know I talked to the Attorney General just before noon. He's willing to hold off any investigation into the King issue until we've had a chance to corroborate the work, but he wasn't pleased with my request to wait." A slight chuckle from Snyder suggested there had been an argument before the state official conceded to the President.

Jason asked, "So what would he gain by his prying into this thing?"

Snyder laughed. "Dean Hawthorne hit it on the head when we met. He'd gain publicity and try to come across as a tough enforcer of ethics in all state agencies."

"Let's hope we can short circuit any further concerns of his."

"I agree," Snyder said, "but let me know how things go. I don't want to get caught short and hear about the problem through the media. And let's move things as quickly as possible."

"I'll do my best. I've told our people not to talk, but refer any questions to Public Relations, but you know how persistent reporters can be."

"I know very well."

Jason replaced the receiver and began signing the daily batch of forms. At the bottom of the stack was the printed budget document and a cover letter to the Dean. He flipped through the pages. Everything looked in order. He signed the letter and on the way out placed the packet on Audrey's desk.

Near his car, he smiled thinking this had been a god day. The excitement of a new venture had somehow meshed with the nitty-gritty requirements of the job.

CHAPTER 13

Jason stood and moved from behind the desk when Audrey announced the arrival of Kathryn Helweg, a post-doc working with King. The young woman smiled tentatively as Jason pointed to one of the chairs around the table. She walked to him and shook his hand before turning toward the seats. Her attire, black skirt, white blouse, sheer hose and heels, and her movements radiated sensuality. Her facial features were exquisite, all the features of the classic beauty queen. Her perfume could be described as enticing. Jason realized he was staring as she sat.

He said, "Thanks for coming in." She sat at the corner next to Jason, primly keeping her feet together, the skirt not covering her knees. She clasped her hands together in her lap and waited, her eyes on his face.

"I've seen you around the building, but tell me a bit about your background." Jason was reasonably sure she had been the person he'd seen huddled with King a few nights ago and recalled King's comment about Riley's fascination.

In a firm alto voice, she said, "I finished a Ph.D. last November at Minnesota and came here in January. After a bachelor's degree in business, I worked for two years, then decided it wasn't what I wanted to do with my life. I returned to the university to major in Biology and continued through the doctorate. I've not worked professionally before, but went straight through all the degrees at the same place. So, the post-doc seemed the right thing to gain experience." She leaned forward slightly as she spoke, her hands resting on the table.

"What project are you working on?"

She leaned back and crossed her legs, causing Jason to glance at shapely legs. "I'm helping with all the projects in Dr. King's lab. He wanted someone with experience to assist in the supervision of graduate students."

"Have you been involved with the work dealing with the relationship of viruses to cell replication?" Jason tried to focus on her face for signals of tension.

"Yes. I'm one of the co-authors on the paper that's been challenged." Her voice was direct, a matter-of-fact sharing of information without hint of apology or concern.

Jason smiled and said, "Actually, that publication is the reason I've asked you to visit. I assume you're aware other investigators in the field have suggested the data were incorrect."

"We all know. Dr. King has talked about the paper with his group. Now we're redoing experiments."

"How involved were you with that original work?"

She looked away, leaned forward again to clasp her hands around the crossed knee. "It was the first set of experiments I did when I came. A graduate student did much of the analyses, but I checked the work and repeated some of the tests when he had difficulty getting acceptable duplications." She paused, then continued, "I did the statistics and wrote the first draft of the paper. Then Dr. King edited and polished the manuscript."

"I take it you didn't suspect anything wrong with the data?"

Shaking her head, she said, "No, and neither did Dr. King, after he'd checked through everything."

"Had you done the same analyses previously or was this a first time?"

"It was the first time I had done that specific procedure, but I've done others like it. I worked through the protocol several times before I did the actual tests. And I could be more help to James if I'd done the procedure." Jason had often done the same thing when he had time to work in the lab.

"So you felt confident of your work?"

She nodded, dark eyes boring into Jason's face, almost a challenge, but something else. Her eyes were a remarkable deep cobalt blue, a coloring he'd never seen before.

"Have you read other recent papers in the field?"

"Dr. King gave me a set of publications when I first came. I've read them all several times. And I've gone back through earlier publications relevant to our work."

Jason didn't feel confident in this exploration, feeling like a prosecutor digging for clues, not wishing to accuse anyone of wrong-doing, but trying to determine where the process could have gone wrong. He asked, "In reviewing those papers and knowing the conflicts with your publication, did you ever consider the data of your paper could have been incorrect? Maybe a flaw in the procedure led the group astray?   Perhaps a misinterpretation of the published directions?"

"We discussed it and went back over our analyses when we compared our data with published findings. We knew ours didn't coincide with papers in the literature, but we recognized our experiments had been slanted differently, to get at another piece of the larger problem." She touched her hair, her eyes glancing away from Jason momentarily. "But we couldn't find anything wrong. All the usual checks and control samples were within the acceptable range."

"Are you working on the new analyses?"

Shaking her head, she said, "No. Dr. King thought it'd be better if everyone from the first experiments stayed clear of these checks, but I'd like to be involved. I don't like my work to be considered wrong."

Jason smiled at the sour look on her face. "Perhaps it's not incorrect. That's why the second experiment is being done. To prove beyond doubt the initial experiments were right."

She nodded, her eyes staring at the floor or her black pumps. She shifted in the chair, recrossed her legs, returned her hand to her knee. "But Dr. King thinks we did something wrong. Now he admits the results were unexpected and blames the student and me." For a brief moment she seemed on the defensive and hurt because King had challenged her work, if not her integrity.

She smiled slightly, a brief display of bright teeth, and added, "He hasn't accused us directly of anything, but I know he believes we didn't do one of the procedures correctly."

"You think Dr. King changed his opinion about the data after the paper was challenged?"

She nodded. "He's concerned about what others think. I know he doesn't like being in the position we're in. You know, suspected of rigging the outcome."

"Who was the student who did the analyses?"

"James Ho. I think James is an anglicized version of his Oriental name."

Jason looked at Kathryn, her eyes not wavering, almost flirting, inviting or challenging. Suddenly uncomfortable, he said, "Well, our discussion has been helpful and I appreciate your openness. And I hope the new experiments will put to rest any questions about the validity of the work."

She stood, pressing her hands along her thighs to smooth any wrinkles in the skirt, saying, "I hope so too. This is all a nightmare."

When he stood, she stepped closer to shake his hand. "Thanks, Dr. Spradlin. It's nice to know who you are. Your post-doc, Angela, tells me such good things about you and the relationship she has with you."

He was not prepared for her behavior or his inner stirrings, wanting to keep the conversation going. He watched her walk through the door, her distinctly female figure and the slight sway of her hips provocative. He wondered if she and King were really having an affair. It would be easy enough to let your guard down around such a enticing woman. But she had been professional in her responses and clearly was irritated at being accused of unethical behavior.

"I'm never at ease doing this kind of thing," Jason said to Lucy, as they parked in front of the Rogers' house at eight. The sun had disappeared and the mid-October evening had turned cool.

"It's hard, but we need to do this." She had insisted they visit Thelma Rogers and had called to set up a time, knowing Jason wouldn't back out of an established appointment with Henry's widow, a woman who'd become a mother figure to him.

Thelma, her mature figure in a print dress, her gray hair neatly combed, smiling, met them at the door and immediately made them feel comfortable. She said, "Have seats. I have coffee made and I'll be right back." She disappeared through a doorway and Lucy smiled at Jason as though saying, "See, it's okay."

Seated across from them, Thelma said, "I'm sorting through Henry's things, throwing out things and giving clothes to Goodwill." She rushed on, "I'm thinking about selling this house and moving to a condominium. It's too much for a single person."

Lucy asked, "So you're planning to remain in the city?"

Thelma shifted in the large chair, "Oh, yes. All my friends are here and the kids are so scattered, it'd be impossible to settle near one of them without upsetting the others. And, they all like to come back here for visits."

"I'll be glad to help with anything around the university," Jason volunteered.

"That's kind of you, but Henry had everything like insurance organized and we'd updated our wills a year ago. It's been easy to

136

arrange things." She added, "Audrey took care of all his papers and personal belongings at the office."

Jason asked, "Did he ever talk to you about problems at the university?" He knew it was unlikely Henry had time to discuss the King issue with Thelma, but he had to be certain. She might know something.

She grinned, "Only if it was in the newspapers and I brought it up. I never knew what was going on in Biology." She refilled their coffee cups and pushed the plate of cookies toward them.

Thelma sipped coffee, then continued, "But I know he'd be pleased you were the new department head. He respected you so much. He'd be happy the department was in good hands."

Jason looked at Lucy, then said, "I don't know if I'll become the permanent head. Applications are due soon, but I'm still thinking it over."

Thelma nodded. "I can understand, but once Henry and I were talking about his successor and he said you'd be an outstanding leader for the department. You should know he'd want you to do it."

Jason glanced at Lucy, but didn't respond to Thelma. He watched Lucy's smile and felt her touch on his arm. He'd never thought Henry would recommend him for an administrative position and wondered if Thelma was really relaying Henry's thoughts correctly.

After a few minutes of reminiscing about Henry and hearing about Thelma's plans, Lucy said, "We're pleased you're doing well, but remember to call us if we can help with anything. Now, we need to relieve the baby sitter and make sure the kids are tucked away okay."

As he backed out of the driveway, Jason said, "Thelma seems in control of everything, as usual."

"She's a steady soul. Henry's death must have been hard for her, but she's coping well."

Both were silent for a while, Jason concentrating on the traffic. Near their own home, Lucy said, "And she let you know Henry's ideas about the next department leader."

Following Jason's graduate class the next morning, James Ho came at the appointed time. The stocky, black-haired man smiled and bowed slightly as Jason approached him, pointing to a chair. Ho's brown suit and matching tie suggested he'd dressed differently to see the department head than his usual lab attire. Maybe he was following Kathryn's example.

"Mr. Ho, I'm pleased to meet you and as you likely know, I'd like to talk about the research project you've been working on under Dr. King." Jason looked directly at Ho's dark eyes behind thick glasses and spoke more slowly than usual, thinking Ho might have difficulty with conversational English.

Ho smiled and Jason continued, "First, tell me about your background."

Ho shifted, his face became serious, as he said, "B. S. degree from university in Taiwan. Now I've come to study here for a Master's and maybe doctoral degrees."

"This is your second year with Dr. King?" Jason recalled seeing Ho in the graduate seminar and around the halls a few times.

138

"That's right. I came a year ago."

Jason said, "Tell me about the kind of analyses you've been doing."

Ho shifted again, his face remaining sober. "I worked on the DNA analyses after the cells had been infected with the virus. We were trying to see if the cells changed because of the presence of the virus."

Jason asked, "Did you find the analyses difficult?"

Ho grinned, "The procedure seemed very hard at first. But I worked a long time to get it right. Also, Dr. Helweg gave me help and she did some of the work."

"Were you confident of the data when you finished?"

"I didn't know, but Dr. King and Kathryn said it was okay. I think it worked out well after I practiced lots of times."

"Do you know other investigators believe your data may be wrong?"

Ho scowled, his features darkened, and his hands clenched. "Dr. King has told all of us about it, but I trust our work. I believe our data are correct."

"And you're not involved in repeating the experiments?"

Ho hesitated and for a moment Jason thought he hadn't understood, then his face lighted and he said, "No. Dr. Helweg has assigned me to other things."

Jason looked at him and said, "I believe that's all I wanted to ask. Thanks for coming by. And I wish you well with your studies."

Ho stood, bowing slightly again, and made his way out the door. Jason watched him, thinking Ho wouldn't have had the expertise to manufacture data. If he'd been involved with erroneous data collection, it had been the result of inexperience and based on poor techniques. Any planned manipulation would have to rest with King or Helweg or both.

Putting away the King file after making notes of his conversation with Ho, Jason pulled the Boseman folder. The department tenure committee was meeting in ten days and he planned to talk to the chair before they met.

Audrey interrupted his concentration by knocking lightly on the door frame. "Dr. Spradlin, Vicki Sanchez would like to talk with you."

"Remind me who she is."

Audrey stepped inside the office and closed the door. "She's a graduate assistant with Dr. Harris."

The reminder on Henry's yellow pad and his conversation with Harris jolted his memory. "Okay, send her in."

"I can ask her to come back another time if you'd prefer."

"No, it's fine." He closed Boseman's file.

CHAPTER 14

A deep frown blanketed Vicki Sanchez's face as she came in. Five-seven, slim, dark eyes, coal black hair framing a long face, she exuded depression and uncertainty. For a moment, Jason thought she might turn and dash out. Wrinkled brown slacks and a faded tan blouse added to her dejected appearance. She made no overture to shake hands, her eyes darting from Jason to the floor.

Jason invited her to a chair at the conference table and sat across from her. He smiled and said, "How can I help you?"

She continued to avoid Jason's face. Her tone a mixture of demanding and pleading, she said, "I want our conversation to be confidential. I don't want anybody to know I've met with you."

"Of course, that's understood."

She waited several seconds, then looked up. "I'm having personal problems with Dr. Harris and I don't know what to do about it."

"Can you tell me what kind of problem?" Jason suspected because of Harris' reputation but he wanted her to say to partially relieve her obvious distress.

"Sexual harassment." Her voice was blunt, challenging, filled with frustration and anger. Now her eyes bored into Jason's face, challenging him to disagree.

Jason waited for a moment, then asked, "Can you be more explicit? Off-color jokes, touching, comments or suggestions?"

Vicki, now looking steadily at Jason, scowled and said, "It started with touching, rubbing my shoulders, back, arms, then he'd put his arm around my waist when the opportunity is there."

"You mean when you are working closely?"

"Yes," she nodded, "or when he stops by to look at my work in the lab. He always pulls me close so our bodies are touching. Once, he rubbed my hips until I moved away." A brief pause, then, "I think he goes out of his way to get near me."

Jason asked, "Has he made comments when he does this?"

"Two days ago," Vicki muttered, "he said he would like to meet for a drink after work. I didn't know what to do, but I begged off, saying I had promised to meet a friend to study and didn't have time. His face turned red and I knew he was mad because I turned him down."

"Has he approached you since?"

"Yesterday, he came by my desk and said he still wanted to meet away from the office to get to know me better in a social setting. I thought his tone was threatening and it sounded like I didn't have a choice. Last night I decided to see you or someone. I'd heard from other students you'd help."

"I'll talk with Dr. Harris today or early tomorrow to get his side of the story." Jason promised her. "In the interval don't meet with him for any reason away from this building."

"He'll be furious. He'll know I came to you." She wiped away the beginnings of tears on her sleeve. Creases of concern covered her face.

Jason smiled, trying to encourage her. "Perhaps, but he'll get over it. And, if he's really guilty of these accusations, you might think

142

about changing major professors." He paused, watching for her reaction, then asked, "What are your interests and background?"

Vicki shifted in the chair, the scowl finally disappearing from her face. "I did a Master's at San Diego State, but I wanted more depth in the ecology of plants, and Dr. Harris was recommended, so I applied for an assistantship. I've been here for a year."

Jason said, "The only other faculty in Biology with expertise in the area is Dr. McLeod. He might take you on."

"I can't afford to lose my assistantship." Her eye squinted with concern. "It's the only income I have and I'm taking out loans to eke by as it is."

"I'll look for some kind of support should that happen," Jason said, "but first let me talk with Dr. Harris. It might work out for you to stay with him."

Vicki shook her head. Strands of hair drooped over her brow. She brushed them away. "I doubt he'd agree to my remaining in his group after he learns I came to see you and I don't know if I could do it after his behavior toward me. Our relationship has changed a lot during the last six months. It's gone from professional mentor and student to people sparring for an advantage in a game. I'm always on guard when he's near. I avoid going into his office."

"Let's see how it goes. I'll have Audrey find you later today or early tomorrow morning after I've met with Dr. Harris, and we'll talk again."

Moving chairs back against the table, Jason said, "Remember, don't let Dr. Harris force you to do anything you don't want to do. If he should pressure you, tell him straight out you've talked to me. Be firm and direct, regardless of what he threatens or promises."

She nodded, took steps toward the door, then turned back and extended her hand. "Thanks, Dr. Spradlin. I'm glad I came to see you."

Jason dug out the file on Harris placed in the stack after his initial meeting. His first suspicion that Harris was lying about the problem had been confirmed. He wished he had some experience in dealing with these issues. No one trained for these jobs. You stumbled into them and did the best you could. He liked Henry's approach—direct, no compromise, but he wasn't sure he was ready to do it that way. Thoughts of his busy but serene research lab nibbled at the fringes of his deliberations.

The glare on Greg Harris' face and his entrance to the office revealed he knew why he'd been summoned. He mumbled, "You wanted to see me." He plopped into a chair at the conference table, not looking at Jason.

Jason sat next to him, staring at his face, and observing the quiver in his hands. Jason said, "A young woman working with you came in yesterday to see me. She complained you've harassed her and believes you're trying to force her into a sexual relationship, something she doesn't want. I promised to hear your side of the story before I do anything."

To Jason's surprise, Harris remained silent, glaring at the table top. Jason pushed ahead. "Remember our previous discussion and your

144

assurance nothing was wrong, but now I've learned there's a real problem."

Harris blustered, "Women overreact these days, all this anti-male attitude in our society. You must know that yourself."

"No, I don't know, but the problem is serious. She was very upset." Jason wouldn't let Harris steer the conversation into a philosophical debate about societal behavior.

His face darkening, his lips almost sneering, Harris stormed, "What a bitch Sanchez has become." He twisted in the chair and his hands were clenched, as though ready to lash out in a physical way.

"She feels violated, Greg. In her mind she had no recourse but to seek help from someone who will protect her. You're damn lucky she hasn't filed a charge of sexual harassment against you. My suspicion is she will if you don't change your behavior." He thought he didn't need to say he'd encourage her if it came to some formal action.

"But, Jason, I haven't done anything wrong. She's taken my actions as something I didn't intend." Harris attempted to look innocent, his hands raised in a shrug, his mouth agape. His attempt to portray innocence failed.

Ignoring the acting effort, Jason continued, "She says you've touched her, pulled her against you and asked her to meet you at some bar. She's highly offended and feels vulnerable If she's right, you've gone beyond the acceptable boundaries of professional behavior between faculty and student."

Still belligerent, Harris stared at Jason. "I can't believe you'd accept her word against mine. I've watched you grow up in this department."

"Greg, I've reviewed your file and your history of sexual adventures with students and other females present a picture that wouldn't serve you well if she files a grievance. It's not a matter of my believing one over the other. If you've given her the impression you're pressuring her for sexual favors, the University Ethics Committee would recommend stiff sanctions without batting an eye. The university administration would have no choice but to fire you. Tenure is not a safety net in these situations." Jason didn't know how strong the committee would be since it would depend on the composition, but he knew it had become much more stringent in the past three years. Universities, like other institutions in society, couldn't tolerate aberrant actions by supervisory or peer employees and be sued for failure to provide a safe working environment.

"So what the hell are you telling me? I'm guilty as charged, without due process." Harris' red face and neck showed his irritation and embarrassment to be placed in the position of defending himself.

"Greg, it's clear the young woman felt compromised, even threatened. I don't know your motives and have only her version of your actions, but she believes you are pressuring her into a sexual relationship and intended to use your position as a major professor and employer to have your way. Regardless of how you view the situation, she's taken your actions as those of a professor demanding a sexual relationship with a student who is in no position to resist. And, to remind you again, your personnel file has notes made by Henry of past incidents, so it's become a pattern for you and makes it easy to accept

146

her version of the events. You need to change before something happens you can't rectify."

When Harris continued to stare and shake his head, Jason added, "I recommend that you apologize for any misunderstanding and move on. But in the future you can't give any impression of sexual expectation. You must behave differently toward Vicki Sanchez. Plus, you can't afford for this to become public knowledge. It would wreck your reputation, maybe your family."

"How do I know she won't still do something silly, like suing?"

"I can't guarantee she won't, but my impression is she just wanted the advances and threats to cease—nothing more. She'd like to continue working in your group if she can be assured there'll be no retribution."

Harris stood, his face a scowl, his posture radiating defiance. "I'll think about it. Maybe I'll talk to her. I need the work she's doing."

Jason walked to the door with Harris, saying, "You have to do more than think about it. You must meet with her and clear the air. And further, I suggest you consider professional counseling to overcome your problem. In any case, let me know what you do in regard to Sanchez."

Jason returned to the Boseman file he'd abandoned the afternoon before. As a result of Audrey's diligence, the file now contained correspondence from previous teaching assessments, notifications of grants received, and the letter from the department committee when Boseman was reviewed after three years at State. Several letters from

Henry about salary raises and the review were present. An up-to-date vita prepared by Boseman completed the dossier.

Jason scanned through the materials looking for some reason to excuse or explain Boseman's lousy teaching record. But every piece of correspondence about instruction chided Boseman to improve. Henry's letter at the last salary review included a strong indictment of Boseman's failure to work on improving teaching and Henry's statement that he would not support him for tenure unless there was a dramatic turn for the better. Clearly this had not happened.

Jason put aside the folder hoping the department committee was prepared to take a stand and reject Boseman. If they didn't, he'd be in the awkward position of recommending against the department faculty committee, an unpopular stance for any head but risky for one with an interim appointment. His thoughts ran through the scenario of options. Not many were available. He remembered Lucy telling him about a faculty member in English who'd been awarded tenure in spite of his lousy teaching record and how the other faculty now resented him because the head wouldn't assign him certain courses to protect the students. Others had to pick up the slack. Biology couldn't afford to have someone like that for another twenty or twenty-five years. He had to do what he could to deny tenure to Boseman.

Harris left Jason's office in a state of deep frustration. He blamed Vicki Sanchez for his embarrassment of being told by an acting head, a guy twenty years younger, to apologize and stay clean. Spradlin hadn't yelled like Rogers might have, but the message was

148

clear—another complaint by a dumb female would land him before the Ethics Committee or worse. He could be out on the street with no recourse.

He detoured to find Riley in his office on the second floor. He walked in, interrupting Riley's shuffling of papers on his desk, killing time until he could leave for the day without averse comments from others. Harris dropped into a chair and muttered, "You were right. Spradlin can be a tough nut."

Looking at Harris' agitated state, something rare in the typically cool professor, Riley asked, "What happened?"

Hesitating as he considered how much to tell, Harris blurted, "This screwy grad student complained to Spradlin. Said I was coming on to her, using my position to coerce her into sex." As he talked, he shifted his feet, brushed a hand across his eyes. "So Spradlin called me in and essentially told me to either stop or be prepared for a formal hearing. I'm pissed because he accepted her story without getting my version. In his eyes, I'm guilty as charged."

With a supportive audience, Harris continued, "So now I have to apologize and stay clear of her." He clenched his hands together, his frustration not abating. "I should fire her ass, but she'd go back to Spradlin and he take care of her and give me hell. Probably take away any salary raise for this year."

Taking on a patronizing tone, Riley said, "I know how he can be."

"I heard." Harris didn't admit that at the time he thought Jason had been right. Riley's messing with Spradlin's graduate student had been over the line.

Riley changed the subject, thinking he'd lead Harris into a more provocative area. "Have you heard about this fiasco with King?"

"I saw the papers. Sounds bad, but it's hard to believe. King is a straight shooter."

Riley smirked, shifted a paper weight from one stack to another, then said, "I'm not so sure. I've learned he's screwing this post-doc." He glanced at Harris and idly moved the glass weight again, continuing, "But I couldn't blame him. She's the sexiest woman I've seen in a long time."

Harris stood. "I know what she looks like, but I'm not so sure of his getting her into bed. I suspect she's lesbian. Anyway, I wanted to let you know about Spradlin. It might be smart to block him from the permanent job."

"I've talked to a couple of others who I suspect will come around to our position after they've seen Spradlin operate for a bit longer."

Harris walked out, thinking about how he would approach Vicki Sanchez. She'd report the outcome to Spradlin, so he had to do something. Bluffing here would likely not work out.

At four-thirty Vicki Sanchez returned. She waited for Jason to move around the desk while Audrey closed the door. Jason noted the same nondescript wrinkled slacks, but a brighter shirt and the slight semblance of a smile. Her hair had been recently combed and lay in neat folds around her face.

As they sat across the table, Jason said, "I assume Dr. Harris talked to you."

She nodded. "Just after noon today. I couldn't see you sooner because your were busy, then I had class."

"Are you satisfied with the discussion?"

"I'm not sure," Vicki said, shaking her head. "He harped on how I'd misunderstood his actions, but he promised to avoid those in the future. Now my concern is he'll hold this against me and my educational experience will be compromised. I've heard of other women being silently punished for standing up for their rights. Something no one could prove, but they knew it occurred."

"Tell me," Jason asked, "the kind of things you believe might happen?"

Vicki shifted, raked a hand through her dark hair destroying the neat arrangement, then said, "I have a friend in another department who resisted the advances of her professor and went to the department head. Ever since then, she's not been supported for travel to scientific meetings, not given the credit she deserves on papers, not recognized in the group for her accomplishments. Little things, but they get to you and deprive you of opportunities others receive. Plus, she believes she'll have a hard time getting a position when she graduates because he'll give her a poor recommendation." She looked directly into Jason's face. "I don't want to go through the same things."

"When you talked with Dr. Harris, did you feel any resentment or did he threaten you in any way?"

She hesitated, seeming to analyze the scene with Harris, then said, "No, but I could tell he was upset and having a difficult time controlling his emotions. He couldn't apologize, but continued to say I hadn't understood and it was his approach to learn more about his students. But he hasn't treated the males the same way."

"Would you rather change professors? Since we met, I've thought more about the possibilities. In addition to Dr. McLeod in this department, several faculty in the plant sciences could provide what you're seeking. I've not called anyone, but I'm willing if we need to."

Her dark eyes bored into Jason's and he could see uncertainty mixed with sadness. She mumbled, "I don't know what to do or what's best."

Jason waited, then she continued, "The research project is exactly what I want to do, but . . . ."

"Let me suggest a possible course of action," Jason said. "Continue with Dr. Harris and see how it works out for the remainder of this semester, until the Christmas break unless there's a recurrence of his demands. Then come back and tell me how it's going. Under the circumstances Dr. Harris probably couldn't admit to you he needs you on the project, but you are valuable to him. And the more you contribute, the more important you become to the success of the research. But, if you suspect you're being denied certain opportunities essential to your continuing growth, or if he approaches you in any way about a personal relationship, let me know and we'll find other things for you."

Nodding understanding, she stood. "Okay, I'll try it, but I may be back tomorrow."

152

"Understand things between Dr. Harris and you will be tense for a while, but give it time to return to the professional relationship you had when you first came."

She shook his hand as they stood. Jason watched her walk out. He moved to the windows and stared across the campus, now with little traffic after the five o'clock rush to leave campus. Under a sky turning grayer, gusts of wind were whipping dry leaves around into apparently random directions as it shifted between the large buildings. He hoped he'd guided Vicki Sanchez in the right direction and wondered if he'd ever know.

He added a note to the yellow pad to check on Sanchez in January if he hadn't heard anything and picked up the Boseman file to take home for one more examination. Then he dropped it back on the desk. Boseman had to be turned down for the good of the department and there was no reason to look further for some way to excuse his performance. Bite the bullet and stand firm.

CHAPTER 15

Jason stepped from behind the desk to shake hands with Pamela Sturgis as she entered the office. During her seven years at State she and Jason had become close colleagues, since she was the faculty member most closely associated with Jason's research interest. They had spent long hours evaluating data from projects, reviewing papers for each other, and exchanging ideas knowing the other would provide an honest opinion without trying to make the colleague feel good but hoping to truly help them. Her white lab coat over dark slacks and paisley blouse reminded Jason he missed the lab activity and the times he'd relied on her judgment. As usual, her short brown hair was neat and her brown eyes and face revealed her pleasing personality.

Pamela handed Jason a folder and said, "I've looked through this NIH Center grant information and we should apply. It'd move the department forward and open doors we've not experienced previously." After several starts to work through the instructions and guidelines for the grant proposal and being sidetracked each time, Jason had asked Pamela to scan the packet, understand the thrust the agency was seeking, and consider the potential for the department and State University. His cursory review of the document had convinced him Biology couldn't do this alone, but would need to enlist faculty from across the university if they hoped to compete successfully.

"Have you thought about who should be involved?"

Always prepared, Sturgis said, "Actually I made a list. It's in the file. John Hadley or someone in his unit may be key, or you may know others in the Med School who would be compatible and interested. Several faculty from this department, Jessica Hobart from Biochemistry, Eleanor Evans from Food and Nutrition, perhaps Joe Bancroft from Psychology could be participants. I've thought about Statistics but don't know anyone I thought would fit.

"I've heard of most except Hobart."

"She came in the fall from a post-doc at Stanford after a doctorate from Berkeley. Good experience with gene manipulation and modification with a focus on enzyme induction. I've talked with her a couple of times at functions of the Women in Science organization. She's bright and seems like she'd be easy to work with."

Pamela continued, "Also, I made a broad outline of the possible approach and the kinds of background information we'd need to incorporate into the proposal. I even went so far as to suggest a set of objectives for us, but others will have ideas as well."

"That's great," Jason said, smiling at Pamela. "Thanks for giving us a start. Suppose I get Audrey to set up a meeting with those you've recommended and let's have a brainstorming session and decide how to go forward from there."

"The thing I haven't done is give a copy of either the instruction guides or my outline to anyone else. If they have those ahead of the meeting, we can save time."

Jason nodded, agreeing with her suggestion. "We'll get that done."

Sturgis stood. "We need to move fast. Only six weeks until the deadline." She returned a pen to the pocket of her lab coat.

"I know and wish I could give it more time than this job allows."

Pamela touched his arm, smiled, and said, "We also need you here. I'll do what I can on the proposal after the group has agreed on the objectives and the general plan."

Ben Rankin passed Pamela at the door. They stopped to chat for a minute as Jason watched his good colleagues. Leaving Pamela and walking into the office, Ben started before he reached the conference table. "Jason, I wanted to touch base about the department tenure and promotion committee. Henry liked to review the candidates with the chairman before we met. I don't know if you wanted to follow his practice. but I thought I should see if you had any words of wisdom for us."

Settling across from Ben at the table, Jason said, "Ben, I haven't paid much attention to such matters in the past, so I didn't know if the committee would talk to me before their meeting or not." Rankin, red-hair, freckled face, always calm and in control, was respected by everyone in the department, thus was often elected for important committee responsibilities. Jason thought of him as the George Stuart of the next generation.

Relieved Ben had made the initial overture, Jason moved to his primary concern regarding candidates this year. "I understand through the Dean that heads make a separate recommendation about candidates to the next level. In getting ready for that, I discovered Henry had major concerns about Terry Boseman. I've worried over his file trying to reach a decision. There's a real concern about his teaching, although everything else seems first rate."

"I've read the letters about his teaching," Rankin admitted, "but I don't know how the committee will weight that, given his solid grant and publication record."

Jason didn't know how far he should push his reservations. He didn't want the committee to ignore Boseman's teaching record, but he knew from previous dealings with faculty committees they'd resent a head's interference into their peer assessment. He decided he shouldn't reveal his own decisions, but hoped they might agree with him.

Jason said, "You understand I won't try to persuade you one way or the other, even if I could, but I hope the committee will consider seriously the negative impact Terry has had on undergraduate students, and probably graduate students as well."

Rankin looked directly at Jason. "You think it's that bad?" He made a note in a small notebook taken from his shirt pocket.

"Yes, I do. Kids are always upset in his classes and trying to transfer out. After I saw the letters and the evaluation scores, I examined the past enrollment figures for the beginning courses. Boseman's sections consistently have the lowest census and always have the greatest number of transfers out. Students avoid him when it's possible. When they can switch sections, they get out of his courses and quickly."

Rankin crossed his long legs, brown socks showing above loafers. "So what are you telling me?"

"I'm suggesting," Jason grimaced, thinking he was pushing too hard, "that the committee think through the potential consequences of giving a life contract to a person who either cannot or does not want to be involved in the teaching function of the department."

Ben grinned, perhaps to lower the intensity of their discussion. "I've never heard you talk like that before. This office has changed you already." He twirled his pen between his thumb and fingers.

Jason grinned back at his colleague whom he respected and liked. "Probably, but I'm worried about the message we send if Boseman is given tenure."

Rankin asked, "Any others you have worries about?"

Shaking his head, Jason said, "No, both Roger Murdock and Elizabeth Givens seem on track okay—solid records in both teaching and research, good contributors to the department."

Rankin stood, tucking the tail of his plaid shirt into khaki pants. "I'll share your concerns with the committee, but God knows how it'll go." Jason hoped he hadn't pressed his position too hard. He'd heard of faculty committees deliberately going against a department head's opinion to demonstrate their independence. Jason wasn't concerned about Rankin, but about others who always exhibited negative reactions to almost anything proposed by the leadership.

Rankin paused in the door. "We're meeting tomorrow and I'll let you know how it goes." He grinned. "Don't let this office change you too much."

Jason and Lucy were well along with their soup and sandwich at Mortimer's when he saw Preston King and Kathryn Helweg being met at the front desk by the hostess.

Aware of Jason's distraction from their conversation, she asked, "What is it?"

"My overactive imagination jumping to conclusions. Preston and his post-doc, Kathryn Helweg, just came in. And as always, she looks dressed to kill or whatever." Helweg's tight gray skirt and sweater caused every male's eye to notice, then stare, as they moved through the crowded restaurant.

Turning slightly and observing for a moment, Lucy said, "She's very attractive, even beautiful, not to mention seductive. But some women always dress like that and nothing is intended, so what's your imagination suggesting?"

"Rumors are she and Preston are having an affair and she's involved with this paper that's being challenged."

"And you think there's some connection?" Lucy grinned.

"There's no reason to believe that, but the thought has claimed a spot in my thinking ever since I talked with her about the data collection."

Lucy laughed. "Maybe you were just distracted."

Shaking his head, Jason grinned and touched her hand. "She has this strange approach, almost like she's coming onto you. But it's," Jason added, "more than her appearance that caused me to be suspicious. Her actions were almost like a challenge. You know,

160

daring me to find the missing piece to the puzzle, although her responses were sensible and agreed with things King has told me."

Lucy shoved aside the sandwich plate. "If she and Preston are so close, there'd be no reason for her to do anything that would harm him. It would also destroy her career if she's somehow connected to the work."

"But it could work the other way. If she made a huge error with the paper, Preston could be protecting her." He shoved aside the plate and sipped coffee, then added, "Or maybe he doesn't even realize what she's done and is so enthralled with her, he can't see the problem in a logical way."

Shaking her head, Lucy argued, "That's a long reach. He wouldn't likely tolerate a wrongful publication just to retain his good graces with a post-doc, regardless of how sexy she is. If they're really involved, both would want the most favorable outcome and would work together to achieve it."

"I understand, but why do I keep thinking she's somehow using him?"

Sliding out of the booth, Lucy said, "Because she came across to you as a manipulator and her appearance is so different from all those drab lab people in the department."

She took his hand as they waited at the cashier's station. "You know, Jason, we're always suspicious of people who act or dress differently."

"Maybe you're right. Time will tell." He made a mental note to find out how the experiments in King's lab were progressing. The time

King had projected would soon be up and the President would be pressing to avoid another call from the Attorney general.

He held Lucy's coat before they stepped out into the cold early November afternoon, but his mind remained on Helweg and King.

As they walked toward the campus, Lucy said, "Maybe she was coming on to you."

Jason took her arm. "Not likely, too old."

"I don't know. Some young women are attracted to the mature types."

Once when they had been bantering about reasons for attractions between sexes, Lucy had told him that some of her friends had warned her about women being drawn to Jason. He'd not believed her, but it made him feel good at the time. And he recalled his own reactions to Kathryn Helweg. She could be quite alluring, even in the office of the department administrator.

He leaned to kiss Lucy on the cheek, whispering, "Maybe, but after our encounters, this mature type doesn't have the energy for other liaisons or whatever they're called these days."

She squeezed his hand. "Tonight I intend to check on your energy."

"Maybe I'll have a nap this afternoon. I'd hate to fail your test."

CHAPTER 16

Ben Rankin returned two days later, a single sheet of paper in his hand. His face expressionless, he handed the paper to Jason as he took the chair adjacent to the desk.

Jason glanced at the summary. All candidates had been recommended for tenure and promotion to Associate Professor.

Trying to mask his frustration and disappointment, Jason asked, "I assume you discussed thoroughly Boseman's case?"

Rankin shifted in the chair, crossed his legs and tugged at his brown corduroy pants. "We spent over an hour debating his problems with teaching. But the majority came down to the position he would improve, and the department couldn't afford to lose his research productivity."

Still struggling to remain calm and objective, Jason asked, "Then it wasn't a unanimous vote in favor?"

"No, but almost. It was four to one in favor. I'm sending you a letter about the specifics and copies of the letters to the candidates, but I thought you'd want to know sooner."

"Ben, I've been surprised about Boseman's teaching evaluations, but I'm convinced he won't improve. Previous correspondence, which the committee saw, warned him about the need to change, but he hasn't. If anything his student scores have deteriorated further over time. I don't know if he can't do better or he doesn't give a damn. My hunch is the latter, because he's a bright guy who's organized and articulate. As best I can fathom, he thinks teaching, particularly undergraduates, is below his station."

Rankin shrugged. "I can't be helpful in explaining his record. I wanted to bring Boseman into the committee and talk with him about the teaching function of the department, but the others didn't agree." He shifted, seeming uncomfortable. "They were probably right. It wouldn't have changed anything."

"Ben, thanks for sharing this," Jason said. I'd like you to keep confidential what I'm going to say next, but I intend to recommend against Boseman. Maybe I'll talk to Boseman before I do anything officially, but in all good faith, I can't support a person who'll be a long-term liability in our most important responsibility as a faculty."

Rankin's mouth gaped open in surprise. "I can't ever remember Henry going against the department committee."

"I haven't been close enough to the process to know, but I'm convinced he would have this time based on the note he left and his letters to Boseman during the past five years." Jason wondered if the committee vote might have been different if Henry were still the department head, but he dismissed the idea as unlikely and just another shred of his inexperience, a colt unsure of new legs.

Rankin rubbed his face as though trying to eradicate a bad memory. "Jason, maybe I shouldn't tell you this, but after I told the committee about your concern, a couple of them became upset that you had tried to influence our vote. I tried to convince them you'd only shared an opinion, but Hugh Riley was livid. I think his outburst clouded the

164

outcome on Boseman. He spent five minutes tongue lashing you for having the gall to interfere and then jumped on me because I'd given you an opening." Rankin shook his head. "It was embarrassing to everyone, but I think he swayed them because they realized he'd give them hell if they went against Boseman. Afterward, I was sorry I'd told them about our conversation. Between you and me, a little more and I would have cracked Riley across the head."

Jason smiled at his friends unease. "But you voted no anyway?"

Shaking his head, Rankin mumbled. "Yes. After our discussion, I remembered my sections of General Biology being overwhelmed with kids transferring away from Boseman. I even went back through several of my class rolls to confirm the numbers adding to my classes after the first couple of days. "

Rankin continued to look at Jason, then asked, "What's with Riley anyway? You must have really teed him off sometime." He raked a hand through his russet hair.

Jason thought back to his early days in the department and his encounters with Riley and his cohorts who had decided Jason should not survive in biology because of his interest in gene therapy and because Henry Rogers had supported Jason's efforts to move the department into a new research area. "We've had several differences of opinions," Jason nodded, "and I challenged him directly a couple of times for snooping around my lab and trying to drive graduate students away. As a result of my complaining, Henry chewed Riley out for his unprofessional behavior with students, cementing the animosity between the two of us. Riley has never forgotten."

"You're right. It made a lasting impression on him." Rankin stood and added, "But I'm afraid the committee made an error with Boseman."

Rankin walked out of the office, hands thrust into his pockets, his head down. Now Jason was placed in the position of either letting Boseman go forward without comment and hope the committee at the college level would correct the error or making a statement openly opposing Boseman. He feared the consequences of not being forthright and not forcing the college committee and the Dean to examine Boseman's credential file with an open mind. In the absence of some dissent at the department level, the college committee might rubber stamp the recommendation. Boseman might well get a free ride and Biology could be stuck with him for years.

He made a note on the yellow pad to visit Dean Hawthorne about his dilemma.

Jason had the notes on the NIH Center proposal from Pamela spread across the desk when Audrey buzzed the intercom. "Dr. King and Dr. Helweg would like to see you, if it's okay."

"Sure, send them in." He piled the papers on one corner of the desk and walked toward the conference table. It was rare to see King in a suit, no doubt for this meeting. Helweg's lab coat concealed most of a blue dress, but the matching medium heels and nylons tipped him off that she was attired in her usual upscale manner.

As they pulled out chairs, King said, "Jason, we've completed the experiments and wanted to let you know the results were the same as those published in the paper." He looked at Helweg, who nodded in confirmation, her eyes glued on Jason's face causing him to remember his comment to Lucy about flirting and challenging. But she could be trying to gauge his reaction.

Jason returned Kathryn's look for a moment, then asked, "So you're pleased and relieved?"

King grinned, "I always believed our first set of data was correct, and now this should silence the skeptics."

Helweg added, "We plan to E-mail the journal editor and then send a short paper for publication. It will serve as a confirmation of the first work."

"This should get us off the hook with Brumfield, but it won't change the stance of those guys who made such an issue of the paper in the first place." King continued, "I never thought they believed the paper was wrong, but they were upset when their theory was challenged."

Jason asked, "So you're guessing they didn't try to replicate your experiment as they told Brumfield they had?"

"That's my guess," King nodded, "but, of course, I can't prove it."

He'd asked previously but thought it would be well to erase any doubts. "Preston, have you been in heavy competition with other labs to be first to demonstrate this viral impact on cell replication?"

King shook his head. "Not to my knowledge. I don't even know who made such a fuss about the paper. If you recall, neither Brumfield nor the media would reveal the names." King's comment reminded Jason he'd never received the communication from Brumfield revealing the complainers. Another promise not kept by the editor who had begun to look like part of the conspiracy against King..

Seeing Audrey standing outside the door and pointing to her watch through the glass panel, Jason said, "Well, you've brought good news. Let's see how the reactions are when the journal publishes your confirmation." He stood, becoming more adept and comfortable in signaling the end of meetings to maintain his schedule after observing the President and the Dean.

As they cleared the door, Audrey said, "I didn't know about interrupting, but you have a meeting in ten minutes with the group about the NIH proposal. It's over in the Medical School second-floor conference room."

As he stuffed Pamela's notes into a small briefcase, he said, "Thanks for keeping me on schedule and I'd appreciate your setting up a time to visit the Dean. It's about a tenure decision."

The group assembled around a rectangular mahogany table in the plush conference room in the Medical Administration building. A matching credenza had a stack of Medical journals on top. Portraits of former leaders of the School adorned the two side walls.

At Jason's request, each of the ten introduced themselves. Jason told them about the call from Nancy Thompson and concluded, "I think we have a good shot at this, and I appreciate Pamela Sturgis's efforts in preparing an outline from which we can build."

John Hadley, a senior faculty in Medicine, said, "This will be an exciting venture and one much needed by the medical profession. but

I'm not so sure you should include my name. I'm planning to retire in two years. I am quite willing to contribute to your thinking, but please don't count on me for the long term."

Pamela glanced at Jason as though waiting for his response, then said, "We'd like to include you. Your experience with medical practitioners is an element vital to our efforts."

Hadley nodded, his gray hair a token of a long career. "I'll be glad to be part of the team and contribute what I can, but understand my commitment is rather short term. And I will try to enlist a younger colleague for the team before I call it quits."

Assuming the lead again, Jason said, "I'd recommend we flesh out Pamela's outline by each of us taking sections of the proposal to work up first drafts, then a couple of us can pull it together in some coherent format. Then everyone can review that version, make additional suggestions or changes, and move to a final document about a week ahead of the deadline. I will include a budget in the draft and ask that you make any adjustments you deem important."

When no one raised questions or recommended a different approach, perhaps because they were relatively unknown to each other, Jason said, "You've reviewed the initial draft and seen the directive from NIH. With that background to guide us, let's spend some time brainstorming ideas about the actual activities we'd undertake to bring practicing physicians up to date in genetic manipulation and counseling of patients with those diseases and related problems. Let's think about what would be useful to them and our methods for delivery of information."

For the next two hours, Jason became immersed in the sharing of ideas with these creative colleagues. Everyone engaged in the discussion and freely injected ides and disagreed with each other to seek a better approach. He left the meeting at five-thirty feeling energized, knowing they'd agreed on a solid plan and put in motion the things they'd need to do during the next three or four weeks. Interim get-togethers had been agreed on by sub-groups as they realized their efforts would mesh better by cooperating across their disciplines. The session reminded him this was the type of activity he most enjoyed, the give and take between scientists seeking the best approach to a common goal with their personal views less important than the overall plan.

Hawthorne pushed open the door to the Dean's suite at seven forty-five the next morning. "Running late this morning. Got caught behind an accident on the edge of campus." He held the door for Jason as they entered a dark room. The odor of furniture polish revealed a recent visit by the early morning cleaning crew.

As he dropped his black leather briefcase and hung a tan raincoat in the closet, Hawthorne said, "Things going okay I assume. I haven't heard from you," he chuckled, " or gotten wind of any revolution in Biology."

"I may be igniting one though." Jason said, taking one of the soft chairs. "That's why I wanted to see you."

Now sitting across from Jason, Hawthorne said, "Bridget said it was about a tenure case."

Jason explained about Boseman and his review initiated by Henry's note, then talked about his rationale for not supporting Boseman for tenure. "Our department committee has recommended favorably, but I intend to go against them."

Hawthorne crossed his legs, and said, "It's fairly uncommon for a head to differ with the committee, but it's been done." His eyes were bright as he watched Jason, understanding the dilemma he must feel.

Jason leaned forward in the chair. "I thought I should alert you and if you have negative reactions, I'd appreciate any advice."

"Tell me more about Boseman's teaching record."

Jason reiterated the details of the evaluation scores, the flight of undergraduates from Boseman's courses, and the assessments by colleagues. "He's been warned several times to improve, but to my knowledge he's never bothered. His scores have never improved nor have his evaluations by faculty colleagues."

"Have you talked to him about the problem?"

"Not in an evaluative sense, but Henry had on several occasions. Every salary letter since his very first year pointed out the need to improve his teaching."

Hawthorne glanced at his watch. "Jason, I'm impressed you're willing to deny tenure in this situation. And, I agree with your rationale. It's a responsible position in the best interests of the department, although faculty may not see it that way at the present time."

Jason grinned at his superior. "Now you understand why there may be a revolt in Biology."

"If there is," Hawthorne stood, "I'll back your decision. I expect the college committee will go along with your recommendation, but there will be a debate about a head and department committee disagreeing. Whatever happens, I'll forward a negative recommendation. Then we'll have to defend our actions to the Vice-President and maybe the University committee."

"Should I tell Boseman about my stance?"

"You aren't obliged to, but it would be proper. He should know how the department head stands before he's reviewed at the college level. In fact, he has the opportunity to prepare a rebuttal to any negative recommendation for consideration at the next level."

At the door, Hawthorne said, "By the way, I liked the budget request from Biology. We'll try to fund your new initiative to upgrade that teaching lab. Maybe not fully the first year, but give you enough to get it off the ground."

"That's good news." Jason walked past Bridget's desk feeling rewarded. His work in putting the package together had paid off for the department. This administrative job wasn't all about finding solutions to impossible problems. You could actually do some creative things.

But now he had to confront Boseman.

CHAPTER 17

Terry Boseman's round face broke into a broad smile as he entered Jason's office, no doubt having been told by Riley that he'd been recommended for tenure by the department committee. Now he was eager to hear the good news from the department head. Boseman, a short, chubby man in his early thirties, usually dressed in sport jacket and tie, but today he'd put on a gray suit and maroon tie in celebration of hearing he was home free, a life contract to do what he wanted to do. His thick brown hair had been combed neatly and parted in the middle.

Jason shook his hand and waited for him to get comfortable in a chair. "Terry, the department committee has recommended you for tenure and promotion to Associate Professor. You'll get a letter from the committee in a couple of days."

"I'd heard through the vine, but I'm glad it's official now." His smile seemed to widen, creasing his features and revealing his teeth that obviously were not in the best of shape.

After worrying about his approach with his own decision, Jason had decided to be blunt and not hedge his words. He said, "Terry, I've spent a lot of time reviewing your file and fretting about your performance in the department, particularly the teaching function. I've decided not to support your case at the College level. I'm recommending against you for tenure and promotion."

He paused, watching the smile disappear and consternation build on Boseman's face as the message sank in, then he continued, "You have a fine research record, but your teaching performance has been consistently unacceptable. It could be described as dismal. I've concluded that the department shouldn't award tenure, or what comes down to a lifetime contract, to someone who does not deal effectively with students."

Boseman's pudgy face beaded with sweat. He shifted in the chair and mumbled, "I don't know what this means." He brushed his face with a hand as though to erase his confusion.

"It means your case will go before the College committee with a split recommendation. That group will then make a recommendation and their decision and that of the Dean will be forwarded for consideration by a university panel and the Vice-President. If both the College committee and the Dean decide against you, your credentials will not be considered further. If there's a split decision or if both support you, the University committee will review the case." He paused and added, "In case you don't know, you have the right to include a letter of rebuttal to any negative recommendation, so you should think about that."

Reclaiming some confidence, Boseman sat up straighter, his hands clenched on the table top, and his face broke into a sneer like countenance. He barked, "Why in hell are you're doing this? I thought the head always went along with the faculty committee."

"Since I've been in this office, I've discovered that's not always true. In fact, the Dean suggested it happens more often than most of us realize for a department head to differ with the committee." Jason watched Boseman's deepening frown and continued, "I discovered Henry Rogers had serious concerns about your situation the day I started this job, but I didn't get the opportunity to discuss it with him. Your file contains several letters from Henry and faculty reviewers about your teaching. Without exception, those letters communicated the need for you to improve your work in the classroom. In fact, Henry's letter last spring included a statement that he would have difficulty supporting your tenure because of the teaching problem."

When Boseman remained silent, staring into Jason's face, balling his hands into fists, Jason said, "What I've not been able to understand is why you haven't paid attention to those warnings. You must have known you were borderline at the three-year review because Henry's letter told you to get help with the teaching issue and improve. Why didn't you do something then?" Jason felt like he was admonishing a rebellious sophomore for failing to turn in his lab reports.

"I can do better, but I couldn't give it the time. I had to have publications to get tenure, so I've put most of my time into the research side."

"That's paid off for you. You've an excellent set of papers, but you have to do both. We can't ignore teaching, the real reason the university hires us." Jason remembered his own early struggles with the dual responsibilities and his frustration at the time and work preparing lectures and instructional materials had taken. It had been more difficult than he'd imagined, but he discovered there was satisfaction in seeing students learn the subject matter and become confident in their use of the concepts. For some reason he recalled the surprise when the feeling of accomplishment had first emerged during a late night help session with a few students struggling to understand a concept related to cell division. Seeing the glimmer of comprehension brightening their eyes and the first hint of smiles had been sufficient reward for his extra efforts.

Boseman asked, "Won't the College committee give more weight to the faculty vote than to your single opinion?" His tone suggested his confidence they would, his tone and posture now challenging.

"I admit I don't know how they'll view my recommendation, but if I understand the Faculty Handbook, they're supposed to give equal consideration to my opinion and the faculty judgment."

Boseman snorted, "So the head has a lot of say in this deal, even if you're only temporary." Disbelief showed clearly in his features, his mouth agape.

Ignoring the act, Jason nodded. "I'm learning department heads and deans have some influence. It's not just a paper shuffling exercise in the administrative offices. Terry, I don't wish to make it sound like I have the final say in tenure cases, but I believe department heads, temporary or not, have to think about the long range implications of such considerations.   Tenure is the most important decision a department makes because in the long term, those individual cases determine what an academic unit will become." He paused, returning Boseman's glare. "We can't afford to have a collection of faculty who don't care about students. Soon we'd be out of business.""

Boseman said, a hint of whining in his voice, "Suppose I promise to do better in the future?"

"Unfortunately it wouldn't mean much. Once tenure is granted, you could continue to do as you've always done and there wouldn't be much anyone could do about it. Decisions have to be made on the record, not on promises. That's why you have the probationary period—to demonstrate your capabilities, as well as your promise for the future."

"What happens if I get turned down?"

"Your employment continues for another year, then you're terminated."

"So I'd have a year to find another job."

"That's correct."

Boseman stood, pulled his coat together. "I still think it'll go okay. My guess is you're the only one with this hang-up about teaching. Everybody knows the students don't give a rip, just so they get a passing grade." Jason realized this statement made in the heat of frustration revealed Boseman's basic attitude toward teaching and students. He wanted to challenge him, but knew it would be a wasted effort.

Jason moved toward the door with Boseman, the last statement still irritating him. "I think your conclusion may be the crux of the problem and I disagree. Faculty should be as concerned as I, if they care about the department, but we'll see what happens."

At the door, Boseman turned back, faced Jason, almost confrontational in his stance, his arms across his chest. "I'll tell you this. If I get turned down, it'll be your fault and I'll hold you personally responsible."

He watched Boseman stride through the outer office, his erect shoulders exhibiting confidence. Jason turned to gaze out the windows, thinking the meeting with Boseman had gone better than he'd anticipated. He'd expected a furious reaction and argument, but then Boseman didn't believe Jason's recommendation carried any impact. Perhaps he was correct. But what was Boseman saying about personal responsibility? Was this a serious threat or just frustration showing and trying to have the last word?

Jason marked through the reminder about Boseman, then added one to work on his letter to the Dean about Boseman. The notion that it'd be easier to go along with the department committee struck him for a moment, but he knew he couldn't accept caving in when he knew he was right.

Boseman left Jason's office in a controlled rage. He'd never been denied anything before in his career. Now this substitute department head intended to disrupt his work and send him searching for a position at some backwater place. He took the elevator to his fourth-floor office, paced around the small space for a few minutes, then tried to work on a journal paper based on a student's thesis project. But he couldn't concentrate, his mind warped by the possibility he'd be out of his slot at State, all because of this idiot in the administrative office.

After an hour he gave up, locked his door and left a note that he was in the library. He drove to the edge of the city and went into the

178

office of the Spencerville Gun Club. The man at the desk asked, "Can I help you?"

Boseman responded, "I'd like to locate a place I can practice shooting. I've been invited for a hunting trip over the Thanksgiving break, but I haven't shot my rifle in years and need to bone up some."

Shoving a printed form toward Boseman, the clerk said, "You wish to join or just reserve a few times to come by. We have a range about ten miles west of here. Fill in your wishes and return it."

Boseman sat at a table in one corner of the office and marked his desire to use the practice facility for five hours in the next couple of weeks, returned it to the desk, paid the fees by credit card. The clerk handed him a pass for the designated times and said, "Just show up and someone will give you directions and instruction if you desire. If you need ammunition or maintenance of your rifle, someone will provide those services."

Boseman left the club, headed to his apartment. Now he had to dig out the rifle given to him by his paternal grandfather on his eighteenth birthday. Much to his frustration, his parents had insisted he spend summers on the Nevada ranch with his grandparents. Then his grandfather had demanded he learn to shoot several different weapons, including this rifle. To Boseman's amazement, he'd become reasonably proficient shooting targets and then progressed to small animals roaming around the ranch and creating havoc with the livestock. But since graduating from high school and entering college, he'd not bothered with the sport.

Now the skill had to be revived and honed in case he needed it. The primary question remaining in his mind was whether to wait for the college committee to render its verdict or proceed with his plan. And he had to figure out where and when he might accomplish his mission.

Throughout his time at State, Jason had used an hour each morning before work to jog, an exercise he'd discovered while in graduate school and had maintained after taking the faculty position at State. If he missed, it was like part of his life and been chopped off. His usual three mile course took him through the park and along the streets to and from their home. For a time Lucy joined him, but since the children, she'd found an aerobics session three days a week during the noon hour. Now she got up when Jason did, made coffee, and had free time for herself before he returned and they woke the kids.

The morning after the meeting with Boseman, Jason entered the park at six, his usual time. He loped along, at intervals thinking about the session with Boseman and his agenda for the day ahead, then his mind went blank for times, enjoying the crisp air and the colors of leaves, still clinging on limbs of maples and oaks. He became aware of a figure approaching from a side trail, but ignored the person since it was common to cross paths with other joggers. Most nodded or waved and kept to their own route.

As they merged, a soft voice said, "Morning, Dr. Spradlin."

Jason slowed to match the other's stride, then looked to see Kathryn Helweg smiling at him. Dressed in a gray sweatshirt with Minnesota printed across the front, purple shorts, white socks and Nike shoes, Kathryn matched his pace, her hair fluttering slightly in the breeze.

"Hi," Jason muttered in his surprise. "I didn't know you were a runner."

Kathryn said, "I've jogged for years, but I've had a problem finding a good route since I came here. Two days ago I found this park, then yesterday I saw you and decided I'd try to connect. I hope it's okay."

"Sure," Jason reacted, thinking he'd had no choice, but maybe the company would be good, keep his mind off work problems for a few more minutes.

Jason increased his pace, not wanting to cut back on his intensity. Kathryn kept even without obvious strain. He asked, "How far do you usually go?"

Turning her head slightly to glance at him, she said, "Three to four miles. I always feel better afterwards." Jason nodded, smilingly accepting the almost universal explanation given by runners when questioned about their phobia.

"I know, plus it seems to reduce the stress of work."

They ran for several minutes, then Jason asked, "Where are you living?"

"In an apartment on Twelfth Street near University Avenue. It's close to the campus, but not right in the middle of all the undergraduates. I'm able to walk to work except when I stay late at night."

"I know approximately where it is. You're not far from the park entrance. We live on Madison, about a quarter of a mile from the park, so I start from home."

They continued for twenty minutes without conversation, then nearing the entrance to the park, Jason said, "I usually walk back to the house from here."

She slowed as he did. "Then I'll see you at work. I enjoyed running with you. I'm apprehensive about being in here alone. You hear so may tales about muggers."

At the street corner, Kathryn said, "If you don't mind, I'd like to do this regularly. I'd feel more comfortable than being alone."

Taken aback and remembering his initial reaction to her in the office, Jason hesitated before saying, "Sure. I go every morning and am usually here by six or shortly afterwards." Usually awake before the alarm buzzed at five forty-five, he pulled on his sweats, splashed cold water on his face, did a couple of stretching exercises, and left through the back door.

"Then I'll be here tomorrow morning. And I'll see you at work." She smiled, then turned away, walking rapidly. If Jason remembered correctly, her apartment would be a couple of blocks east of here.

Walking quickly along the street, Jason wondered if Kathryn's reason for seeking out his regular route was really one of security. He felt strange about the aura of Kathryn, but what could happen at six in the morning, both sweaty and exhausted. And her explanation of safety made sense. A month ago a female student had been grabbed and assaulted while jogging near the campus.

182

Hugh Riley and his group of buddies met at Randolph's for their usual weekly pow-wow. Smiling at Boseman, Riley kicked off the conversation. "I heard you had your meeting with the department head."

Boseman scowled, remembering the no nonsense declaration by Spradlin, and his breaking into a cold sweat. He blurted out the news. "Spradlin won't support me for tenure." His face darkened more and he tugged at the cuff of his blue blazer.

"What a bastard," Riley exploded. "He can't get away with that kind of shit."

Townsend knocked his pipe on the table. "According to the guidelines, he's required to make a separate recommendation."

"Sure, but heads always go along with the faculty committee." Riley settled back in his chair, assuming the posture of an experienced and wise counselor.

Harris chimed in. "But they don't have to. Why make them send forward a recommendation if they always agree." He sipped his draft beer and wiped his mouth with the paper napkin.

Boseman shrugged his shoulders, a suggestion of resignation. "I can submit a rebuttal letter and see what happens at the college level. Maybe I'll start looking for a new job." His paused, his face clouding, his eyes becoming slits. "What I really feel like doing is catching Spradlin alone somewhere and breaking his goddam skull." He snapped in half the pencil he'd taken from his shirt pocket.

Surprised at the unexpected burst of anger from his overweight and out of condition colleague, Riley examined Boseman's face for several seconds, waiting for the rage to abate, then said, "Be careful. Spradlin's a tough character, always exercising to stay in shape."

Harris agreed. "I wouldn't mess with Spradlin. You'll get hurt pretty bad."

Boseman persisted in his anger. "There are other ways."

Riley confided, "Terry, it'll probably go okay. I'll talk to a couple of guys on the college committee. They'll ignore the recommendation of a guy who's in the job because of a fluke and won't be there much longer."

Boseman let a slight smile break through, relief showing in his eyes. "I'll appreciate that." Then his features darkened again as he muttered, almost to himself. "But somehow I'm going to make Spradlin sorry for this crap."

The others looked at Boseman in a different light. They'd never seen him angry. Now his zest for revenge seemed to dominate his thoughts.

Townsend said, "I wouldn't voice that around too much. Threatening department heads is not a healthy action if you wish to remain on the faculty."

CHAPTER 18

At eight-fifteen, Audrey buzzed to tell him Cynthia Pease from Redlake was on line two. Punching the flashing button on the console, Jason said, "How are you and how was Scotland?" He fished a pencil out of the drawer in case he needed to make notes.

"We learned a lot in a brief time. I intended to call earlier but we've been really busy since coming back."

She continued, "As you tried to tell us, the issue is not as straightforward as we'd first believed. There are substantial problems in the cloning procedure, but the investigators there were supportive of our general concept. They kept saying someone will do it soon for the very purpose we're eager to try. If we can become proficient with the biology, the other phases should be easy and the payoffs could be tremendous."

"But it's a big gamble?"

"Of course," Cynthia maintained her enthusiasm, "especially for Redlake. We can't afford a huge experimental cost, but need a project that will reap dividends more quickly than some of our larger, more stable, competitors. We've fretted and worried about this thing since we got back. We'd like to be first, but we can't have a failure. It could be the end of Redlake."

Responding to the deep ambivalence he detected, Jason asked, "So you haven't decided yet?"

She laughed lightly, "You're right. We'd like you to meet with us and review our thinking that has been modified since we last met." She added, "Obviously, as soon as possible."

"Has anyone run this idea by Food and Drug?" Jason knew if FDA took a firm position against the concept, Redlake would either be forced to abandon the idea or be prepared for prolonged and expensive battles with the Federal bureaucracy, a fight they could well lose, costing them thousands of dollars in attorney fees for no gain.

"Brenda is meeting with a Deputy Commissioner in Washington today, so we'd know at least in a tentative sense, how the agency would view a new food product produced by this non-traditional approach."

Jason reminded her of their earlier discussion. "You mean a traditional food source concocted by a modern technique." And he hoped the FDA representative would be candid with Fallon and not lead her on, then have the agency take a different position when the decision had to be made. Plus, the agency was subject to the whims of both the federal administration and the Congress. One representative acting on behalf of some group, even a Redlake competitor, could create havoc and slow the process for months or cause the FDA to back away from their original stance.

"Let's hope it's viewed as modern, rather than bizarre and unacceptable."

Jason said, "I'll arrange my schedule to come in the next three or four days. I'll let you know specifics by this afternoon."

"We could do it over a weekend if that would suit you better."

"Maybe. Talk to you soon." He wanted to help Redlake but the more he considered their goal, the more he believed they needed a different approach than the one they had been working on. To get ready he'd have to review several publications before the meeting, but this was more exciting than arguing with Boseman about tenure. He grabbed his calendar and headed for Audrey's desk.

At nine-fifteen, Audrey buzzed the intercom. "Kathryn Helweg would like a minute of your time."

"Okay, but don't let me run past time to go to the meeting with my graduate students." He stood and walked toward the door, watching as Kathryn moved quickly to shake his hand. Jason was aware of her bright eyes on his face, dark blouse and white skirt, nylons and dark pumps.

She eased into the chair next to his at the conference table. "Dr. King wanted me to tell you we've sent the paper to the journal and that he talked with the editor late yesterday. Dr. Brumfield promised to publish it as a short communication as soon as possible, probably in the December issue."

"Let's hope that clarifies the issue," Jason said, "so everyone can get on with their normal routine."

"One of us will let you know when the paper comes out." She stood, turned toward the door, then retraced a couple of steps to stand near Jason. "I enjoyed being with you this morning." Her eyes were penetrating.

Jason followed her retreat, his eyes drawn to her legs and hips, wondering what game she was playing, confused and concerned about the effect she had on him Maybe he was being seduced and unwilling to admit it. It would be difficult to resist her under the right circumstances and he thought about his weakness in the past. Before his marriage to Lucy, he'd been involved with a graduate student until Henry warned him about the perils of the relationship, although it was clearly a consensual arrangement. The older woman had let him know he was attractive to women, his unruly hair, square jaw, and trim physique, coupled with his supportive personality, invited their attention. At the time he thought she was putting him on, but others had let him know they might be interested in more than a professional relationship. He'd never strayed, nor even been enticed, since his marriage to Lucy. But no one had affected him like Kathryn. Perhaps she was being friendly and he had to learn to deal with all the different personalities in the department. His contacts were no longer limited to those few in his research group.

Pamela Sturgis and George Stuart appeared for their appointment at three. Audrey had alerted Jason they wanted to visit on behalf of the search committee, reminding Jason he was still sitting on the announcement and the letter informing him of his nomination.

As they sat at the table, George started, "Jason, you know why we're here. You've not turned in your application and we want you to do so. The deadline is a week away."

188

Pamela chimed in as though they'd rehearsed their approach. "Some of us are concerned you've decided against it and want you to know most of the committee hopes you'll become a candidate." She paused, her eyes on his face. "Personally, I'll be terribly disappointed if you don't."

"I've thought about it quite a lot," Jason responded to his trusted colleagues, "but I've just not gotten around to putting the stuff together." He didn't tell them he continued to have reservations.

As though reading Jason's mind, George said, "I understand quite well why you wouldn't want this job. It's a pain in the ass most of the time. But the other side of it and what we want you to think about is the department needs someone like you—a leader who's looking at the future and not afraid to make the tough decisions we're going to require. Hell, Jason, you know faculty strut around about having a democratic organization and the influence they can exert, but most of the time when the crunch comes, they'll always take the easy way out. This Boseman tenure thing is a good example."

"I'm surprised anyone knows how I stand on Boseman." Jason had been careful not to tell anyone, although Audrey knew he'd met with Boseman and he'd talked to George earlier about his concerns. He'd voiced his opinion to Rankin, but the committee discussions were supposed to be confidential.

George shifted in the chair and grinned. "Jason, Boseman told Riley about your meeting with him. After that, you might as well publish it in the newspapers. In fact, I heard Riley letting off steam with a couple of others in the hall."

Jason let his thoughts about Riley pass, but said, "I'll talk to Lucy again, then let you know what I'm going to do."

They stood and Jason thanked them for coming in. Pamela said, "You know you'll have solid support among the faculty."

"I'm not so sure of that," Jason laughed, "after Boseman and Riley and a couple of others I've already offended start their negative campaign."

George turned at the door. "If you please everybody, you won't be doing the department much good." Jason remembered Henry saying the same thing during one of their discussions, but he'd not taken it seriously at the time. Now, he understood. But Henry had the security of a real appointment, not an interim fill-in where the future rested on the quirks of a lot of people.

Jason called John Hadley and after the usual greetings and exchanges of progress on the research, said, "I'm surprised you're retiring and wanted to talk about the future of the Wilson's disease work."

"I should have warned you before that meeting, but the discussion about the Center proposal caused me to tell that group. I didn't want to lead anyone to think I'd be around for the duration of the project if we're lucky enough to get funded."

"John, the fact is I'm trying to get my own agenda in line with reality if I apply for this heads job and am selected. As far as our project is concerned, I hope your successor will be interested in the Wilson work."

Hadley replied, "The School will look for someone with an interest in genetic diseases, but beyond that, I have no idea who'll be chosen. But we have another year to go on our present grant and I'll be here most of that time."

"I've thought about it some since you dropped the news. I'll have to decide in about six months whether to request continued support or let the line drop." He added, "I'm thinking seriously about applying for the department head position, and if I should be chosen, I'll have to cut back on my research. Maybe giving up the Wilson's project would be the best thing, especially since you won't be around."

Hadley remained silent for several seconds, then said, "Jason, I don't know what to advise. Maybe see how the search comes out, then decide what projects to keep."

"Maybe we've done all we can do with the Wilson thing. Let others pick it up." When they had started with the research, they'd believed the defect affecting copper metabolism was the result of a single genetic flaw, but as their investigation progressed along with other labs around the world, they discovered the potential of at least five different genes being affected. Trying to correct all of those in afflicted children was almost impossible. But recent developments with the transfer of stem cells had given new hope and additional progress had been made. The scientific community interested in the disease believed they were very close to a solution. Part of Jason's reasoning about dropping the research was a belief they wouldn't be able to unravel the problem much further and it now had become a matter of identifying impacted youngsters and doing routine treatment in major clinics around the world.

A note of sadness in his voice, Hadley said, "Jason, this research has been the best thing I've done and is the single thing keeping me here now. But I've promised my wife to retire and focus on our family agenda for the next few years." He delayed, then added, "I can't go back on my promise."

He didn't want to push his friend further. "You're right about timing. Let's talk again after the outcome of the search. It could be I'll still have the freedom to submit a follow-up proposal."

Hadley laughed. "If you apply, you should assume you're going to become the head. The department will make a big mistake if they pass you by. But however it goes, we can delay any decision until you know."

Jason came to stand near Lucy as she put the last dishes in the washer. "Well, they're both asleep, but I hope soon they'll discover some new stories. I've read this Dr. Suess one at least fifty times. I can recite most of it."

Lucy smiled. "So can they, so don't try skipping pages."

"I've been caught trying to do that, so I know better." He watched her close the door of the washer. "You have a few minutes to give me advice."

Examining at his face and seeing his uncertainty, she said, "Put that way, I will."

He took her hand and led her to the couch in the den, stacking the newspaper on the floor. "Two members of the search committee showed up today. They encouraged me to apply for the head's position, but I told them I had to get your blessing first."

"I'm sure they believed that." Lucy watched his face for a moment, then said, "My guess is you want to do it, as I've said before, and you know I'll go along with your wish. So let's forget blessing."

Ignoring her aside, Jason said, "The last couple of months have been intriguing and I can see how a department head might influence things, but the down side is I've had little time to give my research program. I'm dependent totally on the post-docs and graduate students to keep things running."

"If I recall correctly, Henry had gotten completely out of the research game."

"He had, except for one small project. See, Lucy, I'm not ready to do that yet. And that's what becoming head will lead to in time."

"So what are the other negatives?" She had a way of forcing him to face the real question.

"The continuous confrontation with certain faculty who won't agree with the direction I'd like the department to go. Little things become major issues in their minds. Constant dilemmas that defy solutions."

"Because you have some vision is why most of the faculty want you to take on this task. Faculty complain about everything, but the thing they can't tolerate is having a head who doesn't care about the unit, and them individually and personally. Having two or three who always have other ideas or who resist every new idea keeps the rest honest and thinking."

Jason twisted to look at her face. "I've never heard anyone describe the soreheads as having any useful purpose."

She smiled. "I've tried to figure out why they exist, since they seem never to do anything except bitch. That's the only reason I can find for their existence—to keep everybody else on their toes."

After several seconds of silence, Jason asked, "So you're okay with my applying?"

"Of course, but I don't want you overly frustrated if you aren't chosen. You have to accept that might happen before you apply and get your heart set on the job. Honestly, Jason, my only concern is you'll lose out and be forever disillusioned, even bitter."

"I don't think I'd take it that way."

"Just be prepared to live with the outcome, whatever it is. You can't control the process as a candidate."

The following morning Jason brought his credential file up to date, adding a couple of recent publications, listed several potential references, including John Hadley, Brenda Fallon, Nancy Thompson and Fred Adams. He pulled the position announcement from the folder and wrote a letter of application, responding to the criteria listed by the committee. Then he asked Audrey to proof the entire package.

An hour later she returned. "I didn't find any errors. Shall I put it in Dr. Stuart's box?"

"Please do."

194

Audrey remained standing by the desk until Jason looked at her, then she said, "I'm glad you've decided to do this. It's been easy to adjust to your style. You and Dr. Rogers are a lot alike."

"Thanks, Audrey. You're always helpful and efficient, but let's see how the committee works through all the applications."

"Whatever happens, good luck, but I'd be surprised if they don't select you." She touched his shoulder and eased away, the packet clasped against her chest.

Jason turned to the telephone to call those he'd listed as references.

CHAPTER 19

As soon as Jason emerged from the walkway from his plane at O'Hare, he saw the Redlake trio, Brenda, Cynthia and Eric, sitting near the window of the terminal and staring at the gate. They waved and came toward him. Brenda said, "We're pleased you could come. We reserved a conference space across the street in the Hilton to save time. No reason to spend an hour fighting traffic to our offices."

A five minute walk through the crowded terminal, through an underground tunnel, and up an elevator to the tenth floor brought them to a small conference room. A round table, six chairs, a credenza with a steaming coffee pot with mugs and pastries arrayed on it's surface, suggested an aura of haste. They filled their mugs, grabbed a small pastry, a paper plate and napkin, and quickly found seats.

Not wasting time, Brenda said, "I believe Cynthia brought you up to date regarding the Scotland trip and told you I was meeting with FDA people." Almost without pause, she continued, "The Deputy Commissioner and three of his staff were intrigued by our idea and after two hours of discussion about the potential product and the political realities prevalent at this time, they came down on the side they'd not pose serious objections as an agency, but would demand the usual reviews and testing for safety. On the question of safety, they were vague, since the product we'd present would be a typical meat, maybe somewhat different in composition, but the market is confronted with those variances on a daily basis, as then is the consumer."

Trying to keep pace with the information coming at him, Jason commented, "So it's hard to know what they'd ask for?"

"To some extent. For certain they'll want composition data. Maybe information about the reproductive process. I can't predict what else." She threw up her hands in mock uncertainty. "I'm not worried about composition. Nothing should be different from an ordinary pork product."

Thinking the agency would dream up a set of questions or demands no one could even think about now, Jason smiled. "What are their worst fears? Where might there be opposition?"

"As you could guess, they worry about reactions from the ultra conservatives who will probably object on the basis of religion. One of the staff guys said they've already received letters from some groups—he wouldn't say which—threatening resistance, boycotts of stores, etc, to any food coming from unnatural methods. And we have to assume they would define cloning as an unnatural approach."

Realizing he was posing questions they'd thought about previously, but he wanted to be sure they covered all the likely groups who'd complain, he asked, "What about the traditional agricultural groups? They have a lot of influence in Congress."

"We discussed the possibility, but the consensus seemed to be if we involved growers as part of the enterprise, resistance would be minimal. But Deputy Mendez suggested we talk to the American Meat Institute and an organization of pork producers, the name escapes me at the moment. And we should touch base with the people at the U. S. Department of Agriculture. Mendez thought they might be intrigued enough to support our efforts rather than resist."

"Sounds like you came away encouraged."

Brenda shrugged, went to the coffee urn to refill her mug. "You know the bureaucrats. They don't commit themselves or put anything on record, but I had the distinct impression they wanted us to move forward. They said several times that it would happen soon, but we were the first to approach them."

Cynthia said, "We suspect others may be working on the identical concept, but haven't tipped their hands to FDA. Maybe they won't until they're prepared to market."

"You've done the better thing," Jason said. "Any agency dislikes being surprised, although they're obliged to review anyone's proposal. But if you don't play their game, they'll find a hundred ways to delay your application."

Brenda took the lead again, "We think the climate is okay for us, barring unforeseen resistance from some Congressional or trade group. Our president is close to our Congressional representatives and they'll go to bat for us if need be. Now we need to focus on the science aspects."

When they all looked at him, Jason said, "I've thought some about the problems since Cynthia called. And I've read some background papers I think might be useful. I believe a good thing to explore is the potential for retrieving embryos in an early stage, culture those further in the laboratory and implant them into sows for the normal gestation period. One key is finding the best strain of swine already used in production and then begin running trials to perfect the methodology. Eventually you'll need a herd of surrogate sows to do implants, but the agricultural people already do this kind of stuff with all their embryo transplants to obtain multiple births or to produce some animal with special characteristics, such as when animals fail to conceive by normal mating, or to obtain a horse with potential for speed. One of my post-docs is reading everything he can find and is conferring with faculty in animal sciences."

Cynthia reminded him. "We're going to search for farmers who'd be willing to alter their production strategy and use our techniques rather than relying on traditional breeding methods. They know about feeding, disease and parasite control, and general care of animals, so it's not a jump at all for them. It's just a different starting place."

Brenda added, "If this works as we think, we're going to require a huge number of sows and a lot of manpower to do the actual implants. Maybe veterinarians or animal scientist types."

"As soon as you're certain" Jason said," realizing he was committing to the project, "we could get started on the preliminary lab work. We'll need to learn and perfect the methods for culturing embryonic cells and determine the best time to do implants or transfers. I may want to visit some of the researchers in this country who're into this stuff or perhaps visit with them at a national meeting. If for some reason my schedule won't allow this, the post-doc, Roy Blount, could do it. By then, he'll know more than I."

200

Brenda glanced at her colleagues, then said, "We're moving quickly, so I intend to run a plan by our executive group within the next week. Then, I think we can agree on a contract with you."

Eric, the almost silent member of the group, said, "I've collected all the literature about this procedure and have copies for you." He pulled a thick folder from the stack in front of him and pushed it toward Jason.

Cynthia, from the other side of the table, asked, "Eric and I would like to learn your lab techniques. Is it all right if we spend a few days working with your people once you have the procedures perfected?"

"We can work it out." Jason realized Redlake wanted to reduce their dependence on university scientists and likely move toward their own research and development group. If this venture proved successful, the organization would have the required financial base and technological expertise to achieve that goal. And with Cynthia and Eric they had the nucleus of a research team. Both had doctorates in the biological sciences, but little research experience beyond their dissertation projects. But that would come quickly and with some assistance from Jason's group, they could assume the essential leadership for future ventures.

Two weeks passed without a major disruption. Jason settled into a routine of quickly doing the administrative work, then giving his attention to research manuscripts and revising lectures. The weekly meetings with the research staff were going well, each of the projects in the lab progressing with a limited number of setbacks. Four of the group were preparing abstracts of papers to be submitted for possible presentation at the Experimental Biology meetings in the spring. The late November deadline for those submissions was approaching rapidly.

He spent several hours scanning the publications Eric had given him in Chicago and then shared those with Roy who was busy doing the preliminary laboratory work on cell culture. The more he understood about the process, the more optimistic he felt for the Redlake venture.

Perhaps the best thing that came out of this slack period was his becoming more comfortable in the dual role of faculty and administrator. Having time to focus on his research increased his awareness that it was possible to maintain some research activity and do the routine paper work that steadily and relentless crossed his desk.

Pamela Sturgis brought in the draft of the NIH Center proposal. "I think this has come together pretty well. Everyone gave me their parts on schedule and it seemed to have meshed okay. Now I'd like you to read through it and let's discuss any changes you think important. Then I think we're ready." She placed the thick packet on the corner of his desk.

"I'll look at it today or tonight and find you tomorrow and let you know my reaction, but I'm sure it's okay." He stood and touched his colleague's shoulder. "Thanks for doing this. I know it's been a lot of work."

"It took some time, but it was an interesting exercise. The faculty have several creative ideas and I think we have a good proposal. I'll be interested in your reactions."

"To change the subject," Pamela said, "I'm pleased you applied for this job. As you know, the search committee plans to begin screening applications next week. After that step George will send letters to every one to let them know the status of the search and their individual application."

Jason became comfortable with Kathryn's easy companionship as they jogged each morning in the park. Often they talked about work and university events as they loped, now in sweat suits as the winter weather had taken hold of the area. More often they ran for several minutes without conversation, each engrossed in their own thoughts. His worry about her having some motive related to a sexual relationship lessened, but he was always aware of her impact on his senses. He accepted his susceptibility to her, hoping he would not be tested or caught off-guard. He decided that behind her alluring features was a sensible and intelligent professional.

When she failed to appear two mornings he wondered if she was behind schedule, but abiding by their agreement, he didn't wait for her. On the second afternoon just at five, Kathryn came into his office, passing Audrey and the other clerical staff as they left for the day. Jason glanced up from stuffing papers in his briefcase when she knocked on the door. As usual, her appearance was striking. The navy skirt and lighter blue sweater complemented her figure and jarred his senses.

In spite of his ever present misgivings about her, he was glad to see her and smiled. "Come in. I haven't seen you for a couple of days."

"I hope you didn't wait around for me, but I felt ill the past few days and decided skipping running would help me recover." She stood near the desk watching him close the briefcase.

"You feeling better?"

"I think it was a slight cold or some twenty-four hour virus, but I felt awful. Whatever, I'm better today."

Jason motioned to the side chair and sat at his desk. Aware of her nearness, the scent of her perfume and her legs when she crossed her knees, he said, "So how's work going?"

"Okay, but we haven't heard about a firm publication date for the confirming paper despite the editor's promise to move quickly.. Dr. King thinks we'll hear something concrete by the end of next week. At any rate, we're moving on to the next phase of the project and it's interesting stuff. We're making good progress now that this threat is behind us."

"I'd think the editor will move it forward quickly, but he has constraints. Maybe he's giving those other investigators time to respond, then publish paper and their letters in one issue."

Kathryn shrugged, as though dismissing a boring subject. "Maybe your right, but I really came by to invite you to have a drink with the post-docs in the department tomorrow after work. We've organized a group and get together about twice a month for a bit of socializing,

204

primarily sharing our problems and the work we're doing. Thus far, it's been only for a couple of drinks, but we've talked about a dinner. Most don't know you and thought it'd be a good idea to meet you, so I volunteered to invite you."

"I'd like that," Jason said. "How many in the group?" Jason realized he didn't know the post-docs other than those from his own lab and Kathryn, although they were essential contributors to the research work of the department. They were easily lost in the shuffle between faculty and students with their interactions centered around classes.

"Twelve total, but everyone doesn't make it each time, so it's unpredictable how many will show tomorrow. I'd think most will be there because you're coming."

"Where should I meet the group?"

"Tomorrow we're going to the lounge at the Holiday Inn, the one at University and Ninth. If you like, I'll drop by at five and we can walk together."

Jason thought about his schedule on Fridays. Usually he and Lucy were content to relax at home and unwind after the hectic week. He didn't remember any commitment that would cause him to rush from the session with the post-docs. He said, "Okay, I'll look forward to seeing you then and meeting the others."

She stood and waited for Jason to retrieve his coat. At the outer door, she put her arm through his for a moment and said, "I plan on running in the morning, so I'll see you at the park."

She turned to walk down the hall, heels clicking on the hard surface. He watched her for a moment, then startled by his fascination, turned toward the outside door.

Kathryn appeared at five and waited for Jason to get his coat from the closet and close his briefcase. "I'll drop this in my car on the way out, then I won't have to come back in the building."

They walked quickly in the cold late November dusk, a slight breeze adding to the chill factor, the threat of snow in the air. Talking was difficult in the throng of students and faculty hurrying along the sidewalks, their faces blank, no doubt thinking about plans for the weekend or things they had to accomplish before the next work week.

At the Inn Kathryn led the way to a back table where eight others were waiting, already engaged in a lively conversation about the seminar topic from the day before. As Jason and Kathryn approached, the conversation stopped and they waited for Kathryn.

"This is Dr. Jason Spradlin, the department head," she said, touching his arm. "I'd better let each of you introduce yourself, then I won't embarrass you or myself by forgetting a name." She pulled off her coat and draped it across the back of a vacant chair as she talked.

Jason dropped his coat onto a stack of others and remained standing as each gave their name and the lab in which they worked. The process complete, he took the chair next to Kathryn on one side of the rectangular table. He realized they were almost touching in the confines of the space meant for fewer people. Her leg bumped his when she crossed her knees. She glanced at him and smiled.

206

The waiter appeared immediately to get their orders. Jason noted everyone had a mug of beer and he complied by ordering Killian draft.

Realizing the group, each face expectant, was looking in his direction, Jason said, "I appreciate your asking me to join you, but I didn't prepare a formal statement. Kathryn told me it was a drinking party, not serious business."

Kathryn laughed with the others, then said, "But you would respond to a couple of questions?" Her hand rested on his arm for a moment.

"If they're not too challenging."

"So I'll start," Kathryn said, " by asking about changing roles from a faculty member to an administrator. Is it proving difficult?"

Trying to maintain a light tone in the social environment, Jason said, "That is a serious question for such a gathering, but I'll try. It's been frustrating for me since I can't be very active in the ongoing work of my lab. I depend on Roy and Angela to keep things running and bring to me only the problems they need help with." He nodded to his post-docs across the table as he talked, then waited for the waiter to set down the mug.

Jason continued, "At the present time, I'm only an interim appointment, so I don't know if I'll be in this job after this year."

Roy asked, "What are the problems you hadn't expected? Maybe I should say the challenges."

Jason thought, sipping from the mug. "None have come as a big surprise looking back over the three months. The challenge is knowing there'll be some problem every day, small or huge, you can't predict.

And using your time wisely to solve it, so you don't lose control of any agenda you had planned for the day."

Kathryn said, "So that's the exciting part of the role."

"I hadn't thought about it from that perspective, but, yes, you won't ever be bored."

An Indian woman, dressed in the traditional sari of her culture, at the end of the table asked, "Did you have any training for the head's job and should we consider taking those kind of roles in our future?"

"No preparation at all and that seems to be typical of academic administrators. I found myself in the job when Dr. Rogers became ill. I suspect no one in the academic world ever sets out to become an administrator, but is chosen for one reason or another by colleagues and circumstances."

He sipped beer, then continued, "I'm not a good person to give you advice about assuming leadership positions. I always swore I'd never do it, but here I am, at least for the short term. I would encourage you to establish a solid set of credentials in research and teaching before you consider taking on a head's job. Don't ever get fooled into thinking you can by-pass that step."

When no one posed a question, Jason said, "Let me turn the tables and ask each of you to tell me a bit about your backgrounds and the research you're working on. Maybe three or four minutes each. And since Kathryn got me into this, I'll ask her to begin."

By the time each of the nine had talked, Jason realized he had to get going. He didn't want to delay dinner at home and get the kids off schedule. He said, "I must go, but I'll pick up the tab, since you

208

haven't been too tough on me. And I wish each of you well in your careers. " He stood and found his coat in the pile on a vacant chair.

They clapped softly, causing those at near tables to look toward them, and one voice said, "If I known you'd treat, I would have ordered something other than cheap beer."

Kathryn stood when Jason did and said, "I'll walk back with you."

Jason started to object, but didn't when he realized the group was breaking up and going their separate ways. He held her coat as the others began to find their wraps.

After a block on the almost empty street, Kathryn placed her arm through his. "It's gotten a lot colder," she said, her body seeming to come closer as her hand tightened on his arm.

In the next block the street lamps were spaced farther apart in the interval between the downtown and the campus. Even in the sparse lighting, Jason became aware of a figure on the opposite side of the street, moving at their pace. At intervals the man swiveled his head to glance toward them, as though he was deliberately maintaining an even distance from them.

Jason slowed and caused Kathryn to ask, "What's wrong? You okay?"

He ignored her question and focused on the strange actions of the man across the street. He was certain he'd seen the shape before. His mind raced through the possibilities. After a few seconds, he connected the walrus figure to Terry Boseman. Beyond that, he could not place any significance to his presence, although it was worrisome.

He lowered his voice below the normal. "I think we're being followed by that person across the street. He keeps pace with us. When we slowed he did the same."

They both glued on the figure for the next half-block and experienced a bit of relief when he turned a corner and disappeared into the blackness of a side street.

Kathryn clutched his arm more tightly. "Those kind of actions scare me. Almost every day you read about a woman being assaulted by a freak. I'm glad you were with me."

"It might be nothing, but I understand your concern." If the stranger were really Boseman, Jason knew his target was not Kathryn, but him. Then he couldn't imagine Boseman attempting anything intended to damage anyone.

They picked up the pace again as the cold seeped through their garments and worries about the stalking figure dissipated.

At the door to Quincy, Jason said, "I enjoyed meeting the group. Thanks for inviting me."

Kathryn shook his hand, then stepped closer to hug him. "I'm glad you came. They seemed to enjoy the interactions."

Instinctively, he wrapped his arms around her and held her close for a moment.

She turned to walk inside without looking back as Jason watched her disappear through the door. He turned toward the parking lot and his car, his thoughts on the weird presence of Terry Boseman on an isolated street during a freezing night.

CHAPTER 20

Greg Harris knocked on Riley's closed door, then pushed it ajar to find Riley conversing with Boseman. He retreated a step, until Riley motioned for him to join them, pushing a chair around for him. Boseman shifted his chair to make room in the crowded office.

Riley said, "Terry and I were just discussing our favorite subject, Spradlin."

"I heard he applied for the head position," Harris joined the conversation. "Someone on the search committee let me know. They've received about sixty applications and they're beginning the screening process."

Riley nodded, a slight smirk across his face. "I heard that too. So much for Spradlin's promise to not become a candidate."

Shaking his head in disagreement, Harris said, "I don't think he ever promised. We just assumed he wouldn't."

"Or hoped." Boseman growled, shifting his thick body and crossing his ankles.

Riley waited for a lull, then said, "Somebody told me something very interesting. They saw Spradlin and Kathryn, this post-doc in King's group, walking together along University Avenue. She was holding his arm."

He allowed the tidbit to sink in, the sneer on his face broadening, then he added, "I'd bet my dinner tonight there's something going on.

I'd bet Spradlin is banging her." He leaned back in his chair, waiting for their reactions, looking as though he'd let them in on the secret of the decade.

Harris growled and popped a fist into the palm of his other hand. "And all the while, he's on my case about sexual harassment. What a two-faced bastard." His face flushed as he thought more about the confrontation with Jason about Vicki Sanchez.

Boseman had remained quiet during the exchange, then his voice taking on a note of confidentiality, he almost whispered, "I've seen them together several times. I know they jog together every morning in the city park."

His mouth gaping open, his face appearing incredulous, Harris yelped, "How the hell do you know that? You been following Spradlin?"

"I've tailed him a few times," Boseman admitted, pleased he'd accomplished something the others dared not try.

Remembering Boseman's earlier threat, Riley said, "Be careful. You don't want Spradlin to catch you stalking him. You could land in big trouble."

"Not to mention the police and their concerns about stalking." Harris stood, moving his chair back against the bookcase.

"If this business with Helweg is true," Harris observed, his hand caressing his chin, "we've found a certain way to do Spradlin in for the head's job. Just getting the rumor out will be enough.

Continuing to look down at his colleagues and assessing the issue, Harris continued, "But let's be sure before we spread this around. I get mad when I remember our conversation and his attitude, but he was straight-forward with me. He gave me a way out and he hasn't talked to anyone about it. I respect him for that."

Boseman couldn't let it drop. "But if he and Helweg have a thing going . . . .?"

"All I'm saying is be sure," Harris held his ground. "running together is not enough. Neither is being seen together on a busy street."

"I'll find out more," Boseman volunteered.

Harris and Riley looked at each other, concern about Boseman's true motive, afraid to probe enough to really know. Neither liked the deep scowl on Boseman's face each time he mentioned Spradlin. They knew Boseman had been more than upset about the tenure question and they recognized his demeanor had changed dramatically since that point.

"Let's stay in touch," Riley said, as a way of closing the debate.

As the Thanksgiving break neared, the pressures in the head's office abated as administrative offices began to close things out and wait until after the holiday too initiate new things that would not be settled and drag until after the break, resulting in delays and restarts.

Jason and Lucy tried to utilize the slower pace to accomplish personal issues and protect the actual holiday for family activities. On Wednesday before the break, Lucy scheduled her car for the annual state inspection and the usual winterizing process. Jason had picked her up at the shop and planned to drop her back after work.

As they left Quincy shortly after five, he took her hand as they headed for his Accord in the lot. She related some event of the day that caused both to laugh and edge closer together. For a moment he put his arm around her waist and drew her close.

He opened the door for her and waited until she'd arranged her briefcase at her feet before closing it and coming around to the driver's side. Few cars remained in the lot as most faculty had departed for the day.

Two cars were ahead of them at the four-way stop just outside the parking lot. As they moved, he reminded her she would need the copy of the work order at the car shop. Lucy leaned forward to find the paper in the glove compartment. When they stopped at the intersection and allowed a crossing vehicle to proceed, Jason was startled by a sudden smashing of the driver's side window. Fragments of glass hit his face. Lucy was slammed against the door. Blood gushed from her neck, droplets hitting the window. Jason leaned across the seat to determine what had happened, quickly realizing she'd been shot.

Forgetting the car and the traffic for a second leaning toward Lucy, he allowed it to drift forward. Another shot rang out, smashing the rear window. They were under attack. He had to move from the line of fire. Remembering the hospital was only three blocks away, Jason jammed on the accelerator and sped toward the clinic, blasting his horn and weaving around two slower cars.

He rushed into the emergency parking and pressed the horn to gain attention. Two attendants emerged immediately. He yelled, "My wife's been shot. Hurry."

214

Jason stood mute as the attendants eased Lucy from the car, a third trying to stem the flow of blood by pressing against the wound. She was wheeled into the emergency surgery, nurses scurrying about, a physician running into the unit, his white coat swirling around his knees.

Shocked and concerned beyond rationale thoughts, Jason paced the floor of the waiting area, then remembered he should move his car from the entrance. In the car, he couldn't bear to examine the damage and the blood pooled in the seat. Two shots had hit the car. Someone had intended to kill him or both of them.

As he paced fifteen minutes later, he remembered Lucy reminding him this morning to pick up the kids from daycare. Not wanting to leave the hospital and not knowing what to tell the children, he called a neighbor, blurted out his problem and asked if she could get the children and keep them until he knew the outcome for Lucy. Later, he couldn't remember much of what he'd done as he waited and paced, unable to sit or scan a paper.

He had lost track of the time when a physician came to find him and lead him to a quiet corner of the room. "I'm sorry, we couldn't bring her back. The shot tore through her jugular. She lost too much blood and we had difficulty stopping the flow. Plus, there was other damage to her neck. From all reasonable aspects, she was dead before she arrived here."

Acknowledging the stricken blank of Jason's face, the physician touched his arm. "There was nothing you could have done before getting her here. You took the right action. The damage was just too severe."

The physician reached to touch Jason's face, saying, "You have several cuts on your face and neck, likely from glass shards. Let's check those and check for other wounds." He led Jason toward an examining room. A nurse came immediately and worked her magic, leaving small bandages in four different places on his cheek and neck.

As the nurse prepared to leave, Jason asked, "May I see my wife?"

She nodded and led him into the surgery, then left him alone. Lucy lay prone on a bed, her eyes closed, the torn tissue and blood now cleaned away. But he could see where the bullet had hit and taken her life. He took her hand, continuing to press it for several seconds. He kissed her on the forehead. He pushed strands of hair back into place. For several minutes he stared at her stillness, seeming so peaceful. He remembered her smile, her vitality, fragments of their life together.

Finally Jason turned away, his thoughts overwhelmed with the loss of the most precious person in his life. He couldn't sustain a focus on what he should do next. He paced more, thinking about what had happened. After several minutes, he accepted he had things he must do—take care of his children who wouldn't understand about their mother, call Lucy's parents, let somebody at the department know, call Lucy's boss, funeral arrangements, find the bastard who'd done this. And more he couldn't fathom at the present. He returned to Lucy, kissed her again, wanting to hold her close one last time. He eased off her wedding ring and put in in his wallet.

216

The evening became a flurry of necessary activities. He intended to retrieve his kids but the neighbors insisted on keeping them overnight. He called Lucy's parents in Illinois who couldn't understand for a while. He promised to call them back in a few hours. He called Audrey at home and asked her to let some of his colleagues in the department know. Neighbors dropped by to offer assistance and support. An older woman who lived three doors up the block, brought in a plate of sandwiches.

He spent the night pacing and crying, recalling their life together, alone in the eerie stillness of the house they'd shared. He touched some of her things, holding a favorite robe close to smell her presence again.

As dawn broke he made coffee and found two muffins, then walked along the streets they'd meandered hand-in-hand. Back at the house, he called her parents again to find them more composed and beginning to think about the future. They wanted Lucy buried in the family plot near the church where their marriage had taken place. They volunteered to arrange everything through the local funeral home. Lucy's mother suggested they take the children for a while, but Jason wanted to keep them close, although at the moment he hadn't determined how to accomplish that and maintain his job. The blur had begun to fade. Realities of the future had begun to come into focus, although dim and fuzzy at he moment.

Moving forward took another turn when shortly after eight, Tom O'Hare, the University Chief of Detectives and a detective from the Spencerville station knocked at his door.

Standing in the living room, Tom said, "Jason, I'm sorry about your wife and hate to bother you so soon, but I'd like to move ahead as quickly as feasible in determining what happened."

"I understand," Jason said, pointing them to chairs.

O'Hare said, "Maybe tell us what you remember. We know the general scene and have begun to search the area for evidence."

Jason nodded understanding, raked a hand across his face, trying to recall the sequence of events at the stop sign. He reiterated what he could remember—the stopping for other cars, Lucy leaning forward, the shot, his reactions, the gushing blood, his reactions, another shot, then the rush to the hospital.

O'Hare asked, "Both shots came from the left side of your car, correct?"

"Yes, please look at the car. You can tell from the shattered windows."

"We will on the way out. We'll also look for the bullet. The second one is no doubt lodged in the rear seat or door of your car. We recovered the fatal shot from the hospital."

O'Hare said, "I have to ask this. Has your wife received threats, or have any known enemies? Who would do this?"

"Tom, this was intended for me, not her. It was a fluke she was in my car. Look for people who'd want to get me, not her."

The detectives looked at each other, then Tom asked, "Okay, who might you suspect? Who have you had arguments with recently and irritated them so badly they'd resort to murder?"

Straining to remain focused and shove thoughts of Lucy aside for the moment, Jason thought about his discussion with several faculty since he'd become interim head. None of them seemed likely suspects. Faculty were not the typical sort who killed others in response to professional disagreements.

He disliked revealing names of confidential meetings, but the situation called for complete disclosure if the culprit were to be apprehended and brought to justice. Finally, he said, "I've had heated sessions with two different faculty in the past few days. Talk to Greg Harris and Terry Boseman. Both were upset and mad about my actions, but I wouldn't think of either going this far."

O'Hare wrote the names in a small book taken from his coat pocket. "We'll start with them. Now let me ask if you've heard anything recently from either Jefferson Bell or Archie Smith?" Both men had been involved with a scheme to drive Jason away from State University during his early years because they objected to his research on gene therapy. Their actions had led to the death of a neighbor and the kidnapping of a graduate student. Both were now serving sentences in the state penitentiary.

"No, nothing, but that is all past."

"Some people never forget and always want revenge," O'Hare said. "Let's not rule out some buddy of theirs who has wrestled with his feelings for years and finally decided he needed to act."

Jason said, "Start with the present, but I doubt that will lead to the killer. Maybe it was just random and we happened to some into his sights at the wrong time."

The detectives stood. "We'll let you know. If your car is unlocked, we'll start there." They shook Jason's hand and turned to the front door.

Thelma Rogers came by. She hugged Jason and the children who were sticking close to their father, unsure of what had happened and not comprehending the absence of their mother. After the neighbors had brought them back around mid-day, Jason had pulled them close to him on the couch and attempted to explain their mother would never come home again. Tears streamed down his cheeks as he tried to reassure them by saying she'd gone to heaven to be with God. They cried. He hugged them and promised he'd take care of them and love them more than they could understand. But he knew the vacuum of Lucy's absence would never be filled again.

The matronly Rogers perched on the arm of the couch, saying, "Jason, I just wanted to come by and see how you were and offer my assistance with anything you need. I know how much Henry admired you and predicted wonderful things for you. I hope this tragedy will not alter that."

"There are a lot of things to be figured out." He allowed the children to climb into his lap. "But one by one, we'll get them done."

"What about the children?"

"I don't know yet. It's going to be hard, but I want to keep them close and maintain as much normalcy as possible."

"May I suggest something?"

When Jason nodded, Thelma continued, "I know this wonderful woman who's about sixty-five years of age who might be willing to become a live-in nanny or whatever they're called these days. Her husband recently died and she has scads of experience with young children. I haven't talked to her, but I will if that seems suitable to you."

The idea appealed to Jason. "What would I need to provide?"

"If you could give her a couple of rooms, maybe access to a car, pay her a modest salary, perhaps other things I haven't thought about, I believe she would live in, take care of the children, prepare meals for all of you, all the typical household responsibilities."

"Thelma, that seems a good solution. Please bring her by and I'll work out a satisfactory arrangement. We'll be in Illinois until Monday night, but sometime Tuesday should work."

When Thelma stood, Jason asked, "What should I do with Lucy's clothes. She would want them to be useful to someone and there's no one in her family who could utilize them."

"Everybody does this differently, but Goodwill or some church clothing bank are able to find needy people. My children and I took all of Henry's things to Goodwill. But you may wish to keep some things, maybe a special dress or some item from a special occasion. You must decide what. No one else can do that for you. But you don't have to rush. Take your time and let matters settle a bit."

She touched Jason on the arm. "If it's too hard for you, I'll be glad to do that for you. Or I could help. Whatever is most comfortable."

At the door, Thelma hugged Jason and each of the kids. "Call me about anything."

A week passed in a daze. The trip to Illinois, the funeral service, returning with the children to an empty house. On Tuesday after Thanksgiving with the university back in full swing, a memorial service organized by faculty from English and with Jason's input was held in the University chapel. Almost all of the Biology faculty and staff attended along with those from English and many administrative officials who had interacted with Jason or Lucy during their time at State.

By then Mrs. Lillian Carter, a gray-haired, full-figured woman had come to live with them, using the one-time master bedroom and adjoining bath as her quarters. Jason moved his clothing to the spare room they'd used as a home office. He moved Lucy's clothing and personal items to a storage space in the basement, not ready yet to sort through and give away her things. The most important aspect was the children immediately liked her although they still asked questions about their mother. She was better than Jason in talking through the questions with the youngsters. Within a couple of days Jason knew the arrangement would be good for his children, as well as for himself as he would not be concerned with the daily tasks of feeding and preparing for kindergarten or day-care.

Jason fought through those down times when visions of Lucy seem to penetrate his very being. The worst came after dinner and the kids were in bed. Nothing replaced those moments when he and Lucy had quiet chats about the days events, family occurrences, or plans for the future. Sometimes they just sat quietly, knowing the other was close. He tried not to appear sad around the kids, playing games with them he'd never done before, telling them stories about his own childhood, reading an extra bedtime story if they remained awake. He worried about them although they seemed to be coping okay. And everybody told him that time would help the healing and soften the loss. He wasn't so certain of that advice when he jerked awake in the early morning hours feeling the presence of Lucy, then stared into the darkness until time to get going for the day.

Through it all Jason prepared to continue his career and modified life.

CHAPTER 21

Rifling through the stack of mail that had accumulated during his absence, Jason opened the letter from George Stuart updating him on the progress of the search for the permanent head of Biology. The committee had received seventy applications and now had reduced the number to ten viable candidates. Their plan was to contact references for those ten by Christmas and further reduce the number to three or four. The ten remaining had been invited to update their application, add or delete references, and add new information appropriate for the committee's consideration. Jason stuck the form letter into the file.

Kathryn Helweg came into the office. Jason stood when she came around his desk to hug him. "I'm sorry about your wife. And I'm sorry I wasn't here to support you during that awful time." She stepped back, her eyes on Jason's face.

"I'm recovering and coping," Jason said, "but it will take time. Now I'm trying to get back into the grind of work."

"I won't take your time, but I did wish to offer condolences and ask if I might still meet you for morning runs?"

"I've sloughed off those since the incident with Lucy, but I need to get back to the routine. How about tomorrow, same time as before?"

Kathryn drifted toward the door. "I'll look forward to that."

Responding to a call from Dean Hawthorne, Jason met with the College Committee for Tenure and Promotion. Hawthorne had alerted him the committee had been concerned about the split recommendation from the department and wished to discuss the reasons Jason had gone against the department committee on Terry Boseman.

The large committee, one representative from each of the twelve departments and chaired by Hawthorne, overwhelmed the college conference room. Papers and folders covered the long table and were stacked on the floor along the wall behind each person. A large coffee urn bubbled away on a table in one corner. Styrofoam cups littered the table. The air was dense because of the crowd. Aromas of stale coffee and blueberry muffins mingled with those of bodies crowded close together.

From his assigned space at the head of the table next to Hawthorne, Jason recognized three or four of the members, including Ben Rankin from Biology. Hawthorne introduced everyone quickly, then reminded them of the Boseman dilemma. Jason realized the recap was for his benefit suspecting the committee had discussed the situation just prior to his being ushered in.

Concluding his summary, Hawthorne turned to Jason and said, "Members would like your opinion of Dr. Boseman and your rationale in recommending against tenure for him."

Jason made eye contact with each of the faces, some appearing hostile, others bored. "I attempted to explain my reasoning in the letter, but I'll restate my thinking, then respond to any questions. First,

226

I admit I struggled with Dr. Boseman's situation and I suspect it's an unusual one for your consideration. He has an excellent research record, but his teaching record is abysmal. His file contains several letters from earlier department reviews, from Dr. Rogers, and from faculty who critiqued his teaching performance. However, Dr. Boseman failed to improve and gave scant evidence of trying to become more effective in the classroom. I concluded, based on my conversation with him, that he doesn't believe instruction is an important part of his job and that his research will get him over the hurdle of tenure and through the rest of his career. From my perspective and a review of the guidelines in the faculty handbook, both research and teaching are critical components. Excellence in one, coupled with gross incompetence in the other primary function of each faculty member and the department as a whole, shouldn't merit a lifetime contract. Thus, after hours of deliberation and after discussions with faculty who'd reviewed his teaching performances, I could not excuse Boseman's teaching. I came down on the side that he is responsible and should be held accountable for his total record. His record doesn't measure up in my judgment and I don't want Biology to support such a candidate."

When Jason stopped, a man from the right side of the table, the challenge in his tone betraying his bias, asked, "Did you have any concern you'd gone against your department committee?" He stroked an untidy goatee as though the hair growth demonstrated his thoughtfulness and unique insights.

Looking directly at the man whom he thought was Flynn from Sociology, Jason said, "Of course, particularly since I'm new at this job. But letters and notes in Boseman's file from Henry Rogers were instructive. I knew he intended to do the same as I did."

"So you believe your opinion is better than a group of faculty?" Flynn's voice was clearly hostile, approaching arrogance.

Steeling himself not to lash out, Jason replied, "Not necessarily, but I believe department heads have a difference perspective than most faculty." He smiled and added, "Of course, I was disappointed the Biology committee didn't agree with me."

Most chuckled, but Flynn ignored the aside and pushed his agenda. "What do you mean by perspective as applied in this case?"

"I'm afraid the committee in Biology didn't perceive the long term consequences of giving tenure to an individual who will be dead weight for twenty-five years as far as the teaching mission is concerned. Neither did they consider the potential impact on other faculty . . .."

Shaking his bushy hair, Flynn broke in, "Meaning?"

Jason leaned forward, his arms on the table. "I figured out an important thing during my internal debate about Boseman. That is, when we give tenure to an undeserving individual who will not carry their load in the future, we punish faculty colleagues, not administrators. The record for Boseman is clear. Students flee his classes to cause overloads in other sections, forcing his colleagues to teach larger numbers. Their work loads increased because Boseman was an ineffective, probably uncaring instructor. That's unfair to other faculty, as well as those students who get stuck in his courses."

Ben Rankin interrupted Flynn as he tried to pose another question. "I can attest to Dr. Spradlin's contention as the truth. My sections of General Biology were flooded with students transferring out of Boseman's. I hadn't thought about the implications until Dr. Spradlin pointed it out."

Flynn couldn't let it die. "In his letter of rebuttal to your decision, Dr. Boseman promises he'll give more attention to teaching after he has tenure. I take it you are unwilling to accept his promise."

Jason nodded. "I suspect he told Dr. Rogers the same thing at the three year review and he told me that when I talked to him about my opposition. But we make decisions on the record. If Boseman were deficient on the research side, would we honor his pledge to do better in the future? All of you know we wouldn't, thus why should we award tenure on the basis of a promise to improve teaching?"

Finally Flynn was quiet and when no one else raised a question, Hawthorne asked, "Anything else about Boseman or other candidates from Biology while Dr. Spradlin is here?"

Dave Manly, the representative from Chemistry, said, "I agree with your thinking because I've observed the same thing in my department, but I'm surprised you opposed your faculty. That takes courage."

Jason stood and chuckled. "Maybe I didn't know better."

As he turned to leave, Jason scanned the faces and knew he'd not convinced Flynn, but perhaps Flynn was the Riley version of Sociology.

O'Hare was waiting near Audrey's desk when Jason returned from the tenure session. Following Jason into the office, he said, "I wanted to update you on our investigation."

Jason led him to the conference table. O'Hare continued, pulling out a notepad from his pocket. "First, the two bullets match. Both from a 30.06 rifle. We found shell casings behind a group of shrubs across the street from the parking lot. The shooter had a clear view of cars stopping at that four-way sign. The grass had been trampled over a several day period. He had likely scoped out the position and waited for the right moment. With traffic reduced on that date, it worked out as he planned. And with no residences near, just the park until you proceed another block along the avenue, he would go unnoticed. During the cold weather, no one would be loitering in the area.

"We followed up on your suggestions about possible irate faculty. Harris came across as understanding the conflict between the two of you. In fact, he seemed to appreciate your approach and admitted your stance saved him from more severe consequences. As you'd suspect, there's a bit of resentment in him still and likely will always be there. He recommended we talk with Hugh Riley who according to Harris, knows all the scuttlebutt around the department. So we met with Riley.

"Riley is a strange character. I suspect he opposes everything any administrator proposes. He fosters dissent. We queried him about Harris and Boseman. He became defensive about Boseman, almost as though he was concerned he might reveal something to implicate his buddy. We believe Riley knows something or suspects something about Boseman. We may take him down to the station and put the screws to him, threaten him with complicity.

"Boseman is mad as hell because of your stance about tenure. He couldn't restrain himself from letting his anger show. Based on his responses, we've begun to investigate him further. We intend to discover as much as possible about his background and his activities around the date of the shooting."

Jason said, "I wouldn't think Boseman would have the courage to carry out such an act."

"You can never predict. Sometimes sheer rage overwhelms an individual to the point everything they do leads to an act of violence you'd never consider possible. I suspect Boseman is such a personality."

O'Hare stood, shoving his pad into a side pocket. "On a personal note, how are you doing?"

"Okay, but there are bad periods almost every day. The worst is when I go home at night. It's like the house is silent, even with the kids running around, the television blaring. After the kids are in bed, it becomes worse. That's when Lucy and I had quiet times together. I'll always miss that."

"Passing of time will help."

"That's what everyone says. I hope they're right because it's hard now."

"I'll keep you updated about the investigation." He touched Jason's shoulder before turning toward the door.

The phone rang as O'Hare closed the door behind him. Hawthorne was on the line. "I wanted to let you know the committee rejected Boseman. Your other candidates passed okay. There'll be official letters in a couple of days, but I thought you'd like to know sooner."

"Thanks, but I didn't convince the guy who kept asking questions."

"Flynn never changes his mind. He's one of those so anti-administration he opposes anything he believes a department leader might desire. But you caused most of the committee to think about teaching responsibilities in a way they never considered previously. What you said about sharing the load impressed them, probably because they've all been impacted personally by an ineffective colleague."

"Is this the end for Boseman?"

"Yes, since I won't support him. The letter to him will explain his options for appeal. You'll get a copy. Under our policies he can remain here for one year, but I'd guess he'll start looking immediately."

Remembering the challenge in Boseman's voice when they'd talked, Jason wasn't sure he'd go away quietly. An appeal with lawyers pressing Boseman's case seemed a likely prospect. He said, "We'll see what happens."

The conversation with O'Hare roared back that evening after he'd read a bedtime story to the kids and Mrs. Carter had retired to her room. Jason attempted to watch television, but nothing captured his attention. He switched channels several times, then turned the set off. He wandered around the downstairs rooms for a while, touching things he and Lucy had purchased together when they'd moved into this house. He stared through the kitchen window into the blackness of the back yard, remembering how they'd idled away time on the swing set under the large oak in the corner of the yard, saying little, but comfortable in just being close. Jason tried to shove all those thoughts away. He went to his bedroom, a sterile place with only his personal stuff around. Sleep did not come easily nor quickly as he failed to erase his longings. Finally, sheer weariness overcame his sadness and he slept.

Kathryn was jogging back and forth along the sidewalk when Jason arrived for their early morning run through the park. Without conversation other than brief greetings, they started along the path they typically took. Thirty minutes later they returned to the starting point, breathing deeply, but feeling invigorated.

Pacing along the sidewalk for a brief cool-down, Kathryn said, "I don't know if you've noticed, but a man has been spying on us. I've seen him three or four times, some before you were away and again yesterday. He's usually lurking behind those shrubs over there." She pointed to a group of bare azaleas in the corner of the park across the street from their beginning site.

"You know who he is?"

"I've seen him around the building, but I've never met him."

"Kathryn, this worries me. Let's change our site for a while. How about we meet at the front door of Hastings Gym and jog through the campus?"

"You think this person had something to do with Lucy?"

"I don't know, but let's be on the safe side. I'll see you tomorrow at the same time, but at the gym door facing the quad. Okay?"

"Sure," She touched his arm and turned away toward her residence, two blocks away.

First thing in the office the next morning, Jason phoned O'Hare and told him about the guy trailing him on his early morning runs. He didn't mention Kathryn, not wanting her to be brought in for questioning. "I suspect it might be Boseman, but I've not seen him clearly."

"We're bringing both Riley and Boseman in today."

CHAPTER 22

The weather had turned frigid and both Jason and Kathryn were bundled in heavy sweat suits when they met the next day in front of the gym. As they started jogging, Jason said, "If this cold continues, we'll have to go inside to the indoor track."

She nodded as they picked up the pace, trying to generate body heat. They ran for thirty minutes finding their route through the quiet campus, six laps around the outdoor track, detouring a couple of times through arcades between buildings, then walked the last two hundred yards toward Hastings, an older structure renovated and enlarged as the student body grew.

Jason said, "I'll be away for three days for a meeting. I likely won't see you until next week."

"I'll go alone. It seems safe enough in the cold and I don't like to alter my routine."

Jason touched her shoulder. "Kathryn, I want you to avoid the park until we know more about this guy lurking around. Stay on the campus."

"I will. I'm not worried when you're with me."

Nearing the gym doors, Kathryn asked, "Are you doing okay? You seem quieter today."

"Trying to cope with everything. My kids are too quiet, watching TV but not really seeing the program. I'm not sure what to do to help them get over the loss of their mother."

"It must be very difficult for them, but kids are resilient, so I've been told. And they have a very caring father."

In Dallas for a meeting of molecular biologists, Jason met with three other researchers, each of whom he'd called the week before to set up a lunch meeting in the headquarters hotel. Thinking about the Redlake proposal, he wanted the advice of these guys deeply involved with the essential techniques. He'd asked for a quiet corner and the reservation staff had honored his request. The restaurant, approximately a hundred tables, was filled to capacity primarily by conference participants. The scientists were readily identifiable, name tags on their coats, programs with papers stuffed into the pages, talking and gesturing to their colleagues from around the world. The possibility that this could be his last time at the session gnawed at the edges of Jason's mind.

As they waited for a waitress, Peter Gibbs from Rockefeller, said, I heard the paper your post-doc gave this morning. Good work." Angela had presented a summary of their work on Wilson's disease, a defect involving copper transport, during a morning symposium focused on genetic disorders. After exhausting attempts to identify a fifth genetic error that everyone believed was the last piece of the puzzle, they were now trying an approach using stem cells adopted from a French investigator and supported through a grant from a foundation not bound by federal regulations regarding the employment of stem cells.

Laying his menu aside, Jason said, "We've made progress, but it's slow going. Too many complicating factors when you're dealing with human subjects and we've never been able to develop an acceptable animal model."

Rodney Moak from Tulane agreed. "I understand, but you've made others see this thing can be solved. Keep plugging away. One day it'll be solved. Probably save some lives."

The waitress appeared and they focused on meal orders for a bit, then Jason said, "As I told you when I called, I wanted to pick your brains about cloning methodology. Anything you're willing to share will be useful. Other than read several recent papers and a recent review article, I've not done anything in the area. But so you know my interest, I've been asked by an commercial outfit to help them develop a reliable, and predictable approach. He grinned and added, "I can't reveal to much about their goal, but you can probably guess."

Carl Tahir from NIH suggested, "Clearly the most predictable outcome is when you fertilize, then split the egg to get double the number of embryos."

"What about," Jason asked, "developing the embryos in a culture medium?"

"I've heard of that approach and it seems to work reasonably well. At the blastocyst stage the embryos are transferred to a recipient dam for the remainder of gestation."

Moak added, "Starting with cells from an adult appears very inefficient with present techniques. You never know how it's going to develop, if at all. But the outcomes will improve as the methods become more refined. Almost every week there's a report of a slightly modified approach, some promising, others based on some quirk that won't hold up. I have a hunch timing is the key."

Jason said, "As you'd guess, this company wants a process that will produce the largest number of viable offspring. They can't tolerate a lot of failures."

Gibbs smiled. "So they're going to mass produce a domestic species for food purposes."

"You're right. They hope to market a consistent animal product. Presently, they intend to use farmers who'll provide dams and feed the progeny until ready for market. They haven't discussed the economics with me, but they plan to contract with the growers and share the profits."

"Assuming they have any," Moak grinned. "Sounds pretty risky."

Conversation ground to a halt as their food was placed and they ate for a few minutes before Jason asked, "Have you heard of anyone who's developing the clone completely on an in vitro basis?"

All shook their heads. Tahir said, "I've heard rumors, but nothing more. I'd think it'll be too hard to provide enough nutrients to support cell growth and development. Nature is hard to improve upon."

"That's science fiction stuff," Gibbs said, picking up his coffee mug.

238

Pushing his agenda, Jason said, "Let me bounce an idea off you. Get your reaction. From what I've read, the best approach seems to be to harvest embryo stem cells which will produce the tissues of a new progeny. You could maintain those cells in a culture medium for a long time, possibly several generations, giving you an unlimited supply of cells capable of producing adults. You'd have to restart the process at times, but that's not a huge problem."

Toying with their utensils, sipping coffee, and glancing at each other while he talked, the three stopped, waiting for someone to take the lead.

Moak said, "I've not kept up with this stuff very closely, but if what you describe is possible, I'd think it's the best approach for your company." The others nodded in agreement.

Jason said, "Of course, all the progeny will have identical traits."

"And," Gibbs noted, "you could alter the genetics to change some specific characteristic."

Jason said, "That is the method I'm going to propose, unless you see a big flaw."

When no one suggested a problem, Jason said, "I'll start there and see how it goes."

Gibbs said, "And we'll send you a consulting bill when you strike it rich."

Moak inserted, "I hear you're becoming an administrator. You won't have time for this stuff any longer."

"You're right. I'm a candidate for department head. And you're probably right about the time I can devote to science. However, the search committee may save me and recommend someone else."

Jason picked up the checks from the middle of the table. "Here's the first payment for your consulting work. However it goes, thanks for your advice. Now I need to get to a session where a graduate student in presenting a paper." He knew Ann would be nervous, her first time before a national audience, but she was well-prepared and would do okay. Nevertheless, she'd feel better if her major professor was there in the front row.

Greg Harris found Riley staring out the window of his office when he knocked on the door jamb at four in the afternoon. "Hugh, I heard the cops had you to the station. How'd it go?"

Riley's usual bluster and mischievous nature seemed to have been quashed. His face reflected deep concern, wrinkles prominent across his forehead, something Harris had never seen before. "Those bastards essentially accused me of aiding the shooter in Lucy Bacon's death. They pressured me to tell them about Boseman and his threats against Spradlin." He rubbed his face, trying to erase the ordeal.

"Are they questioning Boseman as well?"

"You bet. I saw him waiting in a little holding room as I left the station. They'll force him to reveal anything he knows. That guy O'Hare knows what he's doing. He sort of leads you into a trap, then slams the net over your head."

"Give me an example."

240

"Well, he came on nice and easy at first, talking about how tragic her death was, and how rarely those kind of events occurred around a university. He asked about my relationship with Spradlin. Then he asked about Boseman and how much we'd talked since Boseman knew Spradlin opposed his tenure."

"I hope you told him the truth."

"Of course. Then he asked about threats Boseman had made, and about Boseman trailing Spradlin. I felt trapped. I had to tell him what I knew or the bastard was going to hold me overnight, and who knows what else."

Harris said, "O'Hare and this city detective talked to me at my house two nights ago. I told them about Boseman's anger toward Spradlin and his admission he had been following Spradlin."

Riley swung around in his chair. "So they knew already."

"Hugh, that's the way investigations go. They compare stories from suspected people and look for holes, then they jump at the first discrepancy."

"This is scary stuff. At one point O'Hare hinted I could be charged as a conspirator. That gets your attention."

"You have to be careful about threats and spreading crap about other people. It can come back to bite you in the ass."

Riley pulled on his overcoat. "I'm going home. Had enough for today." He and Harris walked together until Harris turned away to go toward his own office.

At the same time, O'Hare and Detective Bruce Trout were searching Boseman's apartment using a warrant to gain entrance. They had Boseman in tow after not believing his responses to their questions. He'd sworn he'd never tailed Spradlin, had no particular complaint although he was hurt by Jason's non-support for tenure. But he didn't know what Harris and Riley had revealed.

Jason had settled in his chair for an early morning bout of signing papers stacked up during his trip to Dallas when Audrey knocked on the door and came in to stand near the desk.

She said, "Students from Dr. Boseman's class came in late yesterday. Dr. Boseman failed to show for his General Biology lecture yesterday morning and no one came in to substitute. Apparently a couple of students went to his office only to find it locked. I asked faculty with offices near his if they'd seen him. No one has since day before yesterday."

Jason came around the desk to stand near her. "I assume he's not called in sick."

"No, the office hasn't heard anything."

Thinking about the progression of the investigation, Jason said, "Let me call Detective O'Hare. I know they intended to question Boseman while I was away."

O'Hare came on the line immediately and when Jason told him about Boseman's absence, Tom said, "We had him in for questioning and after that we searched the house. We found a voucher for his payment to use a shooting range, but no weapons. Then we talked to

242

the attendant at the range. He recalled Boseman coming in often in the last month to practice on the rifle range and he knew Boseman owned a rifle which he kept in a locker at the facility. But he wouldn't allow us to search because we didn't have a warrant. Late yesterday, we obtained a warrant for the facility, but we couldn't get there before the place closed. Jason at this juncture, everything points to Boseman as the shooter."

Jason said, "He knew you had the evidence and has fled. Or, he's holed up in his apartment and refuses to respond to phone calls."

"We'll check it out as fast as possible. Be alert. I have the feeling he's a dangerous character ready to explode and he blames you for all his troubles."

Jason replaced the phone and thought about who else Boseman might go gunning for in his frustration and rage. His children might be the idiot's first thought. He called Mrs. Carter and rather than scare her silly by talking about a possible gunman, he suggested he'd pick up the kids from their kindergarten and nursery school today. Thinking about the children further and their joy in going to McDonalds, he said to Carter, "And don't bother with dinner for them tonight. After I pick them up, I think we'll go for a meal together."

Since Boseman believed Kathryn was important to Jason, he wanted to warn her. He called King's lab and asked the student who responded to have Dr. Helweg come to the department office.

Kathryn appeared five minutes later, a white lab coat covering her skirt and blouse. She said, "I'm glad you're back. It's been lonely running by myself."

Jason came to stand near her in front of the desk. "That's what I wanted to ask about. Have you seen this stalker recently?"

Her eyes widened. "Not since we switched to the campus."

Torn between alerting her and scaring her, Jason decided she needed to know the potential scenario. "I don't intend to alarm you unduly, but the police are reasonably certain Terry Boseman was the shooter of Lucy and now he's disappeared. They've warned me to stay alert. And since Boseman saw us together, I want you to be doubly careful until he's caught. He might take out his fury on anyone he thinks I'm close to."

"What must I do. I need to keep working."

"It may be nothing, but if you see him close, get away. Stay with other people if you are shopping or in restaurants. And let's forego running in the park until he's brought in."

She turned toward the door. "I will and you be careful. You're the one he wants to hurt."

The children were overjoyed when their dad came for them. And their excitement increased when he surprised them by asking their preference of fast food places.

They ate hamburgers and fries, stuff he knew was not good for them, but he wouldn't make it a regular venture. He helped them with the wrappings, wiped the excess sauce from their faces, released the straws from plastic coverings. And he kept looking around for Boseman.

CHAPTER 23

On Tuesday of the second week in December Preston King stuck his head in Jason's office. "I stopped by to tell you our short paper was published in the December issue. Brumfield stuck to his promise about quick publication and there were no challenging letters in the issue."

"Maybe Brumfield didn't give them an opportunity since they withdrew their first ones."

Still leaning against the door frame, King said, "Maybe, but I thought they would have raised concerns after such a ruckus before. Could be they've accepted my conclusions or have no rebuttal to offer."

Remembering Brumfield's failed promise to send him names of the disagreeing investigators, Jason asked, "Did you ever learn who were challenging you?"

"No, but I could guess," King responded, now stepping inside to be in front of the desk. "I suspect a couple of people, but I couldn't prove anything. And I don't want to accuse the wrong people."

"I could call Brumfield and press him for the names again . . . ."

His hand on the corner of the desk, King shook his head. "Let's forget it, unless something happens. Maybe confirming the first paper was a good thing to do, but I hated the circumstances and the waste of money and time. Plus, I truly abhor being accused of dishonesty." His face darkened as he turned away.

Jason hoped King was correct and the episode was behind them, but he had a strange hunch the conflict hadn't yet been resolved.

Three days later, Jason's premonition proved correct. The Friday morning edition of the local papers carried a headline on the front page: **State University Biologist Accused.** Details in the AP article named Preston King and recounted the earlier incident, then described his most recent publication as outright manufacture of data to support the initial conclusion. Sources of the accusation were not named, only stating the reporter had based his story on the opinions of highly reputable scientists who didn't want to be drawn in the controversy.

Jason scanned the article a second time, then turned to help Jennifer pull on her heavy coat and mittens. He knew all hell would break loose. The Attorney General would be beating on the President's door and the problems would filter down from that point.

Mrs. Carter had Tony ready to go. "Come on, we don't want to be late." She smiled at Jason as the kids hugged his legs and were herded toward the car. As part of their arrangement, Mrs. Carter had use of Lucy's car to transport children, run errands important to the household, and on some occasions for her personal use. Thus far, the agreement had worked out well and Jason's confidence in the older woman continued to gain traction. Her easy manner camouflaged her stern side as she coaxed the kids to do her bidding. They enjoyed the nutritious meals she had ready on time to meet the various schedules. After dinner each evening, she disappeared into her rooms giving

Jason time with his children, helping them with baths, reading a story, sometimes playing a game with them.

Jason hustled in ten minutes prior to eight, zipping his heavy coat open. Preston King and Kathryn were posed in front of the department door, their faces glum, puzzlement evident in their stances.

While Jason keyed open the door, King said, "I guess you saw the paper." His body continued to sag as though the weight of the universe was tugging at his shoulders, like a fighter ready to cave it in. Kathryn's eyes shifted from King to Jason, apparently unsure of how to respond to the situation. An hour earlier they'd separated at the gym, neither Jason nor Kathryn aware of the coming proclamation at that time.

Jason opened the door, changed the lock so it wouldn't relock behind them, flipped on the lights and led them into his office. Hanging his coat in the closet, he said, "I did. You have any idea of what this is about? No warning from Brumfield?"

"Nothing," King muttered, shaking his head. "Complete shock to me. I honestly thought we'd moved past those things."

King and Kathryn took seats at the table, still wearing their outer coats, faces like zombies, knowing the department leader wanted some explanation.

Jason joined them. "I'd offer coffee, but none has been made yet. As to the charges, I believe we have to become more aggressive. We've sat back and waited for the next shoe to drop, but I'm inclined to take some initiative in getting to the bottom of this issue."

"What can we do?" Kathryn asked, her eyes shifting again to her more experienced colleagues.

Jason didn't like what he was about to suggest, but he'd thought about it on the drive to work and concluded it was the correct approach. "First, I want to be absolutely certain there's not been any cutting of corners in this work. I know you think I'm making another accusation, but for your sake, check through the last experiments one more time. I understand you had an independent group work through the second trial. But be sure there was no collusion with those who did the first experiments. It'd be easy enough to duplicate the first data set without anyone knowing if somehow there was collaboration within the lab."

His face reddening, King sputtered, "I don't like what you're suggesting."

Jason reached across the table to put his hand on his colleague's arm. "Neither do I. I remember that Kathryn and James Ho did the first experiments. Who did the second set?"

Her mouth set in a firm line, Kathryn said, "Robert Tanaka, a post-doc from Michigan State, and two graduate assistants. Robert was responsible for checking the protocols, implementing the controls, helping the students with the analyses, and for the accuracy of the raw data."

King jumped in to continue. "I have complete confidence in his ability and his integrity. He knew we were under the gun to have an independent analysis. I did everything possible to insure the independence of the group. I removed any condition or circumstance

248

that in any was compromise the validity of the experiments. I didn't know at that point if the second runs would support or disprove the original data. I wouldn't let anyone, not even Kathryn, have copies of the first set. It'd be almost impossible to match the two sets, except when both experiments are done independently and yield the same results."

Jason asked, "But the original data were in the publication, right?"

"The data summary and the statistical analyses were of course, but not the raw data. No one outside Kathryn, James and myself have seen those."

Jason asked, "Is Robert smart enough to take the published data and extrapolate to the new set?"

Kathryn ran her hand through her short hair. "It'd be possible I suppose with a lot of manipulation and trying to extrapolate back to the initial data, but that would be more work than doing the experiments again. Dr. Spradlin, your thinking about copying and collusion if all wrong." Her deep blue eyes bored into his face, daring him to challenge any farther.

Thinking further, she said, "In fact, Robert offered to show me the raw data when they'd finished, but I refused and told him to not give it to anyone until he'd done all the calculations. He wouldn't have offered if he were trying to avoid the actual analyses."

In spite of the obvious feelings of disloyalty he was generating, Jason persisted. "And you saw them in the lab enough to know they worked away at the tests?"

They both nodded. Kathryn said, "Robert and the two students practically lived in the lab trying to complete the work as quickly as possible and to do everything correctly. I overheard Robert talking to one student and then making her repeat some phase of an experiment."

Jason smiled, hoping to relieve some of the tension he'd created, then leaned forward, his arms on the table. "I hope you know I've raised these questions so I can be in a position to go all out to support you. I don't want us to be trapped in the middle of some oversight hearing and not be sure we're on solid ground. I believe we are, but you should know if this thing progresses, someone will raise the same questions under circumstances where a lot of people are looking over our shoulders and searching for the slightest hesitation or any indication of your lack of confidence in the work. For the moment, let's see how the next phase plays out."

Standing, King asked, "Do we wait for someone to call us on this or ....?" He shrugged in uncertainty.

"We'll hear something soon enough, but two things. One, I wouldn't respond to any media questions. Second, I'm going to call Fowler and Hawthorne in the next few minutes."

King moved through the door, but Kathryn waited, then whispered to Jason, "Can we have lunch today?"

Audrey stuck her head in the door. "Dean Hawthorne is on the phone."

Unsure of her agenda, he looked into Kathryn's eyes, seeing nothing but those deep blue orbs staring into his face. "Come here just before noon. We'll walk somewhere close."

Watching Kathryn exit the office, Jason picked up the phone. "Spradlin speaking."

Hawthorne's voice was louder than usual. "Jason, President Snyder wants to see us immediately about this King fiasco reported in the morning papers."

The phone dropped with a bang before Jason could respond.

Snyder paced while he talked on the phone, his voice more animated than usual, while Hawthorne and Jason waited at the door to his office with the receptionist. When Snyder saw them, he motioned toward chairs, turning his back and lowering his voice. His conversation continued for three minutes while his visitors surveyed the office and its plush accoutrements.

Walking toward them and dropping into a seat, Snyder explained, "Some reporter from the local paper. I've been bombarded all morning, starting with Attorney General Cline at seven-thirty."

"I suppose," Hawthorne said, "he's gung-ho to start his investigation and accuses us of stone-walling." Hawthorne's voice suggested little or no respect for the politician who had the reputation of doing anything to keep his name in the news.

His face clouded with concern, Snyder nodded. "That's about it. He was on a rampage this morning, full of threats and self-righteous posturing."

Snyder shifted in his chair and continued, "I promised to call back by noon, but I wanted to touch base with Dr. Spradlin, and maybe Dr.

King, before I do." Now he turned to face Jason, his face questioning and hoping for good news.

Jason responded without further prompting. "I met with King earlier this morning. He's distraught, but maintains neither he nor anyone in his lab has done anything wrong. I questioned him and an assistant pretty thoroughly about the precautions they'd taken with this second set of experiments. They're adamant there was no manufacturing nor falsifying of data and that the outcome demonstrates without doubt the validity of their earlier conclusions."

"I take it," Snyder said, "that you believe them without reservations?" His eyes were intent, looking to Jason's actions and expressions for any sign of wavering.

Returning the President's stare, Jason said, "I do believe them. You may recall I had doubts the first time, but King has kept me informed at every stage during this re-run. Looking back to his demeanor the first time and the primary reason I had doubts, I've now come to believe he'd never been accused of wrong-doing before, especially one that became high-profile, and he didn't know how to respond. In many ways he's still that way—like a rabbit caught in the glare of headlights and unsure of appropriate action."

"What do I tell the Attorney General? He won't be satisfied again with my saying we're re-checking the data."

Hawthorne squirmed in his chair, likely wishing to tell Cline to go to hell. Jason intervened. "A significant missing piece of this puzzle is the accusers remain unknown. I doubt the Attorney General would

252

give credence to any other situation in which he didn't know the accusers and their motives."

"Can't we find out who they are?"

"I intend to make some calls when I'm back in my office," Jason said. "I was promised names earlier by the editor of the journal in which King's paper appeared, but he either forgot or avoided me for some reason. And I let it ride since I thought we'd reached the end of the problem. In retrospect, I should have insisted he provide the names."

Snyder nodded and smiled for the first time during the discussion. "You think the editor is involved?"

Shaking his head, Jason said, "I don't think so, but he's caught in the middle of a dispute created by others. They submitted letters of rebuttal to King's first paper, then withdrew them for some reason."

Snyder stood and eased toward the door, signaling Hawthorne and Jason the session was ending. Snyder asked, "What would you think of my recommending to Cline that we turn the matter over to our university Ethics Committee?"

Hawthorne nodded at the idea. "It could be a way of keeping Cline out of our hair, but if Jason is correct, there's been no abuse of our guidelines. I dislike it when we can't put our fingers on the ones raising the questions. The media get all excited then the politicians jump in to get publicity."

Snyder looked at Jason for his ideas. Jason said, "Maybe let the Ethics Committee be Cline's instrument for an investigation, if there must be one. I agree with Dean Hawthorne—we don't know yet who we're trying to satisfy, or why."

Snyder opened the door. "Thanks for coming so quickly. This thing has disrupted everyone's schedule. Stay on it though. Let's get the names of the accusers. We've been embarrassed enough." Jason hadn't heard the stern tone of Snyder's voice before. He didn't know if he were being reprimanded or warned or both. Hawthorne seemed to ignore any threat from the President.

Jason's intention to call Brumfield immediately became side-tracked when O'Hare phoned as he took off his coat. "To keep you updated, we've checked out Boseman's storage space at the shooting gallery. If he had a rifle there, he took it with him. We didn't find it in his apartment so I'm assuming he has it in his car."

"No sign of him, I take it?"

"We've issued an APB and have our patrols on the lookout, but no sighting. Bottom line, keep a low profile for a bit longer."

CHAPTER 24

Jason called Brumfield before another thing could interrupt. As soon as the editor responded, Jason said, "Maybe you don't remember, but we talked earlier about the disputed paper of Preston King and his associates. Now his detractors have gone public with a second charge. This happened as soon as King's confirmation paper appeared in the journal."

"I saw the newspapers. Frankly, I'm irritated as hell, especially after I contacted them and shared a copy of Dr. King's second paper, requesting letters voicing their opinion. Neither replied or let me know they planned to go public."

"When we talked previously, I asked for the names of those raising the issues. I'd really like to have those."

Brumfield hesitated, then said, "Dr. Spradlin, I feel anything I do in this situation will be misinterpreted by someone. I know I reneged on my promise the first time you asked, but after our conversation, I decided it best to let the matter drop."

Jason interrupted Brumfield who seemed ready to continue his explanation by saying, "My concern is Dr. King is being repeatedly placed in the position of defending his integrity while his accusers hide behind the curtain of anonymity. King has the right to know who's challenging him and they have the responsibility of letting others know their positions and trying to convince the scientific community whose theory has merit."

Remembering the President's admonition, Jason continued, "You must know we're going to find out those accusers even if we have to involve the courts."

Still Brumfield delayed, maybe as he considered Jason's implied threat. Jason could almost hear the wheels turning as Brumfield pondered his dilemma. Finally he said, "The letters of complaint came from Alexander Thiele at Oregon West University and Reginald McLean at Northwest University in Seattle. I'll fax you copies of the letters. But I don't know with any confidence they were the ones who raised the ruckus in the second round."

"But you'd suspect them, wouldn't you?"

"It'd be a logical conclusion. No one else has voiced any differences with King."

Ending the conversation with Brumfield, Jason immediately called King, but was told by a graduate student that Dr. King was in the library. Jason smiled, remembering retreating to the stacks to avoid the media, and asked that King call him when he returned.

Then he called Hawthorne and the President's office. Snyder intended to call the President's of the universities where Thiele and McLean worked to let them know, if nothing else, they had faculty who ignored ethical behavior guiding the manner in which scientists operated. No doubt Snyder would let them know his opinion of characters who threw stones in the dark and that State university would not be intimidated further.

256

Thirty minutes later Audrey handed Jason the faxes from Brumfield. Jason glanced at the letters, both stating without equivocation that King's paper was wrong, either based on incorrect data, or the methodology was incorrectly used, or that the authors had manufactured the data. Both demanded the paper be withdrawn to avoid setting back advancements in viral technology. Neither hinted at releasing their disagreements to the media. Comparing the two, Jason was struck by the close similarity of the language, several phrases identical, as though one had copied or paraphrased the other. Both were dated August twenty-second. In his opinion the collusion had been well-orchestrated.

Jason made copies for King, Hawthorne and Snyder so they would have paper evidence about King's accusers and placed the faxes in his growing file about the King fiasco.

The morning mail brought another disquieting communication. A copy of the letter from Hawthorne to Boseman in which the decision of the college committee was communicated had been folded twice. A message had been handwritten across the top—"Spradlin, you're the bastard who caused this. Someday I'll repay you." Signed T. Boseman.

Jason went to Audrey's desk. "How did this come?"

The secretary looked at the letter. "I believe in a regular campus envelope, but I didn't give it much attention until I saw the message. That's scary."

"Let's see if we can retrieve the envelope."

In the trash a mixture of envelopes, now slit open, posed a problem. No ordinary white envelope meshed with Boseman's note, thus they concluded he'd dropped it in campus mail, using the typical brown container on which names were scratched through and the new addressee written on the line following. Audrey pulled one from the stack which had Jason's name preceded by Boseman's and his office number.

Jason called O'Hare to alert him that Boseman was still in Spencerville and had likely been in a campus building within the last two days. The lock to Boseman's office had been changed thus he couldn't have been there, although his books and other personal effects were still housed in the space. O'Hare warned Jason again about being alert for any appearance of the distraught former faculty member. Jason called Mrs. Carter to inform her he would pick up the kids from their respective places at the end of the day.

Just before noon Kathryn appeared and as she waited for Jason to retrieve his coat, she asked, "Is the Campus Diner okay. It's close and the weather has turned awful. It started snowing an hour ago."

Jason wished he'd worn his boots when they walked out, the snow now two inches deep on the unplowed walks and accumulating rapidly, but as usual his winter footwear was in the trunk of his car. As they walked he told her about the flurry of activities around the King paper during the morning. In some ways he felt relieved by the cold and the quietness of the falling snow.

The Campus Diner had been a haven for faculty and students for fifty years according to local historians. The food was simple, filling, inexpensive and palatable. Service was rapid as student waiters earning part of their school expenses scurried around. Today, the air was saturated with vapors originating from the crowd entering from the cold, the mixture of warm breaths and melting snow. Shedding their coats while they waited for a table, Jason noticed Kathryn in heavy slacks and a turtle neck, the first time he'd seen her in attire other than dresses or skirts. She seemed cozy compared to his usual dress shirt and suit. The redness of her cheeks induced by the chilly air only enhanced her facial features. Two males standing near seemed captivated and stared too long.

After they'd been seated in a booth near the rear of the diner and had placed orders, Jason asked, "Do you know Alexander Thiele or Reginald McLean?"

Her eyes widened. "Not personally but by reputation. Both are active into the same kind of work we're doing. They've published a lot of papers I've referred to for background and interpretation of our data. Why do you ask?"

"They were the ones who challenged your first paper. The editor of the journal sent me copies of their letters. I sent copies up to Dr. King's office."

She stopped unrolling the silverware from the paper napkin. "Oh, wow, and you think they're the ones who did this thing yesterday?"

"That'd be my first guess. No one else seems concerned."

"But why? It doesn't make sense."

Jason responded, "It could be neither is guilty but who else sends a letter to the editor then withdraws it. And for two to do it simultaneously is defining."

The waitress placed their chili and coffee in front of them, placed a basket of bread and crackers in the center of the table, dropped their check and moved on without lost motion or spending time discussing the weather.

Kathryn remained quiet for a couple of minutes, stirring the chili and taking a bite. "The reason I wanted to talk to you away from the office is I'm worried about Dr. King. He's becoming more withdrawn and is never smiling like he was when I first came. This stuff is getting to him."

She sipped coffee, screwed her face into a frown and continued, "The lab used to be a happy place. Everybody worked hard, but they enjoyed the challenges and each other. Now it's changed with the secrecy about these experiments and King's moody demeanor, as though he doesn't trust anyone."

"It's been a tough time for him."

"Before these charges, he routinely met with Robert Tanaka and me every Friday to talk about projects and problems. Sometimes we'd discuss future plans and map out proposals for NIH and other agencies. It worked well and I was learning so much. Now he's withdrawn and just says we should work through the difficulties."

"How well do you know him?" Jason remembered the rumors of an affair and wasn't comfortable with his question after he'd asked it, thinking she might suspect him of probing into her personal life, even though she'd opened the door to King's state of mind and their relationship.

Kathryn seemed not to notice. Her facial expression remained the same. "Other than professionally and around the lab, not very well. We had lunch a couple of times in the fall, but I never see him outside the building." She stirred the chili, the bowl almost empty now and grinned, "I know you better, in fact."

To his surprise, he experienced a feeling of relief about her response. He said, "Maybe you know, but in case you don't, there were rumors that you and King were having an affair."

Kathryn's face reddened, telling Jason she may not be as sophisticated as he'd believed. "It's not true." She looked directly at Jason. "I don't know how those things get started."

"People like to talk and anytime they see interactions between men and attractive women, they assume something other than professional activities is going on. It's too bad, but it happens. And universities may be one of the worst places in our society for that sort of stuff."

"So now we're having lunch, the talk will start about us."

Jason said, "Probably, but we'll live with it. People are speculating what goes on between us because we've been running together."

"Good Lord, at five-thirty in the morning." She laughed, her perfect teeth showing as her full lips parted. Her eyes sparkled at the idea.

"I'm relieved you put to rest those rumors about King and you. Now the scuttlebutt about us can have center stage."

"You're funny," she said, but her face turned serious. She seemed ready to reveal some feeling, but then wiped her mouth with the napkin.

Shoving his bowl aside, Jason asked, "Are you getting what you hoped for in this post-doc?"

"I'm learning a lot, but I'm concerned this crap about those papers will haunt me in the future. I don't want to be associated with any group suspected of doing unprofessional things." Her face, dark and frowning, revealed more frustration than she was articulating.

She continued. "I'd planned on staying here two years in the post-doc, but now I'm considering looking for a teaching-research position starting next academic year. Maybe it's time to move on, although I'd hate to abandon Dr. King while this charge hangs over his head, and mine too for that matter."

"I haven't talked with Dr. King about this, but I will if you'd be interested in filling in for Boseman during the spring term. He was scheduled to teach a section of General Biology and a graduate seminar. You could decide the focus for the seminar and see who it attracts. Or it'd be possible to forego the seminar."

Her eyes lighted. "I'd love to do that. It'd give me another experience. Please see how he reacts, but I'd like that very much." She reached across the table to touch Jason's hand.

"One other thing," Jason said, "Boseman is around town and campus." He told her about the message he'd received. She listened her face wrinkling with concern, but didn't comment, sliding out of the booth.

On the sidewalk outside the diner, the snow had stopped although the walks and streets were covered with slush, mixed with ice and salt spread by the road crews. They maneuvered around the worst places, but by the time they reached Quincy, Jason's shoes were soaked.

At the point of separation inside the building, Kathryn said, "See you at running tomorrow?"

"Sounds good. Maybe the streets will be passable by then."

"Plus, we need to keep the rumor-mill going." She touched his arm and giggled.

When Jason drove away from his house the next morning, he became aware of a car following, its parking lights providing the only illumination. When he stopped at a crossing avenue, the other car drifted slowly toward him, but obviously didn't intend to get close. Jason lost sight of the tailing vehicle when he pulled into the campus lot behind the huge gymnasium. His concern disappeared, probably some driver who hadn't had sufficient coffee to become alert yet and was depending on other vehicles for illumination.

Kathryn was waiting at the front doors, jogging in place. They nodded and began their usual route through the campus. Their routine took them around the main quad and past Quincy before they reached the track that provided a smooth surface absent of any distractions. Nearing Quincy on the initial leg, Kathryn touched Jason's arm and pointed. A figure leaned against the corner of an arcade connecting two buildings, both large classroom, office complexes that housed two or more departments. Continuing to the front side of Quincy, Jason grasped her hand and led them into the foyer of their familiar building.

His hand on Kathryn's shoulder as they stopped moving, he said, "That person we saw is Boseman. Go to your office, call Campus Security and the Spencerville police. Stay in your office after you call." Her eyes wide and questioning, she nevertheless moved quickly toward the stairs.

Jason watched her enter the stairwell, then going outside, picked up his pace to circle Quincy, eyeing every potential spot Boseman might be lurking. Thoughts of doing something stupid rather than waiting for the security people kept pace with his running, but he knew Boseman could disappear at any time. He was tired of dodging this threat.

Jason failed to sight Boseman as he passed the rear of Quincy. He cut through an arcade between two other buildings, avoiding a straight path in case the idiot decided to take a shot at him. Veering around the long side of the chemistry building, he spotted movement at the corner he would approach if he continued. He retreated and circled the structure from the other direction, watchful as you can be when you're dashing like a fool on a mission likely to fail.

He slowed as he neared the spot he'd seen the movement. The short plump figure of Boseman leaning against the south wall, sheltered from the slight breeze, emerged clearly as he neared. Noise of a garbage truck making its early rounds worked in Jason' favor as he approached.

Running hard, he rammed into Boseman before he knew Jason was close, knocking him to the ground. His rifle skittered away to rest under shrubs along the wall. Acting quickly, Jason kicked Boseman in the gut, even the heavy coat failing to shield him completely. Trying to stand, Boseman doubled over, his legs pulled under his torso as he fought for breath. Jason yanked him to a standing position, twisted his arms behind him and propelled him toward Quincy. Progress was slowed as Boseman attempted to struggle free, but he had neither the strength nor the physical know-how to overcome the larger, stronger individual. Neither uttered a word although Boseman was muttering curses and threats as they plowed along.

By the time they reached the entrance to Quincy, two police cars had parked along the street. Cops were piling out, grabbing weapons, as a sergeant issued dispersal orders.

Jason yelled, "I have him. Over here."

Glad to transfer Boseman to the cops, Jason led two of the crew back to the spot where the rifle had landed, then returned to Quincy and scurried up the stairs to Kathryn's lab and office.

Kathryn rushed toward him as Jason reported, "Cops have him under arrest."

Her arms around his waist, his around her shoulders, she mumbled against his chest. "Thank goodness. I was terrified he'd shoot you."

They broke apart but their hands remained clasped together. "In retrospect, I probably shouldn't have gone after him, but it worked out okay. Now we can retrieve some normalcy in our lives without worrying about what some fool will do to your children, to yourself, or those important to you."

He pulled her closer. "And you did your part by getting those cops here so quickly."

Kathryn smiled at him. "Let's give up running for today, but I must go home and change clothes."

CHAPTER 25

King appeared at the office door. "Kathryn told me you've gotten McLean's and Thiele's names and I saw the note you left with the letters, but I'd seen those before with the names blacked out."

"Preston, I don't understand to this day why you didn't simply write a rebuttal. That may have taken care of the entire thing."

A slight whine in his voice, King said, "I didn't because there was nothing specific to explain. The bastards said our data were suspicious, implying in my thinking that we'd manufactured the stuff."

Jason didn't want to press King too hard about an issue he couldn't do anything about at this point in the battle. Plus he didn't know what he would have done under similar circumstances, but he thought he would have vigorously defended any allegations of wrong-doing through the usual rebuttal process offered by journals. He acquiesced, "Maybe you were right. Who knows."

Jason continued, standing near King at the door, "I'm expecting to hear from President Snyder about the Attorney General's demand for an investigation. And I have an appointment with a university lawyer to consider what actions we should take against McLean and Thiele. I'd like you to go with me."

"What time?"

"Nine. Come here about ten till and we'll walk over together."

King turned to leave, but Jason said, "I'd like to discuss one more thing. Come, have a seat."

Settled around the table, Jason said, "I need to find someone to take Boseman's position on a temporary basis for spring term. I would like to offer Kathryn Helweg the spot if we can work out an arrangement to not damage your research work."

King seemed relieved this was a topic different than the debate about challenged data. "What did you have in mind? I can't afford to lose the post-doc slot and she's become quite productive."

"Suppose I hire Kathryn full-time on the money from Boseman's salary, but establish the responsibilities so she spends half to three-quarters of her time in your lab. You could take her post-doc money to hire additional grad students or a technician on a temporary basis. Or whatever would be most useful to you. At the end of the spring term, Kathryn would return to you full-time."

King considered the potential for several seconds. "That'll be okay. In fact, you're being more than generous with me."

"I know, but my messing around with your research resulted in a lot of lost time. I hope this can make it up. Gives you additional hands to do the bench work. I'll talk to Kathryn if it's agreeable."

"Seems good to me and it'll give Kathryn some teaching experience. Let me know when I can begin to look for fill-ins."

Jason tarried in his office until five-thirty, but the President hadn't called. Maybe Cline had backed off his threat or he and Snyder had not made contact during the afternoon.

But during the period after normal office hours, O'Hare phoned. "I thought I'd catch you there. We've charged Terry Boseman with murder. He's retained an attorney and no doubt will seek bail, but the Spencerville city attorney will oppose any released time on the grounds that Boseman is a threat to university faculty and administrators. Plus, he likely has sufficient funds to flee the country. You might be called to testify or provide a statement for the arraignment."

"What about his office and personal things. May I box them up and store them until Boseman arranges to do something about them." He'd been reminded about the valuable unused office space when the English department had called him about Lucy's office. He'd promised to clear her things out over the weekend. Another task that would remind him of her and evoke new memories of their life together.

"That sounds good. I'll pass it along to Boseman in case he wants his things taken somewhere."

In her office on the second floor of the Administration Building, Stella Krause shook Jason's hand, then introduced herself to King. "Jason, I haven't seen you in a long time, in fact, not since the Bell trial. Time flies, doesn't it, five years ago. I'm sorry about your wife. I didn't know her, but she must have been a wonderful person. I hope someday our society can agree on more strenuous laws about gun control." Krause had been the prosecutor for the state when Jefferson Bell, a senior faculty member of Biology, and two cronies had been charged with murder and destruction of state property in their attempts to bring about the cessation of gene therapy research. Jason and Lucy had been targets of a bomb. An elderly neighbor had been killed.

"I've been staying out of trouble, or the kind lawyers get involved in, but it's good to see you again." Jason respected this intelligent African-American woman who had guided him through the torturous times with Bell. She hadn't changed, lively brown eyes, black hair cut short, always dressed in a dark suit and contrasting blouse.

"But I'm back with a different problem." He reminded her of the reason for their visit and outlined the series of events related to Preston King and the charges of impropriety. He handed her copies of letters from Thiele and McLean.

"We suspect these same two of generating the media barrage, but we're not certain. Since they challenged the initial paper, it seems logical they'd follow through if they failed in the first instance."

Krause said, "I saw the newspapers. Now you wish to determine how you stop them from further activities, if in fact, McLean and Thiele are the perpetrators. I agree it's a reasonable assumption, but we must be sure."

"Correct. But I want more than that. There has to be a clear admission of their acts and a public statement of apology. What they've done is tarnish the reputation of Preston King and this university."

King interrupted, "I'd be happy to just have them stop this stuff."

"First, let's set out to be certain they were the actual accusers, then there's the matter of understanding motive." Krause reminded them of

270

the legal ramifications. "Depending upon their actions, they could be charged with libel and/or defamation of character."

"I'm prepared to confront them," Jason said, "but I didn't want to damage any case we might have by some inappropriate action."

Krause swiveled in her chair and stood. "Let's start by contacting them with copies of letters to their Presidents." She paused, then said, "Maybe it's more intimidating if the letters come from this office. For some reason correspondence from the Attorney General's office gets attention faster than from an academic department head, no put down intended." Krause, as all university attorneys, were staff of the state's Attorney General. She reported to both the Attorney General and the President of the University.

"We'd appreciate your doing that," Jason said. "We'll draft letters for you to modify and insert your lawyerese language. I want strong statements. They must understand we won't tolerate this crap any longer."

Krause agreed with the approach and indicated she would work on the letters as soon as she had their drafts. To this point, she'd not heard about the threatened investigation by the Attorney General, although she'd likely become involved by the nature of her appointment and location. King agreed to prepare drafts, have Jason review them and bring them to Krause.

Audrey buzzed Jason's line to connect a call from Nancy Thompson, his most prominent contact at NIH. They exchanged pleasantries for a moment. She had heard about Lucy's death and expressed her sympathies.

Getting to the reason for calling, Thompson said, "Jason, I have good news and bad news. I'll start with the positive. We like the proposal from Biology for the Center of Excellence initiative and will recommend the study group give it serious consideration. You have innovative ideas that intrigued the staff and would accomplish important goals of the agency. Unless the study group detects flaws we'd not seen, you can count on funding effective with the next fiscal year." Jason scribbled a note to pass the news along to Pamela Sturgis who'd done most of the work in getting the proposal together, as well as to those faculty across the university who'd joined the effort.

"Now, for the downside." Thompson hesitated as though trying to decide where to begin, then almost blurted, "This business with the King papers is becoming a serious problem. We've received calls from Representative Ladner's office about the publicity. And we've heard through the grapevine that one of King's enemies, or whatever you wish to label them, is from Ladner's district. To make matters worse, Ladner is Chair of the House Committee for Science and Technology that monitors federal agencies involved with science and research funding, including NIH. His aide let us know the Representative may initiate hearings focusing on the ethics of scientists in general with this King fiasco the center of his attention."

"Remind me where Ladner is from."

"The Fourth District of Oregon. He's been in the House for four or five terms and has moved up steadily in the seniority ranks. He became chair of this committee after the last election when the majority shifted parties."

"Is this only a threat or is he going to follow through?"

"We suspect he's testing the waters, so to speak. If there's enough interest demonstrated with Congress, the media, or some lobby group, he'll likely be going ahead. If not, he'll drop the idea, but to be realistic about it, there are a lot of people who distrust the scientific community these days. Ladner will use those concerns to generate sympathetic support for his proposal."

"I can't imagine the public being very interested in arguments between scientists."

"You'd be surprised though at how quickly some of these anti-science groups come to the fore when issues like this King thing is known. They see it as an opportunity to reduce the appropriations for research and shift funds to some pet cause."

Jason's hands were becoming damp as Thompson laid out the potential for political gain by Ladner and others. He asked, "Should we do anything or just wait for the axe to fall?"

"If you have an influential Senator or Representative, talk to him or her. Perhaps that person could head off Ladner, either by convincing him his hearings are a waste of time, or by killing Ladner's request for funding to support the hearings. The latter might be more effective in these tight budget times."

Jason brought her up to date on what they knew about King's accusers, Brumfield's reluctant revelation after hedging for some time, their suspicions that Thiele and McLean were the ones who'd taken their cause to the media, and now the connection between Thiele and the Congressman. Thompson had never dealt with either of the individuals opposing King's work, although she knew they were collaborators and had been supported through the NIH.

Jason said, "They're in the same line of investigation as King, but we can't figure out their motive for these charges and now getting a Congressman involved."

"I'm a blank on that score," Thompson admitted. "Nothing obvious to gain as far as I know, but there's always something driving these types." Jason wondered if her tone and description intended to reveal previous problems with the two or if the possibility of Congressional hearings and probing were irritating her. He recognized agency representatives could be called on for various tasks by the Congress and could waste a lot of time just attending days of hearings.

Jason said, "Back to the good news. When will we know the outcome of our proposal?"

"The special study committee for this initiative meets in February, thus by early March we'll have a final decision."

"Can you let me know what you hear about Ladner's plans. We may not know until some reporter corners us or an article appears in the local papers."

"Sure, but we may not learn until you do. These politicians like to make agencies jump and keep us on the defensive." Her laugh carried a hollow ring.

Jason replaced the receiver and walked to the window. Students hurried along the walk, almost hidden by the mounds of snow piled

274

overnight by the plows. Kathryn's concern about King gnawed at his thinking as he thought about how King might react if forced to appear before a Congressional committee with all the media and bright lights of television. He didn't like his conclusion. Neither did he look forward to informing President Snyder the battle was likely to move to a national stage that could focus damaging attention on King, the department and the University. Jumping into his mind was the nagging question of why he'd ever considered taking on this job when he could have been working away in his lab, ignorant of all the issues confronting his colleague, not to mention the possibility his wife would still be alive.

His thoughts shifted to Kathryn Helweg and their changing relationship. During their early morning runs and other times together, he'd acknowledged he looked forward to seeing her. Beneath her outward appearance that misled most people into believing she used her beauty to manipulate others, he'd discovered a bright, sensible woman who knew her goals and how to attain those. He'd also figured out she was somewhat older than he'd thought, losing years in the business world and then essentially starting over for an different undergraduate degree followed by graduate school and now this post-doc. He wanted to know her better but their respective positions presented obstacles.

Jason opened the door to Lucy's office on Saturday morning, using the keys he'd recovered from her purse before he yielded it and other personal items to Goodwill. Her desk still had a set of papers she'd graded for her beginning literature course. He put those aside to take to the department office. He boxed personal things taken from her desk drawers, several curios she'd placed on book shelves, and copies of the books she'd written, thinking the children would want those when they were old enough to understand their mother had been a respected author. He found her boots behind the door along with a sweater hanging on a hook. He examined the textbooks on the shelves and decided to leave those to be given to other faculty who might use them or donated to the library. Student folders for her advisees remained in the file cabinet, along with notes of a book she'd committed to complete. He'd ask the department head about those on Monday.

His task completed after a couple of hours, he closed the door to the hall and dropped into her chair behind the desk, a place he'd seen her on numerous occasions. Memories flooded his being. Sadness prevailed causing his eyes to water and his hands to tremble. He thought he'd gotten beyond the shock of her leaving him, but the emotions flooded back, almost drowning him for several minutes.

Noise of people in the hall snapped him back. He had to move. He'd promised the kids a lunch at McDonalds.

CHAPTER 26

Jason found Kathryn in King's lab shortly after eight on Monday morning. "I trust you're doing well today," and waited for her to set aside a gel plate she'd been examining. Then he realized no one else had made it in yet.

"I'm feeling better about the situation since our talk," she smiled. "Maybe by tomorrow we can resume running in the park."

"Let's meet at our usual spot, but I came to ask if you could track down the backgrounds of Thiele and McLean. We know they published together and I've learned they've had joint proposals to NIH, but see if they have other connections, went to the same graduate school, things like that." He grinned, saying, "For all we know they could be cousins."

"I'll start as soon as I complete this job. You have ideas of where to begin?"

"Dr. King might know some things about them. Look in Americans in Science or whatever that publication is. You'll know which journals to review. That should give us a start and may be all we need to know about them."

Jason said, "I assume you're going home for the Christmas break . . . ."

She responded immediately as though she had it on the forefront of her mind. "I've decided to stay here. I need to work on lectures for the course I'm to teach. And my parents are going to Europe for the holidays, so I'd hardly see them anyway."

Remembering a couple of lonely Christmas times after his parents died and before he and Lucy married, Jason said, "Would you like to spend Christmas day with us? Mrs. Carter will make dinner and the kids and I will open presents and maybe go sledding or something they enjoy."

Her somber face broke into a smile that made him want to touch her. "I'd love to do that. Should I bring something?"

"No, just come. I'll tell you more about times after I talk with Mrs. Carter."

"Thanks for thinking of me," she said. "I'll bring you something about Thiele and McLean by tomorrow."

She turned back to the gel but Jason knew she watched him leave the lab and head up to English to talk to the department head about the books he'd left in Lucy's office.

Mid-morning Snyder's call interrupted Jason's discussion with Ann about the paper she was preparing for presentation at the Federation of American Societies of Experimental Biologists, shortened to FASEB by the typical attendee or member of one of the groups. The huge gathering would meet in April in several Chicago hotels and the convention center. Ann walked into the clerical office when Audrey indicated the call was from the President.

"Dr. Spradlin, sorry I didn't get back to you yesterday, but Cline was away from his office all afternoon and we didn't make contact until this morning. At any rate, he's straddling the fence. I suspect the Governor suggested he back off and let the university work through this mess without state government interference. Snyder laughed, "I'm guessing of course. Cline would never admit the Governor clamped down on him."

"That's good news, but I talked with an NIH project official yesterday. She's worried Representative Ladner from Oregon is planning to convene hearings about scientific misbehavior, including the King issue brought to his attention by a university professor in his district. She recommended we talk with our senators and influential representatives to head Ladner off. We have some time since the Congress is recessing for the holidays and won't go back into session until mid-January."

A moment passed before Snyder said, "That's bad news. I'd like to discuss this further, but I must talk with a person on another line. But I'll call a couple of our Congressional people today and get back to you."

Kathryn appeared at three the next afternoon. She'd returned to her usual style of dress, looking sophisticated in a solid green wool dress and black heels. Jason wondered what she wore for special occasions and where she found the resources to purchase such an array of expensive clothes.

She sat in the chair across from the desk and said, "Here's what I've found thus far." She handed Jason two sheets of paper. "Thiele and McLean were post-docs in Glasgow at the same time. That seems to be where they first crossed paths and got started on the same research line. Nothing I could find puts them together prior to Glasgow."

"And they've stayed in touch since then?"

Nodding her head, she said, "I'd characterize it as a productive relationship. At least eight journal papers have both names. Five of those publications credit NIH support, accounting for the joint proposals you mentioned. I found two symposia where they appeared on the same program, each making a major presentation but along the same theme. By the way, Dr. King was on one of those programs with them. They collaborate on numerous projects which suggests they work well together. They're likely good friends as well."

"The very fact they're connected is interesting and tells us why they challenged King's paper simultaneously."

He scanned the sheets briefly, then asked, "Remind me if your paper demonstrated something that goes against the line pursued by those two."

"I'd have to read their publications more carefully to respond with any accuracy, but we altered the concentration of calcium from the usual experiments in the area. I'll ask Dr. King. He'll remember about any conflicts off the top of his head."

Jason stood and came around the desk to stand near her. "Thanks Kathryn, This information confirms my suspicions they were in cahoots and have something to gain, either personally or professionally."

Her face frowning, Kathryn said, "I had no idea this kind of sabotage and dirty tricks went on in science." Sadness lingered on her face as she realized nothing in this world escaped evil when reputations were at stake.

"I've never seen outright undermining of another investigator such as this. But I shouldn't jump to conclusions so quickly. There might be something yet unknown."

She ignored the implications of his back-tracking. "I've a lot to learn."

She moved closer, making Jason aware of her perfume, a scent that seemed to pull him toward her. "I'm going to skip running tomorrow, but will see you Christmas."

To his surprise she stepped close, touched his cheek with her lips, her arms on his shoulders. Instinctively, he put his arms around her waist and pulled her against his body. After a brief moment, she turned and walked through the door without a backward glance, her perfume and the sense of her closeness lingering with Jason. Their relationship had just taken another step, but he wasn't certain he was ready for anything resembling meaningful intimacy.

Determined to clear everything on his desk prior to the holiday break, Jason dug into the stack of mail and papers that seemed never to disappear completely. Among the letters was one from George Stuart informing Jason he'd been selected as one of four finalists for the department head position.

Interviews would be scheduled in late January and early February with a goal of recommending the choice of the committee to the Dean by the end of February. A list of groups and administrators to be involved with the interview process was included. Specific dates for visits by the four finalists would be arranged by telephone after the Christmas break. In addition, another letter sent to all faculty invited them to review the dossiers of the four. Audrey would make the materials available for their perusal in the small conference room.

Since the meetings in Dallas, he'd worked as he could find time on the proposal for Redlake. Now with a scheme in order, he called Brenda Fallon. "I've developed the outline of a strategy to meet your goal of producing a transgenic animal with consistent characteristics. I've worked on this a lot, have changed my thinking at times, but now I'm satisfied this can be achieved. I'll fax my ideas to you today. Perhaps after the new year is settled a bit, we could meet to discuss it and then make any modifications you and your colleagues think appropriate."

Brenda responded. "That's great. We've continued to work on the idea and are pretty much decided on a breed of swine. Cynthia and Eric are looking forward to your ideas and we'll get back to you soon after the holidays."

"If we're agreed on this, I believe the next step is trial runs to make sure it all works as we'd speculated."

At Riley's invitation and urging, the trio of Townsend, Harris and Riley met in Randolph's Lounge, a popular hangout for students near the campus. On the final day of exams for the Fall term, the place begged for patrons. Students had fled the campus as soon as their last exam was completed. Two small groups of faculty huddled around tables, celebrating the end of another term.

At a corner table selected by Riley for its privacy, the three ordered draft beer. They clutched pretzels from the complementary bowl. Townsend broke out his pipe, the odor of sulfur and tobacco dented the aroma of beer, broiling hamburgers, and clothing dampened by the light snow that had fallen all day.

Townsend rested his pipe on the table and retrieved a sheet of paper from the inside coat pocket of his wool sports jacket. "I assume you saw the letter from the search committee. You know any of the finalists other than Spradlin?"

Harris responded first. "I've heard of a couple of them. The female, Treadwell, is well- known in her specialty."

"Spradlin's the youngest by several years," Riley snorted. "I gave a quick look at the folders this afternoon."

Riley glanced at the other tables, perhaps to discern if others were interested in their plotting. "We have several openings to do Spradlin in. His little tete-a-tete with this post-doc, his inexperience so he likely will get flustered at the interview, and maybe this flap with King will prove fatal."

Townsend, demonstrating his desire to needle others, said, "We might do worse than Spradlin. First, we know him. The others are complete strangers and we have no idea about how they might respond in different situations." He tamped a new portion of tobacco into his pipe and dug into his pocket for a match.

"Hell's bells," Riley groaned. "You going to jump ship on me?"

Harris had remained silent through the debate, leaned forward and said, "Townsend is right. We could do worse. Look at how Spradlin has handled all this stuff since Rogers died. Then his wife was killed by this idiot, Boseman, who likely was motivated by such crap as you're spewing. And his research keeps going. So tell me, what's your complaint?"

Riley didn't know how to react to such disagreement among colleagues he believed were of the same mindset as he. He drained his mug and said, "I need to get going. But keep looking for anything we can wedge into the debate about candidates."

As Riley departed, Harris said, "You know, Peter, Riley is against Spradlin because he knows Jason will jump his ass every time he starts one of his smear campaigns against any person or policy he's suspects will make him accountable for his performance."

Townsend stood, not replying, and followed Riley into the slanting snow.

*   *   *

Jason used the week of Christmas to spend time with his kids. Each morning, they ate breakfast together without the demand for rushing to the office or school. Mrs. Carter made their favorite foods and told jokes as they lingered over the meal. Then Jason would spend a couple of hours at the office refusing to permit the stack of mail to gain ground during the break. He worked on a paper, had coffee with his graduate students in an atmosphere of mutual give and take, solving problems that had nagged the students. By Christmas Eve, the lab and the building were empty.

Jason thought about Kathryn a lot, remembering their last encounter at the office. He couldn't admit it himself, but he looked forward to spending most of Christmas day with her. At times he felt disloyal to Lucy for even thinking about this other beautiful and personable woman. At other times he accepted his feelings as the way forward. He couldn't live in the past, but he couldn't decide on an appropriate action to get past his inner reservations. And he accepted others would expect there to be a reasonable interlude before a new female appeared in his life.

As they'd planned, Kathryn appeared soon after the early morning chaos around the tree. Jennifer and Tony ripped paper off gifts, yelling with delight, quickly stacking away the practical gifts Jason, with the help of Mrs. Carter, had purchased.

Dressed for outdoor activity, Kathryn presented each child with a gift she'd gotten for them, bringing forth another fit of joy and wonderment.

They sipped cider and nibbled goodies for an hour as the kids adjusted to new toys, a strange person in their midst, and a tiny bit of sadness in the absence of their mother.

Near midday Jason dragged the kids away from their new trinkets and Kathryn to the big hill in the city park. They took turns sledding down the long slope, the kids screaming with joy until the sled tipped and they were flung into the snow. But they wanted another turn.

Kathryn got into the mix easily, giving each child a ride on her back, then pulling the sled back up the grade. By the time they returned to the warmth of a fire in the hearth of the living room, they regarded Kathryn as a new friend.

They fiddled away the afternoon while Mrs. Carter created wonderful smells in the kitchen. Kathryn disappeared for an hour to change from her sledding outfit into a Christmas dress. Jason helped the kids change from their damp clothes into a fitting attire for the holiday feast. He donned fresh slacks and found a red sweater that had been a tradition in his family since he was a small boy.

Kathryn returned near five, the appointed time for Christmas dinner. She'd altered her appearance dramatically, going from a heavy sweater, wool slacks, and boots into a red, knee-length dress with a scoop neck. A single string of pearls accentuated her slender neck. Matching heels and nylons showed off her legs and completed her transformation from a young woman sledding down a hill, yelling in unison with the kids, to a perfectly groomed beauty intent on captivating those around her. Even the kids were awed by her change, especially Jennifer who'd begun to demonstrate interest in clothes. Jason had difficulty not staring as Kathryn sat on a wing-back chair and crossed her legs. He felt like a grub with his slacks and sweater.

During dinner, Mrs. Carter set the tone, passing plates, helping the kids with their food, leaving the table to retrieve some item she'd forgotten in the kitchen, but smiling and laughing throughout.

She engaged Kathryn, asking questions about her experiences. At one point Kathryn revealed her father owned a large department store in downtown Minneapolis. She had worked there during the summers of her junior and senior high school years and throughout her undergraduate years at Minnesota.

Jason asked, "Were you a biology major?"

"Business. My father expected me to take over the store when I'd sufficient experience, and after graduation I worked there as an assistant manager for two years. But I hated the daily grind, selling people stuff they didn't need and couldn't afford, the lack of intellectual challenges—just the whole deal. I rebelled and returned to the university, went into biology and continued until I'd completed the doctorate. My father has never forgiven me for forsaking his dream."

She nibbled turkey for a moment, then continued her biographical sketch. "My dad expected my sister and me to set examples in style and dress. He liked to point us out as the models for other women. And he supplied us with the clothing and accessories to accomplish that. In fact, he still sends me dresses, skirts, blouses, etc. from what he describes as end of the season inventory." She laughed, almost a giggle. "But I suspect he selects things early and doesn't rely on having his choices disappear over the counter."

"So that's how you have all those wonderful clothes."

"Yes, I wear them to work. There are too many to save for special times. Even then, I pass some on to charities."

As dinner ended and the children's eyes began to droop, Jason said to the children, "Go up, brush your teeth, and put on your pajamas. I'll come in a few minutes to read you a bedtime story."

Jennifer surprised them. "Can Kathryn read our story tonight?"

"I'd like that," Kathryn said, cutting off any response Jason might have inserted.

"Then," Jason said, "I'll help Mrs. Carter clear the table."

The chores completed around the kitchen, Mrs. Carter retreated to her rooms and Jason slumped on the couch, reviewing the events of the day, pleased his kids had taken to Kathryn. Noises from above subsided as slumber took charge.

Kathryn eased down the stairs, a smile across her face. "They dropped off before I completed the Dr. Seuss story." She came to sit near Jason on the sofa. She slipped off her shoes and pulled her legs under her. "I enjoyed today. Thanks for letting me invade your family."

"It's nice to have you. The kids like you."

She took his hand in hers and looked at him, their eyes meeting. "Jason, if I may call my department head by his first name, I want you to know I'm attracted to you like I've never been to anyone else." Her fingers intermeshed with his. "I've had a lot of chances to have relationships, but none ever captured my feelings. For the most part, I suspected they wanted to have sex and brag about conquering another female."

Jason turned her hand, looking at the glossy nails, squeezing it a bit. "You know my situation, but I've come to realize I have deeper feelings for you than I reveal. I still think about Lucy at times and those feelings are likely to crop up at times. But I've thought about us a lot in the last few days, especially while Boseman was on the loose. I was concerned he'd go after you in his sick way of getting revenge."

She leaned against him, her face turned to his. Their lips met. Jason pulled her close and their kiss lingered. He caressed her back as she placed her head on his shoulder.

Kathryn said, "So where do we go from here? I understand your being the department head and my being a post-doc under your authority poses a dilemma. But I hope there's a way around that hurdle and we can move forward, know each other in a personal way, and determine how our feelings are after some interlude."

She twisted on the sofa so she was facing him, her legs drawn up on the couch, her torso next to his. Her eyes exploring his face, she said, "I don't believe this is your intent, but just to be clear, I'm not interested in going forward if you see this as an affair or a series of one-night stands."

"Kathryn, that is not my intention at all. I hope our relationship can grow and develop into something important to both of us. My deep feelings tell me it can as we find a way to spend time together away from the office and lab."

He could feel her breasts pressing his chest as he held her as close as possible. He wanted to caress her knee and leg, but resisted the urge, knowing the action might lead them to places neither was quite prepared for. They kissed again, longer than before.

Jason said, "I'm not sure how we do this, but let's not let those hurdles wreck what I believe might be something special."

Kathryn pushed back so she could see his face better. " For a while we can manage to see each other without others knowing. You could come to my place and no one would suspect anything. I know we can't go public until our situation changes."

Jason kissed her again, her lips open, her tongue edging into his. He quashed aside any reservations and moved his hand along her legs, pushing her skirt and slip higher. He stopped before neither of them made the move from which they couldn't retreat.

Kathryn broke the embrace. "Come to my apartment tomorrow night. Jason, we have to make this work."

He walked her to the door, held her coat for her, and they embraced again. He wanted to lead her back to the couch. Rather he walked to her car with her and watched as she backed into the street.

Turning toward the front door, he thought about his life with female companions. There'd never been a serious relationship other than with Lucy, a connection he'd found to be wonderful. He wondered if he were on the brink of discovering a matching experience.

CHAPTER 27

The morning after Christmas Jason went into the office mid-morning after having breakfast with the kids and spending thirty minutes repairing a toy truck Tony had broken in his eagerness to make the toy do something for which it was not intended. He promised to go sledding again this afternoon, but in response to their query, he doubted Kathryn would be available today. They seemed disappointed, but he felt a tinge of joy race through him when he realized they cared about her.

Quincy was eerily quiet as Jason closed the front door behind himself. At his desk, almost bare now, he thought back to Kathryn last evening and their tentative pact. He wanted to do this. He needed to know how their relationship might progress although there were inherent professional dangers for both. They couldn't allow public disclosure until their professional situations changed. He accepted he'd take the risk rather than never know.

To his surprise the telephone rang. He ignored it until the third buzz, then picked up. "Spradlin here."

"Jason, Tom O'Hare. I called your home to be told you were at the office. Must be the only one there."

"It's a very quiet building," Jason responded. "What's up?"

"The Bozeman arraignment went off two days ago without a hitch. The city attorney charged him with murder and life without parole.

The judge denied his request for release until the trial scheduled for late March."

"Will he seek some plea deal for a shorter sentence."

"Wouldn't be surprised. Anyway, I wanted to be sure you knew."

"Thanks, Tom. I didn't see anything in the papers."

After he put the children to bed, an easier task then usual because the afternoon sledding had worn them out, he drove to Kathryn's apartment, finding the address without problems. He parked several spaces from the entrance and waited until he was confident no one was out and about to observe his actions. Sitting in the quiet, he thought about the impending session with Kathryn. He'd decided he had reached the point he needed to move forward and he knew he regarded Kathryn as more than a passing affair. And he believed she was thinking the same way.

She answered immediately the ringing of the door bell. She stepped back to let him in the modern unit. He was immediately struck by her appearance, beautiful as always, the black skirt and white blouse announcing her curved lines. She had changed from heels to flat house slippers reminding him of the difference in height those shoes made. The slight odor of food remained as evidence of her recent meal. A red-white apron draped across one of the chairs at the table.

"Would you like anything, coffee, tea, or . . . ?"

He declined and they sat on the couch. Their hands came together and Jason asked, "Have you thought more about this since last night?" He tried to read her feelings, looking into her eyes.

292

Nodding and smiling, Kathryn said, "Most of the day. I feel comfortable with our moving forward, but I want us together for a long time. The more I've considered everything, I believe this is right for us and I accept the immediate constraints. We can work through those."

She twisted around to place her front toward his. The skirt rode up showing her knees and nylon covered legs. "How about you? You have the most to lose if something goes wrong. You know Riley and his friends would have a field day if they find out we're meeting."

"Kathryn, the worst thing that could happen is I'm forced out of contention for the department leadership, something I'm ambivalent about anyway. Then I'd go back to the faculty and be satisfied doing things I truly enjoy."

Her arms circled his neck and pulled his face to hers. They kissed, exploring, anticipating where this would lead.

Jason pulled away. "If you're not comfortable with this, we can go slower, get to know each other better . . . ."

She shifted to look into his face, while her fingers intertwined more tightly with his. She touched his cheek with her free hand. Her look became sober as though she needed to reveal something important.

"I've dreamed since I was a teen-ager and began to think about relationships with males of finding the right person. Someone who would love me and become a true partner. Because of my parent's worries and warnings, I became very suspicious of men, understanding most wanted only to have sex with a good-looking female."

When she paused, Jason asked, "And now in these circumstances, how do you feel?"

Her eyes still exploring his features, she smiled slightly. "I believe with all my soul you are the right person for me. I have no concern you intend to use me for sexual gratification and move on to someone else. I know your intentions are good."

"You know," Jason responded, "my life has been in turmoil since Lucy's death. Vestiges of her presence remain and I think about her every day. But I've become attracted to you."

He paused for several seconds. "No, it's more than just a physical fascination. It's a feeling we belong together."

Kathryn shifted again, her hand pressing his leg. "I feel that too."

She leaned into him and brushed her lips against his.

They kissed deeply, pulled back then kissed again. Jason stroked her neck, his fingers gently moving across her skin, warm to the touch. He unbuttoned her blouse and ran his hand across her back and neck, aware her skirt her elevated to reveal most of her legs. Jason knew he would have difficulty stopping now as his passion became fully aroused. He moved his hand up her thighs and caressed her crotch causing her to moan and hold more tightly to him.

Kathryn untangled her self and stood, reached for his hand and led him into the bedroom. A full size bed with a small lamp caught his attention for a moment.

Kathryn slipped out of her blouse and skirt and undressed completely.

Following her lead, Jason dropped his clothes on a chair. He moved toward her, pulling her close, feeling the swell of her breasts against his chest.

They eased onto the bed. Jason pulled her against him then moved to be on top, wanting to be gentle as he found her wetness and thrust into her. They moved in harmony, her hips moving to meet his thrusts. She moaned and raised her legs to better accept his movements.

Cradling her in his arms, one hand under her head, his lips on hers, Jason increased the intensity of their union, entering her more deeply and more rapidly as he lost himself in his own desire. Finally spasms swept through both of them, now in utter ecstasy, continuous murmurs and sighs escaping from her open mouth. They lay quietly for a prolonged time.

Coming alert later, Kathryn said, "It was wonderful and I know this is right. I think you do also."

He kissed her gently. "I've come to love you in the short time we've seen each other. I want us to be together."

She pushed herself up so she could look down into his face, then giggled. "And I won't trap you into this by getting pregnant. I obtained a prescription for birth control pills today."

They rested quietly for several minutes, their hands locked together, their bodies touching, each thinking about their future together, and the immediate issues of keeping their relationship secret until the appropriate time to go public.

Jason said, "I should go before I fall asleep and have to creep out in the morning." He pulled her on top of him and ran his hands along her back and hips. They kissed deeply. "And before we start over again." He eased off the bed to find his clothes.

In the early morning hours in his bachelor quarters within his house, Jason came awake. He'd dreamed Lucy had been there and he'd told her about Kathryn. His final vision was Lucy smiling and disappearing.

For the first two days of the spring semester Jason was confronted with a steady stream of undergraduates who required his signature for various reasons. At one point Audrey suggested she could handle most of the concerns, initial his okay, and send them on their way, but Jason felt the need to meet the students, most of whom were majors in the department. He recalled Henry telling faculty the importance of hearing directly from the students and providing necessary support. Henry's way of summing up his admonition had been to say, "Always remember at some future point one of these youngsters will be your boss."

Copies of the letters from Stella Krause to McLean and Thiele caught Jason's eye the third morning back. He scanned them, acknowledged she'd altered his draft and made State's position and concerns stronger from a legal perspective. He filed the letters and wondered how the recipients would react to warnings about their accusations. Krause's statements left no doubt they would be charged in civil court if appropriate explanations and public apologies were not forthcoming.

The President's office scheduled a meeting for Hawthorne and Jason the afternoon of the third day of the new term. As usual when they arrived, Snyder was on the phone. Two minutes later, Snyder was free of the instrument and joined them, saying, "I contacted both Senators and our local representative during the holidays about the potential Congressional hearings. None had heard about Ladner's plans, but all confessed they wouldn't know until Ladner brought it up in committee or approached the House for funding. In short, we're in limbo until Ladner does something to initiate the process."

Jason said, "The NIH representative I spoke to thought it might not come until after the holiday break, but she seemed quite concerned about Ladner's inquiries. Apparently he has no appreciation for NIH and other science agencies."

"That's an understatement if Representative Wray is correct about Ladner," Snyder said. "For some reason Ladner has deep animosity toward biological science research and uses any opportunity to bash the agencies. Incidents like this charge against one of our people is just what he wants. I suspect he's one of those very conservative guys who looks for the worst in anything that might challenge his fears."

"But," Jason reminded them, "I suspect he doing this to benefit a faculty in his district. One of the people bringing charges against King is from Ladner's district and there might be a political payoff involved."

Hawthorne injected, "So he could accomplish two goals. Show support for a constituent and slam NIH. And we're caught in the middle."

Snyder, a prisoner to his schedule, glanced at his watch, and stood. "We'll have to wait and see what happens. I'd suspect if anything comes of Ladner's rumored threat, it'll happen during the third week of January when Congress gets back in session full time."

Moving toward the door, Jason said, "By then, we should have a response from King's accusers regarding our threat to them."

Jason had stewed over a nagging hunch that King's papers contained some error, based on a miscalculation, or misinterpretation of an analytical analysis. It would be easy to do when the tests were being conducted by graduate students without sufficient background to recognize a minor miscue could lead to incorrect data. He'd seen it happen several times in his own lab, but they'd been lucky to detect the error before basing a paper on flawed data.

But he didn't want to raise the issue again. King and his associates had checked and rechecked, remaining confident, almost adamant, they were correct. And having the second set of experiments run by different personnel lowered the odds a repetition of the same error had occurred. Maybe he'd have to live with King's conclusion and hope for the best.

That evening in Kathryn's apartment, they sprawled across the bed, their energies exhausted after a lengthy session of passion. She made circles on his chest, murmuring, "It's better each time. I didn't know sex could be so wonderful."

They remained still for several minutes, then Kathryn stirred. "Let's have a drink. I bought a batch of those wine coolers today. You might like one of those."

In front of the refrigerator, Kathryn volunteered. "Teaching seems to be okay. Having your notes helped a lot although I've changed them in some places." Knowing how hard he'd labored to assemble the series of lectures and not wanting her to struggle with the same task for a one-time run, Jason had brought his notebook to her on one of his visits to her place.

She handed him a glass with a vodka mixture. "But I learned something the first day. Don't wear dresses kids think are sexy. The guys followed my every movement. I felt like a stripper. Since then, I've worn either pantsuits, shapeless skirts or bulky suits."

"I should have alerted you. Remember, these young guys are overwhelmed with hormones and have limited control. They ogle every woman who reveals her true shape." He touched her shoulder. "And you capture every male's attention."

She leaned to kiss him on the cheek. "I hope to continue getting yours."

As they sipped the drinks, Jason told her about his continuing concern with King's papers. "I'm not going to ask for another review, but just trust everything is okay."

She looked at him for several seconds, seeming to realize he was probing for her opinion and perhaps help in achieving closure to his nagging hunch. "That's the thing to do. We've gone over those things too many times. It's not an error in the lab work. It's some personal or political issue being raised by Thiele and his buddy."

"I'm going to put it to rest," he said. "If I raise the issue again, hit me across the head."

"She laughed. "Or I could refuse sex."

Jason pulled her close. "And who's the loser in that game."

Kathryn held his hand as they stood as he prepared to leave. "About the experiments, if it would relieve your concern, I could bring you the lab notes and you could examine them for yourself. But I won't tell King. He'd go berserk if he thought you were still checking his work."

"If you can do that without arousing suspicion, I'd appreciate it. And thanks for understanding my strange obsession."

"One of your post-docs told me you had to be absolutely certain every detail had been covered and could be explained without equivocation. I've accepted that's part of who you are."

Jason nodded. "I know and thanks for understanding. See you at the park entrance in the morning." He kissed her forehead as their hands separated.

True to her promise Kathryn appeared at ten-thirty the next morning with the foot-high stack of lab materials. She placed her load on the conference table. "This is everything, organized by experiment and by steps within each. Please don't let Dr. King know I brought this to you. He'll fire me on the spot."

He'd intended to ask another favor but looking at her face and understanding her reluctance to do anything further in defiance of her boss, he dropped his idea, although it would mean work for someone else. He watched her walk out, an inner voice berating himself about the lack of trust in those nearest you.

Needing to find a suitable reviewer, he pulled King's personnel file, suspecting copies of his recent reprints were included as part of the annual reviews. In luck, he spread the seven publications on his desk and began to compare the citations at the end of each. Several names common to three or more appeared. In addition to Thiele and McLean, another name jumped out—Sylvia Rann, his first doctoral student now at the University of Texas. She was someone who'd have no personal interest in King's problem and someone he'd trust beyond question.

Jason found her address and telephone number in a national directory, waited until the time zone differences were appropriate, and called her. They exchanged the usual greetings and promised to get together at the national meetings in the spring.

Jason explained the threats against King and his nagging dilemma, then asked, "I know this will be a huge imposition, but I wondered if you could do this review for me and come here to do it?"

After a delay, Sylvia said, "I'd be willing to try, but it sounds like an impossibility to find an error in someone else's notes." She paused as he heard a drawer open and close, the pages turning. "I could work it out if I can use Friday and this coming weekend. My teaching commitments won't allow other days away."

Jason responded, "Come Friday or late Thursday. I'll pay your expenses and an honorarium. I'll make housing arrangements and you can do the work at the Union." Jason didn't want Sylvia around the department causing King and others who'd known her to suspect he'd rigged the review by using a former student to do his investigative work. Plus, he didn't want to get Sylvia caught in the middle of this strange affair if for some reasons questions came up about this independent critiques. He grinned at himself, a spy plotting next moves.

"That'll work. I'll fly in on Thursday night and return here on Sunday afternoon."

Jason met Sylvia at the Spencerville airport Thursday night. She had everything in her hand luggage, saving time getting to the Union. The aging structure had been upgraded and renovated several times in its history, served as a modest hotel for visitors to campus who preferred convenience to campus facilities over luxury, and contained a decent restaurant habited by faculty and their visitors.

At the check-in counter, Sylvia reminded him of her previous stay, an occasion that had brought her back for a reunion of Biology graduate students. For a moment they reminisced about that event. Then Jason followed her to her room and showed her the set of notes she would review during the next two days. He reminded her of his dilemma and the potential of being forced to reveal the basic information if Ladner pushed forward with inquiries.

She asked how he was doing and expressed regrets about Lucy, someone she'd known during her days as a student with Jason.

Leaving her, he paused to say, "I won't bother you. You know what to look for, but if you have questions, call me. And save Saturday evening for dinner at my home. I'll pick you up at five, we'll have a drink, then dinner. And you can give me your opinion or findings when I come to pick you up."

"From what you've told me, I take it you'd like no one to know I'm doing this so I'll not come by the department. But I'd like to see Dr. Hadley if that's okay."

"Feel free. And Sylvia, I appreciate your efforts."

CHAPTER 28

They stopped running a quarter mile from their separation point at the entrance to the park, now a daily routine during the work week since Boseman had been arrested. Holding gloved hands, Jason said, "I'll see you tonight and I'd like you to come to dinner at the house on Saturday evening. I'll pick you up around five."

"That's nice." She leaned against him momentarily, then jogged toward her apartment, an easy pace along the sidewalk. Jason watched her until she turned the corner, two blocks from her place.

At four on Saturday afternoon, Jason met with Sylvia in her room at the Union. He'd called her room to be sure she was ready, purchased soft drinks from the café, and climbed the three flights of stairs.

Sylvia was prepared, but sipped the drink first, then said, "I've been through everything and rechecked the calculations. I found two minor discrepancies, but nothing that affects the outcome. As best I can tell, everything was done well. The lab notes are what you'd expect with several smudges and crossouts, but you know that happens routinely. There's no reason to suspect tampering with the data of the second experiment. First, it's not clean enough to have been fabricated and it's clear the people doing the second group of tests had more difficulty and had to repeat steps, but it's documented well and in the end yielded reliable data."

"So bottom line, you're comfortable with the conclusions." He placed the drink container in the waste basket.

"Their data support what they published, but it goes against the prevailing thinking."

"As I understand the area, the theory is not yet firmly established is it?"

Sylvia shook her head, her blond hair moving slightly, a motion he remembered from her student days. "You're correct. It's evolving, but King's paper contradicts it to the extent several investigators will be forced to rethink their ideas. King's paper presents a new perspective that will result in modifications of the commonly accepted theory." She smiled and added, "Just the way science is supposed to evolve to come to the ultimate truth, according to one of your lectures to me during graduate school."

"I still give the same lecture. What about your own work? Going okay?"

"King's publication won't affect me at all. I've been examining another piece of the puzzle and I've used many of the same lab techniques. That's why I'm cited in King's papers"

"Sylvia, your conclusion relieves my mind a great deal. I have been stewing about this for weeks, thinking there must be some flaw King and his associates can't see because they're too close to the techniques."

"I believe I've reassembled everything in the order you gave it to me. I'm pleased I could help. Consider it a down payment on the lessons you taught me. They've served me well."

Jason stood and picked up the stack of King's documents. "If you need a minute to do anything before we go, I'll wait downstairs."

"I'd like to change. Give me five minutes."

On the way to Kathryn's Jason said, "We're picking up Kathryn Helweg who was one of the co-authors. She's a post-doc with King and we've been running together since last fall. I'd like you to keep my next comment in confidence, but the fact is, we're attracted to each other and our relationship is growing."

Sylvia eyed his face from the passenger side, no doubt thinking he'd rushed into another relationship very rapidly. She tested his reaction. "It must have been very difficult when Lucy died. Such a shock to everyone who knew her."

"The truth is, I'm not over that yet. I wake up in the middle of the night, start thinking about her and what I might have done to prevent the idiot from shooting at us. I tried to rationalize there was nothing I could have foreseen, but deep down I keep wondering."

"Because those things occur so rarely in the world in which we academics live and work. So Kathryn is filling a void in your life."

"That's a way to think about it, but I believe it's more."

"Be careful," Sylvia said, reaching to touch his arm. "I have a friend who remarried too soon. Now she regrets doing so and knows she reacted to meet a need. She calls it the rebound effect."

"I've heard of that and I'm trying not to fall into that situation. Each time I interact with Kathryn, I feel more confident we're going to be okay."

In the car after they picked up Kathryn, Sylvia and Kathryn were quiet after Jason introduced them, reminded Kathryn of Sylvia's place in his past and her career progress. "She was my first graduate student and I couldn't have had anyone better. She did some fine work on the Wilson's project. And she's the person I asked to review your data books."

From the rear seat, Kathryn asked, "I'm eager to know if you discovered anything you'd consider incorrect?"

Sylvia twisted to look toward Kathryn. "I told Dr. Spradlin a few minutes ago, I didn't see anything out of order. And I spent the most of two days checking everything. My opinion is the work is excellent, although it suggests a different conclusion than most of the literature. I'd stick by your approach and see where it leads."

Kathryn responded. "That's good news." She laughed. "That's what I have been telling Jason for two months. Nevertheless, I understood his concern to be certain."

"You should know that's the manner in which he works. I remember his probing my data to find flaws, my thinking I could never meet his expectations. But in the end, I realized it was for my own education."

Jason said, "Hey guys, I'm right here listening to your analyses." He pulled into the driveway of his house.

Jason introduced Sylvia to the children and Mrs. Carter. The kids ran to Kathryn, grabbing her around the legs, almost toppling her in their enthusiasm.

The evening progressed nicely, Sylvia telling them about her life in Texas, and Kathryn leading the kids off to read a story just before they disappeared for the night. During the time Sylvia and Jason were alone, she said, "Kathryn is beautiful. I understand why you're attracted. She's also nice and your children like her."

"Is that a tip that we'll be okay?"

"I'm not the ideal person to tell you, but I suspect it is. If she comes into your life as you seem to expect, the children's feelings are important. This from a biologist, not a marriage counselor."

On the following Tuesday the wait for the Congressional shoe to drop was confirmed to be over when Nancy Thompson called. "I wanted to let you know we heard this morning that Ladner has been given the go-ahead to hold hearings."

"Any idea of how soon?"

"We're guessing a couple of weeks. It'll take that long to get things arranged, people called to testify, all the trappings put in place."

She continued, "Ladner convinced his colleagues to fund these hearings on the basis of saving money by rooting out corruption in the scientific community. My guess is Ladner intends to publicize the short-comings of scientists and their waste of public funds as nothing more than a ruse to gain fame for themselves. I suspect Preston King will be one of the first called because of this connection between Ladner and Thiele. No doubt others will be called, but Jason, I think his stated goal might be nothing more than a smoke screen, so the focus on King isn't too obvious. We expect one or two of our project managers will be called to explain our failure to detect flaws in the progress reports."

"Everybody but the politicians know that would be impossible if an investigator were trying to cover up something."

Nancy said, "You're right, even though we do discover discrepancies at times, those are primarily honest errors or plain negligence. When we know more, I'll let you know. If my guess is on target about timing, King may get a subpoena in the next week. You may wish to alert him."

After replacing the receiver and thinking about King, Jason walked to the window and stared across the campus, still a few piles of snow from the heavy accumulation before Christmas. Thinking about King's reluctance to face the issue, his first thought was to let the subpoena arrive without warning and shake him up a bit. But he knew the right thing to do was to alert him and support him through this coming ordeal. He knew Henry Rogers would have taken the latter tack.

He turned away from the window and walked into the hall toward King's lab.

Vicki Sanchez was waiting at the outer door when Jason returned from his lab where he'd been conferring with a graduate student about a question of methodology. His technician had tried to help, but had not succeeded in ironing out the problem. It turned out to be a misreading of the journal article in which the procedure had been published.

A slight tremble in her voice, Vicki said, "Do you have a minute. I came by on the off-chance I could see you for a few minutes." Jason noted the rumpled slacks and blouse, her hair tousled as though she'd not combed it for days. Her face was drawn and colorless, void of make-up. Her eyes rimmed with shadowy circles as though sleep had been an alien experience for days.

"Come to this vacant seminar room." He led her a few steps down the hall, opened the door, flipped on the lights and motioned to a chair. He sat in the chair next to her.

Vicki clasped her hands together, glanced at Jason, said, "I'm concerned Dr. Harris is doing what I was afraid would happen."

Thinking she would elaborate, Jason waited, but after a silence during which she continued to stare at the floor, he asked, "Can you be specific?"

Vicki hesitated, then blurted. "Three of us graduate students are giving papers at the society meetings in April. Yesterday, Dr. Harris told me he couldn't provide travel funds for me. I know he's supporting the others. I stewed about the problem last night and finally decided I should talk to you again."

"Did he give a reason for not paying your expenses?"

"He said there wasn't travel money in the grant I'm on. That's all he would say."

Jason acknowledged that could be correct. Often grants didn't permit travel or perhaps Harris had exhausted the funds. But it was unusual to ask a student to present a paper without some support. He'd been approached twice in the past month by faculty asking for travel

311

money for graduate students from departmental operating funds. He asked, "How have things been otherwise?"

Her face in a frown. "Cold, distant. He talks to me only when he has to. There's no hint of any connection between us. It's as though I'm a robot doing his bidding."

"I assume there's been no further suggestions about a relationship outside the lab?"

Vicki seemed to struggle with her thoughts. "He's never mentioned it since you met with him. He treats the incident as though nothing happened, that the entire episode was only my imagination. But things are definitely different. Dr. Spradlin, the flirtations were easier to cope with."

"Has he demanded more work from you or given you a hard time about your performance?"

"He expects a lot from all of us." She seemed to consider the question for a moment. "I don't think he's asked me to do more than the others, but I work a lot of hours." She crossed one dirty white walking shoe over her knee, baggy brown socks mottled by drops of chemical reagents, a typical characteristic of lab workers.

"More than the other students?"

"I'm in the lab more than anyone else, but I've passed it off as my being slow and methodical." A slight smile as she contemplated the situation. "I haven't minded. I'm learning things which is why I'm here."

Jason asked. "What do you want me to do. Talk to Dr. Harris again or . . . . ?"

"I don't want to irritate him more. It's important I give this paper, but I don't have the money to get to the meetings." She left the obvious hanging.

Jason stood. "I'll check around without talking to Dr. Harris and somewhere I'll find the money to pay your expenses. I'll get back to you in a couple of days."

As he closed the seminar room door, Vicki said, "Thanks, Dr. Spradlin. I'm sorry to keep bothering you." She turned away, her retreating steps not making a sound on the tile floor.

Jason went directly to Miriam's office, a small space opening off the departmental suite, always cluttered with stacks of computer printouts, legers, invoices, and myriad other accounting papers. He closed the door behind him causing Miriam to look up at the unusual action.

Jason said, "Miriam, I'm going to ask you something I don't like doing, but it may be important. Tell me if Dr. Harris has travel funds in the grant on which Vicki Sanchez has an assistantship and how much is remaining."

Her face blank, she turned toward her computer. "Just a minute until I find the account. She punched in numbers, moved through several screens, eyed the results, then wrote numbers on a note pad and handed it to Jason. Eight hundred dollars for travel had been granted. None had been used or encumbered to date.

Digesting the numbers, Jason considered his options, then asked, "How much overhead was allocated to the same grant?"

She flipped to another screen. "Nine thousand, four hundred dollars."

"I'd like you to transfer the department's percentage now rather than on the usual quarterly basis and I'll want to reimburse Vicki Sanchez for expenses to a meeting from those funds."

Then thinking Vicki probably wouldn't have sufficient money to purchase an air ticket, he added, "Let her buy the air ticket directly rather than spend her own money and wait for a reimbursement."

Harris wouldn't give attention to the overhead item, since it was common practice for the department to take one-third of the indirect costs allocated on a formula basis to cover administrative costs for the research, the cost of accounting representing one item. Jason remembered the debate about the policy; investigators arguing they should have all the indirect costs and Henry standing firm that the department incurred expenses related to grants. As a final thrust, Henry reminded them he had the right to take it all and use it for the good of the unit.

Miriam wrote numbers on a pad. "When she comes by with the information, I'll work it out for her."

Jason reached across the desk to touch her hand. "Thanks, Miriam. It's a tricky situation." He knew he could depend on her discretion. Small, gray-haired, blue eyes, keen mind, Miriam could find errors in accounts faster than anyone he'd ever seen.

He put a note in the department mail to Sanchez to see Miriam when she knew the cost of her ticket. Then he scribbled a note on the yellow pad—talk to Harris about Sanchez.

314

He vowed to not allow Harris to play games with a promising student, scratching her way through school, depending on the department to keep promises and act like professionals.

CHAPTER 29

Jason's focus on a memo from Dean Hawthorne regarding a review of the process of arriving at tenure decisions fell aside when Audrey buzzed his line. "Brenda Fallon from Redlake is on the line."

Brenda's familiar voice saying, "Cynthia and I are on the line. We've read your proposal. It looks good to us."

Recalling his reservations and the struggle he'd had in coming to closure, he asked, "No second thoughts about this venture?"

"No, we're gearing up to start."

Cynthia's alto voice. "This is Cynthia. We've found the breed and the specific line we'll start with. We've purchased a dozen sows and two boars."

"You're moving fast. I assume I should get prepared to harvest embryos and refine the lab process." Another note on the pad to get with Roy Blount, the first year post-doc from Colorado, who'd done the background work.

"By all means," Cynthia continued to lead the discussion. "We'd thought if you or someone could come at the right time to obtain the embryos, Eric and I would come to the University for a couple of weeks while that phase is starting up. We'd like to see how it's done."

"I'll line my people up and you let us know when the sows become pregnant. Remember we'll need to move fast since we want cells around the second or third day."

"Remind me how critical is the timing?"

"Very much. We have to retrieve embryos during the blastocystic stage of development." Jason considered the time implications of travel and setting up at Redlake. "Tell you what to do to be on the safe side. Call us as soon as the mating has occurred. We may want to be there by the second day following to conduct some tests. Right now, I think day three at the latest. We'll know better after our first efforts."

Cynthia concluded. "We're probably a month away, but we'll give you adequate notice."

"Sounds good." Jason dropped the receiver gently, thinking Redlake would alert them three or four days ahead. He'd better get moving on the preliminaries although Roy had told him a week ago they were ready. He wanted to check it out to be certain, then grinned to himself remembering Sylvia's and Kathryn's comments about his ultra caution. But thinking about a potential breakthrough was much more exciting then dealing with Harris' behavior or King's issue.

He was still thinking about the conversation with Redlake and making notes about the logistics of starting the project when Stella Krause called. "Jason, I'm sending you copies of the letters I received from McLean and Thiele. Actually from their lawyers and as you'd expect, they reject any hint of wrong-doing and warning us any action on our part will be met with a countersuit. The usual stuff in these situations."

Trying to shift gears from a stimulating project to a worrisome threat led him to say, "I'm expecting King to be called to testify before

318

a House committee any day now. Should someone from your office go with him when he appears?"

"He should have counsel, although as I understand these Congressional hearings, there likely would not be discussions or crosses while he's being questioned. And, you realize you might be called as his immediate supervisor. That happens if they're really trying to place blame on the university."

"I've thought about the possibility but crossed it off as unlikely."

"From what you tell me about the thrust of Ladner's quest, the fact that you were mentioned in the letters to Thiele and McLean increases the potential for your being called to testify. I'm sure you didn't expect that outcome, but it could happen. And they could ask anyone associated with the research in question to accompany King. They'd try to use those associates to cast doubt on his work."

They ended the conversation with Jason trying to suppress a feeling the entire process could be a circus with media swarming over and around everyone in their typical search for a public figure under fire. He couldn't think of a positive attribute to be associated with the event, one he likely couldn't avoid other than disappearing into a foreign country.

An opportunity to confront Harris about Vicki Sanchez came more easily and in a format Jason had not remotely considered when Harris' graduate students presented their work at the weekly departmental seminar. Jason sat in the second row and watched as the three nervously went through the ritual of appearing before the entire faculty, the meeting space crowded with most of the graduate students and post-docs in the department attending. Jason recalled the trauma of those sessions and felt some empathy for the young professionals in training.

Vicki Sanchez, the last of the speakers, came across as thoroughly prepared and presented her material without a hitch, seemingly to have memorized the talk, referring to slides showing data and graphs without a stumble. She appeared poised and confident, although Jason suspected she had inner jitters. Following the unstated custom of dressing better for the seminar, Vicki wore a dark skirt, sweater, and black pumps. She was an attractive young woman when she abandoned the usual slacks and rumpled shirt, arranged her hair, and used a bit of make-up.

Jason watched Harris at intervals during Vicki's presentation. His eyes seemed glued to her as she moved from the podium to point out a cogent point on a slide and then back to the security of the podium and her notes.

At the end of the seminar the students collected their slides and gathered notes while Harris waited, smiling and apparently feeling good the session had gone well. Jason walked to him and said, "They did well. Interesting work, also."

"They've worked hard," Harris responded, "and are doing well with all aspects of the program."

"I understand they're giving papers at the national meeting in a few weeks." Jason watched Harris' face for some reaction, but he remained impassive, any implication passing by.

"That's right. I hope they do as well there as they did today. " Harris still didn't bite on Jason's invitation to discuss Vicki's situation, although he knew department heads signed off on travel requests.

"This was good practice for them," Jason said, then pushing his agenda a bit further, he continued, "I assume you're able to support them all."

Jason detected a slight coloring of his cheeks, but Harris's expression didn't change. "It's no problem. They're all on some grant or I'll do it from my overhead pot."

"Just thought if there's a problem, the department might be able to help." He walked toward the students, wondering if Harris had made the connection between Sanchez and his query. A couple of days would reveal the answer.

Jason said to the three students, now leaving the room. "You did well. Good luck at the meeting."

"Thanks, Dr. Spradlin." A chorus, not quite in unison coordinated with looks of surprise he would even bother to comment.

Moving through the door, Vicki hung back and said softly, "Thanks for your note."

"I suspect it'll work out okay. I expect Dr. Harris will come through in the next couple of days. If he doesn't, see Miriam for help."

Walking together along the hall, Jason said, "You look nice today." Then he immediately wondered if he'd stepped over a line with her.

Vicki smiled, the first time Jason had seen her radiance. "I have a couple of decent outfits for such occasions. Can't risk ruining them in the lab." She touched his arm and walked down the opposite corridor.

Feeling good about the entire episode, Jason wanted to congratulate himself for finessing his way through the morass of personal relationships and departmental politics. Or, maybe sheer luck had intervened this time. And the final word had yet to arrive.

Now after five o'clock and the department dark and silent, Jason thumbed through the stack of afternoon mail. Copies of the responses from Thiele and McLean were on top. He shoved those into the King file after confirming Stella's version of their replies. A letter from George Stuart, outlining the tentative schedules for the four final candidates for the department head's position and confirmed his two days of trial were a month away. He would be the last of the four, a slot he preferred.

With mixed feelings about the correct protocol, he concluded he should be absent when the others came for interviews. He'd heard of them all and knew one reasonably well, yet he didn't want his presence to offer a potential conflict with the outsiders. The downside of not meeting with them might be if he had to work under one of them, he'd like to know their general philosophy about leadership positions and perhaps detect quirks residing within their personality. But out of sight might be the better option for him. He'd have Audrey work on his schedule. Or perhaps days in the library would be valuable—catch up on recent tissues of journals or work on lectures and class materials.

Kathryn appeared at the park entrance at the usual time several days after Jason had spoken with Nancy Thompson about the Ladner hearings. She handed Jason a letter, obviously sent by registered mail. "This came in the mail just before five yesterday."

Jason scanned the page in the semi-darkness. Two weeks hence Kathryn was to appear before the House Committee for Science and Technology and alerted her to be prepared to appear on subsequent days or until notified she would no longer be needed. He folded the sheet along the creased lines and returned it to her.

"Dr. King got the same letter." She stuffed the paper into her pocket as they began to jog along the asphalt trail that wound through the park. The park service maintained the path in good condition and plowed the snow off as needed during the winter months. Street lights mounted at intervals provided sufficient illumination for early morning runners and walkers.

"How did King take it?"

"He disappeared into his office, closed the door for over an hour, then walked out without saying a word to anyone. Jason, I didn't like the way he reacted. I wanted someone to give me advice, but he couldn't help. And you were in those meetings with the Dean. I almost called you at home last night, but decided I shouldn't be such a baby and wait until morning to tell you."

"How about Robert Tanaka?"

"No, he didn't get one."

"I expect he will today, and so will everyone else who's been involved with either of those papers." Fifty yards later, he added, "And I expect to be called also."

They ran in silence for twenty minutes, the cold air exhilarating, their thinking occupied with the unknown ordeal confronting them in the near future. Jason worried about King and how he would handle himself in the public glare with most looking toward him as guilty of criminal behavior. King needed support, but Jason wasn't sure how to give it when King interpreted every overture as another blow to his fragile integrity. He glanced at Kathryn's face, her lips set in determination. She would be the stronger of the two when the Congressman or their appointed lawyers quizzed them about misconduct. But King couldn't avoid an appearance.

Coming toward the end of their route, they slowed to a steady walk. Through his heavy breathing, Jason said, "I'll get everyone together with the university attorneys in a couple of days and decide how we best handle our testimonies."

Kathryn grasped his hand and reminded him. "Tonight is our time together." They had settled on getting together in her apartment at least three times weekly, but varied the days to avoid anyone discovering an established routine.

"I won't forget." Their private times together had been wonderful. In addition to the sex, they talked about their past, their families, childhood adventures, and tried to avoid discussing work. The more they shared, the better he felt about the long-term. And memories of Lucy became less vivid and less frequent. He no longer jerked awake in the early morning hours thinking about her and the sights and sounds of their life together.

Jason's letter came in the morning mail. He asked Audrey to find out through either King or Kathryn who had been notified about appearing and to set up a session with Stella Krause as soon as possible.

Comparing the dates for Ladner's hearings, Jason discovered the Washington appearance would occur during the visit of one of the outside candidates, and if the ordeal dragged, perhaps two of them. A prolonged session seemed likely as politicians relished every opportunity to be in front of cameras and in the center of the public eye.

In Kathryn's apartment, she and Jason sat close on the couch. He confirmed he'd been subpoenaed by Ladner and would probably be expected to reveal how as King's supervisor he allowed such outrageous behavior from a senior faculty member.

She leaned against him. "We'll get through this. In my mind we've done nothing wrong."

"I agree with you and will not accept anything less then Ladner's admission he'd been wrong in stirring this up. Not to mention those bozos who initiated the conflict."

Jason pulled her close, kissed her on the lips.

Kathryn leaned away. "I hope you will agree to my next request." She looked into his eyes for several seconds as though her question might pose a dilemma. "I'd like you to meet my parents soon. I've told them about us and things about you. They've asked that we come there soon."

She'd obviously thought through the logistics. "I know your interview dates will be just before the FASEB meetings in Chicago. That ordeal will be behind you. Now, could you go with me to Minneapolis at the close of those meetings. We'd spend two days, one of which is Saturday, then fly back on Sunday. And no one from State would know."

"I'll be honored to do that. Then you'll know if you have parental approval for our togetherness."

"Everything in my being tells me we're together for a long time, parental approval of not." She kissed him, her lips open, her hand pulling his head to hers.

CHAPTER 30

The group from State University found their way to the large room scheduled for the opening session of the Congressional hearings, guided by Stella Krause who'd been in the Rayburn House building previously and had a general idea of the location. They'd walked from a small hotel arranged for their stay by Congressman Wray's office, an associate suggesting it would meet their purposes and would less likely attract media people than the major hotels near the capitol and adjacent buildings.

Stella led Jason, Preston King, Kathryn Helweg, Robert Tanaka, James Ho, and Cedric Talifero, the graduate student who'd worked on the second experiment, through the huge marble halls to the third floor, an auditorium-like space. Across the front of the room and facing the audience elevated tiers of seats had been arranged behind a polished wood structure designed to give the Congressmen and their aides a sense of security and privacy. Arriving fifteen minutes ahead of the announced beginning time, they entered the space already crowded with television cameras, wires and cables running along the floor. Congressional aides rushed about, placing papers at the seats for the members of the committee.

With the help of an usher, Stella guided them to the section of seats reserved for those to be called for testimony. She pointed out the small table with a microphone where the individual would sit while testifying.

327

At five before the hour, King nudged Jason and pointed to three men taking seats at the far side of the room. "Thiele, McLean, and probably their attorney. Thiele is the short one. McLean, the tall blond."

As he glanced around them, Jason saw Nancy Thompson arrive with three others whom he assumed were NIH staffers. With people still milling around, he made his way to them and shook Nancy's hand. "Well, this will be interesting and maybe disastrous for us."

"You can never tell how these will go," she said. "Usually the opening session is taken up by speeches from the committee members. And they'll all insist on their time before the cameras." An underlying note of disdain for the whole affair revealed itself in her tone.

As she spoke, three Congressmen found their places with name plates in front of their chairs. Ladner, sitting in the middle of the table, banged a gavel, adjusted the microphone in front of him, and announced, "Hearings on the conduct of scientists are in order before the House Committee on Science and Technology." Jason had the impression of a large, almost obese man, but he hadn't observed him when he came in and now could only see his upper body.

Ladner looked at his papers. "This committee has become increasingly concerned about the number of incidents in which scientists have published papers found to be based on incorrect information, some of which was outright manufactured, to bring notoriety to the individual. Much of this reprehensible behavior occurs when the researcher is being supported by public funds and results in this committee and the entire Congress rethinking our positions about

328

the worth of research. Our goal during these hearings is to ferret out such individuals, cut off their supply of funds, and make the public aware of the misdeeds of those who hold the public and the Congress in contempt."

Ladner turned a page of notes and continued, glancing toward the cameras as often as possible without losing his place on the script. He rambled on for a twenty minutes, his tone expressing outrage and dismay at the antics of rogues posing as legitimate scientists seeking the truth. Running out of steam, Ladner stopped his diatribe and turned to the representative on his right who repeated much of what Ladner had said. As soon as he completed his opening, he gathered his notes and eased through a rear exit, having made his mark for the day.

Ladner yielded the microphone to the man on his left. Congressman Wilke started, but his opening took a different tack. "While the distinguished chair is correct we're concerned about the conduct of science, let me be clear that the opposition party will not condone a witch hunt. Several elements associated with the organization of these proceedings suggest that's what we're about, rather than a sincere effort to confirm the ground rules for the behavior of investigators. My experience tells me scientists don't require our help in maintaining appropriate conduct, but ask only that we stay out of their way and provide support for worthy investigations in the public interest."

While Wilke talked, two other congressmen took seats at the table while aides continued to move about, shuffling papers, whispering to each other, coming and going through doors behind the podium. Jason recalled Nancy's comment about a circus.

By the time all members had presented an opening statement, the morning had disappeared. Ladner announced a recess until two this afternoon.

Stella led the group to a cafeteria on the lower floor of the building. They proceeded along a line of assorted dishes and assembled at a table Stella had grabbed for them. Edging along the serving line together, Kathryn said to Jason, "Well, that was a boring exercise, wasn't it?"

He touched her back. "It's what I expected. A lot of posturing and posing for the media. This afternoon might be more interesting." He placed a salad on his tray.

The table remained almost without conversation as the State University delegation thought about the coming ordeal. Stella reminded them to stay on course as they'd discussed back on campus.

At five before two, Ladner and two other members appeared with the usual array of aides scurrying around in the background. Banging his gavel to initiate the afternoon session, Ladner announced that Dr. Reginald McLean would make a statement. He reminded the audience, primarily media types, that statements would be limited to twenty minutes to be followed by questions from committee members or the committee's counsel.

Jason observed closely as the lanky McLean moved to the witness table, arranged his notes, and adjusted the mike.

McLean began, his voice shaky for the initial few seconds, then settling into a monotone. "Congressman Ladner and distinguished members, I appreciate the opportunity to appear before you for the express purpose of publicly identifying an offending group of investigators who are an example of the scurrilous behavior of many in the scientific community today." He paused to gather his breath after the lengthy opening.

Jason noticed King shift and shuffle his feet as McLean continued. "In July of last year, Dr. Preston King and his collaborators at State University published a paper in the *Journal of Cell Biology* which was based on false data. Even after another researcher and I challenged his findings, he persisted and actually published a second paper which he claims confirmed the initial finding. Dr. King maintains his work is valid, although we have tried on several occasions through the established mechanism afforded scientists to set the record straight. Jason noted the blatant deviation from the truth about the actions of McLean and Thiele. He saw King scribble a note in his script.

Jason realized cameras were scanning the faces of the State University delegation, but he couldn't see a monitor from where he sat. King's eyes were glued to the floor. Others focused on the back of McLean's head and shoulders.

Looking up to Ladner, McLean concluded, "We appreciate the time this important committee has given us and the leadership of Congressman Ladner in organizing these hearings. We are pleased to contribute to their efforts in rooting out unethical behavior. It hurts all who labor in discovering the truth." He closed his folder and leaned back in his chair, having delivered the message from the innocent.

Ladner pulled the mike closer and said, "This committee thanks Dr. McLean for his testimony and for bringing this serious matter to our attention."

Ladner scanned his notes, then asked, "Dr. McLean, tell the committee what actions you took when you learned of the publication in question?"

McLean shifted the mike. "We wrote letters to the editor of the journal and requested he obtain a retraction or correction from King and his associates."

"And what happened? Did Dr. King respond?"

"Nothing happened. He ignored the request." McLean paused, then stated, "His refusal to pull the paper only confirmed his misdeed."

Ladner glanced around the room. "And you're absolutely certain the conclusions in the paper were wrong?"

"It goes against all current thinking. King is the only one who has published these kind of data."

When Ladner seemed to have exhausted his queries, Wilke coughed, waited for a nod from the Chair, and asked, "Did you confirm by experimentation that King's data were incorrect?"

"We didn't need to. There's too much in the literature confirming he's wrong."

Wilke's voice took on a sterner tone. "So you assumed he's wrong just because he doesn't agree with the prevailing thinking?" The broad features of Wilke exuded power. His gray eyes seem to bore into McLean who squirmed as though the chair was no longer comfortable.

McLean almost stood, raising his frame to maximum height in the chair. "It's more than an assumption, Congressman. Both Dr. Thiele and I know King's data can't be right. So does everyone working in this field."

Wilke persisted. "I've always been told that science works through these seemingly unexplained findings to eventually discover the real facts. Maybe King's paper is something to be worked through and to determine how his data fit the larger picture."

"It's too far off base," McLean complained, hints of defensiveness showing for the first time. "If we set out to find what he did or how his data fit, it would set the entire field back five years. It'd also mean some of the top investigators in the area would have wasted a lot of effort."

"And if King is correct, that may be the thing to do. If you ignore his work, all of you could be heading down a blind alley. And what a waste that would be." Wilke almost dared McLean to disagree by leaning forward and staring down into the scientist's face, then yielded to Ladner.

Alexander Thiele was called and went through the same litany as McLean.

At the conclusion of his formal presentation, Ladner asked, "Dr. Thiele, remind the committee how you and Dr. McLean are collaborators."

Thiele shuffled at the table for a moment. "We've worked together for several years, have shared projects supported by NIH, and have frequently co-authored papers."

"Thus, you have the same view as McLean about the King papers?"

"I do. We are both certain King is wrong. Initially I believed he'd made an honest error, but when he refused to retract his paper, I concluded he had made an error and refused to admit it, or he had published manufactured data and intended to stick it out."

Ladner smiled, reached for the gavel, but Wilke intervened. "Mr. Chairman, I'd like to ask a question." Ladner scowled but nodded his assent.

Wilke stopped Thiele who had begun to rise. "Haven't you made a big deal out of what may either be a simple laboratory error or a publication which you can't fit into your scheme of things?"

Thiele almost yelped. "No, we know we're right and King's paper is wrong."

"So why can't you leave it stand and continue your work. Won't other scientists ignore King's conclusions if they believe it's erroneous or if they can't figure out how it fits? This won't be the first time an error has found its way into the literature."

Thiele squirmed for a several seconds, his eyes looking toward Ladner. When relief didn't come, he muttered, "We don't want others led astray by King's work. We want it out of the literature."

Wilke stood, lifting the mike to his face, stared at Thiele for a moment as challenging him to stop griping, then stated, "I admire your efforts to protect other investigators, but your self-righteous attitude seems more self-serving than one intended to support others." He placed the mike on the table and walked through the door.

Ladner banged the gavel. "Hearings will resume at nine tomorrow morning."

Jason remained seated watching the portly Ladner descend a set of steps at one end of the rostrum to shake hands with Thiele and McLean. The Congressman's round face gleamed as he offered congratulations on their performances. When Ladner turned toward the State group, most of whom were standing and talking to each other, Jason met his eyes, returning his stare until Thiele distracted Ladner.

Near the exit into the hall, Stella said so each could hear, "Have dinner on your own, but let's meet in the hotel conference room at nine. I'd like to review what's happened and check our strategy for tomorrow, our day before the committee." She smiled into their intent faces. "Maybe tomorrow night we can celebrate."

As Jason waited at the door for Kathryn, Nancy Thompson handed him a note. "You'll be interested in this."

CHAPTER 31

In his room Jason pulled the folded sheet of paper given him by Thompson. She'd written. "One of Ladner's aides has been reviewing the record of grants given to your department. There's an implied threat of pulling support and/or not allowing us to fund pending proposals. Talk to you when I can confirm." 'Nancy' scrawled at the bottom.

He phoned Kathryn's room. Her voice on he line, he said, "Stella wants to have dinner with me. I told her you would join us."

"Is it okay? I won't be interfering?"

"No, it's fine. We're meeting in the lobby at six-fifteen."

Realizing it was still not five in Spencerville, he called his office. After talking with Audrey for five minutes and being told there were no urgent problems, he reread the note from Thompson, wondering what latitude Ladner really had in interfering with the NIH staff. He'd talk to Stella who knew more about the political world than he did or cared to learn.

Kathryn was staring into a display case of clothing available in the hotel shop when Jason walked off the elevator. She closed the distance between them, touched his hand, and said, "If this is not okay, tell me. I saw Stella go to the newsstand."

"I want you to come." He wanted to kiss her, but refrained from a public display bound to travel back to State. Her perfume reminding him of her closeness conflicted with their mutual resolve to avoid any hint of their relationship.

Stella approached saying, "Nothing in the afternoon papers about the hearing. Not enough interest or the session ran too long for the deadlines. Ladner will be upset if there's nothing in the morning editions."

Stella continued her role of guide. "If you don't have a special place in mind, there's a small Italian restaurant in the next block if you don't mind going out of the hotel."

In the cold early evening with darkness causing street lights to pop on, they walked along a narrow street, cars lined bumper to bumper leaving the downtown area at the close of work. Most drivers had cell phones jammed against their ears as their vehicles crept forward like cripples learning to walk again.

The quaint little restaurant had only three other couples this early in the evening. The genial host led them to a table along the wall, linen and silver giving an aura of uniqueness. He lighted candles as they watched, took their drink orders and disappeared in a flurry.

Drinks before them, gin and tonics for the women, Scotch and soda for him, Jason handed Stella the note and observed her reaction as she scanned it. He passed it to Kathryn and asked, "Tell me what you think?"

Stella sipped her drink. "Ladner is a real bastard when he thinks he can get away with throwing his power around. And it's these kind of antics he often tries."

"Can he really suspend our support?" He took the note back from Kathryn and shoved it into his coat pocket.

"I'd doubt it," Stella shook her head. "But agencies are always kow-towing to committee chairs because of the funding issues. Some of these guys will go to any length to force an agency to do their biding about some special interest."

"Like holding up their budgets?"

"That's a key area, but it could be insisting pet projects in their district receive priority over others, even when the peer review process has recommended against a specific activity."

Jason voiced a thought he'd harbored all afternoon since he'd witnessed the treatment of Thiele and McLean by Ladner. "Any chance the charges against King are in this realm? Is Ladner trying to obtain some special treatment for these two, one of whom is in his district?"

"Jason," Stella said, a smile breaking across her face, "you always surprise me by seeing possibilities before anyone else. You're right, it could be his motivation."

Her smile evolving into a chuckle, she turned to Kathryn. "Watch him. He's always ahead of the rest of us." For an instant Jason wondered if Stella had observed his behavior toward Kathryn as something beyond a professional role, but dismissed her comment as nothing more than a playful aside.

Under the table, Kathryn's foot nudged his leg and rested there. "I know. I'll be careful."

The waitress, black dress and white collar in concert with the motif of the place, recommended a salmon and pasta special. All agreed, differencing only in preferences of dressings on the side salads. Stella suggested a white wine as appropriate.

"Who is Wilke?" Kathryn asked, after the orders were completed.

"Wilke," Stella said, "is a long-time House member from Maine and is the ranking minority member on the committee. In fact, until elections two years ago, he was the chairman. He's quite knowledgeable about science issues and has been a strong supporter for increased funding for basic research. Science agencies have great respect for him."

Jason said, "I'd guess he's not so much for our position as he is against this witch hunt by Ladner."

"I'd agree," Stella said. "I'm glad he's attending. He'll keep Ladner focused. Left to his own devices, Ladner could become aggressive in trying to prove King cheated or take the discussions on a tangent to generate publicity."

Ladner has already decided," Kathryn mumbled, "that we did something devious."

Stella sipped her wine, nodding in approval. "Probably you're right, but we still have our day."

Her comment caused Jason to think about King who was key to presenting their case. Turning to Kathryn, he asked, "Do you know what Dr. King is doing for dinner?"

340

"He planned to order from room service. The others were going out to a place Robert knew about."

"I ask because I'm concerned he's holed up alone brooding about this threat and losing his capacity to focus on his response. If he sticks to our plan, he'll be okay. If he doesn't, ..." He left the obvious unsaid and reached for his wine glass.

The audience was substantially larger as the hearings convened promptly at nine the next morning. Publicity in the morning editions had sparked interest by the attendance of eight Congressmen. Jason was pleased Wilke was in his spot.

Ladner went through the preliminaries, giving essentially the same speech he'd given on the opening day, then announced, "Dr. Preston King from State University is called to testify in rebuttal to statements presented yesterday." Jason noted the absence of thanks or any gesture of appreciation by Ladner in stark contrast to his bowing and scraping for Thiele and McLean.

King's mouth was set in a firm line without evidence of any feelings as though being led to his final judgment ordeal. He moved in long strides to the witness table, pulled the microphone closer. Still not looking at anyone, he opened his folder and started. "I appreciate the opportunity to appear and give my version of the events associated with the two papers in question. I call attention to the presence of staff from my research group who were involved with the experiments and suggest each one of them will be able to confirm each phase of our actions. In addition, Dr. Jason Spradlin, my department head who has known from the outset about the controversy, is present and will support my testimony. Our goal is to set the record straight." Jason relaxed and smiled inwardly at King's strong opening, steady voice, now making eye contact with committee members, no hesitation or equivocation.

King referred to the script he'd prepared last week including the modifications suggested by Stella and Jason. King reviewed the sequence of events without apology for not responding to Brumfield's request for a rebuttal to the letters.

His eyes on the committee members, he said, "Dr's Thiele and McLain want you to believe they followed the typical protocol in disagreeing with my paper. They did not. When I did not respond to their charges, they withdrew their letters to the editor. Those were never published. We received copies through the editor but their names and affiliations had been blocked out. Only later when Dr. Spradlin persisted, were we provided copies with all the identification intact."

King told the committee about the second experiment and the efforts made in his lab to clearly separate the analysts to achieve an independent set of data. King stuck to his notes, speaking precisely and objectively, not bothered by the constant movement of aides, whispers to congressmen, passing of papers, nor the apparent inattention of the committee members. He was coming across as professional, confident, without hint of defensiveness.

He concluded by saying, "I knew other investigators would challenge the first experiment because the conclusions demonstrate

342

clearly we've not accounted for the specific role of calcium in this biological process. Thus much of what has been published about viral activity in cell replication is not what really occurs. We checked thoroughly for errors in our procedures, reworked all calculations, and concluded our experiments were correct. On that basis we published the paper. Anonymous peer reviewers raised the typical questions but recommended publication."

King paused momentarily the continued, "The second experiment, done independently by another group in the lab, confirmed the initial findings. The results of these experiments deserve to be examined by other scientists for the purpose of confirming or modifying our thinking, but we stand behind our investigations until someone demonstrates a different conclusion."

He closed his folder. "I'll be pleased to respond to questions."

Ladner, who had been shuffling and scanning papers, seemed unaware that King had stopped. After several seconds of quiet, he jerked up to mutter, "Thanks Dr. King."

Ladner shuffled through several pages, apparently seeking the questions prepared by an aide for King. Then, his voice taking on a challenging tone, he asked, "So your tale is you stick by your story?"

King straightened to his full sitting height, stared at Ladner. "With all due respect, Congressman Ladner, this is not a tale. I am confident our work is correct." A slight titter ran through the audience at King's refusal to be intimidated.

"Even though two reputable scientists have challenged your findings?" Ladner glanced around the room as though pleased he'd found the flaw in King's story. An aide tapped Ladner on the shoulder and handed him several sheets of paper. Jason suspected the aide had prepared a new set of questions while King was talking.

Moving his eyes across the row of Congressmen, King replied, "I fully expected the findings to be challenged because they upset the current thinking about the mechanism of action. I expected others to repeat our experiments for the purpose of detecting flaws or confirming the results. However, the letters from Thiele and McLean were a personal assault rather than a request for clarification or explanation. Neither pointed to a specific potential flaw or questioned the methodology, but made outright unfounded demands for withdrawal of the paper."

"So you didn't feel their letters deserved a response?" Ladner peered down at King as he asked the question.

King leaned forward in the chair. "Had the correspondence focused on the merits of the paper, I would have replied immediately. I would have been willingly to share more completely the steps in our procedure. However, the letters demanded an immediate retraction because in their views, I had manufactured the data. And to remind the committee, the letters were not identifiable at that point and then were withdrawn from the journal. It is difficult to respond to anonymous charges, particularly ones I consider insulting."

"How long have you known McLean and Thiele?"

"Four or five years. We've researched the same topics and have appeared on panels together at scientific meetings. At times we've shared unpublished papers while the manuscript was in the review process."

"Were you surprised they questioned your work?"

"I was insulted by the personal nature of their demand. I was disappointed at their unethical behavior."

"What motivation did they have in challenging the paper? Surely, it's based on a desire to clarify the issue."

King stretched his long legs from under the table and adjusted the position of the mike. "I can't know their motives. But the nature of their approach suggest they have an agenda other than discovering the truth about the issue."

Ladner turned pages in his sheaf. Other members glanced along the row toward him. Finally, he said, "I find it quite disturbing when two outstanding scientists challenge your work, yet you take the position their opinions are not relevant." For a moment, Jason thought Ladner was prepared to deliver a long oration, but then he stopped, waiting for King to respond.

King's shoulders stiffened. He was struggling to maintain his composure and not lash out at the tone of the query. His voice almost a whisper, King said, "An objective appraisal of the entire publication might have been useful. But their attack on my integrity left me cold. Congressman Ladner, as I've said on at least twice in response to your questions, they had nothing to be answered. The crux of their approach was a personal attack. That was it."

When Ladner again paused, Wilke jumped in to ask, "Dr. King, tell the committee in lay terms how your findings upset the apple cart, so to speak?"

King smiled, no doubt thinking there finally had been a sensible question posed. "Our research demonstrates the important role of calcium in the activity of viral agents in cell function. Researchers have ignored the element in that specific context, although it's well known to be involved in many soft tissue mechanisms. If what we've reported holds up, the entire process will have to be thought about differently."

"And I take it, you believe it's a real finding, not an artifact because of some bizarre methodology?" Jason recalled Stella's comment about Wilke's scientific savvy.

King leaned forward as though wishing to communicate better. "The methods we employed are standard except for the injection of the calcium ion into the mixture. I've discounted an artifact."

Again Ladner looked along the row of committee members. "Dr. King, I still find it hard to accept that you don't believe two other excellent scientists. If members have no additional questions, I don't wish to prolong this session. However, Dr. King, I'd like to have all your lab notes brought in for review and I'll plan on questioning members of your research group, as well as your department head, tomorrow morning."

Ladner banged the gavel and declared a recess until nine the following day.

Jason glanced at his watch, only eleven-thirty, irritated they would waste a half-day. He could either remain in his room and worry over notes for tomorrow or visit a museum in one of the world's most interesting cities.

He looked around for Kathryn, saw her standing alone near the railing between the audience and the table placed for witnesses. Except for King, others from State had disappeared. Getting close to her, he asked, "Would you be interested in walking through part of the Smithsonian after lunch?"

"Sure, that would be interesting."

King escaped the gaggle of reporters pressing him at the railing and walked to them. Jason said, "Preston, you handled everything wonderfully. It went well. He shook King's hand, damp from the unnerving experience.

"Thanks, but a couple of times, I wanted to throttle Ladner. What a shit. And his constantly referring to McLean and Thiele as outstanding scientist is sickening. Between us, I'd like to meet those guys in a back alley."

"If the rest of us can measure up to your performance, we'll have done all we can do."

"You will," King grinned. "I'm going to have couple of drinks in the hotel bar, grab a quick snack, then sleep the rest of the day. I was awake all night worrying about this morning." He strode away, intent on his agenda for the afternoon.

Jason turned to Kathryn, touched her hand. "Let's have lunch at the Smithsonian Commons."

Riley and Townsend left the seminar of the first candidate and closeted themselves in Riley's office. The door closed, Riley asked, "Well, what'd you think?"

"Disappointed. No ideas." Townsend tapped his pipe into his palm and dropped the ashes into Riley's waste basket, the odor immediately prominent in the closed space.

Riley dropped into his desk chair. "But he wouldn't rock the boat by making big demands on faculty. He'd be comfortable."

"That's true and it might be good to have a time of stability after the constant push by Rogers to get better as he labeled those curriculum changes and insistence we hustle for outside money." He tamped a new wad of tobacco into the pipe.

Turning up his nose at the aroma, Riley commented, "And we know damn sure Spradlin will be like Rogers or worse. They're cut from the same mold."

In the silence, the only noise the passing of students in the hall as classes ended for the afternoon, Riley broke the interlude. "Just so you know, I'm trying to connect Spradlin with this chick in King's lab. We know from Boseman they jog together. But you know, there's more."

Inhaling and sighing with pleasure, Townsend asked, "What do you mean?" Smoke curled around his head and drifted toward the ceiling.

"Helweg is the most sensuous woman I've ever seen. You know Spradlin must be screwing her. Especially since his wife died."

Interested but wary of his buddy's quest, Townsend asked, "So what are you doing?"

348

"I've been following her in the building for the last week and watching her apartment. Just to see if Spradlin shows up. Thus far, I've struck out, but I have this feeling I'm going to strike gold. Then we can take Spradlin out of the picture."

CHAPTER 32

They lingered over coffee long after most of the Smithsonian Commons patrons had departed for other activities. A mixture of well dressed bureaucrats had mingled with causally clad tourists to savor the excellent food. Now only a few late comers remained.

Jason and Kathryn had talked about numerous issues, primarily things from their past sharing for the first time, both realizing neither knew much about the other except work and their brief times together. Throughout their conversation, quick touches of hands, nudges under the table, Jason had recognized she wanted to reveal something. Twice she had started, then switched to a different topic.

Deciding to help her get the bother on the table, he said, "Kathryn, you're trying to let me in on some secret, but keep hesitating. Go ahead, blurt it out."

She nodded, acknowledging his perception, put her hand on his arm. "There is. Riley is stalking me. I didn't want to tell you while all this junk around King is going on and worry you more. But since we've been here, I've been unable to get his actions off my brain."

"What do you mean by stalking?"

"Riley comes by the classroom when I'm lecturing, stands outside the door which we leave open for air circulation, and stares at me for what seems like five minutes. It's quite disconcerting. Students in the seats near the door have noticed him."

"How long has this been going on?"

She examined the inscription on the saucer. "Two weeks. Maybe longer and I just didn't notice."

She replaced the cup onto the saucer. "But the thing that has scared me happened the evening before we came here. I worked late to complete an analysis in the lab, then ran into the Quick-Stop to grab a loaf of bread. So it was after well after seven when I got home. Riley was parked near the entrance to my apartment, slumped down in the driver's seat to avoid being easily seen. At first I didn't know who it was, but he raised his head enough so the light from the street lamp brushed his features."

She looked into Jason's face. "What do I do? Call the cops? Confront him?"

"Kathryn, Riley is trying to connect us together. He'll do anything to dig up dirt and attempt to head off my becoming department head. Boseman knew we jogged together and I'm sure he told Riley. Now Riley suspects our relationship is something more, something devious, and he wants to tell the world."

She smiled, almost a giggle, "Boy, if he really knew."

Jason returned her smile, pleased she could find a lighter side of this concern. He said, "Don't do anything yet. I'll talk to Tom O'Hare in University Security." He didn't reveal his deepest desire to accost Riley and knock him around.

"But, most important, whatever happens, it won't destroy our feelings about each other." He shoved his chair back, "Come on, let's discover some culture in this place."

The third floor hearing room was active with Congressional aides and media types when Jason led the State University contingency in at eight-fifty the next morning. McLean and Thiele followed behind and found seats across the middle aisle. Neither delegation acknowledged the other.

At nine Ladner entered, apparently in no hurry to get started. He conferred with an aide. Another young woman handed him a folder. He meandered toward his usual place in the center of the long table partially obscured behind the wall blocking the view of the spectators of everything below the Congressmen's waists. While Ladner stalled, Wilke and others arrived to find their seats.

Ladner banged the gavel, glanced around the room, now with a dozen spectators scattered about, and proclaimed, "Dr. King, we received your materials yesterday, but as you might guess, it will require several days for a team of experts to review those documents. No doubt there will be additional questions after the review." Jason wondered if Ladner had the staff to work through King's lab journals or if he would employ a consulting team. The possibility of Ladner's sharing those notes with McLean and Thiele crossed his mind, but he dismissed the idea as too preposterous to merit serious consideration.

Ladner announced, "At this time, the committee calls Dr. Kathryn Helweg to the witness chair."

With no visible signs of surprise or insecurity, Kathryn moved quickly to the seat. Jason knew every eye was attracted to her figure, sheathed in a knee length green dress. Ladner almost leered as he watched her take the chair, cross her legs, and pull the microphone closer.

Ladner asked, "Dr. Helweg, please confirm for the record your position and role in Dr. King's research group?"

Returning his stare, Kathryn said, her voice clear and firm. "I'm a Post-Doctoral Fellow with Dr. King. I've been involved with the experiments in question by doing some of the analytical work and in supervising the graduate student, Mr. James Ho, who did other parts."

"Had you done those procedures previously?"

"Not those specific ones, but I've worked on others quite similar. After trial attempts and with Dr. King's help, I became well versed with the analyses before the actual experiment."

"Did you have any doubts about the accuracy of the data you obtained?"

Shaking her head, Kathryn responded. "No. I'm confident the data were valid. All the control samples indicated the laboratory tests were in the acceptable range of precision for those particular procedures. And we were able to repeat our analyses within reliable limits."

Ladner glanced at his notes, turned a page. "Dr. King testified that he realized the data would be questioned by other scientists. Did you understand why he was so nervous about this work?"

Kathryn paused as though considering the phrasing of her response, but maintained eye contact with the committee members. "It's incorrect to characterize Dr. King's demeanor as nervous, but rather he told us the findings would result in a wholesale examination of the

354

presently accepted theory. That is why we checked the data so carefully."

"And you found no error?"

"We confirmed our initial results." She shifted in the chair, causing Ladner to stare at her again before refocusing on his script.

"And how were you involved with this so-called second experiment?" Ladner's tone took on a more challenging note. Jason wondered if Kathryn had caught the shift.

A pronounced firmness in her voice indicated she had. "I was not. Neither was Mr. Ho. Dr. Spradlin, our department head, insisted that an entirely different group do the second experiment. We honored his request and stayed away from the people doing the analyses."

Ladner beamed, glancing around the audience as though he'd found a major issue, then asked, "Why did the department head become involved? That's unusual, isn't it?"

"I don't know if it's unusual. I've never been previously associated with such an incident."

"Can you speculate?" Ladner leaned forward as though pushing his perceived advantage.

Without hesitation, Kathryn said, "I'd rather not. You should ask Dr. Spradlin directly."

"I intend to do that, but I thought his actions might be interpreted as those of an administrator who suspects one of his faculty has done something wrong and intends to help him cover his tracks." Ladner's short oration caused Jason to remember his suspicion that King had in fact made an error or had manipulated the data when he insisted on the second experiment.

When Kathryn remained silent, Ladner conferred his notes and asked, "And how did Dr. King react when he received letters challenging his paper?"

For the first time on the stand, Kathryn's eyes dropped. Her voice became softer. "He was very upset. He showed the letters to me because I was a co-author. We didn't know how to respond."

"Were you upset also?"

"Of course. The letters accused us of dishonest behavior. They did not point to an error in the publication."

Ladner stared as though intending to intimidate the young woman. "Although those who challenged you have impeccable reputations?"

Returning Ladner's glare, Kathryn replied. "I don't know about their reputations, but the fact they were willing to make charges based solely on their opinions rather than on hard evidence, suggests there might be a flaw in their make-up."

Ladner ignored her thrust. "And it never entered your pretty head that your boss may have been manipulating the data without your knowledge?"

Shifting in the chair and putting both feet on the floor, her back straighter, Kathryn responded. "Congressman Ladner, my head is filled with all the details of this complicated research investigation. The data reported in the journal match precisely those James Ho and I obtained. There was no manipulation. And your continued reference to such acts is an insult to me and all my colleagues."

356

Ladner's face reddened at the rebuff, but without pause, he said, "Unless my colleagues have questions, I have nothing further for Dr. Helweg." He glanced at the others, all shaking their heads.

Kathryn returned to her chair between Stella and Jason, her eyes on Jason's face as she adjusted into the seat.

He whispered, "Good job." He wanted to hug her close, but didn't wish to set off warning signals among his colleagues who were watching their interchange.

Ladner signaled to an aide behind him and took a folder she passed. A moment of scanning the contents, then he said, "It would seem logical to interview others involved directly with this research, but it's obvious the stories have been well rehearsed. Rather than waste the valuable time of my associates and their staff with repetitious testimony, I am calling Dr. Jason Spradlin, the department head for Dr. King and his group, to come to the stand."

Jason could feel the weight of every eye on him as he moved to the stand. He looked upward at Ladner and waited, hoping his countenance didn't reveal his jumping nerves.

Ladner observed, "You seem quite young to be a department head, so tell us about your background."

Jason reviewed quickly his academic training, undergraduate degree from Iowa State, graduate degrees from Wisconsin, followed by a post-doc at a Boston medical center. He concluded, "I've been at State University for eight years and have been the interim department head since September."

Ladner asked, "I assume you became aware of Dr. King's little problem when you took up the reins of the head's job?"

"That's correct. My predecessor had left notes for issues to be followed up on."

"And did you feel compelled to intervene in the situation?" Jason thought Ladner's voice carried a mix of sarcasm and incredibility, but he ignored his intuition.

"I had a responsibility to discover what was happening. I discussed the matter with Dr. King as soon as our schedules permitted, probably within a couple of days."

"What was King's reaction when you confronted him?"

"I wouldn't characterize our meeting as confrontational. He was angry and upset because of the personal nature of the charges."

Ever mindful of the position of the television camera, Ladner gazed around the area, then asked, "Wouldn't you expect such behavior when caught in an unethical act to be defensive and fake anger to hide his transgression?"

Hoping his glare demonstrated his frustration in responding to the same questions over and over, Jason said, "I would anticipate such behavior also from an individual wrongfully accused."

"So why did you intervene—to help King over the mess he'd created, to cover up the situation, or . . . .?"

"My responsibility was two fold. First, to find the truth, then do whatever necessary to set the record straight. Secondly, to protect the integrity and reputation of all faculty in the department."

When Ladner hesitated, Jason continued, "My first reaction was that an error had been made in the laboratory, that no one had caught the mistake, but I remind the committee, the paper had been reviewed in the usual manner without questions. I had my first doubts about the entire confrontation when I read the letters from McLean and Thiele."

"You'll have to clarify why those letters altered your opinion," Ladner, his voice louder. "It seems ludicrous to me."

"First, Congressman, the letters were almost identical as though one had been paraphrased from the other. That seemed strange. Then, both demanded an immediate retraction. And, they accused King of manufacturing data. Further, they did not seek an explanation."

"And you find that unusual?"

"Highly so. Every challenge of a publication of which I'm personally aware, or to any known to faculty in the department, has been based on questions about the experimental design, methodology, or interpretations of data. Outright demands for retraction are foreign, even bizarre, to me."

Ladner switched the focus. "Why did you insist the experiments be done over?" That appears to be a waste of resources if you were confident of Dr. King's original publication."

Jason smiled at the committee members looking intently at him. "Dr. King agreed it was a waste also. But I wanted to be absolutely certain there were no errors. I know from experience that mistakes are easy to make but very difficult to discover retrospectively. All scientists know that repetition of experiments are commonplace, even when there are no questions. It's an integral part of scientific research. You want to be on solid ground."

Jason paused as Ladner turned his head to confer with an aide, and added, "Frankly, Mr. Ladner, if Mclean or Thiele had attempted to duplicate King's work, this entire episode could have been avoided. That's another aspect of their complaint that doesn't hold to the usual protocol employed by researchers."

When Ladner appeared stunned and didn't move ahead, Wilke asked, "You are suggesting, Dr. Spradlin, had they attempted to prove independently the findings in King's paper, they would have succeeded?"

Nodding and smiling, Jason explained, "An inexperienced team in Dr. King's lab was able to do so after a minimum of training and trial runs. I would expect personnel in the labs of McLean and Thiele capable of doing the same."

Wilke maintained the lead. "Suppose for the sake of argument that errors or worse are discovered by the team reviewing King's laboratory journals. Then what/"

"First, I'll be very surprised and they will have to prove to me and a panel I would assemble they had done so."

Wilke continued to examine Jason's face. "Do you believe Dr. King has been wrongfully accused?" Ladner's head jerked up to glare at Wilke.

"Yes, I am convinced he has." Jason eyes shifted from Wilke to Ladner.

"For what purpose would Thiele and McLean do such a thing?"

"I can't answer for them," Jason responded quietly, turning in his chair to glance toward the pair. 'but their actions suggest they set out to discredit Preston King and this specific report. I have no idea of motive." He looked back toward the committee. "But I would like to ask them under a situation in which they're sworn to reveal the truth."

Asserting his authority as chair, Ladner bellowed, "I refuse to accept such a thing. Dr. Spradlin, you owe an apology to Thiele and McLean."

Jason returned Ladner's belligerent fixed look. "May I respectfully suggest the committee attempt to determine the truth rather than assume King's detractors are pure in heart." Jason knew he was pushing hard, but depended on Wilke to maintain some balance.

Ladner's face darkened even more. He leaned forward, the mike almost touching his mouth, his voice louder. "I resent the implications, Dr. Spradlin. We are searching for the facts."

Jason pushed his point, refusing to be cowed. "Then may I suggest the committee hear from McLean and Thiele."

Wilke rescued Jason from a potentially dangerous confrontation by intervening. "Mr. Chairman, you must admit the proceedings to this juncture have been shaded toward trying to prove King's guilt. Thus far, we've heard nothing but reiterations of the same points. I suggest Dr. Spradlin has a valid point and this committee should explore the possibility he's correct."

Scowling at Wilke's reprimand, Ladner twisted around to an aide who shook her head. Then Ladner said, "If there are no further questions of this witness, these hearings are recessed until further notice. As he spoke he shoved back his chair, snatched the folders from the table, and stalked from the room, two aides following closely. None looked back to a surprised audience.

Confusion dominated the scene for several seconds before people began to whisper and then move about. Congressmen and aides picked up their papers.

As Jason stood by the witness table, Wilke came down the steps toward him. 'Dr. Spradlin, I appreciate the testimony of you and your colleagues. I suspect you may be correct about Thiele and McLean, but what is driving them? I've found out they asked Ladner to organize these hearings, but I've not talked with them."

Shaking his head, Jason said, "Nothing is obvious. King's work will cause them to reexamine their own research and alters the theory they've championed, but every scientist expects those challenges. They're experienced enough to cope with those hurdles."

Wilke straightened from leaning against the table. "If you have other ideas, let me know. And I'll keep Ladner under reasonable control." He turned toward the steps leading to the exit behind the platform, leaving Jason wondering if Wilke had read his mind about control.

CHAPTER 33

In the hallway outside the hearing room Nancy Thompson waited for Jason as others brushed past eager to get to their next responsibility or escape for the day. Close to Jason, she said, "I wanted you to know Ladner has asked us to review Dr. King's notes. He almost demanded we find some discrepancy."

Dropping her voice as a couple of Congressional aides passed, she continued, "Our Deputy Administrator is irritated to say the least, but came away from a meeting with Ladner and his chief aide, a guy from Oregon who has the reputation of being difficult to deal with, more than peeved. Nevertheless, I can promise we won't cave in and come up with some fake issue to satisfy them. If we should discover anything suspicious, I'll let you know as soon as possible."

Nodding his understanding of her frustration, Jason said, "If it gets dicey, I'd call Wilke. He thinks Ladner is trying to pull some deal other than punish King."

"I know." She glanced down the hall, seeing only the group from State waiting near the exit for Jason. She said, "I know your people are waiting, but I need to tell you one more thing. We suspect this aide, Clarence Haskell, keeps the issue stirred up with Ladner. He may be the driving force behind these so-called hearings. But Ladner trusts him and depends on him, so Haskell receives a lot of freedom and responsibility."

Edging away toward his colleagues, Jason said, "Keep us posted as much as possible."

Not letting him leave, Nancy asked, "From what you said, I interpreted it as you know already there are no problems with the lab records. True?"

Jason hesitated, then decided he'd trust Nancy not to reveal his actions involving Sylvia. "I had someone from an outside lab inspect the journals. That person found a couple of small problems, but nothing of consequence. The calculations were checked and I'm almost certain you won't find errors or evidence of tampering."

Nancy nodded her understanding. "By the way, Haskell was the one who demanded a list of grants to your department and in a veiled way threatened a cut-off of support. He became particularly interested in those Center proposals since the ratings by the review panel puts you in a solid position for funding."

Unable to resist grinning, elated at the news they'd been successful for a huge grant to take them in arenas of science education and outreach they'd never ventured before. "Maybe we should find out as much as possible about Haskell, including any connections to Thiele or McLean." Having Haskell working in tandem with the two scientists seemed a stretch, but this entire process approached the ridiculous.

"I can't do anything officially without Ladner's office getting wind of it, but maybe there's some way to find out. I'll nose around quietly and see what turns up. But Jason, you or better still, your President or public affairs people might alert your Congressional delegation. One or more of them might be willing to probe into areas we can't touch."

"I'll talk to my President." Jason stepped closer and held her elbow. "Don't jeopardize your career. From the little I know about these Congressmen, Ladner could cause problems for any federal employee he suspects of undermining his agenda." He silently admitted his admonition contained a selfish motive. He didn't want to lose Nancy from NIH. She had become his primary source of information and guidance within the huge agency. But she'd also become a friend he didn't wish to see damaged.

She smiled wistfully. "I'll be careful. I've been around these creepy characters a long time but I have a few friends in Congressional offices."

As Jason turned to catch up with his group, she said, "Take care. Stay in touch."

Stella stepped away from the group as Jason neared. "I was able to get us on the last plane from Reagan, eleven-thirty. I thought you'd rather get home than spend another night here. And I made dinner reservations. We will have plenty of time but we should pack and pay our hotel bills before dinner."

"You missed your true calling, Stella. You should have been a tour guide."

Robert Tanaka, James Ho, King, Stella, Kathryn and Jason were escorted to a corner table in Captain Jim's Seafood Restaurant located on the banks of the Potomac. Smiles predominated the small talk, everyone feeling relieved their day in the spotlight was done.

When drinks were served, Jason raised his wine glass. "Thanks for your good performances." Glasses clinked and they cheered. King and Robert clapped loudly enough that people at adjacent tables noticed and smiled at the celebration.

As the din quieted, Stella said, "It went well. You didn't change Ladner's mind, but you planted enough seeds of doubt and suspicion in the others on the committee."

Kathryn noted with consternation evident across her features. "But most of them were never there. How can they be impressed one way or another?" She shook her head.

"But," Stella explained, "they had associates there, sitting in those seats behind the Congressmen. Through that mechanism, they will know."

Jason said, "I have another piece of good news. Our proposal for the Center of Excellence has been short-listed. We're reasonably sure of funding."

Again, everyone clapped, although some didn't know about the effort. Again, glasses clinked together.

Conversation erupted between those next to each other, then across the table as questions were posed, responses provided, observations noted about the huge restaurant and the throng of patrons.

Sitting between Stella and Kathryn, Jason touched Stella's arm and said, "Nancy Thompson suggested one of our next steps should be to alert our Congressman to the Ladner probe. Do you have contacts or could you recommend how best to do that without tipping off Ladner's office?"

Stella sipped her wine. "Our local Congressman has an office in Spencerville. You could make an appointment to see him or one of his associates. He'll give you good advice. If you'll call me when we're back, I'll find his name and telephone, although I'm sure you can find it in the telephone directory."

Across the table, King squealed, "The best part of the entire deal was to see Ladner scurrying away. Reminded me of a bear lunging through the brush after the bees got to him." Everyone joined in his pleasure, pleased to see him in a happy mood.

The waiter delayed until the laughter subsided, then passed out menus and explained the specials for the evening.

Stella reminded the group and the waiter of their schedule. "We don't need to rush, but neither can we dally if we are to make the plane."

After arriving home near three in the morning, Jason slept until the kids crawled into bed with him. Sitting on Jason's stomach, Tony gurgled, "We missed you. Did you bring us anything?"

"Not this time, but I'll make it up to you next time I travel." He rolled Tony onto the bed and tickled his ribs, peals of giggles squealing forth. Jennifer joined the melee, grabbing Jason around the neck from the back. He pulled her off and laid her on top of Tony.

Escaping, Jason said, "Come on, let's have breakfast."

"We did already. But we'll watch you," Jennifer said.

The morning flew, but soon after lunch the kids disappeared for an afternoon nap. Jason went to the office to find stacks of mail and papers, sorted into priorities by the efficient Audrey. He signed all of the personnel papers and purchase orders before deciding the remainder could wait.

His phone call to Tom O'Hare was rewarded when the detective answered himself. Jason asked, "What are you doing in the office on Saturday afternoon? Maybe getting away from home duties?"

"Something like that. What can I help you with?"

Jason explained Kathryn's suspicions about Riley and said, "Can you do something to stop Riley? It sounds more creepy than dangerous, but it's bothersome to her and disruptive of the class at the least."

"I remember Riley from the Boseman deal. He's a strange character."

"Frankly Tom, I've never considered him to be a physical threat, but he's a pain in the butt around the department, always searching for tid-bits to gossip about. He works harder at that than he does at his job."

"Sometimes those types go along for years causing minor irritations, then something drives them over the edge. Let's not dismiss this. Tell me the details of Helweg's schedule and when Riley would likely show up. I'll check it out."

Jason walked up the stairs to the third floor lab of King. The door was ajar and he heard movement inside. Pushing in, he saw Kathryn bent over her desk, completely engrossed in the task at hand. No one else was at work on this weekend day. A radio aired soft music.

Resisting the temptation to grab her from behind, he spoke. "Couldn't let it wait until Monday, I see."

Startled by the voice, she jumped up, then saw her intruder. She came to him, hugged him around the waist. "No, I need to work on a class exercise for next week. I concentrate better here than at home and especially when no one is around to distract."

She stepped back, her hand holding his. "You want coffee? I made some an hour ago."

"Sure."

He told her about his conversation with O'Hare. "I don't know how he will do his surveillance so don't be surprised if some security guy shows up next week around your classroom."

She smiled at him. "You remembered my concern."

They rehashed the trip to D.C. and the hearings for a few minutes while they sat on lab stools and sipped the brew. Then she said, "This is one of our nights together, isn't it. I can't always remember with our changing schedule."

"Let's make it one anyway."

She moved the mug around on the bench. "If you're concerned about Riley, there is a back entrance. Come in off that side street, then turn right into the alley. Several people park there regularly rather than use the front entrance. It's closer to the elevator for those on the top floors."

Suddenly she hopped off the stool and went to her desk, returned with two papers in her hand. "Look at these job announcements. One in Biochemistry. The other is in the Medical School. But both want someone to teach biochemistry and conduct a research program. Give me advice. Should I apply and to which one?"

Jason scanned the announcements, calls for applicants typically circulated among relevant disciplines and advertised in national journals. Both were faculty positions with long-term promise. "Why not both? Strengthen your odds. I think each has real possibilities for you and could be the answer to our dilemma." As their relationship had deepened and they discussed marriage and the future, Kathryn's future posed a significant issue. She hoped to land a faculty slot, but she couldn't be in the same department as Jason if he became the administrator. And neither wanted her to be forced to leave State, creating a long-distance relationship.

"Then I will. I've thought about the vacancy left by Boseman, but that puts us into an untenable situation if you become department head."

"We should know about that soon. If I don't make it, you would have time to apply." He drained his mug into the nearest sink, rinsed it out, and turned to leave. "I'll see you tonight then."

Jason had hardly settled into his desk chair on Monday morning before George Stuart rapped on the door and walked in. Never one to waste time on small talk, George started, "I know you've been away and wanted to remind you two of the candidates have gone through interviews. The third is coming tomorrow and Wednesday."

"Then everything is on schedule?

"Yes, you are up Thursday and Friday. The first prospect isn't acceptable to the committee but we've not disclosed that yet." George continued, "You know, I'm always amazed someone can look good on paper, then turns everybody off personally, or comes across as a complete ass."

"I suppose leadership comes down to more than a long list of publications and good references from friends."

George shifted his weight from one foot to the other. 'Remember, you have to give a seminar on your ideas about the role of a department head and how you see the future."

Jason grinned at his long time colleague. "George, are you trying to tell me something."

"Maybe," George chuckled. "I want you prepared for this interview. I've seen internal candidates so caught up in the daily routine of their jobs and assume the interview is a meaningless exercise that they come across as not caring enough to give it a little thought." George took a couple of steps toward the door. "Jason, you know how critical faculty can be, so give it some attention."

Jason approached George, grasped his elbow. "I promise to get ready. And thanks for nudging me about this thing." In fact, he'd thought some about the presentation and had made some preliminary notes, but he needed to organize the talk and perhaps think more about the points he hoped to make.

Thinking about the Redlake initiative over the weekend and their need to be prepared, Jason followed George out of the office for an hour in his laboratory office before the daily traffic in the department office became too steady to escape. He motioned for Roy Blount to confer about the status of his efforts.

Roy, a tall string bean with tousled blonde hair and blue eyes, who'd been with Jason almost a year, dropped into the side chair. "I've been working on a couple of embryos I got through a grad student I know in Animal Sciences. I worked on the culturing process and have started the cultures. So far, it's going good." Jason and Roy had worked through the methodology but the growing of cultures was key to being prepared when Redlake called. The procedures had been published, but things never went smoothly until the tiny, but often critical, kinks had been ironed out through trial and repetition. If you failed to get it correct, the whole thing came apart.

"We could be called anytime now by the Redlake people." Then Jason asked, "Is someone in animal science doing the same thing?"

"Some embryo transplant work with different species, mostly cows, but this one student is working with swine."

"So they have no experience with actually culturing and transferring cells?"

"Don't know of any, but they know a lot about reproductive physiology and might be helpful if we run into problems down the line."

372

Jason said, "Keep me up to date. And Roy, don't be reluctant to come to the head's office." During one of the weekly research conferences one graduate student had admitted she wasn't comfortable in bringing questions to him in the department office. He couldn't afford to let that be a barrier between the students and him and allow the research projects to flounder.

Back in the department suite, signing travel requests that had been initialed as okay by Miriam, Jason's concentration of the mindless task was interrupted by Kathryn's appearance. She eased into the side chair and said, "I won't take much time, but I wanted to let you know about this morning."

"Riley showed again?"

"He did, but he'd been watching me only for a few seconds when this campus security guy showed. He said something and led Riley away."

She stood. "I wanted you to know you got security's attention. Thanks. I feel more secure now they're watching Riley."

"Let's see if he shows up at your apartment building again." He watched her walk out, his thoughts for a brief moment on their growing closeness and the unknowns facing them.

He pulled from the stack the next document to be approved or returned for more information.

CHAPTER 34

The third candidate for the department head position, Dr. Joyce Treadwell from the University of Connecticut, arrived with George Stuart ten minutes before eight as Jason scrambled to retrieve folders from the credenza. His plan to avoid Treadwell by working in his lab went awry. He couldn't ignore the two as George led her on a quick tour of the facilities.

At the office door and seeing Jason, George said, "Dr. Treadwell, I'd like you to meet Jason Spradlin, our interim head."

Jason smiled and went to shake her hand. "Welcome. I've heard of your work, so it's nice to meet you personally." Treadwell had the reputation as an outstanding scientist, having won a major award for her research in the zoology of fish. Her photograph had appeared in *Science* and other periodicals circulated among professionals in the biological sciences.

Treadwell's grip was firm. "I've heard of you also and this department has a fine reputation. I'm looking forward to learning more about the faculty and seeing the facilities during the next couple of days."

"I'm sure Dr. Stuart will make certain you have a good visit." The thought entered Jason's mind she might be the best person for the job of leading the department during the coming years. He tried to ignore his growing possessive feelings about the position. However, efforts to obliterate those ideas had proved futile since the interviews had begun

375

and potentially interested replacements had appeared, eager to shove him aside. The positive side of losing out though would be he and Kathryn had more opportunities to seal their commitment absent another professional obstacle. And he could get back to his lab and focus on his research projects rather than be consumed by bureaucratic paperwork.

Jason felt relieved when George said, "We need to move along. I intended to walk through the office, but you were here and suggested we stop for a moment."

Treadwell smiled, "Nice to see you."

"Good luck," Jason responded, watching the tall, brown-haired, middle-age woman precede George through the door.

Sticking with his plan to stay low during Treadwell's visit, Jason retreated to the quiet of his office stuck in the rear corner of a laboratory, a place where he'd spent most of his career at State and still found comfortable.

He'd hardly settled when Kathryn appeared. "Hiding out are you? Audrey told me how to find you."

Sitting in the chair next to his desk, their feet almost touching in the tiny space, she said, "I couldn't believe Riley showed last night in his usual place. He hadn't been there five minutes when two city cops pulled him out of his car and hauled him away. I'd just come home from the lab and passed him, trying to hide in his typical way. Just as I entered the building, the cops drove in. I watched from my balcony, but I couldn't hear anything."

"O'Hare will let me know soon," Jason said. "I assume they arrested him or if not, questioned him over a several hour period."

"Come tell me when you know something," She said, standing, glancing into the lab and seeing no one, leaned over to kiss him on the cheek. "Tonight, remember."

Fighting through the distractions, Jason settled down to work on his seminar presentation, making notes, thinking about how the past months had altered his view about administrative positions, remembering Fowler's warning about becoming contaminated, and Lucy's urging him to give it a try. He made notes about his view of the department's future.

After two hours he wandered into the lab, noted Ann puzzling over a chromatogram, struggled against the inclination to intervene, then smiled as she solved the question. He returned to his desk and focused again on his presentation, now thinking about the type questions faculty were likely to pose, determined not to flounder and please the likes of Riley and his cronies.

Just before noon, O'Hare phoned. "Back to your old haunts I see. Update on Riley—we found him in both places you suggested. After the morning warning by one of our security guys to stay away from Helweg, we let him go. But last night, the Spencerville cops, acting on our tip, found him outside her apartment. They arrested him, brought him to the city jail, and held him overnight.

"This morning, Detective Trout and I interrogated him about his stalking. He vows his intentions were not to assault her, although his real motives remain unclear. The city attorney came in, read Riley the riot act, cited the laws about stalking, but in the end we decided to let him go with a warning. He's on our radar. If he continues with these activities, we intend to arrest him, charge him with stalking with intent to assault, and take him to court. I think he understands we are serious."

"Time will tell," Jason said.

"We plan to watch him at intervals. We just don't have the manpower to put a permanent tail on him, but we know his pattern and can do spot checks. Tell Dr. Helweg to keep an eye out for him. She'll be the first to sight him."

His hideout was invaded again at four when Audrey brought a stack of forms to be signed. She waited until he'd started the routine and said, "Dr. King wants to see you when you have time."

"Did he say about what?" Jason signed another purchase order.

"No, but he seemed upset. I thought it might be about those hearings last week, but I didn't quiz him."

"I'll go up in a few minutes." He initialed a travel request for a technician in Rankin's lab to attend a training session at Perkin-Elmer Corp. as part of a purchase agreement for a large piece of equipment.

Audrey arranged the last document into the pile. "He'll probably go to Dr. Treadwell's seminar which started at four."

"I'll leave a note for him to call me at home tonight if I miss him."

Townsend, Harris and Riley walked to Randolph's for beer after Treadwell's presentation, now an accepted routine after each candidate's visit. Customers filled Randolph's at the end of the day, but they grabbed a corner booth when a group of students left, leaving a half-dozen mugs and the table covered with spillage and condensation.

Waiting for the waitress to wipe the table, Townsend said, "Treadwell might be the one."

Budweiser drafts were delivered, the cold steins foaming over the top. Harris watched his colleagues take their first sip. "It could be different working for a woman."

"You worry about that?" Riley asked, wiping his mouth with a paper napkin.

"I agree with Harris," Townsend muttered, "but I'd take a chance with her rather than with Spradlin." He pulled out his pipe.

Riley nodded. "Let's push for Treadwell."

Harris shook his head. "Maybe we should see how Spradlin's seminar goes before we decide."

Townsend got his pipe going and through a fog of pungent smoke growled, "Maybe he'll screw up and leave it easy to vote for Treadwell." The process agreed to before the screening began allowed each faculty to cast a ballot indicating their top two preferences after all four had completed the interviews.

"Could happen," Riley murmured.

Harris sipped his draft. "Spradlin never fouls up. Have you ever known him to do something poorly?"

Feeling rebuffed, Riley blustered, "But this is different. More pressure. And he's never done this before."

"I'll bet you guys," Harris inserted, "a lunch that Spradlin comes through with the best of all the four." He watched for their reactions.

Townsend said, "You like Spradlin, I've decided, even after all the crap he laid on you when your target student complained."

Harris reddened slightly remembering the incident, but didn't retreat. "I've told you before, Spradlin was straight-forward with me. And he's not harped on it, coming around my lab every few days, looking over my shoulder, checking with the student to see if I've been a good boy. He told me what could happen and that was it."

Townsend puffed as his pipe went out. He knocked it against the table, dropping ash. Grinning, he said, "Hugh, I heard the campus security got on you about gawking at this post-doc you're so enamored with."

"How you know that?" Riley squirmed in his seat, his eyes on the mug.

"Couple of grad students overheard the confrontation and saw him lead you away. Did they arrest you?"

"The bastards are out to screw me. They did arrest me after they found me trailing Helweg near her apartment. Took me to the station, kept me overnight, laid heavy questions about motives. Then this city attorney came in and warned me any more stalking, his word, would lead to prosecution. Scared the hell out of me."

Harris said, "We warned you. This could get serious. You better pay attention to their threat. You know the cops will be watching you for a while."

380

Townsend packed away his pipe. "I need to get going. See you at Spradlin's seminar."

"Not me," Riley said. "I'm not getting near him or Helweg for a long time."

"How did they know," Townsend asked, standing looking down at Riley, "you were tailing her?"

Riley shook his head. "Not sure, but probably Helweg saw me outside her class and notified security. Spradlin hasn't seen me at all."

"Maybe," Harris said, "you should contact your attorney. If the cops pursue this, you could end up doing time."

Townsend walked away. The others followed, edging their way through a crowd at the front door.

Jason had just completed reading a story to the kids and tucking covers around them when the telephone rang in his room. He moved quickly to get it before it roused the little ones and the ordeal would be repeated.

"Jason, Preston King. Sorry I missed you at the office."

"So what's up?"

"This afternoon I had a call from one of Ladner's aides." The tension obvious in his voice, King continued, "He had questions about the lab notes from the second experiment and wants a written explanation. They seem easy enough to answer, but I wanted you to know they're still at it."

"Did he say who is reviewing the notes?"

"He intimated Ladner had brought in an outside expert. He said this consultant discovered the discrepancy, so I assume they've enlisted someone experienced with the procedures. Anyway, he's faxing the pages tomorrow."

"Did you tell him we'd copied the notes?"

"No, remember we agreed not to tell Ladner's crew, although I can't believe they'd think we'd turn over all our work without some record of it."

"I recall Stella insisting we do it." Krause had made an issue of being certain every page could be identified if someone raised a question.

Jason replaced the phone, checked on the kids to find them asleep, their heads peeking from under the covers, faces innocent and unknowing of all the problems in this world.

His urge was to call Kathryn but he needed to revisit his notes for his seminar and organize the major points onto index cards. He recovered his written pages from his briefcase and settled into the task.

CHAPTER 35

At three the next afternoon, Jason walked up to King's lab. He'd stewed about King's absence for a couple of hours after expecting King to come by before noon to show him the questions from Ladner's consultant. Distracted and unable to concentrate, he took the initiative to find him.

Post-docs and graduate students were engrossed in work at lab benches and desks, but King's office was dark, the door slightly ajar. The odor of solvents permeated the air. A fume hood whirred away trying to clear the room, but losing the battle.

Jason found Kathryn at her desk, touched her shoulder and asked, "Dr. King around?"

Looking up and then standing, she said, "He left before noon, maybe even as early as eleven, but he didn't say when he'd be back."

"Do you know if he received a fax this morning?"

"Don't know." She edged closer and in a lowered voice, almost whispered, "Is this about the review of the lab records?"

He explained about King's call last night. "I'm worried they've found a glitch that we didn't catch. If they have, King will be called to explain it to Ladner."

Her face clouded. "I thought we were beyond that."

"So did I." He turned to leave. "Have him call when he's back."

She touched his arm, slowing his retreat. "Are you ready for tomorrow in the midst of all this turmoil?"

"I think so. We'll know tomorrow."

From the department office Jason called Nancy Thompson. To her response on the second ring, he said, "It's Jason Spradlin. I'm calling about the review of Preston King's lab materials. He got a call yesterday indicating errors had been found."

"I don't know, Jason. During the hearings Clarence Haskell asked me to form a team of two or three competent people to do the review. He even volunteered to pay for anyone outside the agency. But two days later, Haskell called to tell me to forget the request. They'd decided to do it differently. At that point, I believed Ladner had abandoned the issue because the hearings hadn't gone as he expected."

"The call to King suggested they've employed someone, the term consultant was used, to do the work."

"Sorry, I can't help. I'm no longer in the loop."

Jason remembered the conversation he'd had with Nancy in the hall after the hearings with aides, media people and others nearby. Now he worried Thiele, McLean or a Ladner aide had seen them together resulting in Ladner looking for another source for his investigation. Why else would he change plans?"

Jason asked, "Can you suggest how I can find out who Ladner is using?"

Nancy's response came slowly, after some deliberation or distraction at her end. "Wilke's office could find out because any expense by the committee would be open to members, but I don't dare inquire myself. My boss has warned us to stay out of Ladner's view until our budget is approved. We encounter enough opposition from him without irritating him needlessly."

"I understand. I'll call around and sorry to keep pestering you."

Jason walked to the window overlooking a major quadrangle on the huge campus. Considering alternatives while watching a maintenance van and three workers take the cover off the entrance to utility lines running through tunnels underneath, he wondered how best to approach Wilke. Then he recalled the brief discussion with Stella Krause in D.C. while at dinner. He'd even found the telephone number in the directory and for some reason put it aside. Retrieving it from the yellow pad, he called Congressman Wray's local office and asked for an appointment on Saturday with either the Congressman or an aide.

Not wanting to get in a dispute with a President who preferred all contacts with political types go through his office or his legislative contact, Jason called Jeff Robinson who had worked with the state legislature for several years. He explained what he wanted to do and was checking to be sure he'd not run afoul of the current University operating procedures by going directly to Wray's office. Jeff assured him it would be okay but if there were questions about the University policies or budgets, please let him know. Relieved he'd cleared one potential hurdle, he focused on his seminar, reviewing his notes and altering the sketch he put on cards last evening.

At four-thirty King appeared, his features revealing frustration, his eyes blood-shot, shoulders sagging, as he dropped into the chair in front of the desk. He stretched his long legs as though to find relief of cramping muscles.

King muttered, "The fax had ten questions, all picky ass, but it's taken most of the day to figure out what they meant and to write a response. At one point, I got so irritated, I went for a walk, then hid away in the fourth floor conference room to finish this crap."

"So what's the nature of the questions?"

King shuffled through several sheets of paper, then pushed the fax toward Jason. "It's fourth decimal stuff," King growled. "Like why a cross-out on page twenty-four, what's the meaning of a smudge or an erasure, how did we calculate the amount of a specific reagent we'd put into a buffer solution, such junk as that. Nothing meaningful."

Jason scanned the fax, acknowledging King's description to be on target. "Maybe the person looking at this is inexperienced in lab work. That's why the naïve questions."

King crossed his feet again, a grimace running across his face. "Or they're very knowledgeable and raise all the mundane details, knowing you'll have to search back to find a reasonable response. Hell, Jason, how do you explain a smudge—maybe he had wet hands when the entry was made, maybe the pencil broke, maybe fifty other possibilities?"

"But you're ready to return the information?"

King nodded, stood without moving for a moment. "But I'll bet I get another batch of similar stuff within a couple of days. It's harassment, it's not seeking clarification."

As King turned to leave, Jason asked, "You okay? You act as though you have pain in your legs."

"Sitting too long. Legs are shot from playing basketball. It helps to move around rather than stay in one position for long periods."

"If you get another batch like this one, let me know. We'll talk to Stella Krause about alternatives."

George Stuart passed King in the door. He handed Jason two pages stapled together. "Your schedule for tomorrow and Friday."

Jason grinned. "Then your work with the search committee will be completed."

George put his hands against the back of the chair. "Except the sorting out of faculty preferences and dealing with the Dean. But the good news is I won't have to accompany you to all the offices around campus as I did the outsiders. But we did schedule dinner with you on Friday evening in spite of some feeling that was not necessary."

"So you know, I prepared for the seminar. I hope it's obvious."

"I'm sure it will be. Good luck with all this stuff. See you Thursday at nine for the meeting with the search committee.

Audrey stuck her head in at five. "Dr. Spradlin, good luck tomorrow. I'm certain it will go well."

As she prepared to lock the outer door, King appeared, this time a grin across his face. He handed Jason a sheet of letterhead. "This was in the afternoon mail. I hadn't opened it until I went back after talking to you."

On letterhead from McGill University in Montreal, Department of Biology the neatly typed message indicated the writer had done the same experiment as King with the same results. He explained he'd read about the conflicts and charges in the newspaper and had decided he should let King know. His lab had been a couple of months behind King with the work and were frustrated King had beaten them to the punch with his publication. Now the McGill paper had been submitted to a different journal.

Jason looked up, matching King's grin. "Wow, this is great news. You know this person, a P. R. Pierre?"

"Not well, but he's published a half dozen papers in the general area. I see him at national meetings, but we've never talked other than to speak and shake hands."

Jason came around the desk to stand by King, looking up a bit to see his colleague's face. "Now, what do we do with this?"

"My first thought was to send a copy to Ladner, but I wanted your advice."

Jason eased toward the window. King followed. Turning back, Jason said, "Let's talk to Krause before we do anything, but I won't be able to do it before Monday."

"If it's okay, I'll go tomorrow while you're trotting around campus doing meaningless interviews with these administrators who know you already."

"Sure, go ahead. Let's talk late tomorrow."

Jason left his briefcase in the office, determined to get sleep and be prepared for the marathon coming the next two days.

Talk over dinner with the kids and Mrs. Carter revolved around their days. Jennifer showed him a sketch she'd done, then they mounted it on the refrigerator, the door rapidly filling with her various pieces of art. Tony wanted something of his up and found a wrinkled sheet with his version of a house and a dog on the lawn.

With the kids in bed and Mrs. Carter secluded in her rooms, Jason called Kathryn. They talked about tomorrow, King's receipt of the letter from McGill that he'd shared with her, mutual promises to get away for a weekend in the near future, and other trivia except for the sound of each other's voices.

*   *   *

Thursday became a blur. From nine to ten he met with the search committee, a group of five biology faculty members, a technician from Rankin's lab representing the staff, two students, and an Associate Dean from the Graduate School. They asked the usual questions of why he wanted the job, his experience, any changes he foresaw, all of which he'd anticipated and thought he responded adequately.

A session with Dean Hawthorne and other department heads in the College preceded a .meeting with a dozen students selected because of their leadership roles in various clubs and organizations. He saw the Director of Personnel Services and discussed retirement possibilities, a reminder for Jason as he'd not thought much about that issue yet. But it did prod him to ask about Lucy's retirement fund now being deposited into a bank account. After some discussion of options, he arranged for the monthly stipend, a small amount given the length of time she'd been employed, to be sent to an investment account. He

389

hoped it would grow and be useful when the kids were ready for college.

Over lunch in the Faculty club he conversed with the Vice-President for Academic Affairs responding to the Chief Academic Officer's queries about the status of Biology in comparison to other departments around the country, what changes he'd like to see occur in terms of tenure, promotion and annual faculty evaluations and raises. After lunch, abbreviated because of the administrator's schedule, he dropped by the Graduate School, then the Research Office.

At three a break had been scheduled to give candidates a free hour prior to their seminar. Avoiding the office and the routine issues that would distract him, Jason meandered into the Student Union, picked up a black coffee at the counter, and found a table in the corner. Thinking back to the groups and individuals he'd met thus far, he was struck by the number of times he'd responded to the same question. And each group had their own agenda. Graduate students pressed him about excessive demands by major professors. Clerical staff worried aloud about potential reorganization and loss of jobs. Some faculty members wanted assurances about fair implementation of policies proposed through the University governance system. Others thought the head should be more aggressive in increasing the operations budget. Several queried him about his likely approach to salary raises. And some watched the interactions without comment or question. Jason wondered if they had no ideas or were reluctant to express them in a public forum.

390

His mind wandered to the issues ahead of him. He thought about the seminar, trying to ignore the King issue, and about his future with Kathryn, the Redlake initiative. He worried for a minute he'd fall asleep and be late for the seminar.

At three forty-five, he went to the rest room, then walked to Quincy, ready for the presentation.

CHAPTER 36

The Quincy auditorium, used as a large classroom during most of each day, was filled to capacity as faculty, post-docs, graduate students, representatives of clerical and technical staff came to hear and evaluate the fourth candidate, a person many of them knew and all had seen around the building. Jason recalled his first seminar at State in this same room, trying to convince faculty he was worthy of a position in this department. His first lecture to a packed house of undergraduates had occurred here. Now the stakes could be considered higher, but he was not nearly as nervous as on that first time when he was trying to gain a foothold in the profession. Nor even for that initial lecture when he had no idea about how he would gain and hold the attention of over a hundred bright-eyed students for fifty minutes.

As George Stuart stood to gain the attention of the audience, Dean Hawthorne and two Associate Deans arrived to take seats in the second row. Hawthorne nodded to Jason as George welcomed the crowd.

George concluded his preliminary remarks about the search process, then said, "I'm pleased to introduce Dr. Jason Spradlin, although I suspect all of you know him. He is the last of the four candidates to be considered for the position of department head. George seemed to hesitate, then added, "I have appreciated the work Dr. Spradlin has done as our interim leader during the critical period following the sudden death of Henry Rogers. Now, he will speak on the topic, "The Role of a Department Head in a Comprehensive University."

Jason moved quickly to the podium, holding two small index cards with the list of sub-topics he planned to address. He looked across the audience making eye contact with each section of the room. Kathryn and King were seated mid-way in the center section. His graduate students were all there in the fourth row. Every eye was on him, but several looked away as he made visual contact.

"I am honored to be among those candidates seriously considered for the position of department head of this excellent department. I have learned a lot since I was asked by Dean Hawthorne to provide continuity after Dr. Rogers died. That experience convinced me to become a candidate, something many of you know I vowed never to do.

"But this afternoon, I want us to think together beyond continuity and consider the significant potential of this department for the future. Dr. Rogers led us to a place of prominence among peers in the world. Many of you contributed to that progress, but he established a vision and an environment for each of us to work and prosper individually and collectively.

"We must stretch his vision if the future is to treat us with respect and favor. All of you know the level of competition in our world continues to be keen and an academic department is no different than any other body in our society. In some respects we confront a more difficult challenge because of the number of groups we must serve, including students, alumni, potential clients interested in collaborative work, university administration, citizens of this state, and the larger profession."

Jason talked for twenty minutes, moving from the podium at times to be closer to the audience, glancing at the index cards when he completed a point to maintain the sequence of his presentation. The audience gave attention knowing he could affect their individual careers if he became the successful candidate. Nods, smiles, nodding of heads revealed he was connecting and holding their attention.

Jason put the index cards in his coat pocket. "Having said several things a department must be and do, I must remind you the head cannot function in a vacuum. Accomplishments during the tenure of any academic leader represent the contributions of every member of the unit. Neither should the leader assume all the credit, but must acknowledge and try to reward the efforts of all who participate. The real challenge for any leader is to maintain the optimum mix of talents and create an environment in which each individual can be nourished and supported. To achieve that goal the department head must be many things—chief advocate, wise counselor, guardian of standards, perceptive listener, kind disciplinarian, controller of assets, and other roles none of us can predict at this point in time.

"I look forward to the challenge. "He smiled across the audience and said, "Now I'll be pleased to respond to any questions."

Clapping began in the middle section and spread across the audience. As it abated, George stood at his seat in the front row and asked, "Any questions?"

For several seconds no one said anything, always avoiding being the first, then one of the Associate Deans asked, "How do you insure the goals of the department are in concert with those of the college and the University?"

"Very carefully." Everyone laughed. Jason waited then said, "Each department head must be involved in those discussions and ultimate articulation of goals and philosophies throughout the University. It's his or her job to make certain his department comes into line with planning throughout the organization. And a head has the obligation and opportunity to advocate ideas generated within his department so those concepts can be modified and adopted by others."

Pamela Sturgis stood in the middle of the audience and asked, "Do you intend to maintain your research program and what kind of balance between administration and other activities do you envision?"

Jason smiled at his close colleague. "I'm sure the mix will change over time, but at the present, I intend to maintain a research enterprise somewhat smaller then the one I now have. I intend to teach a course each semester." He explained further, "By smaller, I suspect one or two projects, three or four research assistants, possibly a couple of post doctoral fellows. Dr. Sturgis, at this point in my career I think it'd be a mistake to withdraw completely from the science. Although I understand most department heads do." He grinned and said, "You know six months from now faculty could be rebelling and the Dean asking for my resignation."

"Have there been any surprises as the interim head?" The question came from Jack Peterson, a senior faculty who always dressed in khaki pants and a dress shirt, usually white or blue, with a tie long out of style, but who knew more about certain classes of fungi than anyone else in the world.

"Jack, every morning." Amid the laughter from his comment, Jason left the podium to stand near the steps down to the level of the audience. "Seriously, several were waiting the day I walked into the position. Most of those have been resolved, but a major concern remains. Much of the job is routine and could consume so much of your time, you'd never get anything else done. But in my short tenure, I've learned to rely on key staff to avoid becoming bogged down in the daily matters that are essential, but not necessarily done by the head. By the way, in case you haven't noticed, we have excellent support staff who quietly and efficiently accomplish many things for this department."

When silence reigned for several seconds, George Stuart stood. "Maybe one last question?"

The session ended. Several colleagues came forward to shake his hand and wish him well. He didn't know if they supported him or if they were hedging the outcome against all possibilities.

George cut off the sound system and walked out with Jason. "You did a great job. I'm impressed by your ability to express the potential of this department."

"Thanks, George. That means a lot coming from you."

"You have only a few sessions tomorrow. We'd timed schedules so candidates would be done by noon. Those traveling could get back home for the next day." He flipped off the lights and pulled the door closed.

King and Kathryn were standing near the water fountain a few steps down the hall. King motioned for Jason to join them and said, "You have time to get a drink? Maybe in one of those joints on University Avenue?"

"I have to be somewhere at seven, but sure."

They walked across a corner of the campus, becoming quiet and isolated as the day ended. Signs of spring were emerging. A few crocuses had made their appearance on the south sides of buildings where the larger shrubs had not shaded them out.

Waiting for the light to change at the crossing, Kathryn said, "You did well. I think everyone was impressed."

"Thanks. I was anticipating questions from Riley but he didn't show."

King said, "I haven't seen him around the past few days. Someone told me he'd gotten in trouble with Campus Security."

King led them into the Campus Bar and Grill and to a booth near the rear of the elongated facility wedged in between larger structures on either side. Most places were filled with students and a few faculty ending their day's responsibilities with friends. King took one side of the booth so he could stick his legs into the aisle. Jason followed Kathryn into opposite seats.

Drinks ordered and delivered, King said, "I went to see Stella Krause as you suggested. She concluded after reading Pierre's letter that we should send a copy to Ladner by certified mail. Someone will

398

have to sign a receipt and a copy will come back to us. She thought do the same for Wilke. That way Ladner can't claim he never received the letter."

Jason sipped his Scotch and soda. "Did she think that would end the deal?"

King nodded and Kathryn responded. "Dr. King asked me to go with him to Krause's office. Stella thought it could very well conclude the argument, but neither Dr. King nor I believe it will. For some reason Ladner hopes to keep the issue in the forefront."

"If this doesn't persuade Ladner to stop, then in my mind there is definitely an agenda we've not figured out yet. Somebody has something to gain but it's hard to fathom what."

King raised his beer mug. "Let's hope this ends it. On a brighter note, here's to Jason for a great presentation. No matter how this search thing goes, I'm proud to be your colleague." He reached to shake Jason's hand. Kathryn patted him on the arm and underneath the table, put her leg against his, sending shivers of anticipation through his frame.

Conversation turned to more mundane items until Jason had to leave for the dinner with the search committee.

At the same time, Townsend, Harris and Riley huddled around a back table in Randolph's.

The usual beer mugs in place and Townsend working at his pipe, Riley asked, "So how'd Spradlin do?"

Townsend said, "Actually, he did well. He made me think about my own career and what I might have done differently. In fact, I could still change and get some things done I'd thought about when I first got into academics. The downside is he's going to expect a lot from everybody. Slackers are in trouble, I'd think."

"I agree," Harris said, sipping beer. "Obviously, he'd worked hard to get ready for the seminar. I know you disagree, but Spradlin is my first choice for the job. He'll demand good effort, but he will help you when you need it. Just look how he's stuck with King in this problem of his. I talked to Preston yesterday and he's committed to Spradlin. King says he'd never taken on those Congressmen and his accusers without Jason's support."

Riley drank a deep swig of beer. "So am I the only non-believer?"

Townsend said, "I haven't fully decided yet, but no, you're not the only one. There'll be some who were shaken by Spradlin's comments about giving your best efforts in everything."

Holding his pipe aloft and sipping beer, Townsend grinned and asked, "So Hugh, you had any more run-ins with those security types."

Riley scowled at his buddy. "Not yet. I'm hiding away for a while."

A group of faculty passed on their way to a table. The woman trailing the others waved her hand to Harris who nodded in return. She stopped. "Greg, join us for dinner if you're not dining with your friends." She followed her colleagues.

Riley, never missing a chance to discover anything that might be a bit unusual, asked, "Who is she? Not bad looking."

400

"Rachel Winter," Harris said. "They're all from Sociology and I think I'll join them. See you guys around."

They watched Harris stand near the table next to Winter, say something which resulted in a laugh, then pulled out the chair next to her. Her reactions suggested she was pleased with his decision.

Townsend chortled, "Another female in his sights."

Riley said, "She's eager, don't you think. To make the first move is unusual even in these days of liberated women." He was quiet for a moment. "But she's not in the same class as Helweg."

"Get her off your mind," Townsend advised, "or you'll end up in the slammer."

Jason arrived as the others were checking their coats at Mortimer's, an upscale restaurant in the downtown area. He realized immediately he was the only single, five other faculty from Biology and spouses.

George came to him. "Welcome Jason. If you're wondering about the mix, we decided to have different faculty have dinner with each of the candidates. That way, everyone and their spouse gets a free meal on the Dean's budget."

"Any particular agenda in this social setting?"

George grinned. "Make sure you use the correct utensil and don't make a pass at some wife. No real agenda. We thought a social affair would be nice after the rush of the day."

The event turned out as George hoped. Jason interacted with faculty he seldom saw, learned their spouses names, heard about children ranging from kindergarten to high school and imagined the issues he'd face as his own kids matured and became more independent. George kept the conversation focused on the light side with no questions about university policies or problems.

In the middle of the entrée as he watched the interactions among the group and sensing the spouses were enjoying the event more than their mates, Jason's thoughts were pulled to Lucy. She would have been the bright star at an event like this, her charm, her outgoing personality, dressed so others acknowledged her innate beauty combined with good judgment. He didn't know why her image suddenly popped into the center of his thoughts now. It had been weeks since that had occurred and he wondered if somehow she was communicating some important message. Then, the woman on his right, an attractive forty-five year old, asked how his children were doing since their mother's death. He explained about Mrs. Carter and how he tried to give time each day to the kids.

As the evening progressed, Jason's mind came back to the future and Kathryn. He'd promised to come by her place if this session ended before ten. He looked forward to seeing her recalling the pressure of her leg on his in the bar with King.

CHAPTER 37

Friday morning went quickly and as George had predicted, without incident. Meeting with offices that had little influence on Biology represented more courtesy than substance. Jason met some new people, discovered aspects of the University he'd never known about, and even saw how interactions could be beneficial to both units. The sessions were pleasant and Jason recognized opinions of these administrators would have minor impact on the final decision unless he somehow insulted someone.

By noon the ordeal had been completed. He reported to George that from his perspective all had gone well. George reminded him that by Monday noon all faculty and other representatives would submit their choices. The search committee would meet that afternoon to sort through the responses and on Tuesday morning would meet with Dean Hawthorne. A decision should be forthcoming from the Dean shortly after that session. But George admitted, he didn't know if Hawthorne needed to clear with anyone above him.

Jason said, "So I should hear something by the end of next week."

"I would think so, one way or the other." George scratched his head, ruffling a few gray hairs. "If you want to know my opinion at the moment, I think it'll come down to Treadwell or you. And you know most faculty lean toward an outsider regardless of qualifications or performance during the interviews."

"I understood that when I submitted my application. Faculty have not seen the idiosyncrasies of the external candidate."

"Jason, understand I'm not saying you're a long shot because I have no idea of how faculty will evaluate the candidates, nor how the committee's recommendation will go." He paused, seeming to be careful of his word choice. "But I thought your seminar yesterday was the best I've heard and I've been to a lot in my time. You challenged us and made us think about our responsibilities to the department rather than give us a bunch of stuff to make us feel good."

"Thanks, George. I thought about it a lot and maybe my time as interim made some difference."

"Probably more than you know."

Edging toward the door, Jason said, "I appreciate your work as committee chair. Everything went smoothly."

Jason returned to the office, a feeling of relief the ordeal was over. Regardless of the final outcome, he'd given it his best shot. And the best feeling was he could look forward to a rewarding career regardless of the decision.

On top of the stack of papers to be signed were two notes, one from King, another from Audrey telling him Cynthia from Redlake had phoned and she'd transferred her to Roy Blount in the research lab. Ignoring the stack, he walked quickly to his lab. Blount had gone to lunch.

He climbed the two flights to King's lab. His office door was closed. A graduate student had his head on his desk, an open book under his arm. Kathryn was at her desk, bent over a computer printout, so intent she didn't hear him approach. She jumped when he tapped her on the shoulder.

Standing, she grinned. "You scared me." She took his hand. "All done with the grilling?"

"I came looking for Dr. King. He'd left a note."

"He left a few minutes ago, but the reason for his note is he received something from Ladner mid-morning. He hasn't shown it to me yet."

Still holding her hand, Jason asked, "You interested in lunch somewhere?" Since I can't locate anyone, might as well spend my time with the best looking woman on campus."

"Don't know how to take that, but sure, lunch would be nice."

Seated across from each other at the same booth they'd had yesterday afternoon, they ordered Reuben sandwiches and tea.

Jason said, "My other message was to see Roy Blount. I'm sure it's an alert from Redlake that they're ready for us to come harvest those cells. I hope it's not until Monday because I set up an appointment in Congressman Wray's local office for tomorrow."

Stirring an artificial sweetener into her tea, Kathryn said, "You know you don't have to go. Trust Roy. You've said he has mastered the technique."

"I feel better if I'm there. I don't want anything to go wrong."

Kathryn poked his arm and said, "If you're going to become the department head, you'll have to learn to depend on others. You won't

405

be able to be closely involved with every little detail. I understand you have this commitment to Redlake, but trust Roy this time."

"I did promise the kids I'd go to the park with them. Maybe you're right."

"I received responses from both my applications telling me they're beginning the review process in a few days and will get back to me. But I was thinking a critique of my teaching might be helpful if somehow that could happen soon. Having student evaluations at the end of the term will be too late."

"I'll get a couple of faculty to sit in your class next week. That'll suffice."

She smiled and shifted as the waitress placed their sandwiches. "If they're okay."

"They will be. A couple of students have told George they like your organized approach and they're learning."

They ate quickly, each thinking about things they needed to get done back at their offices. Jason picked up the check and dropped a tip on the table.

Part of the way back to Quincy, Jason said, "Would you like to come with us on Saturday? We'll watch the kids on the slides and swings, then maybe get burgers somewhere. I'll tell Mrs. Carter she can take the afternoon off."

"I'd better work on my paper for the meetings, but you and the kids come to my place for supper. I'll do something they'll like."

Leaving Kathryn in the foyer of the building, Jason went to his lab on the bottom floor, one taken from Riley by Rogers and given to Jason when his projects overflowed his other space and Riley had not utilized the lab in three years.

Roy was at his desk, looked up when the door creaked. "Dr. Spradlin, we got the word from Cynthia. They'd like us there on Monday." He backtracked to explain. "They moved the boars in with the females this morning and if things work out, impregnation could happen on Saturday or Sunday. We could take the embryonic cells on Monday or Tuesday."

"Roy, can you do this yourself? If you're confident, I won't go with you."

"Sure, I can handle it. I've practiced the technique several times. But if I have problems on Monday, I'll call."

"Then I'm relying on you."

"I'll be ready. And Cynthia has been practicing the procedure also."

"Is she coming back with you?"

Roy reddened slightly. "That's the plan."

"Let me know if I need to do anything to help." He turned away suspecting the blushing of Roy's cheeks implied a budding relationship between Cynthia and him. She was a bright young woman and he was unattached.

King showed at the department office at four-fifteen. "I got another set of questions this morning. Same nit-picking stuff as before. I disappeared into that conference room and prepared responses. I'll put the packet in the mail tomorrow morning."

"Let's see Stella Krause on Monday. " As soon as King left, he called the attorney's office and set up a ten o'clock time on Monday.

Then he turned to the eternal stack of forms to be signed.

Spencer Hayden, Congressman Wray's representative in the Spencerville area, met Jason promptly at the nine-thirty time. He offered coffee and led Jason through a couple of outer offices to a conference area in the back of the building. Only one other person, an older woman sorting through a stack of cards, occupied one of the front spaces. She smiled when Jason passed her table.

Jason explained the events surrounding the charges against King as tersely as he could without omitting important details. Ten minutes of talking led him to say, "It's fairly clear to me that Ladner's bunch, including Thiele, McLean and his top aide, Clarence Haskell, are pursuing an agenda different than he purports in the hearings. I'm hoping Congressman Wray can somehow dig around enough to uncover the driving force behind this stuff. I thought I should start with this office, but if this is the wrong place, straighten me out."

The square-bodied Hayden put his arms on the table. "This is probably good as any. What I do is listen to problems from our constituents, solve any I can, and forward the others to Washington. I've heard about these hearings and read the paper about King's cheating. I'll call the Congressman on Monday and he'll put someone on the trail."

408

"Congressman Wilke suspects Ladner is off base. He or someone in his office likely could be helpful."

Jason stood, thinking this had gone too smoothly, but said, "Thanks for any insight you can discover."

"I'll call you as soon as I know something."

Hayden was making notes on a pad when Jason left the room.

Jason relieved Mrs. Carter by ten-thirty urging her to visit her friends and escape the bedlam associated with two young children for a few hours. He knew she'd made plans to have lunch with two former co-workers, but beyond that, he suspected she'd return soon after, expressing concern the kids would not be okay without her presence.

The afternoon in the park centered around Jason pushing the kids on swings until they were bored, then standing nearby as they climbed the ladder and careened down the slide, screams and giggles resounding. Other children appeared causing lineups for the slide, then they ran to the set of obstacle courses established for small children.

Jason stood and watched somewhat in envy as his childhood had never had these possibilities. A woman standing near asked, "Are you Jason Spradlin?"

He noticed her earlier with two young girls about Jennifer's age. "Yes, I am."

"I'm Maggie Glover. Lucy and I worked together at the University. We've missed her terribly."

Jason looked at her, seeing an attractive thirty-five year old. "So have we, but we're getting along okay."

Now Jason recalled Lucy telling him about Glover and how her husband had walked out one day asking for a divorce, telling her he needed space. He asked, "You're still in English?"

"Yes. I was able to receive some of the books Lucy left. That was generous of you to donate them to the department." She moved closer, almost touching. He had the panicky impression she was coming on to him.

At that moment Jennifer tugged at his slacks. "Daddy, we're ready to go home. I'm thirsty."

"Okay, get Tony and we'll go." Turning to Glover, he said, "Nice to see you."

"Perhaps I'll see you again."

The evening at Kathryn's got off to a good start. They arrived just in time for dinner. She was ready with pizza and soft drinks for the kids, offered Jason beer or wine and they settled around the small table at one end of the kitchen. The kids dug into one of their favorite foods, needing some assistance with the longer slices, and requiring frequent cleaning around the mouth and hands. Then Kathryn offered them ice cream in small bowls. They finished that in a few minutes.

As Kathryn and Jason finished their wine, the kids played with the one toy he'd permitted them to bring after denying the several they'd gathered in readiness for the evening with Kathryn.

Kathryn surprised them by bringing out a board game and dropping to the floor with the two. "Come on, I'll play this with you for a while."

410

"Can daddy play too," Tony asked, his eyes on Kathryn's face.

"If he would like."

The two pulled at Jason until he joined them on the carpet. Kathryn led them through several turns each, explaining the rules and showing them how to count and move their pawns around the around the square until they reached home base. The first one home was declared the winner. By the time Jennifer was declared the champion, the children were ready to move on to the next thing.

Kathryn read a story, the kids resting between her and Jason on the couch. After a few minutes, they both dropped off, eyes closed, breathing interrupted at intervals with gurgles. They stretched the kids out on Kathryn's bed.

As Jason took off shoes, Kathryn walked onto the balcony. She scurried back, her face white.

She grabbed Jason's arm. "Riley is out front."

"Are you sure?"

"I'd know his beat up old car anywhere. And you can see him in his usual pose. Come, see for yourself, but don't make any movement to attract his attention."

Jason eased onto the dark balcony, moved a step toward the railing. He affirmed Kathryn's observation. Riley slumped in the driver's seat, his head turning often to observe people coming and going from the building.

"Call the Spencerville cops."

While they waited, Jason said, "I can't believe he'd risk this after the other time. Kathryn, I think Riley is obsessed with you and those types become dangerous."

She leaned against him. "He's never made a gesture I'd deem out of line. He has followed me around in Quincy at times. I ignored him but it was unsettling."

They returned to the balcony when the flashing lights of the police cruiser wheeled into the lot. The two cops opened Riley's door and made him exit. After a minute of gesturing and apparent attempts by Riley to explain his actions, they escorted him to the rear seat of their car and took off.

They returned to the couch, sitting close, holding hands. Jason said, "On the way over here tonight, Jennifer asked if you were going to be her new mother."

"And your response," Kathryn asked, her eyes on his.

"I told her I'd like her to be, if she's ready."

"You know I am." Then her mood shifted and she moved to face him. "Jason, I love you and hope to spend the rest of my life with you."

"I feel the same way." He kissed her, holding her tightly.

Kathryn pulled away, her hands remaining around his neck. "We could throw the kids off the bed and have sex. But we'd better wait for another time."

"I know. By the way, you were wonderful with them tonight."

CHAPTER 38

The Monday morning edition of the Spencerville *Herald* contained a brief note on a middle page about the arrest of Dr. Hugh Riley, a State University faculty member. He'd been charged with stalking and released on bail. The identity of his potential victim had not been made available to the press. Arraignment was scheduled for Wednesday.

On Monday morning King, Kathryn and Jason received letters subpoenaing them to appear before the House Committee for Science and Technology on Tuesday, April seventeenth. Jason laid it aside until he could talk with the others.

An hour later King appeared in Jason's office as a meeting with an equipment firm representative trying to interest Jason in a new version of a DNA analyzer concluded.

He handed a fax to Jason. "In addition to the subpoena, the latest word form Ladner's aide, Haskell." He slumped into the chair, his posture suggesting his patience was as thin as an old carpet.

Jason scanned the message. *"We have discovered three pages missing from your lab work book. The missing sheets represent notes on or about July seven to nine. Apparently these pages were cut from the book. An explanation and replacement pages are required immediately."*

Jason returned the fax. "Were you aware of missing pages?" He recalled Sylvia's review. She had not mentioned the absence of pages, but it might be easy to not give attention to page numbers when you're absorbed with details of lab procedures.

Scowling and shaking his head, King mumbled, "No, it's another part of their game. I looked through the copy we'd made and we have those three pages—entries made by James Ho and Kathryn Helweg."

Jason pushed back from the desk. "You think these characters are deliberately destroying confidential materials? It's difficult to believe they'd think we're so naïve as to not make a copy."

"Maybe, but if we hadn't, we'd have no proof. It'd be our word against theirs. Or maybe they're confident we'd not copied the stuff. After all, they signed an agreement to preserve all materials."

"Could be they're desperate to find something wrong or super-arrogant." Ladner's actions during the hearings had demonstrated he would use almost any tactic to get his way. Only the presence of Wilke and others had reined him in.

King seemed to be contemplating the possibilities, looking briefly at Jason then around the room, raking a hand through his hair." So what do I do? I can't just ignore them. That'll convince them we cut the pages before we gave it to them, as though we were trying to hide something and hoped they wouldn't notice."

Jason wandered over to the window, his mind churning with possible reactions to Ladner. He'd always believed you had to take the initiative in matters of conflict, just defending your position seemed to invite another charge because you came across as weak or guilty. His participation in basketball and other sports reminded him you had to score points as well as defend your goal.

Looking at King who'd followed him across the room, Jason said, "What would happen if we made a firm statement that the materials were intact when we turned them into Ladner's office, which happens to be true. We'd also take the position any parts missing are the responsibility of Ladner and his associates. Shift the burden of proof. See what their reaction is." He hesitated, thinking more about his proposal. "And we'll word your reply in language strong enough there's no doubt about our stance."

King grinned. "I like it, but it's going to make Ladner mad as hell."

"That's okay. By the way, we need to talk to Stella about the next set of hearings after the Congressional spring recess. I'll have Audrey set up a time for the three of us to see her within the next couple of days."

"I'll bring a draft of my response to Ladner, " King said, turning toward the door, his shoulders straight with new found determination.

His thoughts ranging from the conversation with King and their decision to become more resistant to Ladner's charges to the Redlake opportunity and how Roy Blount was doing with the work there were interrupted by the ringing telephone.

A woman's voice, "Dr. Spradlin, Mr. Hayden asked that I call to tell you. He suggests you contact Peggy Murphy on Congressman Wray's staff. I have her number if you wish to follow through."

"Thanks." He scribbled her name and number on the yellow pad, then dialed..

Peggy Murphy came on the line after two transfers and a lengthy delay. "How may I help you?" Her pleasant voice invited the other party to reveal their problems.

Jason told her about Ladner's hearings and the constant challenging of Preston King. He told her about the hearings and the most recent charge of missing pages. Murphy listened with a question or two as she clarified her understanding. Finally, Jason said, "What I'm really trying to discover is the underlying rationale of Ladner's probing. I don't believe it's merely to discredit Dr. King. There's something deeper and probably more important to him or one of his constituents. And likely this Clarence Haskell is deeply involved."

Murphy replied, her voice soft and with a slight accent Jason couldn't quite place. "I'm not certain I can help, but regardless, I'll have to clear with the Congressman. He doesn't like our inquiring into activities of colleagues."

"Ms. Murphy, I understand the politics to some degree, but Dr. Snyder, our President, has spoken to Mr. Wray about this matter. Also, he needs to know the integrity of a valuable faculty member at State University is at risk. You may wish to review the transcripts of the hearings conducted by Ladner to see for yourself there is a devious undertone. And you may wish to have Mr. Wray talk with Congressman Wilke who suspects Ladner of some hanky-panky. For some reason this Clarence Haskell is out to get King and is using Ladner as his front."

"That's a serious allegation," Murphy replied, her voice more animated now, a measure of disbelief evident.

416

Jason added, as though trying to convince her, "We've received several communications from Haskell. He's either the organizer of the effort by Ladner or he's taken on the task himself after the hearings failed to prove the point he's searching for."

For a moment Jason thought the connection had been broken, then Murphy said, very softly, "I've known Haskell for several years. I'll see what I can discover and get back to you."

"I'll appreciate it very much." Jason experienced a tinge of relief she'd not turned him down.

Murphy continued, "Please understand, it may take a few days and anything I tell you must remain in strict confidence. I'll not be in a position to confirm publicly I was your source. That is, if I'm able to find out at all."

"I'll honor your request."

Jason put the receiver in place very quietly, thinking he should tell King or Stella what he'd done. Then recalling the plea in Murphy's voice regarding confidence, he decided to keep the conversation to himself. The fewer who knew, the more likely any information Murphy gave him would not be leaked.

An hour later, Tom O'Hare phoned to update him on Riley. "As you'd expect, Riley swears he had no intention of harming Helweg but he can't or won't provide a plausible reason for his actions otherwise. He sticks to his story no matter how long we question him."

"Tom, I have an idea he hoped to somehow connect Helweg with me and use that against me any way he could. But it's a guess. The bottom line is, he's followed her around the building, leered at her from the hallway at her while she's teaching class, and waited in her parking lot at strange hours. To me, that constitutes stalking, but I don't know all the legal ramifications of the crime."

"The fact that he ignored our warnings about his actions is a key factor in our case. The City Attorney intends to prosecute him or force him to seek a plea that will cost him money and will go on his record."

"I hope the attorney sticks to his guns. As you told me days ago, some of these guys appear all innocence but then something snaps and they do great harm to their target."

"I remember and the case files are filled with those very things. People, almost always women, are the victims because the law enforcement types failed to understand the motivating forces behind those guys. Whatever, I'll keep you informed."

After the rush of Monday, the week settled into the handling of routine matters. Jason participated in the critique of Ann's presentation to be made at the national meetings. He worked through a manuscript Angela had prepared for publication. He asked Ben Rankin and Elizabeth Chow, a fourth-year faculty member who'd received high marks for her teaching of mammalian physiology, to critique Kathryn's teaching. Roy Blount called on Thursday morning to let him know the procedures at Redlake had gone okay and he would be returning the next day. Cynthia would follow on Monday and she'd reserved a room at the Union. Each day he worked through the stack of travel requests, personnel appointments, expense accounts and other

418

papers. At four on Thursday, Hawthorne's secretary called to schedule an appointment for Jason on Friday at nine. Jason knew this meeting would reveal his future.

Hawthorne appeared jovial when Jason entered his office on Friday morning, immediately telling Jason some joke he'd heard the evening before. Thinking as he laughed this was the Dean's method of making him feel good before dropping the rejection bomb.

The secretary brought in coffee and closed the door as she left. Hawthorne said, as he poured two cups of the dark brew, "I know you've been anxious about the decision. To recap the process following the interviews, the search committee canvassed the faculty and made a recommendation to me. Following the usual protocol in these situations, I discussed the matter with the Vice-President to be certain he concurred. It always takes more time than you suspect it should. But the bottom line is I'm pleased to offer you the position effectively immediately. Hayes feels good about it and even President Snyder asked about the outcome."

Almost speechless after the delaying tactics of Hawthorne, he stammered, "Dean, I'm pleased to accept."

Hawthorne placed his cup on the coffee table. "Of course, there will be a substantial jump in your salary as a reflection of increased duties and responsibilities. I know you would like to continue a modest research effort and teach at least one course each year. That is usually not an expectation of department heads. I'm pleased you will do that and wish more department heads would do so but I recognize the effort required. As a measure of support toward that goal, is there anything this office can do to assist you with that?"

Jason had not anticipated the question and wished he'd discussed the typical stance of the Dean in dealing with new heads with a couple of his administrative colleagues in other departments. He sipped from his coffee as he reviewed quickly the thorny issues surrounding research demands. Typically it came down to money and staff.

Jason said, "The thing that could help most would be stable funding for the technician, Marjorie Yates, in my lab. She's a key to operating the facility and I've depended on soft money to keep her. Having state funding would take some of the pressure off and would secure her future with my program. And it would assure her of a solid future."

"I can arrange for that," Hawthorne said, making a note on a pad on the table. "Have your accounting person call to give her present salary and personnel information."

Hawthorne continued, "You no doubt recall the annual faculty evaluation process. We're ready to begin that in the College. If you need guidance this first time around, either I or one of the Associate Deans can help."

"I remember from the other side of the table," Jason said. "And I might need some guidance in dealing with a couple of problem faculty." His annual conversation with Henry Rogers following completion of activity records for the past year had been scary the first couple of times, then settled into part of the routine of the passing years.

420

"Is Hugh Riley one of those? I saw in the paper he'd been arrested for stalking."

"Riley is the major one, but there are minor issues with two others that I know about. The activity reports may reveal other questions."

"I know this comes at you fast, but what would you like to see happen with Riley?"

Jason didn't have to think very long. "The department would be a much less stressful place if Riley were no longer employed there. He is a non-contributor to either teaching or research. And he can't be trusted to handle any committee assignment because he uses it to create more gossip and dissension. He has tenure and longevity, so firing him may be impossible."

"It can be achieved in other ways," Hawthorne said. "Talk to him about a buy out. We'd provide two or three years salary in a lump sum or in annual increments if he preferred. He would no longer be employed and give up all his privileges as a faculty member. His retirement and insurances would not be affected except for the longevity factor. Make sure he understands the option is no raise for the remainder of his time with us. Plus, this arrest provides us a wedge to force him out. We can't tolerate that kind of behavior."

As Jason waited, thinking about Riley, Hawthorne asked, "What about King? These charges against him are doing the university damage in the larger community, especially among the state politicians."

"King in my opinion is being used by a Congressman to achieve another goal. If you're asking if King is a problem, he is not. He's a solid instructor, productive researcher, attracts good graduate students, dependable department citizen. I hope we can get to the bottom of this persecution soon."

Hawthorne stood, saying, "I'm pleased this worked out for you. I've been impressed how you've done during the interim appointment. My door is open if I can assist in getting past the hurdles new administrators face."

"Thanks, Dr. Hawthorne, I appreciate your confidence and will work at the job."

Near the door to the outer suite, Jason paused to say, "I plan to be away most of next week at the annual FASEB meetings in Chicago. If it's okay, I'll ask George Stuart to handle any emergencies."

"Sounds satisfactory. Stuart is a good person."

The announcement of Jason's appointment was released by Hawthorne by afternoon. Faculty and staff in the department received the message via E-mail followed by a letter. By four-thirty, several faculty had dropped by to offer congratulations.

As Audrey switched off the lights and prepared to lock the outer office, Kathryn came in, waited for the secretary to leave, then pulled Jason's door closed. She hugged him, saying, "It's wonderful news and I'm not surprised you were the one."

Jason held her close. "The wait was the hardest part, but now I have to do the job. And let's trust one of those positions will work out for you."

"I want to get this Ladner business behind us. I'm afraid those other departments will not understand and pass me by because of the black mark I'd bring to their faculty."

Jason said, "I'm working on a new angle to clear King. I believe it will pay off."

"I'll see you tonight," Kathryn said, turning toward the darkened office suite.

CHAPTER 39

Jason always looked forward to the FASEB meeting where he listened to excellent reviews as parts of symposia, heard short papers offering break-through possibilities, and informally interacted with colleagues from around the world. On two occasions during his career he'd been privileged to present papers as part of symposia and he and his graduate students gave papers each year. This year was no exception with both Ann and Angela having papers scheduled. And Kathryn was on a program for a summary of her dissertation work at Minnesota.

As requested in their reservations, he and Kathryn had been assigned rooms adjacent to each other on the tenth floor of a downtown hotel, overlooking part of the famous Loop and not far from the shores of Lake Michigan. They spent nights together but went their separate ways during the day, concerned about their relationship becoming known by others from State. The week sped by with daily sessions running from nine to five, with special events during the evenings if one chose to participate.

Leaving a session late afternoon on Wednesday Jason encountered two biologists from Oregon he'd met in previous years. Without any prior plan or thought, he invited them to join him for a drink in the hotel bar. After they'd been served by a skimpily-clad waitress and had talked about mutual interests, Jason asked if either knew Thiele or

McLean. They glanced at each other and nodded, then Bob said, "They've done work together for several years and we've heard rumors they're planning to leave their university posts and form a company. As I understand, they hope to produce medications based on the work they've done. Beyond that, I know very little."

His colleague, Cedric chimed in. "Why do you ask about them?"

Jason sketched the essential ingredients of the fracas between them and King and inserted his thoughts about Ladner and Haskell. "I suspect they're attempting to discredit King for some reason."

Cedric nodded his head. "I remember hearing about their challenge of a King paper. I read the disclaimer by King in one of the journals."

"Would this paper by King," Jason asked, "somehow throw a snag into their plans?"

Both shook their heads, sipped their drinks, then Bob said, "Maybe if his research suggested there was a flaw in the basic process they intended to use in the production of the medication. I could envision that being more than a snag."

"Any ideas of how this Haskell fits in?"

"Recently there have been brief news blurbs in the state papers about Haskell leaving Ladner's office to take a position in the private arena."

Cedric added his thoughts to those of his friend. "Haskell has been on the ropes for some time with the state people, including the Governor. The opposition party has been trying to nail him with some unethical act for a couple of years and are pressuring Ladner to fire him. He's pretty well lost his influence in Oregon but Ladner sticks with him."

His mind churning with possibilities, Jason asked, "To form a company in Oregon, would they have to file articles of incorporation or some document permitting them to market a product to the public."

Cedric said, "I don't really know, but I'd think so. You could find out through the branch of state government that regulates businesses. Maybe Commerce?" He grinned and added, "You know for Ph.D.s, we know little or nothing about some things."

Jason picked up the check. "You've given me ideas though. I can find out details through other channels."

Bob stood, taking his coat from the vacant chair. "I'm headed for this session over in McCormick Center. A couple of guys are presenting articles I need to hear."

Watching them leave as he dug out money for the tip, Jason felt rewarded. The possibility of Thiele and McLean being thrown for a loop by King's findings seemed altogether realistic. He left the bar, walked two blocks to his room, and called Peggy Murphy in Wray's office. After telling her about his conversation and his growing conviction he was onto the key element in this whole battle, he examined himself in the bathroom mirror, raked a hand through his hair, went into the hall and knocked on Kathryn's door. They were planning to meet several of his former students at a nearby restaurant and he wanted to introduce Kathryn although a residual of wariness lingered about how many people should know about them.

She cracked open the door and peeked through. "Come in, I'm almost ready."

He watched her add the final touches of lipstick and run a brush through her hair. "You look great." The figure-hugging knee-length black dress, low neck line revealing a hint of cleavage, black heels and nylons highlighting shapely legs. A single strand of pearls advertised her sophistication.

"I wanted to impress your people." She turned away from the mirror. "And you still think it's okay for me to come?"

"They have to know sometime and I trust them not to tell others about us." He held her coat, her perfume tempting him to pull her close and forget the dinner. When his fingers brushed her neck, she smiled at him.

Five of his former advisees waited at a large table in the German restaurant when they arrived. He was pleasantly surprised to see the sixth person, Elizabeth Abbott, the woman who'd risked her life to help him overcome the threats of Jefferson Bell and his associates from a fundamentalist church group opposed to gene therapy. They all jumped up to shake Jason's hand or give him a hug. Diners at adjacent tables smiled at their enthusiasm and obvious good feelings for each other.

Jason introduced Kathryn to all—P.V. Rao, Lisa Larkin, Ted Trask, Darlene Moeller and Elizabeth and tried to recall the research projects they'd done for their dissertations. Remembering Sylvia Rann, Kathryn shook her hand then the others. They settled into their places and ordered drinks.

428

As the waitress left, Jason said, "I know you've all heard of the turmoil around me for the past months. I hope that is past."

Lisa piped up. "We heard you've been named department head. That's great."

Wishing to mute their suspense about this beautiful woman with him, Jason said, "I know you're wondering about Kathryn and her place in my life. And so to relieve your curiosity, Kathryn and I plan to be married as soon as we know her position for next year. And we hope that will be soon."

After the congratulations and further visual examination of Kathryn had gone on for a few seconds, Jason added, "Since all of you understand the politics within universities or will soon, we'd like to keep our relationship below the radar until her work place is known. Remember I tried to teach you about confidential matters."

"Among other things," P.V. chirped in, unusual for this quiet Indian now working in Delhi.

Drinks came, Sylvia proposed a toast to Jason and Kathryn and to the good experiences they'd had while at State.

The evening settled in to exchanges of information about jobs, current research, problems confronting them, concerns about tenure, grant applications. They enjoyed the great German food and drink. Then they realized they were the only ones remaining and the staff was eyeing them.

Elizabeth recognized the situation. "I suspect we'd best get going before they usher us out. It's been wonderful to see all of you and we should do this every year."

They meandered out, heading in different directions toward hotels, feeling safe on the streets still busy with convention goers.

Nearing their hotel, Kathryn said, "I felt like an outsider but it's obvious they all have great feelings toward you. That must be rewarding after the hurdles associated with getting a doctoral degree."

"They're a good group and they all thought you are beautiful and I'm lucky to have you in my life." His arm circled her waist.

In her room, he held her coat, then removed his own. He touched her cheek, then turned her face to meet her lips with his. She responded, her mouth exploring his, her hand inside his shirt moving across his chest and mid-section, pulling the shirt out of his pants, nibbling at his shoulders. He eased the form fitting black dress from her shoulders and draped it across a chair. He kissed the top of her breasts, then when she unsnapped the bra, he ran his tongue across the nipples, firm and warm. He ran his hand along her silky legs, caressed her through the pantyhose.

Her skin was burning as he turned her to fondle her breasts, his lips on her neck. She murmured as passion swept over her. He slipped off his clothes then helped her remove the nylons. They came together as they sprawled across the bed, he pressing into her and her hips moving upward to meet his thrusts. They lost track of time. He felt her shudder under him, pulling her hips into his thrusts until he attained the ultimate release and tremors racked his frame. He continued to press her close, knowing his feelings for her would only grow in the future. As the need for sleep began to dominate, she pulled the covers over them and snuggled close to him.

Just before dawn, Jason leaned over her, watching her peaceful slumber, her hair tousled, a slight smile on her face. He eased out of bed, pulled on his shirt and pants, slipped into his shoes, and crept to his room.

On the plane returning from Minneapolis, Kathryn took his hand. "My parents liked you. While we were in the kitchen, my mother told me to hang on to you. That's the first time she's ever said that. Each time before when I introduced a male friend she always suggested I could do better."

"Maybe she was concerned you were running out of options." He squeezed her fingers.

She giggled, "Don't think so. You saw how those guys at FASEB kept looking."

He leaned over to kiss her cheek. "I know. I was ready to hit some of them."

Jason said, "But your father in his way hinted my clothes needed updating." Lars Helweg had insisted Jason visit the store, have the tailor take measurements, then had delivered the morning they were leaving three beautiful wool suits with matching ties. And stashed in a garment bag for traveling.

"I'm sorry he's that way. He gave me four dresses saying I needed to look professional, but they're too dressy for work. He doesn't understand the risks of wrecking good garments in labs."

"But they're sexy, aren't they?"

"Is that always on your mind?" She leaned against him, whispered, "I hope so."

They sat quietly for a bit, watching passengers move up and down the aisle, the stewardess checking on a mother with a small child. Kathryn twisted her fingers into his and said, "In all the rush to get to dinner our last night in Chicago and then all the things my parents involved us in, I forgot to tell you one of the professors from the biochemistry section of the Medical School came to hear my paper. Afterward, he came by to introduce himself, a Dr. Slovensky. He had reviewed my application for the position and said they were impressed and I'd be invited for an interview."

"Great. I've met Slovensky through John Hadley. He had ideas about the insertion of corrected genetic materials when we were struggling with Wilson's disease. He's been around a long time and I've heard as a very young boy he'd been a prisoner of the Germans during the war. I think his parents were killed in a concentration camp."

"He didn't know the schedule for interviews but he did know they wanted to decide soon and may only interview one person, then decide to offer or bring in another if they had concerns."

"Sounds like you're the first."

"I know, but," she pressed her shoulder against his, "I'll avoid those sexy outfits. Just impress them with my intelligence."

The plane began the descent through heavy clouds with air currents bumping the large plane as though it were a weightless object. The seat belt sign flashed on and an announcement informed them to

432

remain in their seats as they would experience some turbulence during the next few minutes. Three minutes later the sun appeared below the clouds and then the ground became visible.

Jason whispered. "Back to the land of sneaking around."

"But that will soon end." She bumped her foot against his leg.

Early Monday morning Peggy Murphy's quiet voice on the phone cut into his attempt to move all the accumulated papers from his desk. "Dr. Spradlin, your request took longer than I'd hoped and we've been busy with the legislative agenda. But I've learned a couple of things and wanted to pass them along."

"I'm sure whatever you tell me will be helpful." He flipped to a clean sheet on the notepad in case he wanted to write something down.

Murphy said, "I am certain Clarence Haskell is ramrodding the actions involving Dr. King. He has pushed Congressman Ladner to reopen hearings week after next."

"Dr. King and an associate have been called to appear."

"That confirms what I've been told about Haskell's agenda. Now the second thing I can tell you is that Haskell is involved with the founding of a pharmaceutical company. The name is Biotech West, Inc. It has a Portland address and documents to incorporate were filed in July of last year. My source wasn't certain, but suspects Haskell is the President of this organization." Jason made notes, now almost certain Thiele and McLean were associated with Haskell as speculated by his biology friends from Oregon.

He asked, "What's Haskell's background? Any connection to the pharmaceutical industry prior to this start up company?"

"He's a lawyer and has been around Congress for fifteen years or longer. He was here before Ladner was elected but joined his staff immediately. He has the reputation of being ruthless when he finds an issue that interests him or can give him additional power." Murphy's dislike of Haskell came across as her tone hardened. It was clear Haskell had established in her mind the attributes of a bully.

"Does he attempt to assist constituents with their problems or causes?"

Murphy hesitated. "I'm sure he does, especially if the individual or group can be useful to him. Many who know him describe him as the non-elected representative or a pseudo-Congressman."

Getting to the point of the King issue, Jason asked, "In your inquiries about Haskell, did you discover anything suggesting some association with either Thiele or McLean?"

"Not specifically, but my source knew a couple of science types had become involved with Biotech West. Their intention, as she understood, is to produce drugs that work against viral infections. But she didn't know enough about that to say with any degree of certainty."

Jason scanned his notes. "Ms. Murphy, this has been most helpful. Thanks so much for your work." Remembering he had to be in Washington for the hearings, he continued, "I'll be in D.C. for the next round of hearings. May I come by and introduce myself?"

434

"I'd like that. It's always nice to meet people we've interacted with. Drop by room 4629 in the House building. I'm here most of each day."

Breaking the connection, Jason leaned back in his chair. All his speculations were coming true. There was not yet a clean connection between Thiele and McLean with Haskell and this company, but it made sense. He didn't have enough to be certain, then he remembered his own advice about being aggressive.

He found the telephone number for the Oregon Department of Commerce through information and called, knowing he'd be forced to weave his way through several offices before getting to the right one. But he could locate the key to this crap about King.

O'Hare phoned mid-morning. "I tried to get you last week but you were out of town. You may have heard that Boseman reached a plea bargain with the City Attorney and the Court agreed. He will serve thirty years with parole possible after twenty."

"You think that was okay?"

"Yeah, you never know how a trial will play out. He could have gotten a more severe sentence, but he may have wiggled free. He'll be an old man when he's out. Wrecked his life and any career aspirations."

"He was also filled with hate and wanted revenge for every little issue that contradicted his personal goals. That's why he failed in his job here. Then he killed an innocent person who gave so much to everyone around her."

After a pause, Tom said, "Sounds like you're not past Lucy's death yet."

"I am for the most part, but it still haunts me at times, especially when I think of Boseman. Tom, we were lucky he didn't kill someone else while he was trying to set me up."

Sitting quietly after the exchange with O'Hare, he wondered about his automatic response involving Lucy. He hoped his lingering emotions didn't contaminate his love for Kathryn. He accepted he'd have to work at control when the subject arose.

CHAPTER 40

At five minutes before nine Ladner entered the hearing room, the same one they'd been in previously, followed by Wilke and two other Congressmen. As usual, aides scrambled about, whispering to the representatives and each other. However, the media was absent except for a couple of young male reporters waiting quietly in the third row, their eyes staring into space, bored and wishing they'd been assigned to a more exciting story. Sitting on the front row reserved for those who would be called as witnesses, Jason's eyes met Wilke's, who nodded and smiled.

Promptly at nine Ladner gaveled the hearings to order. "During this session of the House Committee for Science and Technology, we intend to have Dr. Preston King and Dr. Kathryn Helweg explain discrepancies in their lab journals, including the missing pages we presume contained incriminating evidence. Committee members have been given copies of correspondence between my office and the State University investigators.

"Their testimonies will be followed by a statement from Dr. Jason Spradlin who requested this opportunity. The record will show these hearings are a continuation of the committee's effort to demonstrate the publications by Dr. King and his associates are based on erroneous and manufactured data. This session is also a part of our investigation into the conduct of scientists. This specific example of misconduct was brought to our attention by two noted scientists, Dr. Reginald McLean and Dr. Alexander Thiele to whom we are grateful. We are honored to have both present today although neither will be called to testify." Jason turned in his seat to see the accusers whom he'd not observed when they entered. Seated together in the fourth row, they returned Jason's stare.

"Now I'll ask Drs. King and Helweg to come to the witness table. Since they've worked together on these papers and the subsequent review, it seems appropriate they explain the errors in concert." The smirk on Ladner's broad face revealed his thinking the sinners would finally be forced to confess and seek forgiveness.

Ladner waited for Preston and Kathryn to come forward, turning to take a note from an aide. Then he looked down from the elevated position of the committee members and said, "We will now give attention to your statements."

As they had planned, King started, "At this time, Congressman Ladner, neither of us will make a formal statement, but we wish to respond to your questions related to the paper and the data on which it is based. I request the official record to show that all of our laboratory records, including all calculations and statistical treatment of the data were provided your staff person, Mr. Clarence Haskell, on February eleventh."

Scowling at King, Ladner asked, "Am I correct in stating that on two occasions our staff has discovered discrepancies and have requested clarification?" He glanced along the row of committee members as though letting them know he'd been diligent in his efforts to uncover unacceptable behavior.

King responded. "That's correct. We received two sets of questions about entries into the lab books. On both occasions we responded as quickly as possible to the questions."

"Did you regard those discrepancies as evidence of errors . . . . or worse?"

"No sir," King replied, his voice firm, maybe even challenging. "As we pointed out in our responses, all the questions were about minor, even irrelevant, things, such as numbers crossed out and the correct number inserted, an apparent erasure, or other notes commonly found in data books. In fact, I would describe the questions as nit-picking and without substance. Anyone who has done laboratory experiments and maintained proper logs would understand how these things occur."

Ladner's face hardened, his eyes bored into King's features. "So you didn't give those questions your full attention, but passed them off as inconsequential?"

King smiled at the committee members, an act noticed by Ladner. "That's not what I said or implied. Dr. Helweg and I spent considerable time checking each entry and preparing an explanation. We gave it our full attention for several hours."

"And it's still your contention that none of those questions, some twenty in total, failed to reveal a single error or evidence of misdeed?"

"That is correct." King's tone remained firm and measured.

Ladner shifted papers in front of him. "Then on February twenty, our reviewer discovered three missing pages in one of the books that you claim were intact when the materials were submitted to Mr. Haskell."

Kathryn responded, causing the members to shift focus. "That's correct. We stand by our statement. All materials were complete when turned over to your office."

Ladner smiled as he looked at Kathryn. "And how can you prove to me the pages were not removed by Dr. king or you or someone acting on your behalf?"

Without hesitation, her eyes boring into Ladner's, Kathryn replied. "Because all copies of the materials given to Mr. Haskell were initialed by our attorney and copied in her office. We have copies in our files. Mr. Haskell received the entire record."

Seeming to be taken aback for a moment, Ladner faltered then sputtered, "And how can you explain the missing pages?"

"You'll have to ask Mr. Haskell about those." Then she added in a softer tone. "For the record, we submitted copies of the missing pages, but if those too have been lost, we'll be pleased to provide an additional copy." She smiled, her eyes locked on Ladner still challenging him to query Haskell about the missing pages.

Ladner growled. "I don't like my office being accused of sloppy handling of documents."

Kathryn nodded, saying, "I understand the embarrassment, but Mr. Haskell may have an acceptable explanation of how he mishandled confidential materials submitted to the committee."

Ladner reddened and waved his arm in frustration and anger. "I refuse to have a trusted associate falsely accused . . . ."

440

Wilke broke in. "I'd like Mr. Haskell to be brought in so he can explain or defend his apparent negligence. If he deliberately cut pages from those materials, in my judgment, he has committed a serious violation."

Another committee member chimed in. "I agree."

Jason noticed the reporters leaning forward, scribbling in notebooks, their interest perked by this sudden turn of events in an otherwise expected dull affair. Three other committee members chose that moment to slip into their seats, apparently alerted by aides that the tension was building in a session they'd marked off as of little consequence.

Ladner regaining control but still flustered by the demands of other members, shuffled papers and said, "I'll give my colleagues an opportunity to raise questions."

Leaning forward and pulling the microphone closer, Wilke said, "Dr. King and Dr. Helweg, I appreciate your time today and the efforts you expended on these issues. For one, I accept with thanks your responses, although I've not been privy to the review of your lab journals. But after this exchange, I will ask Mr. Haskell to bring all materials to my office."

When none of the other members wanted to raise questions, Ladner murmured, "Now we'll give Dr. Spradlin time for his statement. Again I remind the committee and the record, we did not request this statement, thus I trust Dr. Spradlin's comments will enlighten us."

Seated at the table, Jason said, "I agree with Mr. Ladner that my appearance is voluntary and I appreciate the opportunity to present certain information I believe will reveal the underlying basis for these sessions and outline State University's plans for responding beyond these hearings." His eyes moved to each committee member as he spoke. Ladner remained impassive, his features dark as he stared at Jason.

"For several months my colleagues, Preston King and Kathryn Helweg, have lived under the spotlight of a public accusation of wrong-doing. I have concluded they have been the target of accusers seeking personal gain and I trust my statement will set the record straight. Thus far, we've been unable to question the accusers, although we will have that opportunity when they are called to testify in the suit we have filed this morning in District Court charging them with libel, defamation of character, and related criminal acts."

Ladner squirmed but didn't try to stop Jason. Other committee members leaned forward. Aides stopped moving about.

"When the accusation was initially made, I persuaded Dr. King to have a different team of laboratory personnel repeat the experiments on which the original paper was based. That exercise was accomplished at considerable expense to the university and used valuable time by Dr. King's analysts. When the second experiment corroborated the earlier work, I knew he was right. Unknown to us until six weeks ago, another laboratory had done the same experiment with the same outcome. That investigator, Dr. Pierre from McGill University in Montreal, sent Dr. King a letter congratulating him on being first to demonstrate a new facet of the problem they were exploring. Copies of that letter were sent to Mr. Ladner's office as well

442

as to Congressman Wilke. In our thinking that should have negated the charge of manufactured data or misinterpretation of data. We believed replication by Dr. King's paper by another investigator, working independently and without knowledge of the King experiments, should have concluded this effort to discredit King and Helweg. "

Ladner broke in. "I did not receive that letter."

Jason pulled a paper from his folder. "The letter sent as registered mail requiring a signature of receipt was signed into your office on March twenty-eight by Clarence Haskell. Perhaps he believed you didn't need to see it."

Wilke said quietly from his end position. "I have the copy here."

Jason continued, determined to get the facts as he knew them on the record. "From the very outset, I couldn't understand the actions of the accusers who demanded an immediate retraction by King and the journal in which the paper appeared. Why not allow the usual mechanisms of science demonstrate the flaws. At no time did Thiele or McLean raise a single question about the experimental methods or the logic underlying King's conclusions, only an orchestrated and unsupported demand for retraction in the public arena.

"It became an intriguing puzzle, but the pieces have come together through questions raised by friends who risked their careers and by sheer luck. I discovered Mr. Haskell is in the process of establishing a company in Oregon to produce a medication to combat viral infections. His method would be based on the work of Thiele and McLean. But the paper published by King demonstrated the methodology they intended to utilize would not work. They were in a

443

bind and probably had investors waiting to support their enterprise. Thus, they needed to get that information out of the scientific literature or be accused of misleading those patrons. They believed they could force King to withdraw his publication. When that effort failed, they somehow through Haskell convinced Congressman Ladner to initiate these hearings as another attempt to discredit the publication. I have confirmed Haskell's intent through the Oregon Department of Commerce. Further, both Thiele and McLean are listed on the request to organize the company.

"State University has filed civil suits against Thiele, McLean and Haskell for actions designed to wrongfully embarrass and discredit Preston King and his coworkers as well as the institution for which they work.. In this respect, I speak with the full support of my President and the Attorney General of the State. We intend to move expediently with this inquiry and I am confident we will demonstrate the three set out to damage an excellent scientist who had made an important addition to the understanding of a vital process."

"Thank you for your attention to my statement." He shoved his papers into a folder and leaned back.

Ladner burst out. "You aren't serious, young man. Threatening a Congressional committee and accusing me personally can get you in deep trouble."

Jason waited for the murmurs to subside. 'We are very serious, Mr. Ladner. We are not challenging the Congress nor its responsibility to conduct legitimate hearings in those areas served by public funds. However, we contend in this specific situation, the Congress has been

444

used by individuals for personal gains. We intend to press charges not against this committee, but against those who attempted to hide behind the structure of Congress for wrongful purposes." He paused, looking at each member, then said, "We trust the committee and the mechanisms of the Congress to examine its own actions in this matter."

Wilke interrupted Ladner's mutterings to ask, "Dr. Spradlin, can you prove the things you have outlined?"

Jason felt confident about the pieces pulled together from his sources. "Yes, sir, I believe when the parties I challenged are brought into court and sworn to tell the truth or perjure themselves, that the scenario I outlined will be essentially correct."

Wilke looked at Jason for several seconds as though weighing his contention, then turned toward Ladner. "May I suggest, Mr. Chairman, that these hearings be in recess."

Ladner banged the gavel. "So ordered."

Jason turned in time to see McLean, Thiele and their attorney rushing for the door. The reporters sprinted out. The audience milled around pointing toward Ladner as he retreated through the exit.

Grinning at Jason, King rushed to shake his hand. "How'd you know that stuff? You should've seen those bastards' faces. Then they charged out of here like they were late for the last plane out."

Kathryn held his hand and hugged him. "Their reactions tell me you're correct."

"I had help with the pieces then it all came together. Stella thought Thiele and McLean might ask for a rebuttal time, but when they scampered out of here, I knew we had them pegged correctly."

Congressman Wilke's voice broke into their huddle. "Dr. Spradlin, my hunch is you've heard the last of these inquiries. I'm fairly confident you are correct about the actions of those guys. Ladner must be embarrassed by having the scheme exposed, but he won't admit he was duped."

Still skeptical of Ladner because of his scornful stares and voice of contempt. "I suspect Ladner was involved from the outset," Jason replied. "If our attorney agrees, we might bring him in as a witness just to hear him confess he knew the whole deal was a charade."

Frowning, Wilke said, "I'd be surprised if Ladner really knew what Haskell was up to, but you may be right to a degree. Ladner should have suspected something was not quite legitimate after the first set of hearings. Most of the committee wanted to drop the matter then, but the system gives committee chairs a lot of flexibility and power, probably too much."

Wilke paused, looking at the three of them, and continued, "But in Ladner's defense, and we're all in the same situation, he depended on staff and trusted they would not abuse their positions." Jason nodded with the realization that the system caused someone like Wilke to protect a colleague, even though they differed on most matters and in the face of unethical behavior.

Wilke turned as though leaving, but Jason held him by saying, "NIH officials have alerted us that Haskell, supposedly acting on

446

Ladner's authority, has threatened to block a major grant we've been awarded. In fact, notification to all recipients has been delayed because of his threat."

Wilke's face hardened, his mouth in a firm line. "I'll check on it. I can promise you neither Haskell nor Ladner will interfere with the agency's normal procedures. We've been through those battles too many times."

"We'll appreciate your efforts to move the process forward."

Wilke shook everyone's hand. "Good luck in the future and I hope I won't meet you again under similar circumstances." His face broke into a wide smile as he took Jason's arm. "You should think about getting into politics."

"Congressman, if you have been around universities, you would know I'm in over my head now."

Wilke laughed, as did King and Kathryn. Wilke turned toward a young man holding a folder in his hand.

Jason glanced at the wall clock. "Maybe we can get an afternoon flight if one of you wouldn't mind checking. But before I leave the building I need to thank someone who helped discover the information about Thiele, McLean, and Haskell. I'd invite you along, but I've promised no one is to know of the person's involvement."

Kathryn looked at King who said, "Wilke is right. What an operator."

They laughed and Kathryn volunteered. "I'll check on flights and let's meet at the hotel as soon as possible."

447

After wandering for a few minutes and asking directions from a custodian working in the hall, Jason found Peggy Murphy almost hidden behind a desk stacked with papers, manila envelopes, file folders and assorted other materials. "Ms. Murphy, I'm Jason Spradlin. I came by to thank you personally for your help."

She stood, a short, brunette going gray haired woman, a pleasant face. "I trust it worked out well." She emerged from her den to shake Jason's hand.

"Yes, very much. Between the two of us, you may have seen the last of Clarence Haskell around this building."

Her smile creased her features. "That would be a blessing. Please call on me again if I can be of assistance." She turned away to pick up a ringing telephone and waved as Jason backed away.

CHAPTER 41

Ten days after their appearance at the committee hearings, the *Herald* headlined an article on the page devoted to national affairs—**Congressman Accused**. The details revealed the House of Representatives Ethics Committee had scheduled hearings on the conduct of Congressman Ladner, Oregon's fourth District, during an investigation into the misdeeds of scientists. In the third paragraph of the article, two sentences reported the resignation of Mr. Clarence Haskell, the Congressman's long time aide.

Jason folded the paper, dropped it onto the end table, and helped Jennifer secure the belt around her coat. Although the beginning of spring had arrived according to the calendar, the weather remained blustery with spits of rain. "Okay, you're all set. Mrs. Carter will drop you off and I'll pick you up so we can have a dinner at your favorite place."

She threw her arms around his neck. "Bye, Daddy."

He watched her go, the idea she would enter first grade in the fall difficult to fathom. The rapid passage of time and the growth of his first born child hinted at his own aging process. And passing thoughts about how Kathryn would mesh into the household of two kids reminded him of the rapid changes coming. He and Kathryn had discussed briefly the potential role of Mrs. Carter after their marriage, both leaning toward retaining her present status, but he'd not discussed possibilities with Carter yet.

Stella Krause had assembled them in a conference room within the University Attorney's suite, always neat and tidy without the typical debris in public places.

After the usual pleasantries and discussions of the news about Ladner, Stella said, "I brought you together because the attorneys for McLean and Thiele wish to make a deal rather than battle it out in court. I want your thoughts and ultimately your approval of any bargain."

King, sitting at the end of the table, his long legs stretched beyond the width of the rectangular furnishing, asked, "What have they proposed?"

"They suggest," Stella said, scanning notes she'd apparently made while conversing by phone, "that Thiele and McLean will pay you seven hundred thousand rather than the million we placed in the court document. They will issue public apologies through the news media and in a letter to the editor of the *Journal of Cell Biology.*"

Kathryn asked, "What do you think? You know more about these deals than we."

The attorney replied, "I'd be inclined to accept their offer. You never know how the court will rule. And we will insist on seeing the apologies in print before we close the negotiations."

Jason added his thoughts. "I'd like to see the bastards squirm on the witness stand. I think the deal is acceptable, but the decision is up to Preston and Kathryn."

King rested his arms on the table. "I'll live with that but I would have preferred to see them hauled into court and made to reveal their sneaky intentions."

"If we're in agreement, I'll inform them this morning. Now, perhaps a more difficult issue is how do you wish the funds distributed? I've discussed the matter with the Attorney General and with the Vice-President for Administration. They're in agreement neither the state nor the university have a stake in this settlement."

The three looked at each other, their faces blank, having never considered the options. Jason broke the stalemate. "Since Preston bore the brunt of the attack, he should receive the majority of the proceeds. Kathryn should receive a share, and maybe those two graduate students and Robert Tanaka be recognized with smaller amounts. As to precise numbers, I don't know."

Stella reminded them. "The Attorney General will expect to recover expenses but those are minor. He may want reimbursement of my expenses for the trip to D.C. for the first hearings and incidental costs of telephone and preparation of court documents. I'd guess that would be less than two thousand."

"Any court costs related to the filing of the suit?" Kathryn asked.

"Maybe another two thousand but I could demand Thiele and McLean pay those. And your department incurred expenses in getting you to Washington."

Jason said, "I can get Miriam to come up with the exact numbers. I'd estimate five thousand for plane tickets, hotels, meals, maybe other small items."

Stella said, "Okay, let's say ten thousand for expenses. May I propose the following division—four hundred thousand to Dr. King; two hundred thousand to Dr. Helweg; thirty thousand to each of the other three, leaving ten thousand to cover costs."

King jumped in. "Sounds good to me, but I'd like to use the money coming to me as a reserve for things needed from time to time in my research lab."

Kathryn followed quickly. "I'll put mine with Dr. King's with the proviso that if I locate a position at State, I could use those monies as start up funds to get research underway."

Jason said, "I applaud your generosity, but maybe each of you should take fifty thousand for personal use. Put the rest into a fund for your professional use, equipment, travel to conferences, things that come along the university can't support."

King and Kathryn nodded at each other. King said, "Let's do it that way."

Stella laughed at the looks on their faces when they realized what they'd agreed to so quickly. "I'll set it up. And those grad students and Mr. Tanaka will have more money than they've ever seen before."

"Remember," Jason said, "their careers could have been tainted before they began if Thiele and McLean had prevailed."

Standing, his long frame looming over the others, King said, "We need to celebrate—do something other than just go back to our desks and mundane tasks. Tell you what, let me treat all of you to dinner at a really good place. How about Saturday night if it'll work. Stella you can be my date."

Jason had never seen King so animated, his usual calm demeanor had been overrun by this sudden enthusiasm. Then he realized the pressure his colleague had been withstanding for months had finally been taken from is shoulders.

Walking toward Quincy in the bright sun with the clouds breaking up and the temperature rising, Kathryn said, "I sent my teaching evaluations to Dr. Slovensky yesterday. Now I must wait to hear from them."

"Comments from the reviewers were excellent."

"I didn't know how it would go although I believe the students are learning. The test scores on the last exam were quite good, only a few failures out of the hundred and fifty."

Jason asked, "Shall we go together for dinner Saturday?"

Kathryn glanced at him, waited for a group of students to pass. "You know they'll suspect something if we show together."

Jason grinned, wanting to take her arm. "I believe they already know there's something special between us. We could even tell them our plans."

"Let's don't do that yet. Keep them guessing."

"We'll talk about it more tonight."

She bumped her shoulder into his. "Sure we will."

With the fiasco surrounding King concluded, Jason turned his full attention to the department and the future. He had fragments of plans to try focusing the department on two or three major subject areas and make their mark nationally for those rather than continue to cover the spectrum of subjects found in most traditional biology departments. He wanted to involve the entire faculty in that discussion and to have all on board if possible.

He started the annual conferences with faculty in the department. He'd spent hours reading their activity reports piled on his desk when he returned from the D.C. trip. He'd made notes about issues the faculty member had raised or things he wanted to communicate. He'd asked Audrey to schedule thirty minutes for each and to begin with Riley. He wanted to get past that confrontation then exchange ideas and hopes with those who year after year did their job and were happy to be in the department.

After considering the future of the department which would have three or four vacant positions by the end of this academic year, he talked with Roy Blount about filling his faculty position on a temporary assignment for the following year, teaching a section of General Biology, and keeping the Redlake work going. He made it clear to Roy he could be a candidate for the permanent slot, although there was no solid promise he'd be the successful applicant. Roy had done an excellent job with the embryo culture efforts and now they were preparing to impregnate a dozen sows owned by a grower near the Redlake facility. If that succeeded, Redlake intended to expand the process as rapidly as possible and soon be able to mass produce meat

454

from a lean, rapidly growing animal for the consumer market. But there were still questions to be resolved before there could be a predictable and reliable product attractive to customers. In the recesses of his thinking, Jason had some concerns the Food and Drug Administration would raise obstacles to an animal not bred in the traditional manner, even though the outcome was the same. Those from the far right wing of society still harbored reservations, even outright objections to anything resembling non-traditional methods. He made a note to discuss his concerns with Brenda Fallon in the near future. Redlake couldn't afford to have a disaster after the huge investment.

As the spring semester approached the end, Riley, Townsend, and Harris held their last meeting in Randolph's Bar and Grill on the Friday afternoon prior to final exam week. They settled around the usual table with steins of draft beer sweating in the humid establishment filled with students celebrating the end of classes.

Townsend raised his glass. "Here's to another year and a good summer."

His two colleagues touched their mugs with his, then Riley said, "This may be my last time with you guys."

Both his pals were taken aback for a moment, then Harris asked, "Are you resigning? Is that what you're telling us?"

Nodding his head, Riley said, "In a manner of speaking, but the university is buying out my last years. I had my conference with Spradlin two weeks ago. Without much of the usual stuff that goes on in those reviews, he came right out proposed a buy-out and termination of my appointment. He had it all figured. Three years salary in either a lump sum or spread over the three years coupled with my resignation effective at the end of this spring term."

"But," Townsend said, "you can't be fired like that with tenure and all the years you've given State."

Riley ran a finger along the side of his stein. "Spradlin admitted that, but he let me know I'd never receive another raise. In my mind, it's a wash. I was able to have a few days to consider the options, especially the payment schedule. I decided to take the salary over the three years because of tax implications and get the hell out of there. I told him this morning. I figured why spend five more years with Spradlin on my back and giving me hell every time I turned around."

Harris asked, "Did this arrest enter the discussion? I've heard if you commit a felony, the university can get rid of you, tenure or not."

"Never came up. But Spradlin did tell me straight out I'd become a liability with all my gossiping and sneaking around to find out stuff about others. And he had all my teaching evaluations laid out to show I'd not done very well. In his words I was doing more damage than good."

Harris spoke up. "I thought my review went okay. He congratulated me on my new grant and the productivity of my research. He did ask about my relations with Sanchez and indicated he was pleased he'd not heard anything more about it. He led me to believe I'd receive a decent raise for next year."

456

Riley asked, "Peter, how about you? Are you on Spradlin's list to go?"

Townsend placed his dead pipe on the table. "We had a good discussion. I admitted I could do a better job of teaching, that I'd not maintained currency with the senior course I've had for years. In a non-threatening manner, he asked that I give my responsibilities more work and cease voicing rumors about my colleagues."

"So you came out pleased?"

"Challenged to do better is how I perceived the review. Spradlin let me know he expected more in the future, but I'd come to that conclusion myself after hearing his seminar during the search."

"Bottom line guys," Harris summarized, "Spradlin will be tough if he thinks you're a slacker and you will always know where you stand with him. Not much different than Rogers, but maybe higher expectations. He wants Biology to be outstanding rather than average."

Townsend nodded, fingered his pipe and put it into his coat pocket. "You're correct, Greg. The memo he sent two days ago about giving the department some focal areas rather than covering the waterfront is the first shot."

Riley finished his beer. "Keep in touch with me. I don't know yet if we'll remain in Spencerville. My wife likes it here and knows a lot of people. But part of my probation deal with the city attorney is I leave the area or report to a court appointed officer on a monthly schedule. In fact, I might try to land a teaching job with one of the community colleges within the area. I'll let you know. Now I need to begin cleaning out my office so I'm out of the place by the time I turn in my final grades." He stood, shoved the chair in place, and meandered through the crowd.

His buddies followed.

At the door, they stopped and looked back. Townsend said, "Greg, let's keep this going next year."

"I'd like that but without Riley, it won't be the same."

"My suspicion," Peter said, "is Riley will be around just to keep up with things."

CHAPTER 42

Even in northern Minnesota the July days were warm, then the nights cooled requiring a jacket if outside and a blanket on the bed. On their third night at the upscale lodge, Kathryn and Jason had consumed a great meal of soup, salmon, mixed vegetables, rice and the chef's own baked bread and outstanding desserts. Wine and coffee with dessert had more than filled them. Hand in hand they meandered from the restaurant toward their suite in one of the rustic buildings that had been built fifty years ago and upgraded a couple of times. Now it was a posh resort offering a variety of recreational activities, fine dining and a wide range of personal services.

Inside their cabin, Jason kissed her and led her to sit on his lap in one of the comfortable chairs. "Your mother seemed to get over our insistence we have a small, family-oriented wedding."

"She will remind us on occasion, but ignore her. She'd always dreamed of huge church affairs with bridesmaids, receptions, organs, the whole bit. My sister went through that, planning and scheming for weeks, altering dresses, worrying over the best floral arrangements, trying out an organist, all that, and her marriage lasted three years."

"I suspect we will do better." They had married in the Helweg's home church with their Lutheran minister officiating. Her father had without their prior knowledge provided the attire for both of them. He'd sent a black suit and muted tie for Jason. For Kathryn he'd had his in-store designer create a white dress, fitted bodice, tight at the waist, then flaring out from the hips to mid-calf length. The old man was rewarded when everyone raved about how beautiful she was in the lovely dress.

A few friends and several relatives sat in the front pews of the huge sanctuary. A reception followed in the recreation hall of the sprawling church. Then they escaped, flying in a small commuter plane to this isolated but luxurious place.

Her eyes on his, inserting her fingers through his unbuttoned shirt to caress his chest. "We will for certain. I can't imagine going through life without you. And we've been blessed thus far. Everything we hoped for has worked out. My position in the Med school, your headship, Mrs. Carter agreeing to remain with us."

"Are you past your reservations about her?" His hand skimmed across her knees.

"For the most part. I want to become the person your kids call mother and having her around puts a damper on that coming true."

"But the plus side is she'll take a huge burden off both of us by taking care of the daily chores to keep the household functioning. You need to focus all your attention on your work and gaining tenure rather than become bogged down with household chores. And we did agree with her we'd review the arrangement in a year."

Kathryn snuggled closer against him. "She had concerns herself, not wanting to be in the way of a new wife."

"The new place will help with that." They'd discussed the arrangement with Carter and her desire for some privacy and their need for freedom from a third party. In the end, they'd purchased another house, one with a built in apartment in the basement. Carter could call it her home without their interference and they would have full use of the main house absent her presence after the evening meals. They all agreed it was a strange set-up but it could work. And the best thing was the children had come to love and depend on Carter while seeming to adore being with Kathryn.

He moved his hand along her leg. They kissed deeply, trying to please each other as their passion deepened. Soon with their clothes in disarray, they moved to the bed.

After a week they flew to Spencerville. Arriving mid-afternoon, they went by the office before facing the turmoil of moving into a new home and melding Kathryn's personal belongings with his. Kathryn went up the stairs to King's lab to check on any mail or messages on her computer.

Jason stared at the desk, piled high with messages, personal mail, stacks of papers to be reviewed and signed, a message from Audrey welcoming him back and informing him nothing urgent awaited him.

He pulled out the yellow pad from the drawer. All items had been scratched through. He tore off the several pages he had filled after the few notes left by Henry. A blank page waited for the first entry in the new era for both the department and for him personally.

THE END

ABOUT THE AUTHOR

S. J. Ritchey served as a faculty member and administrator at Virginia Tech. He began writing fiction after his retirement and has short stories in magazines and in two collections published by Blue River Writers.

The author lives with his wife, Elizabeth, in Blacksburg, Virginia. They spend summers at her family cottage on Lake Couchiching near Washago, Ontario, Canada.

462

Contents

CHAPTER 2

LISTINGS, LISTINGS, LISTINGS - LISTINGS AND LISTING SYSTEMS

CHAPTER 1

BUYERS, BUYERS, BUYERS - BUYERS AND BUYERS SYSTEMS

Foreword

Recently a new Salesperson revealed to me what most newly licensed individuals experience... *"Bruce, when I got my real estate license, it seemed like they gave me the keys to the car but then nobody taught me how to drive it."* There's a lot of wisdom in that analogy and...no doubt a lot of frustration for people starting out.

In his first book, ***List to Last***, Stephen Silver focused on prospecting for, closing on and managing listings. In his second book, ***Foundations for Success***, Steve takes you through a very detailed process of "how to drive a car." As a new REALTOR®, you need to take time to develop your business without wasting time and money. You'll learn how to:

- Develop a simple business plan that will take you on the trip from where you are now to where you want to be.
- Avoid the most common traps in which new REALTORS® get caught.
- Implement the systems that help you:
  - Become organized, in terms of managing time, finances and clients.
  - Connect with and cultivate the leads you'll need to develop in order to secure a consistent, reproducible business.
  - Manage listings and buyers from start to finish.

This book provides specific business building exercises for you to complete that will utilize the information provided and get you on track to success fast. You'll see how you can achieve the success you deserve and grow your business at a significantly greater rate than you ever thought.

I have known Steve Silver for a long time… he knows the business inside out and is an excellent "driving instructor." Follow these steps, take them on chapter by chapter and you too will be "a great driver". Good luck…turn the key and start your engine!

Bruce Keith

Bruce Keith is a leading Motivational Speaker and Trainer for sales organizations in North America, specializing in Real Estate Sales.

He has been in real estate in excess of 27 years, including 16 years as a top Coach for thousands of Sales Agents. Learn more at www.BruceKeithResults.com.

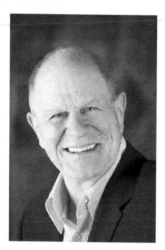

Acknowledgements

Bruce Keith, mentor, coach and long-time friend, for sharing his experience, his encouragement and recommendations, which made the publishing of this series possible.

Aileen Simcic, my best friend and business partner, for her support and encouragement through the many years of our shared real estate practice and beyond and her husband, Christopher Hairrell, for putting up with it all.

Bohdan Uszkalo, friend, business partner and general wild and crazy guy, who always had a joke (not always great) and an encouraging word.

Gerald Tostowaryk, whose personal and professional life defines the meaning of ethics and character and who kept me pointed in the right direction when I needed it.

Dan Gitzel, friend, Broker and mentor, who gave me the chance to find my way back to what I love, teaching and helping others and without whom none of this would have been possible.

David Yunker, ever present and ever available friend, mentor and sounding board, without whose guidance and advice this work would have oft gone astray.

Virginia Munden whose example of dedication to teaching and mentoring has been an inspiration and for taking the time from her ridiculously busy schedule to help me get this book into a readable condition.

George Zanette, friend and trusted advisor, whose advice has been instrumental in getting this book into a format that makes sense to more people than just me.

ACKNOWLEDGEMENT

Christina Davie, friend, major support and chief architect of my endurance, without whom I would have either called it quits or be sitting in prison for murder.

Josie Stern, friend, inspiration and SuperREALTOR®, for demonstrating, on a daily basis, that the main thesis of this book, having and consistently using systems as well as an unwavering commitment to client service, are the only ways to succeed in real estate.

Peggy Urieff, Associate Broker with Coldwell Banker in Roseville, CA, who graciously allowed me to include her outstanding website, www.popbyideas.com, in this series.

To my family; my father Gerald, and daughters Arielle and Andrea, who endured my neglect, ordered in food, and my mood swings and still gave me their unrelenting support, encouragement and love. Without you, this would never have been possible.

And finally, to my amazing partner, Harvey, best friend, kindred spirit, inspiration and dearest, most loving man I know. I can't imagine my life without you in it.

Introduction

Systems for Success

Real estate sales can be a siren song to many. To those outside the business it appears to be an easy way to make money. Watch any of the home improvement channels and you can see people flipping this house, flipping that house, real estate agents selling million dollar properties to the first people that walk in the door, turning junk homes into gorgeous properties and renting them out to the first group through. And all this happens during an hour-long show. So many get into the business with the dream of earning a huge income in their first few months, but it's a sad fact of life in the real estate world that almost 50% of new Sales Representatives fail and are out of the business within the first year of graduating from the training programs. And a further 50% of the remaining aspirants drop out within the second year.

This happens for a wide range of reasons, but the most common one is that the initial training programs don't adequately educate them on the realities of life in the real world as a REALTOR®. They're taught how to avoid getting into trouble with the provincial regulators. They're taught the basics of real estate law and they're taught such useful tools as the length of a "chain", metes and bounds or the Torrens system. There's little to no training on what is truly necessary to succeed in this most competitive business, systems.

That's why this series has been written. It's designed to provide new salespeople with the information, tools, skills and systems they'll require to help them get through those first couple of difficult years.

In this series can be found a step by step approach to implementing the systems that every successful real estate salesperson requires, beginning with business planning and time management and moving through organizational systems, prospecting, working with sellers and buyers and much more. Tools and business building exercises are included, both in the series, the workbook and online at www.foundationsforsuccess.ca which will assist the salesperson in developing those systems, their skills and confidence.

On the Right Foot will introduce you to the Business Plan, the real secret behind getting started without falling into the traps encountered by most new Sales Representatives. It will also introduce you to the key components of success, consistency and organization; doing what needs to be done, when it needs to be done, as often as it needs to be done, in every aspect of the business, including time, client and financial management.

Good Hunting will familiarize you with various types of prospecting techniques, and even more importantly than the types of techniques, you'll learn to develop the mindset required to be consistently successful at it. You'll be shown how to develop and maintain one of the most important long-term prospecting activities, a farm, an activity which will establish you as the best known and most knowledgeable REALTOR® in the area. We'll review the many different active forms that prospecting may take, including making prospecting calls, door-knocking, Open Houses, converting For Sale By Owners, networking, trade shows, and participating in client and community events.

Volume 2 will examine not just lead generation but will also help you develop a complete and organized lead follow up system, so that the leads you generate result in ongoing and future business. You'll read about how to follow up with leads rapidly, effectively and to set them up on a program that keeps you in touch with them until they're ready to act.

In **Listings, Listings, Listings** you'll read about, and prepare a listing system that differentiates you from other REALTORS® and helps influence people to want to work with you before they actually meet you. It discusses listing presentations that demonstrate to the potential client that you're able to provide them with the value they're seeking and what they feel is important, not what you believe your value is. You'll also learn to develop a highly organized listing system that ensures you follow a consistent process for every listing, thereby reducing or eliminating the possibility of missing any steps throughout the entire sales cycle.

Volume 3 will also review and discuss offer management, a key component of a well-constructed listing system. The management of offers, both single and multiple, can easily become disorganized and chaotic without a standardized method of handling the many aspects of what can be a complex procedure.

In **Buyers, Buyers, Buyers** you'll read about different buyer demographics, what the average buyer in each is looking for when purchasing a home and the questions that will help you determine what your client is looking for, what type of buyer they are and that will help you narrow down their needs and wants. By following the systems in this volume, you should be able to review the properties for which they're looking and help you find them the right property in the least amount of time.

As in Volume 3, this volume will help you develop a buyers' system, including an offer management system for your buyer which will enable you to protect your client's interests while obtaining the property with the least amount of difficulty.

And in **I'm Just Sayin'**, you'll be introduced to a critical skill you'll need to develop, objection handling. Using the BASIQ technique, introduced in this volume, you'll be able to quickly and easily determine what the true objection is and by asking the right questions and listening carefully to the answers you'll have the opportunity to understand what the client's concern is and, even more, how to handle it.

The next critical skill you'll need to cultivate is your communication abilities, in order to eliminate the major source of complaints against REALTORS®, a lack of communication or a miscommunication that was never resolved. This volume will discuss how your ongoing task will be to, through the use of open ended questions and active listening techniques, fully grasp what your client is trying to communicate to you as well as ensuring that the client is able to clearly hear and understand the information you're providing.

You'll also be introduced to negotiation, which, if not prepared for, can be a very disconcerting experience. You'll learn how to work towards a win-win resolution, how to prepare for the negotiation and how to develop and execute an effective game plan, complete with specific strategies to achieve the desired outcomes.

And last, this volume will provide you with direction on marketing and advertising. As with any other system, your marketing strategy must planned out for the year so that you don't miss any component or spend money where you needn't, a major point of failure for most new salespeople. You'll learn how to write ads that appeal to buyers.

And finally **The Workbook** will provide you with a weekly, step by step approach to building and managing your business. You'll have opportunities to develop, in a logical, proven, sequence by completing the exercises provided, the systems, skills, and tools you'll need to smooth out the learning curve, reduce the time required to implement the systems needed to ensure their success and begin earning a steady, reproducible and predictable income in a shorter period of time.

However, it is not the end of what you need to do and what you need to learn. As with any athlete, learning the rudiments of the sport is just the beginning. Stop learning and perfecting your skills and techniques and you end up being nothing more than average at best. Professional and high caliber amateur athletes all recognize that the key to ongoing success is to have someone who can teach them and hold them accountable for their performance, forcing them to take absolute advantage of their strengths as well as to face their weaknesses and overcome them; in other words, a coach. I strongly urge you to consider working with a real estate coach who can help you hone your skills and techniques as well as provide you with additional tools and skills designed to test your limits, push you to excel and ensure you reach the goals you'll set for yourself.